William Black

Kilmeny

William Black

Kilmeny

ISBN/EAN: 9783337039714

Printed in Europe, USA, Canada, Australia, Japan

Cover: Foto ©Andreas Hilbeck / pixelio.de

More available books at **www.hansebooks.com**

A Novel.

By WILLIAM BLACK,

AUTHOR OF

"GREEN PASTURES AND PICCADILLY," "ADVENTURES OF A PHAETON,"
"A PRINCESS OF THULE," "A DAUGHTER OF HETH," &c.

HARPER & BROTHERS PUBLISHERS

NEW YORK AND LONDON

In einem Thal, bei armen Hirten,
Erschien mit jedem jungen Jahr,
Sobald die ersten Lerchen schwirrten,
Ein Mädchen schön und wunderbar.

CONTENTS.

KILMENY.

CHAPTER I.

MY MASTER.

I WAS not born to command men. The keen, audacious spirit which plans the building of bridges, lays down great lines of railway, and gets up prodigious companies was always a mystery to me—a mystery as depressing as the things themselves. I used to be afraid of large mechanical works—used to wonder what sort of men first undertook to raise immense viaducts, drive tunnels through mountains, and plan huge ships. The mere size of a church made me sad. And when I met men who seemed to have splendid, matter-of-fact strength in their faces—men who had hard, clear, literal views of things—who were on equal terms with the newest enterprises, and were capable of imagining even newer and bigger things, I almost feared them. A tall man overawed me as a big building did. Then the great, rich people, who had such a royal way with them—the men who could stare a beggar out of countenance, who could quite honestly look at a tradesman or a waiter as a sort of divinely appointed slave, who could do cruel things when the law allowed them, and laugh over the misfortune of their weaker opponent—they, too, were among my mysteries. The world was too big and strong and rich and hard-hearted; and I feared it.

I used to make a world of my own, in which there were no gigantic walls, or gaunt buildings, or lonely squares with cold iron railings and melancholy trees. It was a world which I must have borrowed from some theatrical scene; for it only consisted of an Irish lake, surrounded by hills, under moonlight. I used to imagine myself living always by this lake, and listening to the old

Irish airs, which seemed somehow to hover round about it, and be its very atmosphere. At night I would lie in a boat on the still surface, with the moonlight on the sedges and trees; and the melody that always came then—like the lake itself speaking—was, "Silent, O Moyle, be the sound of thy waters!" Fancy falling asleep to that pathetic wail! Then for the brisk morning breeze and the sunshine—the joyous "Garryowen" falling into the plaintive minor of "Shule Aroon." And somehow that always led on to "Love's Young Dream"—the old air which no repetition can rob of its exceeding sadness—sad as love's young dream itself—which is the saddest thing a man meets with on this side of death.

I suppose it all arose from my being physically not the equal of my neighbors. I saw big, strong, handsome men, and they were to me as demigods. Was it not their right that they should have plenty of money and beautiful wives, and a fine, domineering manner, and a splendid carriage to whirl them homeward to their grand dinners? Notwithstanding my having been born and bred in the heart of an English county, I was small and slight; I was sallow of face; I was hungry-looking; and they used to say that my eyes stared like those of a young crow. Once Big Dick—of whom you will hear more by and by—in a kindly mood, begotten of too much beer, said to me—

"Look here, Ted, I'll tell you what you are like. Did you ever snare a rabbit, and take it up before it was dead? Did you ever catch it by the back of the neck, and look at its wild, frightened, big eyes, that were full of fear and trouble? You always look to me like a caught rabbit, half dead with fright, and like to cry, if you only could. My sister had eyes like you. I wonder if *you* would cry, like her, if you heard pretty tunes? Ted, I think you were meant for a girl."

I did not tell; but that I used to cry bitterly, in secret, over certain kinds of music—especially some of these Irish airs I have named—was too well known to myself. You must not suppose, however, that this altogether arose from physical weakness. So far as muscular force went, I was strong. I had a broad chest. My arms, rather long, were tough and sinewy. When the fit came across me, I used to torture myself with physical exercise, to get rid of my plethora of nervous strength. I will say nothing of my having seen a boy, twice as big as myself, beating a little girl one day in High Holborn. I so nearly strangled him that the sight of his face has never been erased from my memory.

I used to have my dreams, of course. I used to imagine myself one of those big, handsome, florid-faced men, with lots of money, with beautiful women my friends, with the power of going whither I pleased, with the delight of having no master. Oh the luxury of lying in bed as long as you might wish! Oh the happiness of walking out in the sunny forenoons—with no fear of coming work—to saunter idly by the gray Serpentine, and watch the blowing of the leaves of the trees! To have no master and lots of money! But it was not for me—I was too small and insignificant. These things were for the big and proud.

You may ask how such a one should have a story to tell; and I reply at once that there is nothing heroic of my doing which I shall have to record in these pages. But I have a tenacious memory: life has seemed very various, and, on the whole, very beautiful to me; and I venture to set down some sketch of what I have seen and known, that others may judge whether they see the world with the same eyes. Hence I must beg the reader to regard the following narrative as wholly impersonal; the word "I" will occur frequently, too frequently; but it will merely represent a lens, and the reader is asked to look at the picture only. There are some, curious in such matters, who may be inclined to analyze the peculiarities of the lens by watching the distortions they will find in the pictures; they too, I hope, will not be disappointed, if frankness will help.

Now if there was anybody likely to cure one of mooning and day-dreaming, it was my master. His name was Weavle, but we generally called him Weasel. He was a carver and gilder in High Holborn; and he employed three men and myself. He was in a fair way of business, dealing more with artists than with the general public, and hence it was that I came to know so many artists. His shop adjoined the Royal Oak Yard, and the work-room windows looked into the stone square of the old Royal Oak Inn, into which, every forenoon, the Buckinghamshire omnibus is still driven. How I used to look out of the dingy gray panes, and envy the rosy and happy faces of the people who came in, with the light of the country in their eyes, and the keen breeze painted on their cheeks! How I used to envy the people who got up on that coach, and were taken away out of the great close town! But to my master.

Weavle was a short, thin man, round-shouldered, with a pale face, a bald head, and small reddish-gray eyes. He was querulous and captious as an ill-bred and angry woman; he had a shrewish tongue, a diabolical temper, and a nature so indescribably petty and mean that I despair of conveying any notion of it. He walked about in thick, soft slippers, for the express purpose of catching his men in some small delinquency; and then he would stand and scold with a spite and ingenuity of epithet that were wonderful. It was, I believe, the thing dearest to his heart, this angry declamation, in which he exhibited a marvellous power of saying everything that could wound a man's feelings to the quick, and humiliate him before his fellows. He laid traps for the men. He slid about like a spectre, and watched them with the eyes of a detective. And he never went out of the workshop without turning sharply round to see if any one were grinning over his washerwoman speeches.

The very keenest pleasure I have in life is this. Sometimes, even at this remote period, in this remote and foreign town, I dream for a whole night that I am again under Weavle's domination. I have to submit to the insult of his stealthy footsteps, to the virulence and meanness of his scolding; the old pain and heart-sickening return, the bitterly cold mornings, the dull days, the hopeless labor, the weary struggle against poverty. The daylight breaks, and I fancy that I have to go and submit to that cruel, mean old man. And then, slowly, as if sunshine were filling the room, I begin to have the consciousness that there is no Weavle, that all the bad time is past, that I am my own master, with my own plenteous time, and my own plenteous money—that I am FREE! It is almost worth while to have had one's heart-blood sucked for years by a Weasel to know the intense, strong joy which accompanies that conviction.

The man was not always mean and offensive; at night he slept. And if in his dreams he ever saw a company of angels, I know that his first instinctive impulse was to watch them, lest they should be stealing their master's time.

It was this poor little tyrant who first taught me to love the great, generous forces of nature. It was when I thought of him, and of his unutterable pettiness and suspicion, that I grew to know and love the sea, the long swathes of light across the blue, the far-off coast-line, and the moving splendors of the clouds.

Even at this moment I cannot bear to look on a river or an estuary. There must be no land on the other side, nothing but the great plain on which the winds came down darkling, or on which the sunlight sleeps still and warm, blurring the horizon-line with a mist of heat. Indeed, the whole bent of my life, physical and mental, has been escape from Weavle. That I am now free I have already hinted, and I propose to tell the story of my release.

Perhaps you ask if my companions regarded Weavle as I did. First let me say a word about them. Big Dick was a man who stood six feet one in his stocking-soles; he had a massive and strong frame, a fine chest, tangled black hair, and a handsome face, flushed by much drinking. His wife was dead. He had a little boy, whom he had handed over to his sister, thus leaving him free to follow his own courses. And regularly as Saturday came round, so regularly did Dick get drunk; and drunk he continued until the following Wednesday. Then he would come in to his work, his big scarred hand, with its protuberant knuckles, swollen veins, and horny finger-tips, trembling and uncertain, his eyes bleared and lustreless. He was gruff, and would not speak to us then. By Thursday the black-sheep feeling wore off, and he set to work to make up for lost time. He was a splendid workman, and by the Saturday had always amassed as much wages as he wanted for his needs. He was remarkably good-natured, and being "a rare handy man," was in much request among the neighbors. He could glaze and paint, and hang wall-papers, and work in stucco—in short, he could do everything, and he was always ready to do it as a neighborly turn, if you allowed him his necessary liquor. Dick good-humoredly said of his master that Weasel could not hold his tongue if he tried, and that he did not mean half of what he said. When Dick got into trouble, he bore the rancorous and scurrilous speechifying with resignation, and only gave a sigh of relief when Weasel slipped out.

But you should have heard what Joe Risley had to say about my master. Throughout the trade Joe was known as "The Royal"—because, on Coronation-day, Joe had dressed himself in a Coronation-coat, and, having got a little tipsy, made a rush forward to the Queen's carriage, in order to shake Her Majesty by the hand. Joe very nearly lost his ear by a dragoon's sword, and was picked up from among the horses' feet with his coat rent in twain. Perhaps it was this circumstance that had made "The Royal" a furious, bitter Radical. He was a dark-whiskered cadaverous man, with big, lambent black eyes, a weak chest, and a shaky frame. He had read extensively—especially in history; and when woke up by some argument into fierce fight, the eyes used to glow, and the frail figure quiver with excitement. But he rarely spoke of these things except when he was drunk; and then he would describe to you the scattering of the Allies at Austerlitz with sweeps of the arm that threatened all the glasses near him, or he would pronounce a panegyric on Napoleon which might have done Hazlitt credit. Napoleon was his great hero. He forgave the conqueror his despotism in view of the terror he had struck into the hearts of "the leagued band of kings." It was as well that Joe seldom became excited about politics in the shop; for then he used, in his enthusiasm, to destroy the gold-leaf,* sending fragments flying into the air as if he were Napoleon blowing into chaos a whole worldful of diplomats. "The Royal" looked upon Weasel as the personification of the tyranny of money, and used to curse him between his teeth as a usurper and an aristocrat.

"Kent" is hardly worth speaking about. He was a pale, flaxen-haired young man, who got into a terrible fright when Weasel caught him doing anything and began to rage. I scarcely think he had any particular desire or aim in the world. He was content if he got his work done in good time; and sometimes, but rarely, he took a holiday, which he spent in lying upon Hampstead Heath. He seemed to have no friends; and never went down to Dartford, his native place. His real name was, I think, Taplin or Toplin.

Such were my companions in Weasel's shop; but they were very differently situated from myself. They were men, and independent of other men. They could spend a half-crown without thinking much of it. Above all, they were free to work when

* I need hardly say that Weavle cheated. He never allowed a leaf of "deep red" to be used where "Dutch metal" could be used in its place; and, instead of the ordinary varieties of "lemon," he had all manner of foreign abominations, which invariably turned green or black in course of time. Big Dick rebelled against this more than against the scolding; for he was proud of his work, and he did not like to let a frame leave his hands which he knew would change its color after being hung up in some gentleman's room, and subjected to London gas for ten or twelve months.

they pleased, to be idle when they pleased. If the whim came into their head (that it never did was always a puzzle to me), they could have snapped their fingers in Weasel's face, and gone off to spend a whole day on the banks of the Serpentine, assured that next morning they could get work elsewhere. At least they could take a holiday; and my notion of a holiday was always associated with the Serpentine. I loved that little bit of water as if it had been the sea. I used to make it a sea by sitting down on one of the benches and shading my eyes so as to hide the opposite bank—so that I could see nothing but the gray rippling water, hear nothing but the wind in the trees overhead; and then I grew almost faint with the dull dumb joy of being alone by the sea. I forgot the rich people who were riding up and down the Row behind me; I saw none of the poor idling loungers who stood at the end of the lake, and threw crumbs or stones at the ducks. There was nothing before me but the wind-stirred water, and where I could see no more water, I imagined water until it touched the sky. Sometimes I fancied I could hear the sound of waves on the far-off coast; sometimes I fancied I could see, just on the line of the horizon, a faint white speck of a ship appear, catching a touch of gold from the sunset. The Serpentine is small and insignificant, doubtless; but so is a sea-shell, and the sea-shell, if you are alone, and if you listen closely, will tell you stories of the sea.

As I dreamed there, on certain rare occasions, I grew to think that life, for me, was scarcely worth the having. My existence was a blunder. I was not fitted to cope with the forces around me, and wrest from them that alone which would have made life endurable. I had no clear idea of what that was: I only knew that it was unattainable. What lay before me? A life similar to that pursued by my companions in Weasel's shop would have been sufficiently distasteful, even had I had the fine physique and good-humor of Big Dick, the keen interest in political affairs of Risley, or even Kent's imperturbable temperament. What was the use of me to anybody—to myself even? The mere object of keeping one's self alive with nothing to look forward to but the endless round of work, in which one could take no interest, was disheartening in the extreme. Many and many a time I wished that I could compress my whole life into a few moments, and make it useful to some one who would kindly thank me for it. One of those beautiful women, for example, who rode by! Could I not throw away my life at her feet, doing her some slight service, and earn from her the gratitude of a smile? My life was a weariness to myself: could I make it heroic and worthy even for a second, by yielding it to the service of one of those peerless women, who were so far away from me—so cold and beautiful and distant?

As I sit here, under a blue and Southern sky, thinking of that old, sad, ridiculous time, some one looks over my shoulder, and reads these words, and laughs.

CHAPTER II.

MY HOME.

It was the month of primroses; and the wind blew fresh and mellow with the promise of the summer. Even in the London streets there was a strange sweetness in the air, and a new, keen light in the sky. And on that morning, when I was free to go home for a whole couple of days, the spring seemed to have taken a clear leap ahead, and got into a fine breezy summer warmth. As I made my way to the Great Western Railway Station, the gray dawn broke into a pale saffron, and the light lay along the tall, silent houses and their rows of windows. Beautiful houses they were—up by Park Lane and Connaught Place and Eastbourne Terrace—but I was no longer oppressed by them, or by the grand people who lived in them. I snapped my fingers at the closed white shutters and the lowered green blinds. I laughed aloud in the empty streets, to the amazement of solitary policemen. I skipped and hopped, and tried to jump impossible jumps; so that I reached the station half an hour too soon, and speedily got sobered down by the melancholy gloom of the place and the official gravity of the porters.

But then again, as the train got out and away from London—leaving Holland Park and its tall houses pale and silvery in the east—and we were among the warm bright meadows and fields—with the sunlight shimmering over the young green of the trees—with the sweet, pure, spring wind rushing through the open windows of the carriage—with the joyous motion of the train, and the thought of utter, unrestrained freedom and pleasure for two entire long days—was it possible that I should feel unkindly to any man or place? I blessed London—after Notting Hill was long out of sight. I began to think "Kent" almost an enlivening sort of person, and very nearly forgave Weasel.

There were to be grand doings at Burnham House, and at Burnham, the little village down in the heart of Bucks, where my father and mother lived. Miss Hester Burnham, the last of that long line which had given several prominent names to English history—particularly during the great King-and-Parliament struggle—had just come home from France to live in England. My father was head-keeper at Burnham—a man who ought to have been born in feudal times; and it was somehow his notion of what was right and proper that I, though having nothing to do with Burnham, ought to be there when this important event came off. Fain would I have gone down on the top of the coach that daily leaves Holborn for these quiet Buckinghamshire parts, and done the journey in the old picturesque fashion; but I should have reached Burnham too late in the evening; and so I had to take rail to Wycombe, and walk across to that little village which has been for centuries a sort of appanage to Burnham House.

I had very little interest either in Miss Hester Burnham or in the doings that were to celebrate her return. I remembered her only as a little girl, with dark hair and staring eyes, who used to ride about on a white pony, and was greatly petted by the farmers and their wives—indeed, by everybody. Doubtless Miss Hester was now a fine lady, come home from France to set up her state in the great old house, where her people had lived for centuries. Indeed, so little did I think of the whole matter that I forgot that Miss Hester could scarcely be sixteen years of age.

So it was that, when I reached Wycombe, instead of walking straight over to Burnham, I set forth on a ramble across the long chalk hills and through the dense beech-woods which were once so familiar to me.

How well I knew every house and orchard and field, as the road gradually rose and brought into view the deep and pleasant valleys that were now so deep and warm! Night after night, in my poor London lodgings, I had laid with open eyes and dreamed of these woods and hills and hollows; and lo! here they were

—not as I had imagined them—but under the bewildering glare of the spring light.

Yet the day was not one of strong sunshine. There was a thin, transparent yellow mist, that did not so much obscure the sunlight as conceal the directness of its rays; and while you could not turn to any point of the sky and say the sun was there, you felt that it was all around you, shining in the intense pellucid green of the young hawthorn leaves, and causing the breaks in the distant chalk-hills to gleam like silver. Then all the wonders of the spring were out—the rich-colored japonica in front of the laborers' cottages, the white masses of petals on the great pear-trees, the big flowers of the cherries, and the rose-tinted scarcely unfolded apple-blossom, sprinkled here and there with little bunches of woolly leaves. Here, too, were all the spring flowers about the hedges and banks; and the spring freshness and brilliancy upon the young leaves of the chestnuts and the elms and the ash. The limes were black yet; the tall and graceful birch had only a tinge of green on its drooping branches; and the interminable beech-woods—the glory of Buckinghamshire in the time when they grow red and orange and crimson—showed as yet only a dull purple, caught from the ruddy and twisted buds. And over all these things brooded the warmth of that pale yellow light—so calm and still and silent, but for the pearly music of a lark that was lost in it; and the woods, also, and the long low valleys, seemed to be hushed into a drowsy silence, broken now and again by the clear, strong piping of a thrush in one of the blossom-laden orchards. It was all so different from London.

Through these beech-woods, strewn with dead leaves, and matted with brier and breckan, I joyously went until I issued upon the summit of the hill, upon the steep side of which is cut the great white cross that can be seen all the way from Oxford. The old grand picture of that immense intervening plain was once more before me. Princes Risborough, with its red-tiled houses and its church, lying down there under the faint blue smoke of the village; the long white road leading on to Bledlow; the comfortable farmsteads smothered among orchards; then the great patchwork of fields with their various colors—the red and brown fallow, the dark green of the young clover, the fine tint of the wheat, here and there already yellowed with charlock; the sharp, black lines of the hedges gradually getting closer and fainter as the eye rose to the horizon, and there becoming a confused mass of misty streaks; on the right the remote uplands, with their larch-plantations, and here and there a white house shining in the sun; down on the left the continuing line of the chalk hills, rounded and smooth, where they became visible from among the dusky stretches of the beech-woods; and far on in front, half lost in the shimmer of light along the edge of the sky, the pale blue plain of Oxfordshire, indeterminate and vague.

How long I lay on the shoulder of White-cross Hill, with the dazzling glare of the concealed sun lying warm and crimson on my shut eyelids, I cannot say. I was outside of all distressing conditions—absolutely free, and without a thought for anything or anybody, including myself. It was enough to be in the fresh and beautiful air, to be alone, to be able to dream. And it seemed to me, as I lay there, that there were fairies hovering over me, and that the warm spring air, blowing over my face, was only their tickling my forehead with their small handkerchiefs. Or was it with spikes of feather-grass? I lay and pictured their walking around me in all sorts of picturesque and shining costumes—the small gentlemen with helmets of acorn-cups, and shields made out of the shell of the green beetle; the small ladies with parasols formed out of a curved rose-leaf, and bonnets of white larkspur. Then, somehow, a thought of Weasel intervened; I got up impatiently, and made to go down the hill and get back to Burnham.

I then found that a pair of new boots I had put on that morning—assisted, doubtless, by the mad jumping and hopping of my progress to the station—had severely hurt my feet. Indeed, when I reached the foot of White-cross Hill, I found it impossible to put one foot to the ground, so intense was the pain which the pressure caused. Under the circumstances, I took the only course open to me—sat down, pulled off my boots and stockings, put the latter in the former, and, slinging the whole over my shoulder, prepared to walk barefooted until I should near Burnham. Perhaps by that time I might be able to pull my boots on again; if not—and the chances were against it—I should have to put a bold face on the matter, and walk with absurdly white feet up to my mother's door.

But, as I yet rested, I heard a pattering of horses' hoofs, and, looking around, saw a couple of riders coming along the white road. The glare of the light was in my eyes; but I could make out that the one was a young girl, the other a youngish gentleman, though considerably older than she. It struck me at the moment that very likely this would be Miss Burnham; and so I sat still, that I might see her well as she passed. Besides there has always seemed to me something very fine and stately and beautiful in the position of a woman (who can ride at all decently) on horseback, and in these days lady-riders wore long skirts, which greatly added to the effect of their appearance. So they came cantering along the dusty road; and just before they reached me, the light was so altered that I could distinctly see them.

My first thought was, "How quickly girls grow in France!" My second, "What a sweet face!"

Pale it was, and dark (at least it seemed dark in shadow), scarcely surrounded by loose masses of brown hair that the wind had blown back from her hat. You could not tell what the features were, for the wonderful eyes of the face caught you and kept you there. As she swept past, she drove a single glance right through me; and I thought that I had seen a vision of all the sweetness and gracious kindliness of womanhood revealed by this one swift look. Here, at least, was a gentlewoman in nature, one who was not supercilious, or cursed by conventional pride. I looked after her, and I said to myself, "There, now, if you could do any service to one such as she is, life would not be quite worthless."

Then I saw her, before she had gone twenty yards, pull up her horse. Her companion, a young man of about twenty-two, fair-haired, apparently tall, and with cold gray eyes, followed her example.

She said something to him—he shrugged his shoulders—and, as well as I could hear, said he had no coppers.

"Give me silver, then!" she said, with a sort of girlish petulance; and then he handed something to her.

She wheeled round her horse and rode up to where I sat. I could not understand all this. She held out her hand. I rose, expecting her to say something. She still held out her hand, and I, reaching up mine, received into it a half-crown. Still I stood, stupefied, wondering what the beautiful blue-gray eyes, under those long black eyelashes, meant; and then, before I had recovered myself, and without a word, she turned her horse again and rode away.

It was all the work of a second; and for some little time I was too bewildered to know what had occurred. At last, when I saw the white half-crown lie in my hand, a sensation which I shall never forget came over me—a sensation of consuming, intolerable shame. This was what the kindliness of her eyes meant, that I was a beggar and she pitied me. I felt my face grow white and cold, and then burn red with confusion and anger. To have alms thrown to me by the wayside, to be treated as a common beggar—the very thought of it seemed to crush me with a deadening, burning weight, that was scarcely relieved by wild anticipations of revenge. Was not my mother a gentlewoman, too; although only the daughter of a poor clergyman, when my father, then a young gardener, got so madly in love with her that even his notions of duty were unable to prevent his running away with her? And was not his careful and respectful behavior to her—now that they had been married something like eighteen years—a wonder to the neighbors, and a greater wonder to my mother's old friends, who had prophesied the usual consequences of her folly? Nay, had not the Burnhams been always tenderly considerate to my mother, though she was only the wife of their head keeper; and who was it that taught this very Miss Hester the little accomplishments of a gentlewoman before she went to her Parisian schools? These things, and others, I thought over; but the accursed white half-crown lay out in the middle of the road, whither it had rolled after I flung it violently to the ground; and the mere sight of it seemed to make my eyes burn.

And yet she had a kindly face. I could recall the very look with which she had regarded me; and somehow it took me back to old times. But to receive alms from her! I sat down by the wayside once more, and buried my face in my hands, and burst into bitter tears, the bitterest I have ever shed.

CHAPTER III.

MY UNCLE JOB.

The broad gray front of Burnham House has stood these couple of hundred years and more at the head of one of the finest avenues in England—an avenue about a mile and a half in length, and at least three hundred yards broad, leading up from the valley in a straight line to the building on the top of the hill. Many a goodly company has cantered up and down that splendid ride, with its dense, mossy, close green turf, its patches of furze and broom and breckan. On either side stands a row of magnificent Spanish chestnuts; on the one hand skirting the woods that slope down to the Amersham road, on the other forming the boundary-line of Burnham Park. The House itself, fronting this spacious avenue, commands the broad valley that stretches for miles eastward; and from almost any point around you can see from afar the gray frontage of the old building, gleaming like gold in the sunshine, high up there among the trees. Just outside what is called the "ladies' garden" stands the little old church, whose walls are covered with marble memorials of the Burnhams; and from thence a narrow road, dividing the park, leads across the summit of the hill to Burnham village and Burnham Common. The place, with all its historical associations of the times of the Civil War, is little known by Englishmen; but it is familiar to Americans, and Frenchmen visit it, and Germans write about it; and in St. Petersburg you can buy photographs of Burnham and Burnham Church, and of the monumental stone erected to John Burnham, the friend and colleague of Cromwell.

Before coming near Burnham, I cooled my feet in a small stream that runs along the valley, and managed to pull on my boots again. The pain of walking was intense; but I did not mind it so much now. When I got to the lodge, I went in and borrowed a spade from the lodge-keeper.

"Why, I bain't a wolf, Mahster Ives," said he; "you needn't speak to a mahn as if he wur a wolf."

"I didn't mean to be uncivil," I said.

"It wur only my fun," he said, bringing the spade; "but you do look a bit vexed and hout o' sorts."

That I might not be seen by any of the people who were now at the House, I passed into the wood by the side of the avenue, and made my way through the thick undergrowth to a deep cleft or dell in which we children, who had the *entrée* to the woods of Burnham, used to play. We had had a notion of getting up some kind of grotto there, and a large number of big stones were still strewn about the edge of the wooded pit. The biggest of these I placed on my shoulder; and then made my way down through the tangled brier and bushes to the bottom of the dell. There I dug a hole about a foot square and a foot deep. I flung the half-crown into the hole—I think I struck at it with the spade in impotent rage—and, covering it up, put the big stone over the place.

"That is the first alms I ever had offered me," I said aloud—and my voice had a strange sound in the dell—"and that is what I did with it."

I took the spade back to the lodge-keeper.

"Why, Master Ted," said he, "you look as if you'd gone and buried your sour looks. You be younger and brighter by a dozen years than you wur when you axed me for the spaäd. And it's a good spaäd, too."

"It's a capital spade," I said. "Did Miss Burnham pass up to the House lately?"

"Yaäs, she did."

"On horseback, with some one with her?"

"Yaäs."

"Who was he?"

"That be a son o' Colonel Burnham's—Mr. Alfred—and he be a divvle to curse and swear, he be."

"I suppose he means to marry Miss Burnham?"

"Lor' bless ye, there wun't be thoughts o' marryin' in her 'ed for yurs yet. And when she do marry she'll marry a properer mahn than '*im*. I bain't much of a weatherwise mysel', but I doant think much o' that ere 'errin'-gutted young feller. He's bin to college, I reckon, and learnt to play cahrds, and swear at ye as if ye wur a deäd stoat."

I saw that old Joshua Tubb knew very little about Mr. Alfred

Burnham, but that he was inclined to guess the worst, probably by reason of his having suffered a little of the young gentleman's strong language.

"He's living up at the House, I suppose?"

"Yaäs, and his father, and lots mower on 'em. The old plaäce begins to look live-like now."

I went up by the side of the avenue to cross over to Burnham, keeping out of the way of the House. It seemed to me just then that all the hateful influences I feared and loathed were within that gaunt gray building; and that it also held the first human being who had ever thought so meanly of me as to make me a beggar. If you consider that it was at the very moment when I was rejoicing in my freedom from that sense of constraint and inferiority which the town pressed down upon me that she appeared, and again brought home to me the immeasurable distance that lay between my insignificance and helplessness and the beautiful independence and strength and power of the rich and lovely, you will understand how I felt towards her. I had begun to forget what I was: she came, and seemed to say—

"You have no right to rejoice in the free air and the light. You must not imagine yourself equal with other people, even by forgetting their existence."

When I reached the small cottage, fronting Burnham Common, in which I was born, I found my mother training some creeper up the outside wall around the window; while my father stood by, waiting upon her and assisting her as he could. They were very unlike—he a tall, brown, sun-tanned keeper, with a hook nose, gray eyes, scant whiskers, and ruddy hair; she a small, tender, black-eyed woman, who had at one time been very good-looking, and who even now was pretty and neat and engaging. This little, sensitive woman, who never spoke a harsh word to anybody, who could not even scold an unruly dog, had this big man her absolute slave. I think he was fonder of her then than when he persuaded her to run away from her father's home with him. Naturally, he was rather overbearing in his manner—at least he was extremely practical in his aims, very plain-spoken, and inclined to regard everybody who did not agree with him as more or less of a fool; and yet with her you could see that he was almost studiously courteous and gentle and tender. Even his manner towards myself I attributed in part to the notion he had somehow got of my mother and myself being of a different race from his own—or being somehow superior to the people round about. It was this feeling, I imagine, that induced him to send me to London, when the situation in Weasel's place was offered, rather than allow me to grow up to the ordinary routine of farm work.

After the customary greetings and inquiries, I went inside to get a pair of slippers, and sat down in our little front room, which looked out on a bit of garden and on the common. By this time the sunlight had so far dispersed the faint swathes of mist as to show along the sky a strong glow of pale gold, streaked across with bands of cirrus clouds, which gleamed white and silvery in the warm yellow light. Burnham village is very pretty and picturesque in its high-lying position; its few scattered cottages and gardens fronting the undulations of the furze-covered common, and looking towards a long stretch of woodland beyond, which encloses the small colony and shelters it from the wind. I was gazing out from the shadow of the room upon this secluded little place—so warm and silent under the heat and light—and was relapsing into the old feeling of dreamy contentment, when a sudden apparition awoke the bitterness and shame I had experienced in the morning. Miss Hester Burnham walked up to the little green gate, and entered our front garden. She came forward, with the sunlight and a smile on her face, to shake hands with my mother; and, but for the difference in dress, I think you could have taken them for mother and daughter. I was too exasperated and ashamed to pay attention to such things; but I can look back and see that at this moment, standing in the sunlight of the garden, she must have been exceedingly pretty. The slight and girlish figure was small and delicate, exquisitely proportioned, and gracious and graceful in every motion. Her eyes seemed to be darker than my mother's eyes; but they were not. They were of a soft grayish blue, quiet and tender in expression; but what made them dark in appearance was the long and almost black eyelashes which deepened their meaning, and added singularly to the beauty of her profile. Then her eyebrows were high, finely curved, and black; and a profusion of dark hair fell about the rather pale face, and down on the white small neck and the delicate small shoulders. As for her features—you could not see them for looking at her eyes. They may have been regular, irregular—anything: all you could distinctly say was that there appeared a singular light and life about them, with an occasional touch of gravity which was beyond the girl's years. The eyes seemed to have too much sympathy in them for one so young; and yet in their wise truthfulness you could see that there was no trace of affected interest. I can remember how she looked into my mother's face, with those tender, thoughtful, and beautiful eyes. I can remember, too, that she was dressed very neatly —in a tight-fitting, slate-gray costume, that had lines of white about it, and just a touch of scarlet ribbon near the neck. She wore a small gray hat with a single gleaming red feather in it; I think she had a riding-whip in her hand; and she had a sprig of crimson heath in her bosom.

"Mrs. Ives," she said—and her voice had the soft, contralto mellowness that made my mother's voice so tender and pleasant —"I must trouble you again; I really think you must let me coax you to live at the House altogether. I very, very much want you to come now and help me among all those tiresome people. Can you come at once?"

"Certainly, Miss Hester."

"Then I suppose I must go in and wait until you're ready?" she said, with a sort of girlish impatience that made my mother smile.

"No, Miss Hester, you need not wait; I will be over at the House in a few minutes."

"Then I *will* wait. You see how you have spoiled me with your kindness; and so—and so—"

I heard her come into the passage; and I rose.

"My son is within," said my mother.

"Oh, that's Ted," I heard her say, "who used to be my great friend, and my champion when I got into trouble with old Joshua. Is he in here?"

The door was opened, and she advanced a single step. I saw the peculiar, frightened glance she directed towards me: then her face grew scarlet, and for a moment she stood in direful confusion. For myself, I said nothing and did nothing; but my blood was up in rebellion, I knew.

Then, with a wonderful graciousness and the frankest of smiles —I could not help admiring the ease with which her fashionable education enabled her to extricate herself from this embarrassment—she came forward, and held out her hand, and said—

"May I beg you to forgive me?"

I said, coldly enough perhaps—

"I have nothing to forgive."

Her eyes met mine for a moment; and I knew that her woman's wit—wonderfully ingenious even in a girl like that—was wrestling with all the circumstances of the case. Then (all this had happened in a moment, and her hand was still extended) she said in a low voice that was intended not to let my mother hear—

"I will take it back, and then I will ask you to forgive me. It was a mistake—I am very, very sorry."

Then it flashed upon me that I could not give her back that accursed piece of money which was lying buried down in the dell; and I knew she would fancy that I had accepted the alms—that I had already spent the money. The horror and agony of that one moment was worse than all that had gone before. If there was one thing I was proud of it was my pride. It was my only possession: I had need to preserve it. And now the only creature belonging to those gifted people who held the world in their hand who had ever descended so far as to speak to me (and in the old days to be a sort of patronizing little friend to me) had offered me alms, and she would imagine that I had sold my birthright of independence for this wretched bit of money.

"I—I have not got it—I cannot give it to you," I stammered; and then, half conscious of the wonder and astonishment of her eyes, I went past her, and out of the room, and out of the house.

I went out into the cool air of the afternoon, feeling that I had the brand of Cain on my forehead. Was I not a convicted pauper? I walked away from Burnham, over the park, into the strip of wood by the avenue, and down into that dell. The stone was still there. My first impulse was to dig up the half-crown again, and take it to her, and throw it at her feet; but how could I make the explanation? No; it should remain there, and she might think of it all just as she liked.

At that moment I heard voices above—of two men who were walking along the avenue. I heard some snatch of conversation like this:

—"Not much, certainly. But there is the House and grounds—a fortune in themselves."

"You would not sell them?"

"I would, if I had the chance."

"Then, I suppose, you'd send that poor little girl adrift, and spend her money on Clara Beauchamp. Well, Alfred, you have got a wonderful decision about you, to put it mildly."

"Clara is a devilish fine girl; though she ought to have taken some other name than Beauchamp when she started on her career. As for my cousin Hester, you know I shall be compelled to get money somewhere, and she has got such a d—d smooth temper, she would stand anything—"

That was all I heard; but it was enough to suggest many things. And the most probable theory of the aim of this conversation which I was forced to hear was so mean and repulsive and depraved that, at the time, it delighted me. These grand people, then, were occasionally in straits like others. They were not immaculate, either. They had their meannesses—perhaps more absolutely gross and mean than was possible with lesser people in lesser circumstances. To be looked upon as a beggar was bad enough; but there were more despicable beings in the world than beggars.

When I got out of the dell, and looked up the avenue, I saw that one of the two men who had been speaking was the gentleman who had been riding with Miss Hester in the morning. Then I turned my back upon Burnham House, and hoped that I might never see it again.

I walked over to my Uncle Job's farm—some two miles off; and there I spent the evening and the whole of the next day. This Uncle Job was my father's elder brother—an old bachelor who had, by rigid parsimony, worked his way up to the tenanting of a farm of over two hundred acres. Many things contributed to make him a sort of outcast from among his neighbors. To begin with, he went about in a frightfully unshaven and ragged condition, with an old, smashed, and sun-tanned hat, a wisp of dirty black silk tied around his neck, no collar, an old and shabby coat, and a pair of tight and dirty corduroy breeches; while his unwashed and unshaven face was ornamented with a curiously large gray moustache, which was ordinarily besprinkled with snuff. He smoked a short clay pipe, and puffed out all manner of socialist and revolutionary speeches along with the smoke. He never went to church. He had been the friend of a God-forgotten Major who used to dwell in a lonely house near Crutchett's Coppice, and who was supposed to be a monster of wickedness, and to have murdered his wife. It was found at his death that the Major had provided that he should be buried in the neighboring wood, instead of in consecrated ground: was not this sufficient proof that the devil was sure of his prey? My Uncle Job was left as perpetual guardian of the Major's house; and that had now fallen pretty much into ruin, because, as everybody knew it was haunted, nobody would live in it. The experiment was tried once, and the people were glad to get away. In the dark of an evening the noise of carriage-wheels was often heard without—on the carriage-drive and at the hall-door: when the occupants of the house went to the window nothing was visible. Loud laughter, coming from the neighboring wood, used to startle the people at dead of night; when they opened a door suddenly, a sort of scuffle was heard, and sometimes the faint echo of a laugh a minute afterwards. But the climax of these visitations was that the owner of the house, going home one night, distinctly saw a gray dog-cart, with a white horse, standing opposite his door-steps. He went forward: as he approached it faded away, and he walked right through it. That same night no one in the house could sleep for the shrieks of laughter heard all around the place. Next morning the man left, with all his family, and nobody had ventured to sleep in the house since.

Uncle Job was very unwilling to speak of these matters. He growled in his bitter way at the superstition and folly of the people around; but he would never say distinctly what the occupant of the Major's house had told him when he left.

"Darn the fools," he used to say, sitting at his fire of a night, with the small black pipe in his mouth, "they'd believe anything if the pahrson 'ud only tell it them. But the pahrsons are too lazy nowadays to invent new stories—they stick to the hold ones, Ted. They keep to the hold stories, and they've shot the dower agin the new ones. They be rare fond o' tellin' ye o' the plagues o' Egypt; but what I says is, Why didn't Moses try the Egyptians wi' a plague of pahrsons?—that's what I say. And that's a rare good un' too, about the sun standin' still. Bah! It's my opinion that if the sun stood still, it was because it was so darned astonished at Joshua's cheek in askin' it."

I think there can be no doubt about my Uncle Job having been a frightful old ruffian. But the cool way in which he disposed of his respectable neighbors, and maintained the independence of his position, was fine in its way. I walked over his farm the next morning with him. Job had his small pipe in his mouth, and his hat drawn over his forehead to shelter his eyes from the sunlight.

"The pahrson doan't come to my shop," he said; "I doan't go to his. I be as good a mahn as he—I be. No, I doan't say as goin' to church is a bahd thing, but there's a rare lot o' hypocrites as goes, and what I say is as it's better not to go unless you can haet up to it—that's what I saäy. They go to church, and talk o' the blessin' o' bein' poor, and try to make one another believe as they believes it; but it's my opinion as bein' rich isn't so much of a curse arter all; and I doan't see as they throw any o' their money into the sea, or much of it into the poor-box, for the matter o' that. Yes, they talk o' being poor, and yet they want to farm their two thousand and their three thousand acres, and keep a lot o' families starvin' as ain't got a bit o' land to work on. It's one mahn eatin' up the livin's o' eight or ten—that's what it is, Mahster Ted. What I say is, every mahn should ha' an acre—a mahn an acre—then there 'ud be no starvation or Unions."

"Why do you farm two hundred acres yourself, Uncle Job?" said I.

"What 'ud be the use o' me givin' up my patch o' ground? what could a mahn get wi' his spade out o' an acre o' this darned stuff? Now, lookee there, Mahster Ted — look at that divvelish little dell as I ploughed for the first time last spring."

We were now on the brow of a hill, above the long valley in which the straggling village of Missenden, with its red brick houses and its pale blue smoke, lay under the early morning sunshine. And right in front of us, at the other end of the valley, rose the great avenue that led up to Burnham, and the House stood soft and shadowy there among the blue mist of the trees, with a flush of pale yellow across its frontage, caught from the glow of the east. Job paused on the edge of a deep hollow at one end of this field, and blinked at the sunshine, and puffed his pipe, and said—

"As I was a ploughin' theär, I turned over cannon-bullets as was fired all across that valley from Burnham House by Holiver Cromwell."

I asked Job how he knew that the cannon-balls had belonged to Cromwell, but I was aware that the people living in this district attribute all historical relics to the time of the Civil War. There seems to have been in history an absolute blank, so far as the Missenden valley is concerned, between that time and this; the people speak of 1640–50 as of yesterday, and there is scarcely a stone or tree in the parish that has not somehow been mixed up in the great struggle between the King and the Commons.

"How do I know?" said my uncle. "Who ever came into this part of the world to fire bullets except him? Ah! those wur grand times, when gentlemen knew what wur expected of gentlemen, and went out and fought for the poor people as was being taxed. They're talkin' in the newspapers, as I hear, o' spirit-rappin', and all that darned stuff, and it's my opinion that the pahrsons are only humbuggin' us about the joy o' goin' to 'eaven, if we're to be sent to attend on a lot o' darned old women, and play accordions for them. But what I say is, if it wur possible for ghosts to come back, what d'ye think, Mahster Ted, 'ud Ireton and Cromwell and Blake and Burnham — to say nothing o' them as wur on the other side—think of our fine gentlemen now, ruinin' themselves and their families wi' horse-racin', fightin' in theatres, gamblin' wi' blasted furreigners in Germany, and the like? Look at the House there—isn't it as fine a house as any in England? And them as has had it — bah! — and him as is goin' to have it—"

"Who is that?" I asked.

"Why, I bain't a prophet, be I, when I say as I know Mahster Alfred Burnham ain't got a darned farthin', and that his father has plenty to get beaver* for, let alone him; and when I sees him ridin' about day arter day with Miss Hester, and looking so particlar attentive, I don't need to be Eliza — Elijah I mean — to say as there's somethin' hup. Well, she ain't got much money either, as I can hear on; but he'll get a rare good sum for the old 'Ouse. I dunnow if he can sell the church, too. It wur a pity if he couldn't make some use o' them vallyble bits o' marble as have all the Burnhams' names on 'em."

"You don't think he would sell these, do you?" I asked.

But at this moment the bell of Missenden church—high up on the hill there, above the gray old abbey and the small river and the broad meadows—began to toll.

"Darn them bells!" said Uncle Job, turning away testily, "let's

* *Beaver*—food.

go around to the other side of the hill, and get out of the way o' their noise. I hate 'em. They 'mind me of a funeral; and they say to me as the people who go to church are so darned respectable and solemn and proper; and they tell me what yur respectable people think of me—and that is that I am a flamin' old cuss, who ought to go and bury myself, because I doan't shine my boots, and go and snivvle in a church pew, and promise to obey all the ten commahndments, and ten mower, if Providence 'll only make me better off than my neighbors."

I don't think old Job Ives was a very profitable companion, as he went about on a quiet Sunday morning, down in this Buckinghamshire vale, railing and cursing against his kind. However, I hated Burnham, and I remained at my uncle's farm all day, creeping over to bid good-bye to my father and mother after dusk, when no one from Burnham House could see.

CHAPTER IV.

MY FRIEND.

I RETURNED to London, and to Weasel's shop, with a great purpose in my heart. I was determined to be Correggio, or Isaac Newton, or Edmund Kean—anybody of such transcendent genius as should make the world pause and wonder. It was not alone the small world of Burnham that I wished to conquer, but that greater world which had cast me down and made a beggar of me. I should be even with it; and, if I spent my life in the struggle, would in the end force it to recognize in me its equal. What were the means? An astounding audacity, assumed for the purpose; backed by a resolution to explore all the various branches of human knowledge. There was nothing I did not attempt. Greek was my first effort; though I begin to perceive now that life is not long enough to let a man learn Greek. French, and a little German, my mother had taught me; and, while I still coached myself up in these languages, I took to the indiscriminate study of everything. I had no master or instructor or guide. I gathered up pence, and bought second-hand books in Holborn. I began to fancy myself learned in hydraulics, and could turn you off at a moment's notice the proper angle for a sluice-gate. I regarded myself as profound in chemistry; and only wanted some apparatus to increase considerably the list of non-metallic elements. I studied astronomy; and knew that, with the requisite time and instruments, I should have discovered Neptune. I studied botany (theoretically, alas!), and had my own notions about the protoplasmic movement and origin of life. For amusement, I drew, and dabbled in water-colors. I made the absurdest efforts to excel in all these things, that I might wipe out, some day or other, the cruel stain that Hester Burnham's silver coin had left upon my hand.

I pass over all this foolish time, and arrive at a period when a little further knowledge had cooled my hopes, if not my impatience and desire. My great and faithful friend, now as then, was an artist to whom I had occasionally to carry home picture-frames. He and I somehow became acquainted: he took a sort of fancy to me; and I used to spend all my brief snatches of leisure in his studio in Granby Street, Hampstead Road. His name was Owen Heatherleigh; and I thought at first that he had no friends or relations. I discovered afterwards that he had plenty of both; but he went near them rarely. He was a man getting on towards thirty, with rough unkempt hair and beard, a broad, honest, powerful face, with a gash upon one cheek which he had received while studying in Germany; large, brown eyes, a good, handsome figure, and slovenly dress. His history, as I heard it from himself, bit by bit, was a peculiar and sad one. He was of very good family: his father was a squire in some remote district in Westmoreland; and, some ten years before I knew him, Owen had the misfortune to fall in love with a young girl, the daughter of the village schoolmaster. His parents would hear nothing of the match. But the girl loved him; and he had just come home from a German university, full of ambition and independence and the fine feeling of youth. He left his father's house, and never set foot in it again.

"I used to go and see her every morning, from my lodgings," he said one night to me, as he sat before the fire; "and they had a little room prepared for me, in which I used to work at my water-color sketches, that were, of course, to make a fortune for us both. You know what I am, Ted: what I think about many things. One day I went up to the window of the cottage: it was open—summer-time, you know. She was singing—it was an old, poor piano—but my little girl had the tenderest voice. She was singing some religious hymn or other; and I caught the words, 'Nearer, my God, to Thee, nearer to Thee,' uttered with such a pathetic abandonment that I dared not to enter the house. I felt like a murderer who had wandered near a village church, and heard the people singing. I stood outside and asked myself if I could destroy that beautiful, simple faith of hers. If she were to marry me, would she not either break her heart over my condition, or could I, on the other hand, crush out all the tenderest and holiest aspirations of her sweet young life, and leave her the prey of doubt and despair? Still she sang, and you might have imagined that the angels themselves were listening to her. I hurried away from the place as if I had been an evil spirit; and—God forgive me! but—I fled here to London. I think it was not more than three months after then that my darling died; and when I went down there, I went into the churchyard and saw the flowers on her grave. She died without ever knowing how wholly and perfectly I loved her, or what it was that had caused me to leave her. Some half-hour before her death she asked for her prayer-book—there was a primrose in it, you know: that was all . . . I never kissed her."

Such was his story.

At another time he told me why he was so lazy—he who could gain reputation and money by every half-hour of work he chose to expend.

"I came up to London again, resolved to make my own way, and be equal with the people who had cut me on poor Hettie's account—"

"Was her name Hester?" I asked, with a sudden accession of interest.

"Yes. But I found it was no use. What was the good of working yourself to death to amass money, when you found yourself baffled even in the poor competition for the honor that money can give you by people who never worked a stroke in their life? They had all the chances on their side; I had none. Had I made a lot of money, I should still have been looked on in society as a poor devil of an artist—a man who had to earn his bread—whom one might patronize—who was your servant when you paid him. I gave up the fight," he continued, recovering his gayety of tone,

"I take my ease. I have educated myself into tastes that are easily gratified. I like beer better than all other drinks. I prefer a pipe to any cigar you can give me. I work as little as I can. I have a fine constitution, and am content to enjoy laziness. I lead, on the whole, a remarkably jolly life. As we used to say over in Heidelberg—

'Ein starkes Bier, ein beizender Tobak,
Und eine Magd im Putz, das ist nun mein Geschmack.'"

"You have the beer and the tobacco; but I don't see the well-dressed girl," I remarked.

"Not when Polly Whistler comes to look us up?" he said.

But if there were any girl in the world whom it was unlikely Owen Heatherleigh would care about, it was Polly Whistler—the strapping, frank, good-natured model, who had a tongue as keen as her wit, and a heart as soft as her big black eyes. Polly was a very respectable girl, be it understood. She only sat to two or three artists whom she knew, and who were known to each other; and she was a good deal more scrupulous about her costume than many ladies who would have regarded her with anger and disdain. Sometimes I used to think that Polly cared more about Owen Heatherleigh than he suspected, or than she chose to show; but then again the suspicion was dispelled by the open manner in which she "chaffed" him about his misogynist habits, and suggested that if she were his wife she would improve both his chambers and himself.

I remember walking up with him one evening to his studio; he had been insisting on my going to live with him, help him in his work, and share the profits. The mere suggestion of such a thing set my head spinning with wild anticipations; and I eagerly went to his lodgings to talk the project over.

When we entered the large room we found the lamp already lit—throwing a dull light on a great, gloomy screen, on the various sketches and pictures hung around the walls, on the littered and dirty apartment, and on a row of dusty and sepulchral plaster busts set along a high shelf. Polly was seated by the fire.

"Well, Polly, are you here?" he said unconcernedly, taking another seat.

"Yes," she said, turning her bright, frank face to us with a smile; "my old woman went out to a concert with one of her neighbors, and I didn't care about sitting in the house alone."

"Quite right too. Sitting alone begets gloomy fancies."

"That's why you are so particularly dull at times. I came down here thinking to put your place a bit to rights for you; but I was too lazy, or tired. I was to tell you from your landlady, though, that two gentlemen, who would not leave their names, called to-day and will be back again to-morrow."

"Good!" said Heatherleigh to me. "I swear they want to offer me a commission to paint a picture for the Prince of Wales."

"No," said Polly, with her black eyes twinkling maliciously, "I believe they are like the unbelieving Jews—they seek a sign."

"You are very wicked, Polly, do you know?" he said carelessly, filling a pipe. "You will never be tamed and made respectable until you marry. I wish I were the happy man."

"I wish you were," she said, with a laugh. "But no. You will never be such a fool as to offer to marry me; and I shouldn't be such a fool as to accept you, if you did."

"I hope I shall never get fond of you, Polly," he said.

"Why?"

By this time the smile that her chaffing had brought to his face had quite died away, and he was staring pensively into the fire. When he spoke it was as if he were speaking to himself.

"Because the chances are you would die."

"Good gracious me!" said Polly.

"I sometimes have a notion," he continued, rather absently, "that the unknown presence of some fatal malady—some predisposition to death—may lend to women's faces a sort of expression, or tenderness, or sadness, that is peculiarly attractive to some men. The man does not know why he is attracted by this expression—he only knows that all the women he has loved have died off one by one, while they were still young. It is only a theory, you know, but there are some men who are unlucky like that."

"Well," said Polly, "of all the agreeable topics that were ever started, this is about the most lively. It all comes of your sitting indoors, and taking no interest in anything—not even in your painting. An artist has no business with philosophy—has he, Ted?"

For she called me Ted, too.

"Why, no," I said; "but Heatherleigh dabbles in philosophy in order to excuse his idleness."

"Well, Polly, suppose we start another topic. Suppose we take you into our confidence, and consult you about this young gentleman's prospects. I propose to assume the garb of an old master, and have him for a pupil—a student—a disciple. In time he will be able to paint all my pictures for me; and I shall have all the money, while he reaps all the praise. I propose taking a junior partner into the business; he is to do the work, while I get the profits. What do you think of it, Polly? Did I ever show you the things he has done? They're not very good, you know, my lad; they're chiefly remarkable for cheek. But in a short time, you would, I think, be able to paint a good many bits of my interiors for me, and so forth. What do you say, Ted?"

What could I say? Here were two of the very kindest beings I have ever met in this world laying their heads together to help me; and the astonishment and gratitude with which such a circumstance filled me almost blinded me to the obvious fact that Heatherleigh was trying to disguise the nature of his offer. To be plain, he, too, was conferring charity upon me. I knew that for a long time I could not be of the slightest use to him. Besides, he did not want to make money either by my efforts or his own. He worked by fits and starts—and after he had got a check from a dealer, he relapsed into his dawdling ways and indolent, abstemious luxury. He had an amazing gift or trick of manipulation—painting cost him neither study nor pains. He could turn off, when pressed for money, a picture in an inconceivably short space of time; and, if it was not a striking or original work, it was still out of the common run of picture-dealers' pictures. There was not a particle or trace of genius in his work—no bold conception or lofty aim, or sharp and luminous interpretation; but there was an easy and bright cleverness which had a certain individualism of its own, and which procured a too ready market for all that he produced. I think he was quite conscious of all this, and that the knowledge helped to confirm him in his indolent ways. He was not even gifted with the vague hope that he *might* become a great painter. He painted when his funds became low, or when he took a sudden fancy to dress himself remarkably well and give a few companions a dinner at Richmond. He was a handsome man, as I have said; and, when he chose, he could throw off the roughness of his present mode of life, and astonish one with the extreme elegance and finish of his toilet and general appearance. His hands were fine and delicate; he had small feet, and a certain air of refinement and ease which became his intelligent face and well-set neck. When he thus dressed himself, he completed the metamorphosis by becoming absurdly critical in all such matters as wines, cigars, dishes, dress, and manners. He was only acting a part, and imagining what he might have been had he not quarrelled with his family; and yet he acted the part so naturally that his companions, chiefly artists, used to be greatly impressed by such evidences of culture and high-breeding. Next day you would find him laughing at his own folly—dressed in an old velveteen jacket, with his hair uncombed, his waistcoat open and showing a shirt liberally stained with megilp and color, his delicate fingers sticky and dirty with varnishes and oils, and on the table beside his easel a short clay pipe and a battered pewter pot filled with half-and-half.

"I say that you are too kind," I replied—"that I should not be worth my keep for a very long time, if ever."

"You don't understand, Master Ted," said he; "I am entering upon a business speculation. I am buying up rough land, out of which I mean to get great harvests yet. I mean to make an artist of you, Ted."

"Make an artist of yourself!" said Polly.

"I mean to buy you out of the hands of that charming person, Weavle. I shall hold you as my slave and bondman; and then, when I am an old man, grown white and lean and shaky, you shall work for me and pay my little bills, and I shall bless you. You are not bound by any engagement to Weavle?"

"No."

"Nor by any promise to your parents?"

"No."

"What do you say, then?"

"I say that if you give me this chance I will do my very best in whatever way you want; and whether I succeed or not, I shall never forget your kindness to me—about the greatest I have ever received."

"Bravo!" cried Polly, with a sort of sob—indeed, nothing could equal this kind creature's intense sympathy with everybody and everything around her. "But do you know, Ted, what you have to go through before you become an artist?"

I professed ignorance; and inwardly hoped that Polly did not mean that I must grace the occasion by kissing her.

"There never yet," said she, "was an artist, or an author, or a poet, or anybody who had to live by his wits, that was of any good until he had met with a terrible disappointment in love. You must have your heart half-broken, Ted, before you can do anything. You know, they say that a reaper never does any good until he has cut himself with the sickle; so an artist must get wounded and hurt in the same way before he discovers the way to touch people. We must get your heart broken, Ted."

"Isn't it a lucky thing that there are so many women," said Heatherleigh, "whom Providence seems to have appointed for the purpose. I can easily supply him with any number of young persons whose profession is to break your heart with the most charming air in the world. Let's see: I wonder whose house I ought to take him to—to get him broken in, as it were. The air of Lewison's drawing-room—I call his place the Æsthetic Grotto—is too fine and clear for a vigorous, strong flirtation; and yet there are some promising young executioners to be met with there. You remember what Alfred de Musset says:

'J'aime encore mieux notre torture,
Que votre métier de bourreau.'

There is Bonnie Lesley, as they call her, for example—"

"What?" I said, "the girl whose face you are constantly sketching?"

"Even so, young sir."

"If she is like your copies of her, she must be something better than what you say."

"Oh, she is pretty enough, and sweet enough, doubtless," said he. "At least, I presume she is good-looking. In my young days, you could be sure of a woman's being beautiful, because you had a chance of seeing her face."

"I am certain," said Polly, "you have painted her face oftener than she has done. I saw her once in Regent's Park—recognized her directly. I should fall in love with her if I were a man."

"Very likely," said Heatherleigh, "and, if you were a man, you would probably regret it. However, I am glad to hear you say a kind word for her, Polly. You women are so very distrustful of each other."

"I suppose it's because we know ourselves so well," said Polly, with a sigh.

Heatherleigh now rang the bell, and begged his landlady to send up supper. It was soon on the table—cold mutton, pickled onions, water-cresses, cheese, and half-and-half, with a small bottle of stout for Polly's exclusive use.

Polly Whistler and I frequently supped there; and at these modest entertainments the girl really made a most charming companion. She had an inexhaustible fund of good spirits; and she had a playful, ingenious wit that I have never seen approached by any other woman. Of course, the brilliant and sharp and odd things she was constantly uttering lost none of their effect by the freedom of her manners, or by a half-dramatic trick she had of giving them point and expression; and yet there was never a trace of rudeness or bad taste in anything she said or did. Heatherleigh used to lie back in his big wooden chair, and listen with a sort of lazy enjoyment and paternal forbearance to her rapid talk, her bright laughter, and her shrewd and humorous hits. He, too, in his indolent fashion, would often meet her half-way in these sarcastic comments on men, women, and the accidents of life. She used to laugh and talk and jibe for the mere pleasure of amusing her companions and herself; but you could see that in his lazy epigrams upon human nature there was just a touch of bitterness—as if, unconsciously to himself, he was exhibiting marks of that old and useless struggle against the hard, resisting mass of the world. There was a half-concealed pungency about his wit that made you think he was scarcely himself aware of its acrid flavor; and to one who was accustomed to his ways, his sayings had the unusual merit of appearing to be dragged from him. I never saw him talk for effect—even in trying to amuse a girl, when a man is scarcely expected to be accurate, honest, or sensible. He and Polly used to relish these quiet little meetings keenly; and I—why I thought there never were in the world two people who enjoyed themselves so thoroughly and in so innocent a fashion, who were so good-natured and disinterested and frank and kind to everybody, high and low, whom they met. But I knew they were exceptions; for the average of human nature was as yet represented to me by Weavle.

Then we went to see Polly home. She lived just round the corner, in Albany Street, behind Regent's Park; and when she bade us good-bye, she said she should some day go to see my picture in the Academy. The words thrilled through me, and for a moment I could see nothing of the dark houses and the pavement, and of my two companions—but instead a great room filled with fashionable folks in splendid attire, all come to look at the rows of brilliant pictures. If I could but get a modest corner there! I said to myself, with a strange throb—and if, by chance, my obscure and little effort were to be glanced at, even for a moment, by—

"Thank you, Polly," said I, with the old consciousness falling down on me again; "my work has already been seen on the Academy walls, and I suppose it will be again—on the frames."

So we turned away, Heatherleigh and I, and walked carelessly onward. It was a beautiful night, still and mild, with a full moon shining on the pale fronts of the tall houses that lie along the north side of Regent's Park, and glittering here and there on the glossy leaves of the young birches. There was almost no one to be seen along the white pavements; but occasionally we passed a house the windows of which were lit up, gleaming warm and red into the pale gray light outside. We walked around Regent's Park and Primrose Hill, and along the Finchley Road towards the neighborhood of Hampstead; Heatherleigh talking of many things—of the project he had proposed to me, of Polly Whistler, and, latterly, of that old dead love of his, and of all the beautiful hopes and aspirations that lay buried in her grave. He seldom talked of her; when he did, there was something to me almost terrible in witnessing the emotion of this strong man—of the piteous way in which he used to look back and wonder how the world could have compassed this cruel and irremediable thing that was to haunt the rest of his life with its shadow. And yet there was a sweetness in the memory of it, I think, as I think there is in the memory of all our great sorrows—so long as these have not been the result of our own wilfulness or folly.

"Come," he said, "let us talk of something else. Do you know I regard Polly Whistler as the most heroic little woman I know? How Polly would laugh if you were to tell her she was a heroine. Did you hear, just as we walked off, an angry screech of a woman's voice from inside the house?"

"Yes."

"That note of kindly welcome was sounded by her mother,

who, I suppose, has returned from her concert in a state of intoxication. Fred Ward told me this morning of the frightful persecution the girl suffers at the hands of this woman, who spends all her earnings, and threatens her if she does not bring home more money. When she is in one of her drunken fits, she follows the girl through the streets, and goes up to the studios after her, and insists upon getting money."

"Fred Ward," said I, "must have been putting more imagination into his story than he ever did into one of his pictures. How is it Polly never hinted anything of the kind, but, on the contrary, has always spoken very generously and nicely about her 'old woman?' How is it that the old woman never pestered you for money?"

"There's the odd thing," said he. "You know Polly only sits to three or four fellows, all of whom I know. Every one of them, it seems, is familiarly acquainted with the mother, except myself; and Ward told me that Polly had made very great sacrifices that I might not know, and begged them all not to tell me. Indeed, the old woman, it seems, holds up a visitation to my studio as the highest threat she can use, and Polly will do anything rather than that I should learn what sort of a mother she has got. Ward says it is time that this terrorism should cease, and that I ought to explain to Mother Whistler that she had better drop it. He says, too, that the girl's conduct towards her mother is simply admirable—in kindness and forbearance and good-nature. But now I can look back and explain a good many things about Polly that used to puzzle me sometimes."

"Well," I said, "if I were you, I should not tell her that I knew. The girl doesn't want you to think ill of her mother; give her her own way."

"I'll consider about it," he replied; "but if I could get a private word with Mrs. Whistler, at some sober moment, I should like to tell her what might be the result of her conduct upon a girl less determined in character than poor Polly."

It was nearly one o'clock when we drew near Primrose Hill again. The streets were now quite deserted, and there was scarcely a light to be seen in any of the windows of the tall, pale houses. As we came around by Albert Road, however, we observed one house in which the lower rooms were yet lit up. Heatherleigh crossed over, and we paused in front of the railings.

"That is the Æsthetic Grotto," he whispered; "I wonder who are inside at present?"

The windows were open and the Venetian blinds were down; the latter, from their sloping position, showing only gleaming lines of the roof and chandeliers inside. Presently a girl's voice was heard—a pure and high soprano, that rose clearly and fully above the delicate rippling accompaniment of the piano. In the stillness of the night we heard every tone and modulation of the exquisite voice, and I, for one, stood entranced there, drinking in the beautiful, touching melody.

"I think it is Schubert's," said Heatherleigh; "the Lewisons are mad about Schubert."

At length the song was finished, and the blank stillness that followed struck painfully on the ear.

"They are unusually late to-night," said Heatherleigh. "They keep open house every evening, for everybody who has musical or literary or artistic tastes. The place is a perfect den of big and small celebrities, and sometimes they have the most brilliant little gatherings."

After a moment, he said, with a smile—

"Do you know who was singing that German song, just now?"

"How should I?"

"It was Bonnie Lesley, as they call her."

CHAPTER V.

IN REGENT'S PARK.

On the first morning that I walked up Tottenham Court Road towards Heatherleigh's studio, with the old shadow of Weavle removed from over me, I felt that the world had grown immeasurably wider. It was the morning of the first of May, and all the sweet influences of the season were added to this one supreme sensation of breadth and life, and a joyous and active future. I imagined myself then going to conquer the world. I felt the delight of anticipation tingling through me. I straightened up my shoulders and sniffed the fresh morning air, which was sweet and grateful even in this dingy district. I clenched my fists, brought them up to my chest, and shot them out again as if I were knocking down a Weavle on each side. To my horror and surprise, I found that, as a matter of fact, I had in my blind exultation dealt a severe blow to an elderly gentleman, who had been crossing the street, and was just about to step on the pavement.

"You great, lumbering idiot!" he said.

I turned and made the most ample and profuse apologies, which he cut short with—

"Go to the—"

I did not hear him complete the sentence as he angrily turned away, but I can imagine how it ended. Yet I would have braved any amount of anger to hear those words "great, lumbering," applied to me. Was it, then, that I might not be so deficient in bodily presence as I had imagined? I regarded myself in the window of a shoe-shop. I did not cut a distinguished figure—that was clear. I was obviously taller than the old gentleman whom I had hurt in a sensitive place, but then he was of the barrel order of human architecture. For the rest, I had not much in my appearance on which to pride myself. There was a certain lean and hungry look on my pale face, which the staring dark eyes and rather beak-like nose did not diminish. By accident, my hair had been allowed to grow long, and, as I looked at myself in this extemporized mirror, I could compare myself to nothing so much as a hungry Italian refugee, who had lost some notion or idea when he was young, and spent the rest of his life in wistfully trying to recall it. Pictured against the rows of shining boots, my face must have seemed that of one unsatisfied, meditative, melancholy, and perhaps a trifle older-looking than I ought to have been at my years.

"Good-morrow to the youthful Apelles," said Heatherleigh, when I entered. "You have come betimes. I presume you mean to set to work immediately."

He was lying in his big easy-chair, his leg over the one arm of it, a clay pipe in his mouth, a volume of Bain in his hand, the breakfast things still on the table. He certainly had not washed, and you could only say by way of courtesy that he had dressed.

"If you please," I said.

I felt very nervous all the same, and looked timidly around to see if there was anything I fancied I might be able to do for him. I glanced at the picture which was on his principal easel. It was a remarkably clever study of a lady of Charles II.'s time, seated in a high-backed chair, with a couple of spaniels playing at her feet. There was absolutely no idea or aim whatever in the picture; he had merely taken this pretty and cleverly painted face, and surrounded it with a few appropriate accessories.

"What do you think of that?" he said.

"I don't see what you mean by it," I answered, frankly.

"I will tell you, then. I mean money by it. It is a sketch I made for the market some eight months ago. I had the good sense to be ashamed of it, and turned its face to the wall. I took it down this morning, and mean to finish it—why? do you think?"

Of course, I had no idea.

"Because Professor Bain has just been pointing out to me that I have a natural genius for being happy. In the country, I have the keen pleasure of Self-conservation—the storing up of physical health and nervous energy; in the town, I have the indolent pleasure of Stimulation—drawing upon that store of superfluous vitality. If Stimulation were out of the question, and all our pleasures only increased our health! As it is, however, it seems to me, my Pupil, that I have not been balancing the two—that I must have more of Self-conservation; and as I propose, consequently, to go into the country, I took down that picture to find the means."

"I shall be very glad, Master, if you will instruct me in Philosophy as well as in Art," I said.

"That notion has just occurred to me. But then, you see, the old teachers of philosophy were accustomed to talk to their disciples under the trees and in the leafy alleys of Academus; and, accordingly, the best thing I think we can do this fine morning is to take a walk in Regent's Park. What do you say?"

"It is for you to decide, of course," I answered; but the notion of thus being able to walk out anywhere in the hours which ought to be devoted to work was thoroughly bewildering to me. Nor could I throw off an impression that there was something wrong in the proposal; and that, if we did go out, we should be "caught."

"I must dress," he said, getting up out of the chair; "and, meanwhile, I will put you on your trial. You see I have sketched in behind the lady that screen over there. If you like, you can try your hand at finishing it—keeping it very quiet. Use my palette until I get you one for yourself. There, sit you down."

He left, and I sat down before the picture with fear and trembling. My hand shook so that I could scarce squeeze the color out of the tubes; and my eyes seemed to throb and burn. The screen was an old, tattered thing, which had at one time been covered with colored maps. Now all these had subsided, until the surface was a mass of cool grays, with here and there just a touch of warmer tint, where Africa or England was vaguely visible. It was an admirable bit of background; but how was I to attempt it?

I wonder if Heatherleigh purposely delayed his return. At first, it seemed to me that every moment the door leading into his small bedroom would open, and that he would walk over to the picture to see that I had been too nervous to begin it at all. Then the brush began to work a little better; and although my eyes still throbbed and burned so that at times the whole screen and room faded away and left only a spotted mist there, I felt, rather than saw, that the screen in the picture was beginning to look somewhat like the actual screen beyond.

This was not by any means the first time I had attempted painting in oil. Many a chance effort I had made to wrestle with the stronger medium; although I always returned to water-color as that which I could use most easily. It is well known that tyros paint more presentably in oil than in water—their experience of both being equal; but I had dabbled in water-color for two or three years, while my acquaintance with oil was exceedingly limited. From the moment, however, in which I had accepted Heatherleigh's offer, I had industriously experimented with a few of the cheapest tubes and some bits of board, until I could fairly copy the different colors and hues of the objects around me. Yet to have my clumsy manipulation placed exactly side by side with Heatherleigh's dexterous and clean touch was a cruel test.

At length the door opened, and he walked across the room. The brush fell from my hand, and I had nearly dropped myself, for my head was swimming with the superlative concentration of the last half-hour. Very probably, too, my face was a trifle paler than usual; for I noticed that he regarded me curiously before he looked at the picture at all, and that he kindly placed his hand on my shoulder as he proceeded to scan the wild effort I had made.

I felt myself grow hot and cold alternately in that moment of dire suspense; and when he said, with a tone of surprise, "By

Jove!" it was as if a blow of some sort had struck me. I dared scarcely say to myself what that exclamation might mean.

Then he said, quietly and cheerfully—

"Whatever made you try to paint in all that accurately in five minutes? Of course, it won't do, you know; but the effort you have made, and the result you have gained, in a few minutes, is astounding."

I rose up, keeping firm hold—I know not why—of the brushes and the palette.

"Do you think," I said—"do you consider—"

Then I felt that I was reeling, and knew vaguely that he put out his arm quickly to catch me. After that a blank. When I came to, I found that I had fallen backward, striking my head against the table. Heatherleigh led me into his bedroom, and made me bathe my head in cold water. After a few minutes I was all right.

"Come," said he, with a quiet smile on his face, "take my arm, and let's go for a walk in Regent's Park."

We went out into the cool, fresh air: and I was proud of the exhaustion I felt, for I knew it had been incurred in that one terrible effort to cut forever the chain that bound me to Weavle and the old hard times. But was it of any avail? He had never answered my question; and I dared not ask it again, lest he might tell me, in tone if not in words, that I could never be useful to him—that the dreams I had already begun to dream were visionary, impossible, hopeless.

After a few minutes' silence he said to me, gravely and kindly—

"If you don't find some means of curbing that impulsive and impetuous will of yours, I fear your life will be neither a long one nor a happy one. If you suffer your temperament to lead you into the habit of desiring successive things so earnestly that you lose all consciousness and judgment in striving for them, you will find yourself subjected in life to a series of the bitterest disappointments, and these revulsions might have a disastrous effect on one so sensitive as you are. There is nothing of an intensely dramatic or tragic kind that I can imagine as being unlikely to fall in your way. You are the sort of man, for example, who, if I mistake not, would coolly and deliberately blow out your brains if some woman you had set your heart on proved unfaithful to you."

"You imagine all that," I said, "because I tried hard to paint the screen. But I didn't know that I had been trying hard until it was all over."

"Precisely," he said; "you entirely abandon yourself to a passing mood or fancy. I have remarked it several times. Now what would be the result if you happened to set before you one supreme aim—if you staked all your chances upon one throw?"

"In what direction do you mean?" I asked.

"In any. You say to yourself, *I will never cease striving until I have painted a Madonna to eclipse Raphael's*, or *I will win such and such a woman, or die.* You are just as likely as not, in either case, to aim at something quite impossible. The result?—when you find yourself cheated in your notions of your own power, when you find the chief object of your life removed from you, what is more likely than that you will suddenly put an end to a wretched failure—by a pennyworth of poison."

"You want me to confine myself to easy possibilities?"

"To possibilities."

"Who is to tell me what is possible to me? Suppose I have an unconscionable craving, that might make me hope to win this or that prize? Or don't you think that one may feel the delight of striving for anything—however impossible—a greater happiness than the achieving of some small immediate success? You yourself—don't you constantly aim at something new and unknown in a picture, and chance the failure?"

"No, I don't," he said, with a laugh. "I know very accurately what I can do; but I am out of court in the matter. I know that I am myself a failure; and the knowledge doesn't bother me. All I say to you is this—take heed not to set your desires too high; for to you a disappointment might be a catastrophe of a sudden and final kind."

For me to set my desires too high! I inwardly laughed at the notion. Was it not enough that I was permitted at times to break through the hard conditions of life by dreaming?—by dreaming of things which were possible to others, but which were to me forever impossible.

So we went around and entered Regent's Park. Heatherleigh kept talking of all sorts of things—following, as usual, the most diverse moods of morbid introspection, of gay raillery, of bitter sarcasm. Yet all this was colored by a broad, warm light of kindliness which, I suppose, partly owed its origin to the evident enjoyment he had in exercising himself in any way. Life was really a happiness to him; and his sharp speeches, and brooding analyses, and light-hearted jocularity were as great a delight to him as the physical acts of breathing and seeing and walking—all of which he enjoyed with an enjoyment that was at times just a trifle too conscious. I do not believe that he had a single care to cloud his mind. He had long ago cut all connection with whatever relatives he may have had; and was free from necessary friendships and forced duties. His few acquaintances were of his own manner of living; and he could obtain their society just in such proportion as he chose. He could make more money than he needed; and the labor was neither painful nor irksome to him. He had no particular aim or desire to torment him; he rejoiced in his physical strength, in his mental clearness, as he rejoiced in the flavors of food and beer and tobacco. How a man, living under such circumstances, failed to become a selfish misanthrope, I never could understand.

"Don't you ever mean to marry?" I said to him, this morning, as we were passing the Zoological Gardens, and were coming in view of the broad park, that lay green and beautiful in the May sunlight.

"Sometimes I wish somebody would take the trouble to marry me," he said. "I think I am in the position of a good many unmarried men. They know they could be very affectionate and contented if they married; but they know the bother and peril of looking out for a wife, and don't care to run the risk. You glance around the circle of your acquaintance, and see a number of more or less sensible, pretty, and well-meaning girls. You can't marry one of them without spending ever so much time and anxiety in finding out her disposition, and also without encountering the nuisance of rivalship. Then you may either find yourself mistaken and be disgusted with your waste of trouble, or you may really fall in love with her, and find her perverse or inclined to marry somebody else—and so on; while all the time you are losing the best years of your life in this perplexing and irritating, and often profitless search. Of course, I am talking of men who are a little anxious about the sort of woman they mean to marry. At your age I fell in love with everything that wore ear-rings, and would have married anybody capable of saying 'I will.'"

"Yet men do marry," I said, "in spite of all the current talk."

"Oh, yes," he said, "in the mean time they do. But if our young men cultivate their present notions and habits, we shall soon have this world getting so far to be like heaven that there shall be in it neither marrying nor giving in marriage. At present—"

Either he paused or I forgot to listen. For some minutes I had been gazing vaguely at two figures which were walking slowly towards us under the trees. While they were yet a long way off, the lines of sunshine falling across the path from between the branches gleamed upon them from time to time; and it seemed to me that the materials for a very pretty French picture were there before us—in the straight road, the long and narrowing avenue of trees, the bars of sunlight, and the fashionably dressed ladies who were walking together. Without thinking of them, I was admiring the contrast in their costume. One of them wore a tight-fitting dress of black silk and crape, with a rather lengthy train that added height and dignity to her somewhat short and slight figure. Even at that distance I could see that she walked with a wonderful ease and grace, that made the girlish little person look almost majestic. *Incedit reginâ.* Her companion, on the other hand, actually shone in the sunlight; for she wore a gauzy white dress, the upper and tight portion of which was touched here and there with bright blue, while the under part revealed a bold dash of color in the gleam of a blue silk petticoat. Then she wore a small white hat, with a blue feather in it; and she had a bit of blue near her neck; while she carried in her arms a white Pomeranian dog, which, like herself, wore a collar of blue satin ribbon, with absurdly big bows. She had profuse golden hair, and a bright complexion that the twilight of her white parasol scarcely dimmed. Indeed, so very brilliant and beautiful was this apparition, that as the belts of sunlight through which she passed broadened, and as she came nearer, I could not keep from regarding the harmonious taste of the dress and the singular effect the whole figure produced in the alternate green shadow and yellow sunlight—insomuch that I paid no attention to the other lady by her side.

I suppose we all of us often look at people without seeing them—stare in their faces, while thinking of something else, and are yet quite guiltless of intentional rudeness. I know that I had fallen into a sort of trance, and heard nothing more of Heatherleigh's voice, when I suddenly observed a smile of surprise appear on the face of the girl in white and blue. I knew, rather than saw, that Heatherleigh lifted his hat, and went forward to speak to her. At the same time, as I was naturally passing on, I caught a glimpse of a pair of eyes that *had been* looking at me. I only remembered, a minute afterwards, when the cold shiver had gone out of me, that these dark, luminous, gray-blue eyes had also a certain surprise in them—perhaps a kindly surprise, and inquiry.

Heatherleigh stopped and talked to the two girls for several minutes, and I was glad. I never could understand the easy dexterity with which the matter-of-fact people in the Scriptures encountered the most startling and unexpected things—how this man answered directly and frankly the questions of an angel; how the other accepted some great miracle as a thing of course, and only to be considered as getting him food or water. Why were they not wholly paralyzed and overwhelmed with wonder? why did they not instinctively beg for time to comprehend and realize the mystery before them?

"What a singular coincidence!" said Heatherleigh, laughing, when he came up. "I was just going to speak of her in connection with your marriage topic. Do you know who that was?"

"The lady in blue and white?"

"Yes."

"No, I don't."

"That, Master Apelles, is the young person to whom Polly and I mean to hand you over in order that your artistic education may be completed. That is she whom her numerous admirers and victims call 'Bonnie Lesley.'"

"You have warned me effectively," I replied.

"That may have been a mistake of mine, from an artistic point of view," he said, laughing. "But perhaps if I were to tell you why I like to run down that young creature, you might be inclined to take up the cudgels for her, and impound me. After all, she is a very nice sort of girl. She is staying at the Lewisons' at present, as I imagined when I heard her sing there. I fancy she lives there chiefly now. I told her the service I wanted of her as regards you. She was very willing; and hopes you will go with me to the Lewisons' house on Thursday evening. It is only one of their ordinary evenings—æsthetics and mild refreshments. I promised you would come with me."

I looked at him: I thought he was joking; but he was not.

"One or two young men about town come in evening dress," he continued; "but Lewison doesn't care about that element, and discourages it. His wife likes it, for the sake of her young-lady friends, and of course where Bonnie Lesley is, there young fools are sure to be."

"What did she do to you," I said to him, "that you should be so bitter about her?"

"She once made me believe that she had a heart; but I discovered afterwards that it was only an organ with two openings, situated in a cavity of the chest, for the convenience of the lungs."

"I fancy I can understand."

"No; don't mistake me: Bonnie Lesley and I were never lovers. But of that anon. What I want to say to you is this: mind, in speaking to her, not to ask her too particularly where she has lived—I mean, in what particular place she was brought up."

"Where do her parents live?"

"She hasn't any."

"Her relations, then?"

"She hasn't any. I don't think she ever had either the one or the other. I imagine that on some hushed, warm afternoon in summer, when everything was lazy and quiet and solemn, somebody down in some still valley saw a small angel, dressed in blue and white, with a tiny white hat and a blue feather, drop quietly down from the clouds. And she has grown up to be Bonnie Lesley, and the hat has grown with her. Really there seems to be a good deal of vagueness about her antecedents. For myself, I only know that she is acquainted with some parts of France and Germany. Whoever called her Bonnie Lesley must have supposed she was Scotch; but, if she is, she must take uncommon pains to conceal the fact. She has her notions of form and color, too, has that young woman. Do you know what she said of you?"

"No."

"That you might, with proper dressing, resemble either Dante, Schiller, or Vandyke. She preferred Vandyke herself; and I promised to get you to buy a big brown beaver, with a broad and dashing rim."

"Tell me honestly—did you or she speak of me at all?" I said.

"I give you my word of honor that she expects to see you at the Lewisons' on Thursday next."

"What did the lady who was with her say?"

"The girl in black? Nothing particular. By the way, I did not catch her name when I was introduced to her."

"I can tell you that," I said: "it is Miss Hester Burnham."

"What?—the girl who has got the big house down in that valley you are constantly talking about?"

"Yes. My father is her gamekeeper. I suppose she, too, is staying at the Lewisons', and I dare say you would consider it rather a good joke if I were to go there and meet her on equal terms!"

"Monsieur, you mistake. When you enter the Æsthetic Grotto you leave all such considerations behind. Besides, what does it matter to you whether your father is Miss Burnham's keeper, or the devil, or a bishop? You are an artist. I have given you the royal accolade. You are the equal of all men upon the earth, even if your purse be rather short, and your reputation nothing to speak of. But if I had known that the quiet little girl was Miss Burnham, I should have looked at her attentively. I only know that she had singularly fine eyes, and a soft and pretty voice."

I was unwilling to let him imagine that because my father was a gamekeeper (though even that suggested the propriety of my not meeting Miss Burnham) I did not wish to go to the Lewisons' house. So I told him the whole story of that visit to Burnham, which was yet fresh and keen in my memory. When I had finished, he looked at me curiously, and said—

"You are a strange creature. I can't make you out."

"If you had been in my place," I asked, "wouldn't you have felt as I felt?"

"I should have laughed at the whole affair. I should not be glowing with indignation and anger and wrath as you are now. Come, suppose we go to Lewisons' on Thursday. Suppose we beg Miss Burnham to rebel against her womanly instincts, and speak the truth for once. Suppose we ask her—"

"If I go," I said to him (while I felt my face flush), "it will be to meet her as an equal."

"Bravely spoken," said he, "but you forget one thing: it is very unlikely she will be there. The Lewisons' house is not a hotel."

CHAPTER VI.

THE ÆSTHETIC GROTTO.

But long before Thursday evening my courage failed me. I had had wild ideas of revenge and self-assertion, and all the rest of it; but not even these would permit me to be guilty of an impertinence; and an impertinence I certainly considered the notion of my being present as a guest in any house where Miss Burnham was also a guest. I told Heatherleigh I would not go.

In the mean time I applied myself earnestly to whatever snatches of work he allowed me to undertake. Looking back at that strange probationary period, I can scarcely say whether I had grown bold enough to consider certain dreams of mine possible of realization, or whether it was only the fever of impatience and desire, begotten of a certain extravagant purpose that had nothing to do with art, which drove me into constant and painful effort to leap over necessary study and achieve definite results. Heatherleigh looked at the matter from a practical point of view.

"You are still laboring under the habit you acquired in Weavle's place," he said, "of thinking that you must constantly be working. Why, absolute idleness is the very commissariat of art—that fine, receptive calm in which you are storing up, unconsciously, experiences and reflections for future use. You work as if Weavle were constantly at your elbow."

Polly Whistler took great interest in my progress, and used to tell the most audacious lies in the form of criticism upon my labors. I was so very grateful for her encouragement and kindness, that I was nearly falling in love with her. But Polly had a fine, practical way with her, which not only instantly detected any such tentative lapse from the explicit relations existing between her and the people around her, but also set the matter straight again with a surprising and business-like swiftness. Early love, of this nebulous and uncertain kind, thrives upon secrecy, but is killed by frankness; and Polly was uncommonly frank.

"I'll be a mother to you, if you like," she said to me, in her merry way, "but you mustn't fall in love with me, because then you would get angry because I didn't fall in love with you. It seems to me a pity that men and women can't be friends with each other without falling in love and spoiling it all, becoming jealous and cantankerous and exacting. Everybody should take a lesson from Mr. Heatherleigh and me."

I looked up at her as she uttered the last words, and she inadvertently dropped her eyes.

To return, however, to the proposed meeting at Lewison's house. On the Wednesday, Heatherleigh brought me a positive assurance that Miss Burnham could not be present on the following evening, and also Mr. and Mrs. Lewison's cards, with their compliments. In the end I went.

This was my first introduction into anything like society; and for a time I could scarcely tell, myself, what my first impressions were. The chief thing that struck me, I think, was the extreme quiet and repose of the people. They seemed to live in a delicate atmosphere, which caused small sensations to appear large to them. They never had to emphasize what they had to say; and there was a general apprehension of minute points and appearances which made me a little nervous. The very air of the room seemed to be fine and watchful and critical.

Mr Lewison was a tall, fair man, with a partially bald head, dark blue eyes, and a red moustache. He had a peculiarly bland, easy manner about him which puzzled me; because it seemed to lift him so entirely above that sphere of struggle and competition and passionate impulses with which I was familiar. I think he had been in business; at any rate, he was now living as a private gentleman, his chief amusement being the making of his house an open resort for all sorts of artistic and literary persons.

When Heatherleigh and I entered the large and brilliant room there were not more than a dozen people there. Miss Lesley was at the piano, singing a rather commonplace ballad in her splendid style. She had an excellent soprano voice, tenderly expressive, and perfectly cultivated. There was a gentleman by her side, in evening dress, who was turning over the leaves of music for her.

I was introduced to Mr. and Mrs. Lewison, and found myself surprisingly at ease with both. Indeed, I found at this time that, however apprehensive I might be about meeting any stranger, I had no sooner begun to enter into conversation than my embarrassment vanished. Besides, all the responsibilities and formalities lay upon Heatherleigh.

When Miss Lesley had finished singing she took the arm of the gentleman who had been waiting upon her, and crossed the room towards us. I saw with dismay that her companion was Mr. Alfred Burnham. Instinctively I glanced around the room again to see that she whom I had feared to meet was not there. No; there was no one even resembling her.

The young man with the hook nose, the cold gray eyes, and closely cropped yellowish hair moved off to another part of the room, and Miss Lesley was left talking to Heatherleigh. Then Heatherleigh introduced me to her; and, somehow or other, I found myself seated beside her on a couch, turning over a collection of proof-engravings.

I had listened to her voice but for a few moments, when I began to wonder how Heatherleigh could have spoken so unfairly of the girl. Was it to surprise me with the contrast? She had a face that, in spite of its full-grown and developed beauty—its broad, fine tints, and dazzling complexion—was almost childlike in its simplicity of expression: large, blue eyes of great tenderness of color and depth; a full little mouth, rosy and plump; a somewhat low, smooth, Grecian brow; and great masses of yellow hair, that were artistically arranged and decorated with a broad band of violet velvet. She wore a low white dress, with a train of heavy violet satin, and there was around her white neck a thick gold serpent, whose diamond head and ruby eyes, lying upon her bosom, scarcely rose and fell as she breathed or laughed. That this glorious creature should waste upon me—upon me alone—a single thought or word would at another time have seemed incredibly absurd to me; but under the spell of her voice—which had a scarcely perceptible lisp that was singularly quaint and attractive—I forgot all considerations of whatever kind, and went on talking to her as if I were in a dream, only to hear the sound of her voice in reply.

She asked me if I liked the song she had sung. There was but one answer to the question: perhaps I did not limit my expressions as I ought to have done.

"I am so glad," she said, with a pretty smile in her eyes, as she played with an ivory paper-knife that she held in her tiny white fingers, "because here, you know, they don't care for anything but classical music. I feel very guilty when I sing anything that is simple and commonplace, and I am so pleased to discover that some particular one here or there has been enjoying it. You like ballad-music, then?"

"I never heard any kind of music, played on any kind of instrument, that I did not like," I said, enthusiastically, but with absolute truth—"so long as it was in tune. I am like a confirmed drunkard, who will drink anything that will intoxicate him; and the effect that music has upon me is more intoxication than anything else."

"But Mr. Heatherleigh says you are an artist. Why, with such a passion for music, did you not become a musician?"

"I am neither an artist nor a musician, nor anything else that produces," I said; "but there is no sort of art that I do not enjoy. As for being a musician, I dare say I should keep in tune if I played on the drum."

"But if you enjoy every kind of music," she said, with a kind of childish wonder, "what is the value of a compliment from you? Perhaps you thought the song I sung rather stupid, although you like the jingle of the music."

"Well, I did," I said.

"But you must prefer some kind of music to other kinds."

"I should have preferred hearing you sing a German song that you once sung when I was listening outside at the railings."

"Ah, do you like German music?" she said, turning her large and beautiful eyes upon my face, and blinding me. "I love it. I think it is charming."

Now "charming" is not exactly the adjective which I should have applied to German music. I never could see prettiness in the sea. But then Miss Lesley was a very young girl; and very young girls are not always apt at choosing the proper word to describe their emotion or opinion. If you had looked at the perfect flower of her face, at its changing lights and tenderness, you would have seen that the pathos and utter misery of the old German ballads, and the mystic grandeur of the German classical music, were somehow themselves expressed there.

We talked of all manner of things—of the pictures before us, of artistic subjects generally, of the people in the room. On the last point, she was very confidential; describing not only the one or two celebrities present, but also her own impressions of them.

What chiefly struck me about her was her childlike desire to obtain information. Once or twice I turned and regarded her, to see if she were making fun; but no—the large, infantine blue eyes still begged for the knowledge she had demanded. She was so anxious to acquire a correct taste in artistic matters, she said. She did not wish to appear stupid; and she would be very grateful if I would privately give her some little assistance.

"You see how I am situated," she said, as she pretended to turn over the engravings which neither of us heeded. "I meet here men and women who are profoundly learned in subjects of which I know nothing. I dare not speak of these things and confess my ignorance, or they would look upon me as a barbarian. Now, with regard to old pictures, the only rule I have been able to make out for myself is to admire whatever is very dirty, very ugly, and indistinguishable. In crockery—enamelled *faience*, don't they call it?—in china and glass, and such things, I find my only chance is to seize upon what is more than usually absurd and extravagant. If the lizards, frogs, and eels on the plate are very ugly and ridiculous, then one is safe in praising it; and if the drinking-glass be dirty, of a bad shape, and useless, it is certain to be some rare specimen of Venetian or some such ware. I find it the same in other things. If one is turning over a collection of ferns, for instance, one may be certain that the ugliest and most insignificant are the rarest. Of course, it is only my ignorance that makes me think so, and I should be so grateful to any one who would kindly explain to me the real beauty of artistic marvels. But then, it would have to be quite secret—this instruction. When grown-up people learn to dance, you know, they are very much ashamed of the process, and make it quite private. Suppose you were to go and bring me the black thing that Mr. Lewison has just put down—on the top shelf of that Chinese whatnot."

It was a Japanese jug in bronze, with a curious handle, and a long, slender spout. The design of the jug was very graceful, and the workmanship remarkably delicate. I fetched it, and showed it to Miss Lesley, who regarded it with that air of pretty wonder which was almost the typical expression of her face.

"Shall we go into the room opposite?" she said. "They use it as a sort of picture-gallery, and I suppose you have not seen the pictures."

She took my arm, and we left. The large room we found to be lit up, although there was no one in it. There was an imposing array of pictures all around, and one of them especially having caught my eye as I entered, we went towards it. I can remember only that it was the figure of a young man, who sat dejected and alone amid a curious flood of golden light. The whole character of the painting was Greek; and it was apparently decorative in treatment. Despite the obvious mannerism of it, it was a work of singular power.

"Isn't it very pretty?" she said, with the same expression of gentle wonder on her face. "It was done by ——, who is a great friend of ——'s, the poet, whom you will see here to-night, most likely. It represents some story, Mr. Heatherleigh told me; but he did not say what it was."

"I know the story," I said, as soon as I heard the name of the young poet, who had then just made his appearance, and who was puzzling the sober-minded critics with the reckless inpertinences and wilfulnesses of his unmistakable genius.

"Will you tell it to me?" she said, sitting down upon a couch.

"How can I translate it into prose?" I answered. "However, the story is of a young Scandinavian poet who dies. You find him in the world of spirits, wandering about moody and discontented. Odin comes to him, and asks him why he complains. He says it is because the maiden whom he loved on earth must now have grown old and gray and wrinkled, and when she, too, comes into heaven, he will not be able to recognize her.

"'Does she love you still?' asks the god.

"'Her love is like mine,' says the poet; 'it is the same always.'

"So Odin sends him down to earth, and bids him seek out his old love. He wanders about, and cannot find her. At last he enters a chamber, and finds there the dead body of an old and wrinkled woman, and they tell him that the dead woman is the woman he loved. At first he is sorrowful, and then he is glad; for he says, 'I still love her; and now I shall know her when I get back to heaven.' So he bids farewell to earth again, and prepares to meet his love grown old and careworn. But he is just entering heaven when he sees before him, with a smile on her face, the very maiden whom he knew in his youth. She comes forward, and takes him by the hand; but he is half-afraid, for he thinks that Odin has played him a trick.

"'Are you really my little Frida, whom I loved long ago?'

"'I am your little Frida; don't you know me?' she asks.

"'But I saw you lying dead; and you were old and gray.'

"'And don't you know,' she says, 'that the gods have decreed that whoever loves truly shall always be young? I shall be always to you your little Frida, whom you loved long ago.'"

When I had finished my poor effort at conveying a notion of the story, she sighed gently, and said—

"How very pretty! Do you know many of these stories?"

"No," I said, "for that is the story of a modern poem; but old Scandinavian and German poetry is full of such legends."

"I should like to listen to them forever," she said, with a sort of pleased curiosity in her eyes.

Then we rose, and made a tour of the pictures. Her remarks puzzled and perplexed me. It was not that she made any great mistakes, or talked nonsense; but that she seemed to have the same appreciation of every quality of excellence. Nothing seemed to affect her beyond a certain point; and everything seemed to reach that point. We crossed a very pretty hearth-rug, and I drew her attention to the quiet and artistic pattern of it—so different from the staring bunches of red roses and white ribbon which I had seen in upholsterers' windows. Well, she appeared to be as much struck by that as by a small moonlight scene of Turner's, which was a wonder of idealized and yet literal faithfulness. Sometimes, when a particular picture seemed very striking or powerful to me, I almost begged her to be a little more enthusiastic in her admiration, and then she always was—in words. By this time we had grown quite familiar with each other. She confessed afterwards that she was astonished by my easy frankness; but then I knew nothing of the reserve that society demands, and she undoubtedly failed to impress it upon me. She so little overawed me that I began to wonder what most affected her—on what side of her character she was most receptive and impressionable. For pictures, it was clear, she cared little; or, rather, she had a general liking, which may have been indiscriminate through imperfect education. But she was never moved by a picture; and I gathered from her admissions that she had no great preference for any kind of music. I wondered whether, on hearing Mozart's Sonata in A sharp, or one of Mendelssohn's splendid choruses, she would only express a faint surprise, as she did on meeting a masterpiece in painting. Or was it that all the artistic side of her nature was cold and shallow, while in matters of personal feeling she was receptive and warm and deep?

Perhaps some temporary indisposition might have blunted her artistic perceptions. I have noticed that people who were ready to overpraise mediocre work, and be quite enthusiastic about good work, when they entered a picture-exhibition, passed over with indifference or cold distaste the very best pictures when they drew near the end of their visit—so powerful an agent is physical fatigue in destroying the keenness of the æsthetic sense. Perhaps Miss Lesley had a headache, or was annoyed by the non-receipt of a letter; and only out of courtesy expressed a vague acquiescence when I ventured to praise a picture.

At all events, on the emotional side, no one could question the generous width and tenderness of her nature. To look into her eyes was to kill doubt. The warm love-light of them seemed to thaw reserve, and draw you closer to her. You could not help speaking in a low voice to her; you could not help, if you looked at her eyes, unbosoming your most secret confidences and begging for a return of this friendly frankness. She seemed to have around her an atmosphere of warmth and kindliness—an atmosphere silent and delicious, that predisposed you to waking dreams. To be near her was to breathe poetry; and yet, when you regarded the statuesque beauty of her bust and neck and head, the fine play of color and light in her complexion, the warm, supple contour of her face, and the life and tenderness of her eyes, you were puzzled to understand why this glorious woman should, even in one direction, exhibit a hardness or thinness of character that seemed so inconsistent with her soft and stately and yielding beauty.

I was recalled to myself by hearing some voices, and when I looked up (we had again sat down, and I was listening intently to what she was saying) I found Heatherleigh's eyes fixed on me, with a peculiar, mocking expression in them. He had been led into the room by Mr. Lewison, who was talking to him; but when I looked up he was quietly regarding us both, with a sardonic smile on his face. It was a smile that seemed to me to have something demoniacal in it. Did he imagine, then, that I was inclined to play Faust to his Mephistopheles? No sooner had Miss Lesley perceived their presence than she asked me to take her into the other apartment; I gladly consented, and so we walked across the room.

A little incident occurred as we were going out.

"Miss Lesley," said Mr. Lewison, "do you know why, according to Mr. Heatherleigh, we ought to be thankful that we are Christians?"

"No," she said, simply.

"Because, if we were not, some other nation would probably try to make us Christians."

She uttered a musical little laugh and passed on. But when we had got outside into the hall she said—

"I do dislike conundrums. I never discovered the fun of a conundrum even after it was explained to me."

"But that isn't quite a conundrum," I said, with some surprise; "he means that the process of being made a Christian against your will is rather—"

"I beg you not to waste your time in trying to explain a joke to me," she said, laughing, but still with the most obvious candor and honesty. "I assure you I never could understand the simplest of them. People will not believe me; but I cannot even understand the meaning or enjoyment of a pun. They show me that they say two things, using the same word in each; but I don't see the fun of it—I don't see why they shouldn't use another word. Don't you think me very stupid? Of course, I know it is clever to make a pun; but, if I laugh at one, it is merely as a compliment, as you are expected to admire a painting you don't care for."

Then she seemed to recall herself, shrugged her shoulders slightly, and laughed the pretty little laugh again.

"There are some people one cannot help talking freely to; and perhaps I have been creating in your mind a notion that I am a monster of ignorance and dulness. Is it so?"

Now I never could pay a compliment to a woman. If I liked her, and admired this or that in her character, I could and always did become enthusiastic, and was in nowise loth to let her know my exaggerated opinion of her excellences. But absolutely to pay a compliment, in the form of a compliment, to a woman who drove me into it—no. I remained silent—perhaps a trifle vexed that I could not easily fence off the question as any one accustomed to the small word-warfare of society might easily have done.

Fortunately we were just entering the other room; and so my embarrassment was partly concealed.

"Why she *has* come after all!" exclaimed my companion.

The next moment I caught a glimpse of a small darkly dressed figure; and I knew that it must be Miss Burnham. I dared not look her in the face—indeed, I scarcely knew what I did, as Bonnie Lesley relinquished my arm and went forward to greet her friend. Was it she or I who effected the separation? I only know that I walked away, without once turning my head; but I heard Hester Burnham's voice, and I fancied a tall gentleman who was by her side must be Colonel Burnham. I went to the other end of the room, to a small table which stood in a corner and was covered with works in *terra cotta*, and there I busied myself partly with them and partly with devising some means of escape. I had no time to think of how I had been led into the trap; my only desire was to get out of it. It was clear that Miss Burnham had arrived unexpectedly; and I knew that in any case Heatherleigh would not have intentionally deceived me; so there was nothing for it but to get quickly away from the possible inconveniences and annoyances of this ill chance.

I could not walk out of the house and go home, without offering some apology or explanation to Mr. or Mrs. Lewison. But to get out of the room was my first consideration; afterwards I could seek Heatherleigh and Mr. Lewison, and make some sort of excuse.

I turned; and there they were—those eyes! She came forward to me—she was alone—and held out her hand. Did not I remember the exact counterpart of this little scene, happening in my mother's room long ago? There was the same friendly light in the wonderful, wise eyes; there was the same queenly ease and grace in the position of the small figure—the same tender entreaty in her voice, as she said—

"Have you not forgiven me yet?"

And I was possessed by the same insufferable sense of clumsiness and boorishness, as I stood there perplexed and embarrassed, wishing the floor might open under me. Of course, I knew that she wanted no forgiveness—that she did not imagine she had done me any wrong. I knew that the solicitude of her voice and the look in her eyes were but part of that polite training which people in her position necessarily acquire by good example and tution. It was her sense of courtesy that made her come as a beggar to me, and endeavor to put me at my ease by assuming an attitude which was absurd. If she had accidentally hurt the feelings of her coachman or cook, would she not have been equally desirous to rectify the wrong? And here was I, not able to meet her on equal terms—not knowing in what fashion to put aside this inversion of our natural and real relations. If I had been educated to the fine sensitiveness and delicacy with which well-bred persons treat such matters, I should have been able to let her know that I understood an effort of courtesy which was prompted by her sense of duty to herself—that I accepted it for what it was worth, and held my position in the affair as nothing so long as she was satisfied—that I did not mistake her humility, but rather looked upon it as a species of proper pride.

All this passed hurriedly and confusedly through my mind, with the painful conviction that she must be imagining that I took her words literally. Imagine a man so unacquainted with the symbolic usages of society as to take the phrase "your obedient servant," coming from a stranger, as literal, and presume upon it! In lesser degree, such was the position I saw that I should assume in Hester Burnham's eyes. Finally, I blurted out—

"You are very kind, Miss Burnham. But you know that you have nothing to forgive. Why should you take the trouble to recall that—that mistake?"

She looked at me for a second; and I thanked God I had nothing to conceal from those calm and searching strange eyes.

"You won't shake hands with me?" she said.

It seemed to me that she sighed as she spoke. I could have flung myself at her feet, had I not been vexed at the same moment with the thought that this look of hers was another bit of that delicate by-play which an extreme social courtesy demanded. And it seemed to me monstrous that, merely to preserve her personal pride in being just and courteous to all persons, she should go the length of talking to me, who must be an insignificant nothing in her eyes, in a way that otherwise might have driven a man mad. Had she but meant what her look and speech and tone conveyed, I would have said to her, "You are too kind to one such as I am. What can I give you in return for your kindness? I have nothing of any value, except it be my life: if it will but give you five minutes' pleasure, I will lay it with joy at your feet."

What I did say was this—

"I hope you won't speak of it any more, Miss Burnham. It is too small a matter for you to think twice about."

And as I did not consider it was for her and me to shake hands, I did not offer her my hand.

She turned away then, a little proudly perhaps, and took the arm of Mr. Alfred Burnham, who was coming towards her. Mrs. Lewison came and sat down beside me. I don't know what she talked about, for Hester Burnham was now singing.

Then I left the room, and found that Heatherleigh, with one or two other men, were in the smoking-room up-stairs. Heatherleigh was in an excellent humor; and as he lay in a chair, with his great frame stretched out, he poured forth a continual stream of quaint and odd suggestions, happy repartees, and occasional sharp sayings, that sometimes hit one or other of his companions a little severely. For instance, when I entered, a young man, elaborately dressed and scented, was railing against women, quoting ancient authorities to prove that women were regarded as of the brute creation, and finally declaring that he believed them to be a superior species of monkey. Heatherleigh was irritated, I could see; and no sooner had the philosopher advanced this opinion of his, than Heatherleigh, with a sharp glance, said—

"That is why you don't marry, I suppose—fearing the ties of consanguinity."

Now there was a good deal more brutality than wit about this remark; but I constantly observed that, on this one subject of woman, Heatherleigh never would suffer in his presence the little affectations of cynicism which are common in ordinary talk. On any other topic it was absolutely impossible to stir him into anything like a temper. If you flatly contradicted every position he took up, and went dead against his most favorite opinions, he would lie with his head up in the air, and a quiet smile on his face, as if he were balancing your theory alongside his own on the point of his nose. He would play with your opinion as he played with his own, and would put it into comical lights with an easy grace and wit which were irresistible, because they were the offspring of a fine fancy and a tender disposition. You might tickle him all over, and he would only smile; but when you spoke sneeringly of women (as many of his bachelor artist acquaintances were inclined to do) you pricked his eye, and then he would spring up and deal you a blow with the utmost savagery of which he was capable.

I wanted him to go home; but a message came at this moment to the effect that supper was ready. Heatherleigh insisted on my staying; because, he said, Bonnie Lesley had complained to him that I had run away from her, and because she expected me to take her in to supper.

"Is there anything particularly laughable in that?" I asked, seeing that there was a curious smile on his face.

He looked at me for a moment.

"Well," he said, "men like to see other men innocent and gullible, for it flatters their own astuteness. Of course, too, it multiplies their chances of existence. But you are so very, very believing and simple, Ted, that you are a positive wonder. The Midianitish woman has already captured you, merely by staring at you."

I was very vexed to find myself incapable of replying to his raillery; but it was on Miss Lesley's account that I was vexed. It seemed to me unfair that Heatherleigh should, even in joke, talk of Bonnie Lesley as of some interested and deceitful woman, and I could not help recalling my suspicion that something underlay this fun—that Heatherleigh had some cause to feel spiteful against her, and was thus revenging himself in a petty and unworthy way. Nor was this impression lessened by some chance remarks made by Miss Lesley herself, as I sat next her at supper.

"I don't believe," she said, "that artists have souls. I believe that artists and actors and authors—all the people who have to live by art of any kind—sell their soul to the public, and leave none of it for home use. They can assume various characters, and pretend to have a regard for this or that, but it is only a pretence. They are empty inside. They have neither a soul nor a heart—they have sold both to the public, and live upon the result. Oh! I know it."

"Do you mean—?"

"Look at Mr. Heatherleigh," she continued. "He could act being in love with any woman, and she might believe him, and yet I am certain that his profession has taken it out of his power to be seriously and honestly affectionate towards anybody in the world."

"You are quite mistaken, then," I said. "You will meet with

very few men who are as generous and disinterested and affectionate as Heatherleigh."

"Oh! I am so glad to hear you say that," she replied, with that air of pretty wonder which was so irritating, for it left you in doubt as to whether she understood or believed or cared for what you had been saying.

But it seemed to me that she knew, or fancied she knew, something more of Heatherleigh than she chose to express, and I hoped that my true and honest friend had not suffered by some mischance in her estimation. Indeed, I ventured to press my opinion on the point, for it seemed to me almost painful that these two, who had so much that was beautiful and lovable about them, should be separated by some misunderstanding. She listened to all I had to say, and appeared deeply interested. Nor had I any desire to cut short my speech, for it was an indescribable pleasure to me to watch everything I said reflected sympathetically in the large and expressive eyes. The various phases of attention and deprecation and astonishment that passed over them were so singularly beautiful. But a quiet astonishment was their normal expression, and it was so far normal that it seemed to answer what you were saying, when she herself was thinking of something else. She appeared to have some curiosity to hear what you said, and every new sentence seemed to convey another pretty little surprise to her, but in time you began to see that all your efforts to interest her only awoke the same result. It was not that she was preoccupied or absent. But she seemed so contented with herself (as surely she had a right to be), that she cared only for the pleasure of sitting still, and being tickled by small novelties of information. I grew to wonder whether, if a lightning-bolt shot past her, and split the mantel-piece beyond, she would do more than turn the big, child-like eyes upon the place, and regard it with a bright and pleased curiosity.

On our way home Heatherleigh did not choose to speak about Miss Lesley, and I was rather glad of it. But he questioned me about Hester Burnham, and I told him minutely and accurately everything that had occurred.

"You are a perpetual conundrum to me," he said; "I can't make you out. I never saw such exaggerated self-depreciation joined to such insufferable pride."

CHAPTER VII.

SOME OLD FRIENDS.

I FEAR it will be impossible for me to convey to the reader any sense of my great enjoyment when it first began to dawn upon me that I was really of use to Heatherleigh. Those who have been delicately brought up, with wide possibilities around them, with ease in money matters, and innumerable avenues of pleasurable activity lying in front of them, cannot understand how hard and gloomy and dismal was the pall which had hung over my life, and the presence of which had always seemed to be inevitable. And now there was a rent overhead, and a stirring of free wind; and a ray of Heaven's own sunlight fell upon me, and found me without words to express my gratitude.

Heatherleigh, in his lazy way, used to make fun of me (in order to protect himself) whenever I ventured to hint of the debt I owed him. Generous to a fault, he shrank with an exceeding sensitiveness from being considered generous, and you could not have made him more uncomfortable than by showing him what you thought of his goodness. So I nursed my great debt towards him in my heart; and wondered if ever I should have the chance of revealing my respect and admiration and affection for this good man. I used to think that if he and I were to love the same woman, and she loved me, I should leave her, for his sake.

"What an irritating fellow you are!" he said to me, one day, when I was beseeching him to go on with some work, that I might get something to do. "Why can't you take life easily? Nobody will thank you—certainly not I—for worrying yourself to death."

"But I cannot help it," I said. "Weasel put the notion into my blood—and it will always remain in it—that I ought never to be a moment idle in working-hours. I can't help it. I *feel* wretched unless when I am working; and if I sit talking to you I have an uneasy feeling that some one may open the door, glide in on slippers, and scowl and scold. I never enjoy taking a walk in the daytime—I expect to see some one somewhere who will ask me why I am doing nothing while all men are working."

"You are like some unfortunate wretch who has been all his life in prison, and who sickens and dies in free air for want of his ordinary employment of scraping the wall with his finger-nail."

"This morning, coming down here at half-past ten, I saw Weasel in the street, and I half expected him to come up and ask why the devil I was so late, and if I wasn't ashamed to be cheating my master. Just now, I'd much rather work than sit talking like this."

"Confound you, do you think I am going to pander to your diseased appetite? If you must work, work at home, and don't bother me."

"I have been working at home."

Then I told him all about it. I had been trying a picture on my own account for some months. I began it in the early part of the year, and, as the daylight widened, I rose earlier and earlier, until now I got between five and six hours at it every morning before I hurriedly swallowed my breakfast. I used to get up at four, paint until ten, and then eat something or other and be down at Heatherleigh's studio by half-past. There were many reasons why I did not wish Heatherleigh to know about my laboring with this picture, chief of them being that I did not wish him to see it until it was in some sort presentable; although, had I shown it to him, I might have spared myself an immense deal of toil and vexation. I was working without tools, to begin with. I had to place one chair on the top of another to form an easel; then the canvas was tied to the back of the upper chair by a bit of string, while I sat on a stool. The colors I had bought were of the cheapest kind; but I had acquired under Heatherleigh considerable experience in heightening and tempering dull or crude pigments. Of course, I had no models; but the recollection of form was always easy to me. And yet the amount of pain, physical and mental, that the incessant struggle with my own ignorance and inexperience gave me, was indescribable. Again and again I painted portions over—here rubbing out the damp work of the previous day, there coating over what was too dry for that operation. It is conceivable that the canvas got into a deplorable state; and at last I drove a knife straight through it. It was my second effort at the same picture which was on the stocks when Heatherleigh spoke; and of it, such as it was, more may be said hereafter.

In the mean time Heatherleigh besought me to moderate the vehemence of my labor. He professed himself unable even to supply sketches for me to fill up. He was growing too rich, he said—he should have to die and leave his wealth to the hospitals. More than one dealer owed him money—an unprecedented thing—which he had never asked for. And with that he suddenly slapped his knee.

"Ted," he said, "I have a grand idea. Let's both put on a spurt for the next month or five weeks. The Lewisons are going down to Brighton in June; and you and I will go too—for a grand long holiday of magnificent laziness. We can make up by that time £200, I know; and we will go fair halves in it. Now don't blush like a school-girl, whether you are vexed or pleased—you do three fourths of the work, and you ought at least to have half the money. Or we will have a common stock, if you like it better. Is it a bargain—five weeks' hard work, and then a month at the sea?"

The sea! I heard the sound of waves then, as clearly as I can hear them now, down on the beach there. As clearly as I behold it now, from this window, I looked through the mist that was before my eyes, and I saw the great, breezy, green plain in the sunlight, with the joyous white laugh of its running waves.

Then I told Heatherleigh how there was not even a river down in the Missenden valley in which I had been brought up; how the farthest views you could get from the chalk hills only revealed extensions of a great cultivated plain; how the sea and all its strange associations—so different from those of the land, so beautiful and wild and terrible—produced a sort of delirium in me; and how even the remembrance of it was to me full of the sadness which is somehow interwoven with the beauty of all beautiful things.

We talked of Brighton then, and of the sea, and of what was to be done there. Miss Lesley was certain to be with the Lewisons. Perhaps the Burnhams would be down.

"I know several other people," said Heatherleigh; "they are

all nice sort of people, who have the courage to leave the London season at its height, and catch the flush of the year at the sea-side."

The very next day I had to go down Holborn; and I met Big Dick and the sleepy-headed Kent, who were on their way to their dinner. I went up and spoke to them, and I felt like an impostor with them. Kent was very respectful, and I hated him for it. Big Dick was more natural, and talked pretty much in his usual fashion; but of course I had grown a good deal older since I was his apprentice, and there was a difference in his manner too.

"Let's go into this doorway," said Kent, glancing at my fine suit of gray clothes and my hat. (I was on a diplomatic errand for Heatherleigh, and had got out of the ordinary slouching studio-costume.) "You won't care to be seen with the likes of us."

"Don't be a fool," I said, rather angrily, and kept standing in the middle of the pavement.

I was debating in my own mind how I could offer them something to drink without appearing to be ostentatious (for I knew they were rather sensitive on that matter of treating, which is a point of honor among working-men), when Big Dick, having more moral courage than I, proposed (and I was heartily glad) that he should stand something. The doorway which Kent wished to shelter him led into a chop-house, in which there was also a bar; so as we were going in, I said—

"What do you say to our all dining here, instead of your going home?"

"All right," said both of them; and so we went in and sat down.

They asked me to order the dinner, and I did: a very good dinner—mutton-chops, vegetables, gooseberry pie, and bottled stout.

"Well, I'm d—d glad to see you, Ted," said Big Dick, shaking my hand again with his great horny fist, "only I suppose we must call you Mr. Ives, eh?"

"You may if you like, Mr. Richard Primer," said I—at which profound joke Kent laughed consumedly.

"And what a change there is in you!" said Dick. "Why, you were a poor little devil when I knew you—all eyes, you know, and looking as if you was afraid everybody wanted to eat you. And now you've grown tall and straight, and the worst of you I can say is as you look too like a b—— Frenchman or Italian. But that comes through your way of life now, I dare say."

Kent had been looking at me steadily for some time with a sort of wonder in his sleepy eyes. At last he said, cautiously and with nervous politeness—

"I hope we're not detaining of you."

"I wish you wouldn't talk like that, Kent," I said, nettled beyond endurance; and this woke him up somewhat, for by and by he said, when the stout had warmed him a little—

"You'll be marrying presently, and then there'll be Mrs. Ives, as well as Mr. Ives, and lots of little Iveses."

With that Kent stretched his gray eyes to their uttermost, endeavoring to control his merriment; and then half shut them again, and abandoned himself to a roar of laughter over his wit.

"But I've good news for you, Ted," said Dick, laying down his tumbler. "There's an awful revolution round there at Weasel's. Weasel used to be a great man to you—I know you was frightened of him. Ha! you should see Weasel now. He's married—married a big, strapping woman as warms him, I can tell ye, when he gets into a bad temper. There's no cantankerousness 'll do for her. She can give him a hot un when she likes; and the scoldin's all the other way now. Of course he's the same to us—mayhap he revenges hisself on us for what he gets from her; but doesn't he get it! She comes down to the shop and lays about her like a good un; and Weasel, with his whitey-brown face, stands and bites his lips, and then drives the things about when she's gone. Lord bless ye! he can't call his soul his own."

"He never could," I said. "If he has one, he must have borrowed or stolen it."

Well, I don't see anything particularly brilliant in that remark; but its effect upon Kent was alarming. He had been drinking a good deal of bottled stout; and what I said about Weasel's soul sent him into a prodigious fit of laughter, with which doubtless the beer had something to do. He laughed till the tears ran down his face; and then something stuck in his throat, and he gasped and laughed and coughed until he was blood-red. Seeing that he was in the same good-humor when he recovered, I proposed that we should have a pint bottle of old port with our cheese, to which they agreed; and before the dinner was over we had entirely established our ancient relations.

"I'm proud of ye, Ted," said Kent, whose lazy gray eyes had never been so excited for years, "and I say as you are a credit to the shop that brought you up. And we'll dance at your wedding."

Then came the question of paying. I said, carelessly, that I should much prefer to pay for the whole; but I saw by Dick's face that he was a little hurt by the proposal, and he dissented from it in rather a stiff and formal way.

"Come, then," I said, "let's toss for it."

Now there is a favorite trick among the Missenden boys (and probably among boys elsewhere) by which you can toss up a penny, put it between your hands, feel with your thumb whether tail or head is uppermost, and change the coin according to what your opponent calls. I was never very dexterous at this piece of juvenile legerdemain; but I succeeded in convincing both Big Dick and Kent that I had lost both times, and so they let me pay the small bill. It was a very pleasant dinner, that in the Holborn chop-house; I have since then risen from many a grander banquet having enjoyed myself considerably less. When we parted, I believe Kent was in such good spirits that, at my request, he would have gone straight into the shop and challenged Weasel to a hand-to-hand fight.

However, to return to this projected trip to the sea. As I was going home that evening I met Polly Whistler; she turned and walked up Hampstead Road with me, and I told her what Heatherleigh and I proposed to do. Polly's face grew a trifle thoughtful for a moment; and then she said, with what seemed to me a rather affected carelessness—

"I suppose Mr. Heatherleigh expects to meet people he knows down there—the Lewisons, perhaps?"

"Yes, he does."

"And that girl, Miss Lesley?"

Polly was looking hard at the ground.

"Yes, I think she will be there also."

"I suppose Mr. Heatherleigh means to marry her?"

"Marry her!" I said, in astonishment, and—shall I confess it?—with a sharp touch of pain.

"Why not?" she said, with a smile that was peculiarly unlike her ordinary frank smile.

"Don't you know the manner in which he always talks of her?" I asked—"quite unfairly, I know; but still he does it."

"That is only his way," she said. "He never likes you to know that he is fond of anything or anybody, and makes fun over it in order to hide himself. If he were dreadfully in love, and going to be married to-morrow morning, he would spend to-night in satirizing us poor women-folks as hard as he could."

"Then he is not dreadfully in love, for he never attempts anything of the kind."

"But you say he talks in that way about Miss Lesley. Now, what sort of a girl is she?"

So, as we went on, I told her all I knew of Bonnie Lesley, and of her fine and handsome appearance, her childlike and winning ways, and her kindness to myself. Polly listened very attentively, and put two or three questions the drift of which I could not quite catch. Then she grew a little more cheerful.

"You are likely to be dreadfully spoiled by women, Ted," she remarked.

"Why?"

"I don't know. There's something about your manner—something desperately direct and honest—that provokes one's confidence. Don't you remember I talked to you immediately after I saw you just as I would talk to you now? And so this Miss Lesley has been making great friends with you. What does she say about Mr. Heatherleigh?"

"Nothing. I think there is some misunderstanding between them. He is constantly gibing at her, and making epigrams about her; and she is very cautious in mentioning him at all."

"I'm glad you and he get so pleasant a subject to talk about all day. It must be such a variety from the constant talking shop that you men are so fond of. We women never get a chance of talking shop—unless when we talk about babies."

Polly said this in the most artless manner, but in a second she had caught herself up, crimsoned deeply, and then burst out laughing. To hide her confusion, she stooped and picked up a pin that happened to be lying on the pavement.

"There," she said, showing me the pin (though there was still a laugh lurking about the corners of her mouth), "how many times have I laid the foundation for a fortune? You know the stories of the industrious young men who picked up a pin, and then heaps of money came to them through it. But here have I been picking up pins for years in the expectation of getting only a small competency, and it never comes. What are you laughing at?"

"At your ill-luck in never getting a fortune," I said, boldly; wherewith she laughed too.

Having once got into these good spirits, she rattled on like a mad thing. She took my arm, and we strolled along carelessly towards Hampstead, she all the while telling stories, and making the oddest remarks about the people passing, and laughing in her quiet and discreet fashion. First she began about a lady in her neighborhood, a widow, who was famous for the number of her suitors, and the rapidity with which they were changed. She described the various lovers, and their mode of making love; although I am positive she never was inside the house, nor heard one of them speak.

"The one she has got just now," continued Polly, "is the smallest man, I believe, in the world—so small and thin and pale. I used to call him the widow's mite; and she heard of it, and said she would teach me better manners if she laid her hands on me."

This led up to another experience of Polly's. She had been going on a bitterly cold winter night to visit some one at Stamford Hill; and after the omnibus was packed, a rather good-looking young girl appeared at the door and looked in.

"Come in," said an elderly gentleman,—"come in, my girl, and you can sit on my knee till you get out."

Rather than wait half an hour in the cold, the girl, blushing a little, did as she was bid, and was subjected to a good deal of quiet and harmless joking by the passengers, who were going home to their suburban houses, and all of whom knew the old gentleman who was so complaisant to the new-comer. He himself was very good-natured and jocular, and made some remote hints about his wishing that he was not married.

"Then," said Polly, "the old gentleman asked her where she meant to get out. 'Clarence Lodge,' she says. 'Why,' he says, 'that's my house!' 'Are you Mr. Sandemann?' she asks. 'Yes,' he says, beginning to look uncomfortable. 'Then I'm your new servant, sir,' she says, and you may imagine how all the gentlemen roared. But did you ever notice, Ted, that in getting into a 'bus, or anywhere, women are far less courteous to each other than men are to each other? Men seem to have some idea of fairness, and let the first-comers go in; but women will squeeze and elbow and push themselves foremost in defiance of justice. Of course one of the fine ladies you visit wouldn't do that. She would let anybody who had the vulgarity to take precedence take it, and would only show her contempt with the tip of her nose. I am beginning to think that all fine ladies are my natural enemies."

With this sort of nonsense (which gained not a little from Polly's bright eyes and her low, delightful laugh) an hour or two passed very pleasantly, and it was getting towards dusk when we came down Hampstead Road again. I thought there was something more in that vague dislike to fine ladies than lay on the surface of her foolish talk, and I noticed that Polly more than once turned the conversation towards Bonnie Lesley. She was careful about what she said, but indirectly she uttered some rather cutting speeches about this poor girl, who seemed to be more suspected the less she was known. Polly had not even seen her. And, having cogitated over the matter, I, in my wisdom, evolved these propositions, to account for the mystery.

1. Heatherleigh has been, and perhaps is, in love with Miss Lesley.

2. She has refused him, and promised to keep the secret.

3. He is vexed, and makes epigrams about her fickleness, simply because he happened to be in love, and she wasn't.

4. Polly is in love with Heatherleigh, and, without having seen her, is jealous of Bonnie Lesley, and consequently spiteful.

There were some few points which did not seem to me to square with this theory, but it was the best guess I could make at the position.

CHAPTER VIII.

POLLY'S MOTHER.

I THREW myself into that five weeks' work with all the energy of which I was capable. Look at the splendid prize that was to recompense our labor. To Heatherleigh a month at the sea-side was nothing; to me it was a treasure perpetual, inexhaustible. While I worked I dreamed of it. That gaunt and dusty chamber in Granby Street seemed to smell of sea-weed, and the stillness of it was like the murmur of a shell. People who have repeatedly spent a month at the sea-side know how short a period it is, but I looked forward with a kind of wonder to the idea of rising morning after morning, and still finding one's self confronted by the great width of water. I liked the labor, and I liked what was coming after it. At present, the excitement and the interest of hard work; in the future a blaze of sunlight, and tingling breezes, and the glories of the sea.

And it was during this period, too, that I first definitely saw that my work was of some value to my benefactor and friend. Not only did I do the greater portion of most of the pictures, but I goaded him into what work he did undertake. But for me, I think the scheme would have been abandoned. Many a time I went up in the morning, and found him lounging in his easy-chair, absorbed in one of his favorite treatises.

"I don't think I shall go on with that picture to-day," he would say; "what is the use of bothering? Let us go down to Rotten Row, and stare at the people."

Then I would remonstrate, and remind him of our compact.

"You are the most uncompromising, persistent, stiff-necked brute I ever met. What is the use of life, if you must subject yourself to all sorts of needless martyrdoms? You will worry yourself now, and, when you find yourself at Brighton with nothing to do, idleness will drive you mad."

"Idleness hasn't driven somebody else mad whom I know," I said.

"You haven't enough of reflection in you to know that the intentional idleness you propose to have at Brighton would be a nuisance, while the chance idleness you take at the suggestion of a whim is always charming. So soon as a man is over-conscious that he is doing something, the enjoyment of it flies. I have a notion that you could make one of those mad harlequin-dancers miserable by getting him to read a treatise on anatomy. Indeed you would destroy his chances of living. Show him all the delicate mechanism of the bones and sinews, and he could never afterwards fling his limbs into contorted forms without a vague fear, which would render the performance a failure."

Now, if I had let him go on, there would have been no more work that day. He would start some such subject, and pursue it through all its phases, comic and serious and practical, with his hands crossed on the crown of his head, and his legs stretched out and crossed in front of him. As I have said, he had no sort of interest in painting as painting. To him it was merely a profession which yielded him an easy life, plenty of leisure in which to indulge his habit of indolent day-dreaming and listless speculation, and as much money as kept him comfortably, or allowed him to be generous when he wished.

Something else in his book had struck him; and he was anxious to explain to me how the writer was wrong in assuming that civilization would in time work frightful mischief by developing the cerebrum at the expense of the cerebellum.

"That's all very well," I said, "but—"

"It is absurd," he persisted. "The physical conditions of life will prevent it. So long as men have got to contend with cold and rain, and the toil and exposure of agricultural work, the race will never so exclusively cultivate its intellectual powers as to improve itself off the earth. It seems to me—"

With that I sat down at his easel (not mine) and began working at the picture. But I had been merely a dummy listener; he continued his meditations all the same, and it was only when I began to meddle with the face of his heroine (a very good likeness of Polly) that he started up, and took his palette and brushes in hand.

"After we get down to the sea-side," I said, "I will lie on the beach if you like for hours, and listen to everything you have to say about harlequins or priests or philosophers."

"You have the determination of ——," he said, naming an historical personage who may have been determined, but who was notoriously unsuccessful.

At length the time drew near; and, although we had not got in all the money, it was worked for and available. Heatherleigh, having taken down some checks to be cashed, came back with a pocketful of bank-notes. He counted them out — one hundred and sixty pounds odd — and then he quietly told off eighty of these and placed the money before me on the table.

I was the possessor of eighty pounds in hard cash—it was my own, my very own.

"Heatherleigh," I said, "let us have a walk through Kensington Gardens and around the Serpentine."

"Why, you positively love the Serpentine, I believe, you abominable Cockney. And you going to the sea to-morrow!"

Nevertheless we went; and as we drew near the small lake, the sun had set in the northwest, and after the red light had quite faded down, there was a strange pale "after-glow" in the sky, while a gathering mist fell over the water, causing the opposite shore and its trees to recede into a vague, ethereal distance. I had grown to love the Serpentine in the old days of my bondage, when I used to steal out alone in the evening, and sit on the cold wooden seats, as the stillness of the night fell. And now, as we walked across the damp grass, the various sounds of the day ceased, and the place was solitary and quiet; while the wandering white of the fog settled thicker over the farther side of the lake, and through it we saw the far gas-lamps burning sharp and red. Then, as we lingered a while, a strange golden moonlight crept up the skies and made the faint streaks of the clouds visible; while it touched the trees also, and glimmered, a trembling line of yellow light, along the shore. You forgot that you were near a great city, and the poor Serpentine became lonely, mystic, magical.

Did Heatherleigh guess why I wished to come hither? Many a time, in the old days, I had wandered around the small lake, empty-hearted and empty-pocketed. In all my dreams, did I ever anticipate that within a year or two I should walk over that damp grass, and around that mystical shore, my own master, with the art that I had loved as an amusement now become the sole occupation of my life, with a future full of freedom and beautiful possibilities before me, with eighty pounds of savings clasped tightly in my pocket?

"What are you thinking of?" said Heatherleigh.

"Of the power that this money gives me. Couldn't I live for a whole year, doing anything or nothing, just as I liked, upon it? I could set eighty wretched creatures wild with delight by giving them a sovereign apiece. I could take fifty pounds of it, and buy a small, little brooch, with curious stones in it, and I could send it, without being known—"

"To whom?" said Heatherleigh.

Then I burst out laughing; for I knew it was time the farce should end.

"Here," I said, "take the money. I have no right to it. I wanted to have the sensation of having it, and of coming down here to crow over the notions that Weavle used to give me."

He refused to take it.

"I won't have it," I said, simply enough, "because you know as well as I do that I have no right whatever to it."

"Well," he said, "you are still to me that perpetual conundrum that I can't make out. Where were you born, Ted? Had you a father and mother? I believe you are a sort of will-o'-the-wisp—there's no catching you. You have the courage and determination and self-reliance of half-a-dozen men, and you have the sensitiveness, and finical, particular, humbugging nonsense of a thousand girls; and all this confusion of character you exhibit with a simplicity which astounds me. Brought up as you have been, you should be as hard as steel, cautious, keen, avaricious—"

But I need not follow him into his theory about the manner in which I had come to develop those wonderful qualities he had discovered. When he finished, we were still walking around the Serpentine; and the moonlight was now full and clear in the skies.

"That bodes well for to-morrow," said he.

"But," said I, "you haven't taken the money. If you like, I will accept ten pounds of it; and let the rest go into our general fund for housekeeping at Brighton."

To this he agreed; and next day we proceeded to get our things in readiness for starting. Polly Whistler called around in the forenoon; and then I persuaded her to go out with me, and help me to purchase with the ten pounds a dress for my mother. We went to a big place in Tottenham Court Road, and Polly was quite grand in her manner as she insisted upon seeing pretty nearly everything in the shop. At last she confessed herself pleased; and the parcel was ordered to be sent on by the Burnham coach to its destination.

Further, I persuaded Polly to dine with us, and, finally, to come and see us off.

"It is a heart-breaking thing to part with you, Ted," she remarked; "but we must teach ourselves to suffer. Besides, my old woman is a little wild to-day; and then I like to give her the house to herself."

"She has been trying to keep you in order, Polly," said Heatherleigh, strapping down his portmanteau.

"And she *can* keep people in order," said Polly. "If she had been Nebuchadnezzar's wife, she'd have made him pare his nails precious smart!"

I could not help admiring the good-natured way in which the girl joked about this affair, which was certainly no laughing matter to her. To listen to her, you would have imagined that her mother's only fault was a certain impatience of people who did wrong, and a desire to have her own way in ordering her house. Polly said nothing of the persecution and insults, and often bodily pain, she suffered at the hands of that bad old woman, whose drunken madness had long ago made her forget that she was a mother.

There was some commission which Heatherleigh had undertaken that prevented our catching the afternoon express. There was nothing for it but to sit in patience, with our portmanteaus at our feet, waiting for the recusant messenger, the while Polly chatted and laughed, and pretended to make love to me.

Our fooling was suddenly interrupted by the sound of a loud voice on the stairs—a woman's voice, shrill, angry, intoxicated. How it flashed across me that this must be Polly's mother I don't know; but I shall never forget the quick gesture and look of the girl when she heard the noise. She instinctively caught my arm, as if for protection, while she darted a terrified, anxious glance towards Heatherleigh. It was as though she had cried to me, "Ted, save me, and don't let *him* know!" In that brief second the whole nature of the girl was revealed; and I said to myself, "She loves him with her whole heart."

Instantaneous as was the warning given, and dumb as were her directions, I had sufficient presence of mind to go quickly to the door. I went outside, and shut the door behind us. The woman was on the stairs, directing the fury of her speech, along with much gesticulation, upon a maid-servant, who, from underneath, was protesting against the strange visitor going up-stairs unannounced. My appearance on the scene turned the flood of her wrath upon me.

"I've got you, have I? I thought it was here you'd be found; and it's time I had a chance of speakin' hout. You're Mr. Heatherleigh's friend, are you; and what have you done with my daughter? I say, what have you done with my poor girl, that's bein' made a byword of among a pack of wolves? Oh, don't pretend to pacify me—I heard o' your goin's on this morning, and buyin' a dress for a respectable girl as belongs to a family as 'zpectable as yours. And are you not ashamed of yourself, sir—my poor lamb among them wolves? But I'll have the law on you, I will, I will, I will!"

"Don't be a fool," I said; "hold your tongue, and come down-stairs and tell me what you want."

"Is my daughter in that room?" she screamed, at the pitch of her shrilly voice.

"If you don't be quiet, I'll have you turned out of the house," I said, and then added—determined to avert the shame of an exposure from poor Polly—"Is it money you want? I will give it to you, only don't make such a hideous noise."

"Merciful 'eavens!" she yelled; "he wants to buy me as he has bought my daughter. Oh, the wretch! Oh, the vile, wicked, traitorous—"

I caught her by the arm, as I thought she was going to tumble down the stairs.

"Would you lay hands on me? You think you'll buy me—"

"Why, you old humbug, I wouldn't give twopence for a dozen of you," I said, when I saw it was impossible to restrain her violence by persuasion.

With that she caught me by the coat, dashed past me like a wild-cat, and entered the room. I followed; and whatever there may have been of absurdity or comicality in the old woman's ravings on the stair, was forgotten now in what I saw before me. Polly stood motionless, her face bent down and quite pale. Her lips were trembling; but that expressed only a tithe of the humiliation and shame that seemed to cover her whole figure. She had heard what had been going on outside, and she stood there absolutely stupefied and speechless by the cruel shame and mortification that she must have long dreaded. Heatherleigh stood at the other end of the room, with a look of wonder on his face that soon gave way to indignation and anger. For the old woman at first confronted her daughter, and made such speeches as I need not write down here. It is not a pleasant thing to hear a mother mouthing out lies against the character of her daughter, wounding her at her most sensitive points, and outraging even the bystanders' sense of decency. She spoke so rapidly, too, that the mischief was done before either of us could interfere; but Heatherleigh, with a quick flush on his face, went forward and caught her by the shoulder.

"You shameless creature," he said, "do you know what you are doing?"

Here Polly, still looking down, came forward and interposed between them.

"Mr. Heatherleigh, she is my mother," said the girl, now crying very bitterly. "Mother, come away."

But the infuriated woman drove her aside, and held her ground, while she confronted us with an intoxicated stare.

"Good-bye, Ted," said Polly to me, holding out her hand. Then, I think, she directed one furtive glance towards Heatherleigh, and went away. The mother remained behind.

"Good-bye," I had said to her, knowing that it was the last time she would ever enter that room, in which we had spent so many innocent and happy evenings.

"Do you know what you have done, you foolish old idiot? Do you know what you have done?" said Heatherleigh, with his face full of mortification and anger. "Do you know that you have tried to destroy the character of an honest and industrious girl, who has hitherto kept you and indulged your beastly habits? Do you know that you may have sickened her of her honest life? Do you know what has happened within the last few minutes—that you have outraged the feelings of a sensitive girl, whom you ought to have protected, and may God forgive you if anything comes of your drunken insanity!"

He snatched his hat, and hastily went out. It was half an hour afterwards when he returned. By that time the old woman had gone. Heatherleigh's words had partly sobered her; she had begged my forgiveness, and burst into a flood of alcoholic tears. When Heatherleigh came back, I noticed that he was rather pale, and there was a thoughtful, fixed look in his face.

All the way down in the train he scarcely spoke. Neither of us cared to read by the light of the dingy carriage-lamp, and so we lay and stared out into the dusk. There was a faint light out-side, owing to the moon, but the moon herself remained hidden.

Presently he said to me, looking up from his reverie—

"Did you ever hear or see anything like that?"

I knew what he meant, and I said—

"It is the last time Polly will ever be in that room."

"I followed her," he said. "I overtook her, and, do you know, she would scarcely speak to me. The poor girl seemed quite dazed and bewildered—no wonder. I could have strangled that incoherent old idiot who went raving on and seeing nothing of what she was doing. And yet Polly should not have been so much put out. When I told her we all understood that her mother was talking nonsense, she said nothing but that I was to go back again, and leave her to go home alone. I don't understand it."

"I shouldn't wonder if Polly never spoke to you any more," I said.

"Why?" he asked, with a quick glance of surprise.

"I don't know. I don't think she ever will."

The apartments which Heatherleigh had secured for us were in King's Road, and therefore fronting the sea. But as we drove down from the station and around to the house, I could see nothing but a dusky gray where the sea ought to have been. I heard the murmur of it, however, far away, like innumerable strange voices.

Supper was prepared for us. Afterwards Heatherleigh smoked a solitary pipe in silence; and then we retired to our respective rooms. Mine was a small chamber, near the top of the house, fronting the sea. I could not sleep for that strange noise, that seemed so wild and distant and yet so sadly familiar. I must have lain and tossed about for a couple of hours or so, I think, and then I began to perceive that the room was full of light, and on the wall, near the window, the moon was gleaming in slanting squares.

I got up and went to the window, and involuntarily I uttered a cry of astonishment and joy. The world outside was all aglow with moonlight of a soft and greenish-yellowish hue, the large, full moon herself hanging up there over the sea and throwing a great, broad lane of glittering light on the water. Every object was sharply and clearly defined; from the palings along the Parade and the boats on the gray beach to the fleet of fishing-smacks whose black hulls lay and rolled in the flood of moonlight. And I could see the waves now—tiny waves that came gently in, and broke over with a murmur which was repeated and echoed in the stillness of the night. The picture was magical, wonderful. I listened to the sound of the waves, and gazed upon the splendid pathway of silver that lay and quivered on the great gray plain of the sea, until I was numbed with cold. Then I hastily dressed myself, sneaked down-stairs, opened the door of the house stealthily, and was outside.

There was not a human being abroad at that hour; this whole, beautiful world was mine. I walked away from the houses—eastward, past the chain-pier, the dark masses of which were touched with the moonlight, and past those long terraces of tall buildings that gleamed gray and ghost-like in the silence of the night. I wandered on, along the smooth turf of the cliffs, meeting no one but some solitary coast-guardsman—a black figure seen vaguely against the gray-green of the sea. The moon was at my back now, but all around was the wonderful, calm, clear light; and so I walked on until I stood over Rottingdean, the small hamlet that lay dark and silent under the throbbing eastern stars.

Here I went down on the beach. The tide was some distance out; and there came a breezy odor of sea-weed from those patches of rock out there, among which the pools of water glimmered white. I lay down on the shingle, under the great cliffs, that echoed back the long rush of the waves on the shore. I could now see the distant lamps of Brighton, the black line of the pier, the specks of fishing-boats, and the moon that seemed to belong to that side of the picture; while before me stretched the vague and mystical sea, and overhead dwelt the silence of those splendid constellations that were now growing faint and wan. Was that the famous jewel of the Harp that gleamed so palely there? The twisted snakes of Cerberus were cold and dead, and the flaming points that used to stud the aerial harness of Pegasus were scarcely visible. Hercules himself seemed sick and pale in the moonlight; or was it another strange light that now began to show in the east, bringing with it a stirring of cold wind? I know that when I returned to Brighton, and got into the house again and tumbled into bed, a glow of pale saffron was shining along the level coast by Shoreham and Worthing; while high up in the east there were flakes of red in the sky, and all the new motion of the dawn.

CHAPTER IX.

LEWES CASTLE.

I AWOKE in a torrent of adjectives. Heatherleigh was standing by my bedside, heaping reproaches on me for lying so long on such a morning, when, as was evident from the great splatches of sunlight on the wall of the room, the weather was lovely. He was dressed remarkably well—in a fashion which set off his handsome figure; and you would have failed entirely to recognize in this tall and gentlemanly looking man, with his accurate gloves, the easily negligent tie, and the large brown beard which was exactly that of the "swell" of that time, the indolent student-painter who a few days before was lounging about a dirty room in Granby Street in shabby clothes, with unkempt hair, no collar, and an old wooden pipe. The odd thing was that in either case there was not the least self-conscious assumption. He was as natural in the one condition as the other; although I think he greatly enjoyed the sudden contrast of these twin modes of living, and went to extremes in both to increase his pleasure.

"Why, it is past twelve," he said; "I have been riding with Bonnie Lesley since half-past ten. Ah! I thought I'd wake you up with that bit of news. Fancy our having been at Rottingdean while you were lying asleep, like a pig, in broad daylight."

"I was at Rottingdean this morning before either of you," I said; and then I told him how I had wandered about all night.

"Madness! my boy, madness!" he said. "But come, dress yourself smartly; you are due at the Lewisons' at one, for lunch; and Miss Lesley sends you her kind regards, and hopes you will spend the afternoon with her. This is a compliment, mind you; for she is holding quite a court down here."

"I hope you have made friends with her again," I said.

"Oh, Bonnie Lesley and I have always been friends—of a kind," he said.

When I went down-stairs, and went to the front window, the world of Brighton was out driving and riding and walking in the glowing sunlight, while a gentle sea-breeze came over the far blue plain, and brought with it coolness, and the odor of sea-weed, and the plash of the waves on the beach. What a gay and brilliant company it was, to be sure—the twos and threes of ladies who lay lazily and proudly in their phaetons and landaus; the packs of rosy-cheeked girls who cantered past on horseback, accompanied by a riding-master or their papa; the incessant strolling backwards and forwards of men and women dressed in the extreme of fashion, and having the air about them of the superiority of conscious wealth and beauty! This was the world which I was asked to enter—I, a waif and stray, a nobody, an insignificant fraction of that other world of hard work and narrow means, of small hopes and few enjoyments. I did enter it, almost against my inclination; and I saw for the first time how these rich and beautiful people passed day after day, week after week—the round of brilliant pleasures they enjoyed, the gay scenes and pleasant excitements which were always pressing upon them, their courteous ways and manners, their kindness, amiability, frivolity. Anybody acquainted with the ordinary life of fashionable people could describe it in a few words; but to me it was all new and wonderful.

At one o'clock we presented ourselves at the Lewisons'. There were a number of people there; and they were quite different from the people I had met at their house before. The æsthetic element was nearly wholly absent. Instead of sculptors and authors, and what not, the party consisted of very grand people who happened to be visiting Brighton—among them a viscount. I looked at this gentleman with awe. He was a small, thin, gray-haired man, who paid particular attention to his plate, and muttered to himself his comments on what other people were saying. His wife was a young and pretty woman, who exhibited all the little coquetries of a girl, and was especially amiable to Heatherleigh, beside whom she sat. I sat between her and Miss Lesley; and when the viscountess happened to say something to me, which she did with a smile that made you fancy you had known her for years, I was in great straits to know whether I should, in answering her, address her by her title. As I was not quite sure, however, what that was, I forbore, and hoped I was not guilty of some appalling rudeness.

But for my being beside Bonnie Lesley, perhaps I should have been overwhelmed by this assemblage of grand people. No sooner, however, had we re-established our old relations with each other, and these consisted of many little secret understandings, which were very pleasant to ourselves, than I forgot all about the other persons present. She and I talked exclusively with each other, despite the efforts of one or two gentlemen to engage her in conversation across the table. I noticed that more than one of them regarded me with a stare of stolid surprise, when she persistently turned and talked to me in her confidential way.

"You have no other companion, then, down here than Heatherleigh?" she asked.

"No."

"Don't you find him dull at times?"

"Never. He is the best companion I could wish for."

"How strange!" she said, with a pretty smile. "But, even if he is so pleasant a companion, you can't always go about with him. You will see him captured by somebody when lunch is over; and he will be taken off to drive with some of those ladies. So shall I, probably; or perhaps some of those gentlemen over there will thrust themselves upon us. Now, what do you say to our going off at once, the moment they rise from table? The mail-phaeton is to be round in a few minutes: what if we slip down-stairs, and go off without warning?"

"Nothing could be better."

"You won't be afraid if I drive?"

"Certainly not. But you need not drive, unless you like. I have had lots of experience with horses in the country."

"Thank you, but I am passionately fond of driving; and as they never will let me take out those horses by myself, I mean to secure them to-day by stratagem."

So it was arranged; and I was delighted with the arrangement, not expecting that it would lead to a little scene. The moment we were free, she and I slipped out of the room, and I went down-stairs, while she went to change her attire. The carriage was there, and I had had sufficient acquaintance with the horses at

Burnham House to see that one of the pair harnessed to this phaeton was rather a restive animal, which the groom was trying as well as he could to pacify. Presently Bonnie Lesley appeared, with a flush of pleasure on her fine face. More than one passer-by turned to look at her as she got up into the high seat, and took the reins in her fingers, while the other hand, small and tightly gloved, held the whip in the most artistic fashion. Suddenly Heatherleigh came running down.

"Really, Miss Lesley, you must not—"

"I will," she said, rapidly and in a low voice, while she cut at the neck of the restive horse with her whip. The animal would have sprung forward; but Heatherleigh had rushed to its head (displacing the groom) and tried to hold it. Of course the horse plunged and reared.

"I tell you, Miss Lesley," said Heatherleigh, "you will kill yourself and him, too."

The girl's face turned white with a spasm of anger.

"Are you afraid?" she said to me, abruptly.

"No."

"Will you go with me?"

"Certainly."

With that she made a cut at the neck of the near horse with her whip, and then caught the other, which Heatherleigh was holding, over the ear. Both horses sprang forward, nearly knocking him to the ground; and the next minute we were dashing madly along the Parade, while Miss Lesley sat cold and firm, without moving a muscle.

Then she burst into a laugh of downright, unaffected merriment.

"I hope I didn't knock him over; but I half expected he would come out, and I was determined to have my own way for once. I am so very much obliged to you for coming; and I will take the greatest care of you. No, you needn't laugh: I fancy you looked afraid when you got up."

"If I had been afraid," I said, "I should have been none the less delighted to come."

"Why?"

She withdrew her eyes for a moment from the horses' heads and fixed them on my face with her ordinary look of bright wonder. Under other circumstances I might have felt embarrassed by this awkward question; but driving through the cool wind, in the brilliant sunlight, and perched up beside the handsomest woman in Brighton, who could have failed to acquire some boldness?

"The pleasure of being beside you might make one risk a much greater danger than this; and you knew that when you asked me to come."

She laughed a charming and unaffected little laugh, and was evidently greatly pleased—why, I was, long afterwards, to find out.

"Shall we turn and drive back along the Parade and the King's Road?"

"As you like."

"People will stare at us, if I drive."

"Why should you care?"

"There are such a lot of carriages out at this time."

"Come," I said, "confess that you want me to urge you to do it—and I do."

She wheeled round the horses very cleverly; and soon we were again clattering along the Parade. When we got into the thick of the carriages in the King's Road, it was astonishing to see the number of people, mostly gentlemen, who bowed to her. Every one looked at her—as well they might; for in all that brilliant throng there was neither girl nor woman to be compared with her.

"There is Mr. Heatherleigh," she said to me.

He was seated in an open carriage, with two ladies and another gentleman. As they approached, I saw that one of the ladies was the viscountess whom I had seen at lunch, and I supposed that the gentleman opposite her was her husband. He and Heatherleigh had their backs towards us, and, of course, could not see us.

"I am getting tired of this. What do you say to going for a short drive into the country?"

Having made some inquiries about the horses of the man who was in the small box behind, it was finally arranged that we should drive to Lewes. I was glad to get away from the crowded thoroughfare, and into the sweet-smelling country roads. The summer was at its brightest and greenest; and we had no sooner left the town, and got into the quiet of meadows and cornfields, than Miss Lesley regained her equanimity, and began to talk in her usual cheerful and confidential way. Indeed, I was very much struck by the rapid fashion in which vexations passed off her mind. While she had been bitterly angry with Heatherleigh at the moment of starting, three seconds had sufficed to chase away her resentment and restore her ordinary good-nature. Her temper was like a delicately balanced pair of scales: a touch of your finger would produce a great disturbance, but the disturbance never lasted above a moment.

What a pleasant drive it was, through the cool avenues of trees, and out again into the glare of the sunlight, with the broad white road lying like a line of silver between the dark-green meadows and fields. Here and there they had begun to cut the tall clover, and from the cleared portions of the fields the piles of gray-green hay sent us the warm, sweet odor which makes the summer gracious. But for the most part the grass was still standing; and the light breeze that went over it stirred the smooth velvet plain into waves of shimmering gray, while it rustled across the great cornfields and swayed the as yet unripe ears of the wheat. The country was as still and silent as the unfathomable blue that stretched overhead; you only heard the far-off call of the cuckoo from some distant wood.

At length we reached the old-fashioned and picturesque town, with its quaint and clean streets, its sudden descents, its ancient churches, and its fine old castle. If a stranger wished to see a typical English country town, homely, quiet, and bright, with neither the pestilence of manufactories in the air nor the vices of fashion visible in the streets, could he do better than visit Lewes? I had never been to Lewes; but I was proud of it, for Miss Lesley's sake. She, too, was a stranger to the place; and, after she had delivered over the horses to the man to be put up, we started on an exploring expedition. We went down the hilly streets, and through quiet thoroughfares, and out to the precipitous chalk hills which surround the outskirts; then we returned to the Castle, and clambered up the wooded old ruin, where the sunlight was straggling down through the elms and chestnuts. We were the only visitors; and when we had got right up to the top of the tower, we found ourselves alone, for the portly and good-humored seneschal remained below.

The view from the top of Lewes Castle, as everybody knows, is one of the finest in England; and on this particular day the splendid plain, with its woods and hills and valleys, lay in the warm sunshine and shone. I think such a view, whether in sunlight or not, is rather saddening—perhaps it was so to me because it so closely resembled that stretch of Buckinghamshire country which was connected in my mind with so many old memories. However, Bonnie Lesley leaned on the parapet, and gazed long and wistfully over the great extent of country that lay so peacefully under the summer sky. Suddenly she spoke, and I saw that she had not been dreaming dreams of by-gone times.

"Did you think I was very angry when Mr. Heatherleigh tried to stop the horses?"

"Yes."

"You saw how soon I got over it?"

"Yes."

"Would you consider that a fault?"

"What, a fault to get rid of anger?"

"Yes."

"I should consider it—and did—a sign of great good-nature."

"Mr. Heatherleigh would say it was a weakness."

She turned and said this to me with a show of petulance, and there was a kind of wonder in her eyes.

"I think you mistake Heatherleigh altogether," I said, "or else there is a misunderstanding on both sides."

She laughed.

"Is that a question? There is no mystery between us. He says I am incapable of mystery, among other things."

"Heatherleigh couldn't say anything so idiotic. Why should anybody want to be mysterious?"

"Perhaps it isn't mystery, entirely, that I mean. But, tell me, you and he are very much alike in your tastes?"

"Very much, indeed."

"You care for the same sort of people; you have the same notions of things; you have the same sort of nature, in short?"

"Pretty much the same in most things," I said, "but very different in others."

"You like the same sort of people?"

"Yes, I think so."

"And you said it was a pleasure to you to come with me?"

"You know that it is."

She laughed again.

You must remember that this was the first "fine lady" with whom I had ever been privileged to be on any terms of intimacy;

and that I found nothing singular or abnormal in her peculiarly frank way of talking. I was not aware that there was a touch of the *Bohémienne* in her manner and conduct. I knew nothing of the extreme restraint that society imposes on the speech and general relations of young and unmarried folks. I saw that, among other people, Bonnie Lesley was as reserved and ceremonious as any; and fancied that there was nothing unusual in her childlike confidence and her self-disclosures, when it had pleased her to break the bounds of formality between herself and me. And this boldness of hers naturally encouraged me to be bold. I did not know that I was sinning against the laws of society, and offending the canons of good taste, in showing her what I thought of her good looks, and in expressing gratitude for her special favor to myself.

Doubtless she perceived this; and was provoked in exaggerating the license of her frankness through some notion of the humor of the position. If she encouraged me, my simplicity encouraged her. My ignorance of the customs of good society had produced in me that peculiarity of which Polly Whistler spoke—I was unable to see why a man and a woman should not be as intimate in their confidences as two women, and I never could teach myself the least embarrassment in speaking honestly to a woman. This much by way of explanation, or excuse, for much that happened then, and will have to be recorded afterwards.

"Will you consider me egotistical," she continued, "if I ask you to tell me what you think of me?"

"I daren't," I said.

"What!" she replied, turning her eyes upon me, with a look of amused surprise in them, "are you afraid to tell me the truth? And is it because you would have too many cruel things, or too many pretty things, to say to me? But do let me hear what you would say, in any case. I shall not be angry."

"Well," I said, "I think you are very kind."

She shrugged her shoulders.

"I think you are very courageous and independent in your kindness. For instance, you leave all your friends to come here with me, who am almost a stranger to you, and you make friends with me instead of—"

"All that is nothing," she said.

"Then you are very amiable."

"Well?"

"And remarkably good-natured."

"Well?"

"Very frank."

"Well?"

Here I stopped, not knowing how to describe her disposition further, whereupon she cried out impatiently—

"Don't you see? That is the very thing. I am amiable and good-tempered and kind: is that all you say? Why not say I am desperately revengeful or cunning or passionate or morose—anything gloomy and deep and hideous? He says there is no background to my disposition—"

"And pray who could have said anything so abominable and wrong?" said a new voice, and Heatherleigh appeared at the top of the stairs, and stepped out upon the leaden roof of the tower.

Miss Lesley turned with a start to see who was the speaker, and, when she saw who had overheard her, she stamped her foot with an involuntary spasm of vexation. Then she crimsoned deeply, bit her lip, and turned contemptuously away, pretending to look out upon the plain.

"Pray forgive me for breaking in upon you, Miss Lesley," said Heatherleigh, who seemed rather amused by the scene, "but I could not help riding after you to see that no danger befell you. Come, don't be angry, if I interrupted your *tête-à-tête* at an awkward moment—upon my honor, I had no intention of doing so. I have been waiting for you at the foot of the tower for a long time; then I thought I'd be able to point out some objects of interest to you if I came up."

"You are very kind," she said, coldly.

"Come, Ted," he said, "be my intercessor. Plead for me."

But Miss Lesley turned around, with a smile breaking through the coldness of her look, and said—

"We will forgive you, if you fulfil your promise. Tell us everything you know about the place."

Which he did—for he had lived in Lewes, and studied its history and traditions and legends; told us such stories of friars and kings and knights, of battles and sieges and monkish exploits, that the place appeared to me enchanted. It seemed as though that old and beautiful and picturesque time was divided from us by some thin veil of mist; and that, if we went down there, might it not return to the still, quiet town? How long ago was it that the cold winter days awoke to find the Saxon farm-people overlorded by the fierce and drunken sea-pirates of the North, while Alfred the King and his small court lay hiding in the swamps of Athelney, planning a sudden raid upon them? How long ago was it that Canute, sailing through the yellow sea-fog of the morning, heard the monks of Ely singing, and bade his knights row near the land? The time came quite near to us; English history seemed to be around us; and as we leaned upon the old wall and looked down on those fields and mounds into which generation after generation of Saxons and Normans and English had peacefully passed, there came up to us the slow, soft notes of an organ, which was being played in one of the churches. It was probably only the work of some amateur player, trying over some new chants; but as it reached us—so faintly that we lost it occasionally—it seemed a breath from these old forgotten times, full of mystery and pathos and sadness.

Miss Lesley uttered a light cry; she had dropped her glove over the wall.

"Jump down for it," she said to me; "or shall we all go down? The horses must have rested sufficiently by this time; and that young one especially gets fidgety if he is kept long in strange stables. I hope he won't run away with me."

"If he were a more intelligent animal, he might be excused," said Heatherleigh, with a smile.

Bonnie Lesley blushed slightly, and said, rather inappropriately—

"Oh, you think that men are superior to all the other animals?"

"In some things only," he said. "As food, for instance, men are inferior to sheep."

I could not help reflecting what a rejoinder Polly Whistler would have made at this moment. Indeed, I sometimes wished that Miss Lesley, with all her splendid graces and accomplishments, could possess herself of Polly's wit and gay humor and brightness. But would not a perfect woman be a monster? Surely Bonnie Lesley had enough of what was beautiful and desirable in woman!

When we had gone down to the hotel, and ordered the man to get out the horses, Heatherleigh came up to me, and said (Miss Lesley was not within hearing)—

"You can ride, can you not?"

"No; but I can stick on the back of a horse like a leech."

"Will you ride my horse home, and let me go in the phaeton?"

"Are you tired?"

"No—"

"Then why do you want to exchange?"

"I can't tell you just now—"

"Well, I'd rather go back in the phaeton. You seem not to like Miss Lesley; why should you want to go with her?"

"Very well," he said, turning aw...

There was no look of disappointment or vexation on his face; but there was a meaning in the tone of his voice which I could not understand. Then his anxiety that she and I should not go off together—his sudden appearance at the old castle—this present desire to separate us—what could it all mean?

Was he jealous of the favor which Miss Lesley, in her thoughtless good-nature, was so liberally extending to me? I was irresistibly driven to this conclusion; and my old friend, if he should happen to read these confessions, will understand that I now record the fact with shame.

That notion took possession of me, and by its false light I read all the occurrences which happened at this time. On that very night—after Bonnie Lesley had driven home in time for dinner—Heatherleigh and I dined at a big new restaurant in West Street. He spoke of what had happened at Lewes Castle.

"I only caught the last sentence; but I knew that she had been speaking of what I had said about her, and as I did not wish to hear more, I broke in upon you."

"Then you did say that?"

"I did, and do. The girl is in many respects a very good sort of creature; but she has no more permanence or depth of character than a sheet of tissue-paper."

"Her good-nature—"

"Her good-nature is negative. It is the absence of the power to be really angry. She has not depth of nature enough even to feel a proper resentment against anybody or anything. She has no emotional capacity whatever. She admires everything in a pretty and careless way, and admires everything to the same extent. She loves and hates and wonders, all in this slight and superficial fashion—"

"For goodness' sake, stop," I said to him. "When you begin to talk about Miss Lesley, you lose your reason. What has she done to you, that you should be so savage? And if she is so feeble and frivolous a creature, why were you so anxious to enjoy her society that you rode all the way to Lewes, and why did you want to go back with her in the phaeton?"

He looked at me for a few seconds.

"Yes," he said, "you have your troubles to come; and it doesn't matter which woman it is who opens your eyes. Do you remember when Polly and I were talking nonsense about the necessity of a young artist's having his heart broken?"

"Yes."

"And I proposed to make Bonnie Lesley the operator in your case."

"Yes."

"That was a joke; and I did not think that Bonnie Lesley would have taken the whim that she has taken. But if I were to tell you why the girl is petting you, you—with your sublime faith in the virtue of everybody—would not believe me."

"Certainly not," I said, "if you proposed to tell me that the girl was acting unworthily. Why, it is too absurd. Take your own position—that she is kind to me for some particular purpose of her own; and how does that affect me? I find a warm-hearted and generous girl, whom everybody (except one) admires; and she chooses to make friends with me, who am too young to be of any importance to her or to anybody else—"

"Younger men than you have run away with pretty girls, and married them. Consequently, younger men than you have been led into the notion that they *might* do so, and, finding themselves mistaken, may have had their faith in human nature destroyed and their lives ruined. I warn you, Ted, not to continue your friendship with this girl. I rode out to Lewes to separate you; and I would have ridden as far again; for your sake alone, understand me. Perhaps, as it was, I saved you from a danger that might have befallen you in a few minutes—"

The thought that these words suggested was so horrible that I started back from it. I sprang to my feet—my face, I knew, was as white as death, and my heart seemed choking. I said to him—

"You have been my friend, and I am grateful; but, as sure as I live, I will never listen to another word from your lips."

I rushed out of the place: he followed, but he had to stop for a moment or two to explain to the waiter. This saved me. I walked about all night; and took the first train in the morning for London.

CHAPTER X.

POLLY AND HE.

I WAS hasty enough, I know; but I was beside myself with indignation. For Heatherleigh to talk of my losing faith in human nature through some possible underhand dealing on the part of Miss Lesley seemed absurd when I considered that he, without any proof or reason or excuse, suggested about an honest and good-hearted girl what his words dared not state explicitly. What danger?—and to me! Why, so great was my sense of that beautiful creature's bounty in even regarding me and speaking to me, that I should have been only too willing to suffer anything to give her a moment's pleasure. And it was out of the question that any suffering of mine could affect her in any way. Suppose she was one of those impossible women who are supposed to go about the world in order to imperil men's souls by breaking their hearts—suppose she liked to boast of conquests as a savage points to the number of his scalps, was it likely she would care to make a conquest of me? There were a dozen men in Brighton at that time anxious to have the honor of being her victims. They hovered around her, knowing that all of them could not marry her, and certain that all, except some particular one, must be disappointed. To catch a smile or a word, or the pleasure of handing her a fan, they sought her society at this risk; and it was not to be considered that she should turn aside from these suitors, who had every advantage of age and position and money, to me, as one likely to flirt with or make love to her. Why she should in any case have shown me such favor was sufficient of a mystery; and it was explicable only on the ground of her disinterested good-nature and that independence of kindness which I had observed in her.

As I was going up Hampstead Road to my lodgings, on the morning of my hurried departure from Brighton, I met Polly

Whistler. I shook hands with her heartily; for I was glad to see some face that I knew. It was my first estrangement from Heatherleigh; and all the world seemed to have grown cold and distrustful.

"What are you doing here, Ted?" she said.

"I should like to tell you, Polly; but it is a long story. Where are you going?"

"I was to sit to Mr. Frances at ten o'clock, in place of that Italian girl—only for the costume, you know. I don't look like an Italian peasant girl, do I? However, come along with me, and I will tell him I can't sit for him this morning. He must wait for her until to-morrow. Then we can take a walk in Regent's Park, and you will tell me all about it."

"But you will lose the sitting," I suggested.

"I don't care now," she said, rather sadly. "I used to like to gather a few shillings you know, and buy little things for the house; but my mother—"

I understood the mother not only took the girl's earnings, but sold such little ornaments or luxuries as she chose to buy. So Polly and I went around to Regent's Park; and I told her the whole story. She was deeply interested in it.

"And do you think he is in love with her?" she asked, with her eyes fixed on the ground.

"No," I said; "I can't say that. A man would not talk about a woman in that way if he was in love with her."

Polly was very thoughtful for some time. We sat down on one of the benches underneath the great lime-trees fronting the broad stretch of the park that lies south of the Zoological Gardens. It was here that I had first seen Bonnie Lesley. There were few people in the park at this time; and an unusual silence dwelt around, for the leaves of the trees scarcely stirred in the warm sunlight.

"You think he would not talk like that if he was in love with her?" said Polly. "Did you never imagine the position of a man who is compelled, in spite of himself, to love a girl whom he considers unworthy of his love? Don't you think he would be bitter against her, and bitterer against himself? Would he not be likely to laugh at the folly of being in love; and sneer at those feminine arts by which he had been captivated? Would he not revenge himself in that way, and cover his own weakness, of which he is ashamed?"

It seemed to me that this bright and happy girl must have had her moments of cruel and sad reflection before she could have hit upon a notion like that, the truth of which flashed upon me at once. But was such the position of Heatherleigh?

"Come," she said, with a laugh, "what have you and I to do with love-matters, Ted? They are for rich people, who have nothing to do but choose whom they will marry. We have our living to look after; and it takes us all our time, doesn't it? I wonder if, in the next world, we shall be able to get free of all these things, and speak to each other of what might have been here below? It would be like a Sunday out for us poor people, if we were to get such a chance. There—will you look at this thing, that I copied the other night?"

With a sort of assumed carelessness, she slipped into my hand a bit of paper, which I unfolded. There were some verses on it, written in her own handwriting, which I knew. It was very correct and precise, but a trifle stiff: she had taught herself.

The verses, so far as I can remember, began with these lines—

"If you and I were only ghosts,
Cut off from human cares and pains,
To walk together, at dead of night,
Along the far sidereal plains—"

and went on to say how they would forget all the cruel conditions that had separated them here on earth, and talk to each other of all they had been thinking when these things had kept them asunder. Indeed, the lines, touchingly pathetic here and awkwardly constructed there, were so obviously a reproduction of what she had been saying, that I cried out—

"Oh, Polly, you have been writing poetry!"

"Nonsense!" she said, with an embarrassment and blushing I had never seen her exhibit. "I told you I had copied it."

"And you told me a fib."

She put her arm inside mine (she had slipped the paper into her pocket meanwhile), and said—

"Come, let us go into the gardens. I have got a shilling, if you have. And you shall tell me of all you mean to do. I insist first, though, on your making friends with Mr. Heatherleigh."

We passed into the Zoological Gardens, and we strolled about the walks, sometimes talking about Heatherleigh and Bonnie Lesley, sometimes talking about the animals in the cages. Polly was in better spirits now; and went on chatting in her usual bright and happy fashion. I wish I could remember a tithe of the remarks she made about the animals—mad interpretations of their feelings and opinions, humorous touches of description, and comical comparisons of every kind. From cage to cage we went, from enclosure to enclosure, and there was scarcely a bird or a beast that she did not endow with human feelings, and wonder what each was thinking of at the time. Some of these anthropomorphic fancies were extraordinarily ingenious, and they flowed out so freely and spontaneously as to charm one with their constant variety and novelty. She had just described the opinion probably held by a very mangy-looking hyena about Offenbach's music, as played by the band of the Coldstream Guards opposite its cage, when her arm, which was inside mine, gave a sudden start. Heatherleigh approached.

The expression of her face changed instantly; and she seemed anxious to get away without speaking. However, he came up, and shook hands with her, and asked, in his old friendly way, how she was. She answered him very coldly; and, saying that he probably wanted to speak to me, was going off by herself.

"Don't go away like that, Polly," said he.

"At least let me go with you," said I.

"There now," he said, with a peculiar smile, "are my two best friends—about the only people I care for—in league against me, and going to cut me! Have I deserved it? At any rate tell me what I am accused of."

"I don't accuse you of anything, Mr. Heatherleigh," said Polly, in a low voice, "but I wish to go home."

He looked at her for a moment with a strange look in his face—a look of infinite compassion and tenderness. I thought he would have seized her hand. But he only said, in a graver voice—

"Don't let any misunderstanding remain between us three. Life is not long enough that we should waste it in quarrels; and friends are not so plentiful that we can afford to throw them off. Let us sit down on this seat. There now. As for you, Ted, I will bring you to your senses in a moment. You misunderstood entirely what I meant about Miss Lesley. But say that you didn't; and I profess myself all the same very sorry, and I will never say anything against her again. It was entirely for your sake that I spoke: you will find that out some day, when you know both her and me better. I say that I regret having said what I did: will that do?"

I nodded.

"Shall we be friends, then?"

"Certainly; I don't see how we could have been anything else under any circumstances. But your conduct towards her is a mystery to me. You say that some day I shall think otherwise about her. You don't suppose I am in love with her? But, so far as I do know her, I know you do her a great injustice, and last night what you said was simply—"

"There, there," he said, "we'll have no more about that. I regret it; and you will think no more about it. Is it a bargain?"

"I am only too glad to be friends with you again on any terms; but it is you who will think otherwise in time—unless your present opinion of her is only a pretence."

"And now for you, Polly; what have I done to you that you should try to avoid me?"

"Nothing at all, Mr. Heatherleigh," said Polly, casting down her eyes; "and you know it."

"Why, you used to be as frank with me as the daylight, Polly," he said. "When I came around the park in search of Ted, and when young Cartwright, who saw you both, told me you had come in here, I said to myself that I should have an ally in bringing him to reason. Instead of which I have both of you to argue with; and the mischief is that I don't know what it is we have to argue about. *You* are not in love with Bonnie Lesley, Polly?"

"No."

"Then what is the matter?"

"You forget how we parted last," she said, in a low voice.

"But what has that to do with me?" he said, taking her hand.

She drew her hand away, and said—

"It has nothing to do with you, Mr. Heatherleigh, of course. but—but I don't wish you to speak to me any more—"

She hastily rose from her seat, and left, with her back turned to us. He would have followed her; but I restrained him.

"Don't shame her any more," I said; "she is crying."

He bit his lip, and sat silent for a moment.

"That old idiot!" he muttered; "why should her nonsense be regarded by us who are sane?"

"By and by Polly will have forgotten much of what her mother said, and may not be ashamed to meet you; but at present—"

"Well, at present?" he said; "wasn't she chatting just as usual to you when I came up?"

"That is another matter," I said, looking hard at him.

He did not seem to draw any inference from the words: he was staring at the path, drawing lines on the gravel with his stick. Eventually I persuaded him to go over to his rooms, saying that I would follow him.

Then I went in search of Polly, and found her.

"Is he gone?" she said.

"Yes," I said.

She pressed my hand; and we went slowly towards the gate, without a word.

"Really," I said to her, in crossing over the park on our way home, "you put too much importance on what passed that night. Heatherleigh understands that your mother did not know what she was saying; and he is very sorry that it should have occurred, and is vexed that it should alter in any way our old relations. Don't you remember the jolly evenings, Polly, when we three used to sit all by ourselves after supper, and chat until near midnight? You know, the autumn nights will be coming on again; what shall we do with ourselves if we are never to meet as we used to do?"

"You are very kind, Ted," she said, "but that is all over."

"It isn't all over, Polly. When Heatherleigh finally comes back from Brighton—"

"Do you think I can ever enter his house again, considering how I left it?" she said, with just a touch of indignation in her voice. "Do you think a woman has no sort of self-respect, even although she is a model? Oh, I hope I shall never, never see him again—for it kills me to think of his standing in that room and listening to all the cruel things she said of me."

I saw her mouth quivering, and her breath came short and quick. Then she said—

"You told me you had a picture at your lodgings, Ted."

"Yes."

"Could I—could I be of any use to you? We are both poor, you know—at least I am; but I have plenty of time, and I should like to come and sit for you. Will you let me do that in return for your kindness?"

"But why should you cry about it, Polly?" said I.

The tears were streaming down the poor girl's cheeks. As we passed along, I knew that Heatherleigh was watching us from under the shadow of one of the trees; but she did not see him.

CHAPTER XI.

MR. ALFRED BURNHAM.

I WENT down to Brighton again with Heatherleigh, and re-entered that strange world of indolent enjoyment, of luxury and gayety, of day-dreaming by the sea, of listening to Bonnie Lesley's pretty voice, and looking at the pretty wonder of her child-like eyes.

What chiefly astonished me in this new world was the life led by the young men—the young Olympians of handsome figure, of faultless dress, and unlimited command of money, who drove their mail-phaetons in such splendid style, and had such a fine indifference to the presence of waiters. Rather against my will, I was dragged into their society by Heatherleigh, who knew several of them who were living at various hotels. So far as I was concerned, I could not help admiring the free and easy manner with which they used to try to convince me that I was their equal. I was too much impressed by their manner of living, however, to think of myself in the matter: it was enough for me to watch the actions of those young favorites of fortune, with their irresistible coolness and self-possession, and their unconscionable expenditure in flowers, gloves, and cigars. How little they thought of tossing up as to who should pay for a dinner for four or five of them, which cost, at a moderate computation, eighteen shillings a head! How carelessly they would hand a half-sovereign to the leader of the band which used to play in front of the hotel at night! With what indifference they wrote off to Poole to send them down a couple of suits of clothes! And with what a royal magnanimity they dispensed shillings and half-crowns to anybody who did them the smallest service!

There was one among them who was never guilty of these thoughtless acts of generosity or extravagance; and that was Mr. Alfred Burnham. Miss Hester Burnham, I heard, had come down, and was living with her aunt—an old lady who had a large house at the extreme east end of Brighton. This lady I had never seen; but I knew she was not very favorably disposed either to her nephew, Mr. Alfred Burnham, or to his father and her brother-in-law, Colonel Burnham. Such, at least, was the gossip down in Buckinghamshire, and it was so far corroborated by the fact that Mr. Alfred Burnham, instead of living at her house, stayed at a hotel.

I detested that man, and everything I saw and heard of him at Brighton increased the bad impression I received from his cold and calculating eyes, his thin lips, and selfish, hard face. He was handsome enough, in one way—indeed, he looked like the best type of young Englishman, with the emotional and moral qualities withdrawn. He had a good physique, good complexion, and excellent manners, of a somewhat indifferent and *blasé* kind. To women he could be exceedingly agreeable, when he chose; and then he would turn away, with a half-concealed look of weariness, as if he rather pitied their folly in being pleasant to him. In the company of men, he was chiefly remarkable for his constantly watchful habit of making the most of current circumstances—of winning bets, and extricating himself from the necessity of paying anything. He did not seem to care to shine in any way. H never boasted of anything—not even of his successes with women. He acknowledged himself ignorant of politics; was rather inclined to be a Conservative, as he considered the Radicals "such a pack of d—d cads;" he hunted sometimes, but he had no good runs or exciting escapes to recount; he shot sometimes, but cared nothing about it.

Here is a little incident which I used to think revealed his nature admirably.

He and two or three others, with Heatherleigh and myself, were going into the Grand Hotel. I may say here, *par parenthèse*, that I had no scruple about meeting *him*. I did not care whether he remembered or not that he had given me half a crown by way of alms. I disliked him, and had there been any disposition on his part to recall that incident at the foot of White-cross Hill, I should not have been ashamed of it in *his* presence. As it was, he made no difference between me and the others, except that he never tried to make bets with me.

As we were going up the steps, I saw him linger behind, and drop a stone on the ground. I could not understand why a man should have been carrying a stone in his pocket, but paid no particular attention to the fact. We went into the billiard-room, somebody having proposed that there should be a game of pool before lunch. Some played, others looked on, and bet upon who should divide. I happened to sit down beside a young barrister, with whom I had become acquainted.

"I fancy you noticed Burnham drop a stone as we came in," said he to me.

"I did."

"Come out with me, and we'll have a lark."

We left the billiard-room together, and when we got outside he picked up the stone which Alfred Burnham had dropped.

"Now," said he, "he's up to some trick. He means to bet about that stone—either the distance it lies from the pavement, or its weight, or something like that. He's always at it; and he's not above trying any sort of dodge if he thinks he can get a fiver out of you. Suppose that we get a bit of string and measure how far the stone lies from the pavement, and then we can have it weighed?"

He put the stone down again, and we accurately measured the distance. Then we went into the tobacconist's shop at the corner and had the stone weighed—seven ounces thirteen drams was the result. Finally the stone was put back in its place, and we returned to the billiard-room.

Burnham was in high spirits; he had won a sovereign, betting three to one that Heatherleigh would divide the last pool. He offered to toss double or quits; but the offer was declined.

We went into the room in which luncheon had been prepared for us; and sat down at the prettily decorated table, with its colored claret-glasses, its vases of flowers, and—not least attractive—its handsome wine-coolers, out of which the rounded heads and golden necks of two champagne-bottles peeped. And out there the gay crowd rolled past in its handsome carriages, and there was a glow of brilliantly tinted parasols, and bonnets and dresses, along the pavement; and then, out beyond that again, lay the great white sea and the sunlight, and the far-off specks of sails.

Heatherleigh was sitting next to me, and I begged him to tell me whose guest I was.

"I don't know," he said; "it doesn't matter."

"Don't you know whose wine you are drinking?"

"I believe a person of the name of Röderer is the excellent author of it. Don't distress yourself. We were hustled in here indiscriminately by two or three men, and if there is any one of them whose bread and salt you would rather not eat, we shall forbid his paying his share. Have an honest care of your stomach, Ted; and leave Alfred Burnham alone."

"I wasn't talking of Alfred Burnham," I said.

"No, but you were thinking of him when you asked that question. There is old Ebury, at the end of the table, preaching about the benefits to civilization that the Italian canal, in which he is a shareholder, is going to produce. He may talk about the Italian canal till Doomsday; but it is his own intestinal canal he is thinking of."

At this moment I overheard Mr. Alfred Burnham beginning to talk rather loudly about the fun of making absolutely absurd bets.

"Why do you treat Alfred Burnham so defiantly—so cavalierly," continued Heatherleigh. "Has he done you any injury? Why, you speak to him as if he were a beggar—"

"That is *my* rôle," I said, laughing.

"Ah, I remember," said Heatherleigh. "But you don't blame him for that?"

"I don't blame him for anything—I dislike him; and I shouldn't eat or drink a morsel or drop at this table if I thought he was going to pay for it."

"Be at rest on that score, Ted; Alfred Burnham never pays. It is a point of honor with him; and I am glad there is one thing on which he follows a principle."

Burnham was now engaging the attention of the men nearest him by describing the various bets he had seen made. The running of rain-drops on panes, the motions of flies, the chasing of waves—anything in which no possible calculation could be made be preferred.

"For instance," he said, getting up and holding his table-napkin in his hand (although lunch was not nearly over), "I shouldn't mind having a bet about the weight of anything lying out there—a stone, or a bit of dry stick."

With that he looked out of the window.

"Are you good at guessing right?" asked my friend, the barrister, whose name was Tilley.

"I take my chance, like everybody else," said Burnham. "For example, I will bet you anything you like that I will go nearer the weight of that stone lying out there than you will."

"Sit down, you fellows, and drop your betting," said some one.

Burnham, however, ordered the waiter to go out and fetch in this particular stone. He brought it, and it was handed to Tilley.

"I don't mind having a bet with you," said he.

"What shall it be?" returned Burnham, carelessly. "Ten, twenty, fifty, a hundred?"

"Anything you like—say fifty."

"All right."

By this time everybody at table was listening.

"Send it off to be weighed," said Tilley, "and make the waiter bring back the weight on a bit of paper. You and I must write down our notion of the weight, and hand the two slips to Heatherleigh."

"Very well," said Burnham, with a laugh. "I suppose we must be particular when fifty pounds are in the case. Or, what do you say, shall we double?"

"I don't mind."

A minute or two afterwards the waiter returned, and gave Heatherleigh the third slip of paper.

"I find," said Heatherleigh, speaking with official gravity, "that Burnham guesses the weight of this interesting piece of stone at eight ounces, which is a very near guess, as it weighs seven ounces thirteen drams. But I find that Tilley is even nearer; *for he guesses it at seven ounces thirteen drams.* Accordingly, he has won the bet."

Heatherleigh must have seen through the whole affair when Tilley's paper was handed to him; but he made the announcement quite gravely. It was received by the others with an explosion of laughter. Burnham was beside himself with rage; for not only had he lost the money, but he saw that his neighbors perceived he had been caught in his own trap. He tried to laugh, and said to Tilley—

"You think that a good joke?"

"Well, I do," said Tilley, who was laughing heartily.

"I'll tell you what I think," shouted Burnham, entirely losing command of himself, "I think you are a d—d swindler."

Tilley was about to drink some claret out of a tumbler. The next second the wine was thrown into Burnham's face. Then ensued a pretty scrimmage, two or three men holding Burnham back by main force, and everybody begging everybody else to be quiet. Tilley stood calm and collected at the table. At length Burnham, vowing unheard-of things, was persuaded to go to his bedroom and change his stained waistcoat; while Tilley sat down, and asked if anybody was willing to cash Mr. Alfred Burnham's note of hand for a hundred pounds.

"I will—when you get it," said his neighbor.

Burnham did not reappear; and Tilley—who made no secret of the way in which he had trapped his opponent—finished his lunch in peace. From that day I noticed that the men rather fought shy of Mr. Alfred Burnham. When, through habit, he offered to bet, they declined.

"Lucky for him the Lewisons have not heard of that prank," said Heatherleigh to me.

"Why?"

"Because he would not be allowed to visit there, and it is only there he has a chance of meeting your friend, Miss Hester."

"Then you think—"

"That he means to become an honest man so soon as he can marry her and get her money to live upon. They say these two are engaged."

Heatherleigh was silent for a long time.

"She reminds me so much sometimes of that girl—whom—whom I told you I used to know. She has the same sort of manner, and her eyes have the same strange expression. Sometimes I look at her and think that— Bah! nonsense! What is she if she is capable of thinking of marrying *him?*"

CHAPTER XII.

AT SHOREHAM.

Some local club or society having resolved to hold its annual fête at the Swiss Gardens, Shoreham, Mr. Lewison, who knew several of the members, was asked to form a party to go there. He accordingly did so; and Heatherleigh and I were among the number invited. Some started from Mr. Lewison's house; others drove over by themselves, in their own carriages. Among the former were Heatherleigh and myself, and, as the party was successively told off, it happened that we were ordered to accompany Miss Lesley.

It was a very pleasant morning, with a cool breeze blowing in from the sea that tempered the fierce heat of the sunlight. Miss Lesley was looking particularly handsome; and she was particularly gracious. Even Heatherleigh's coldness seemed to be thawed by her obvious desire to be pleasant and friendly; and he chatted with her in a better-tempered fashion than I had ever seen him exhibit towards her. Once or twice, however, when he happened to say something to me about painting or poetry, or some similar topic, and when she joined the conversation, he turned to her with a polite and cold attention, which plainly said, "I don't choose to have *you* talk on such subjects."

This was unfair; because again and again I had noticed in the girl a desire to appreciate and understand these things, which deserved every encouragement. I have already said that it seemed to me the artistic side of her nature was singularly unimpressionable—that she seemed incapable of receiving artistic influences; but surely it was all the more creditable to her that she should be anxious to be able to take an interest in such matters. Even to assume the interest she did not feel was in itself a virtue. Most women in her position would have used the prerogative given them by their surpassing loveliness to despise what they could not comprehend, and banish any mention of it from their circle. To hold in subjection a court of lovers, to look like some glorified Cleopatra, would have been sufficient for them; and they would have laughed at and scouted the intellectual cravings which they could not understand, even as modern interpretation will have it that the object of Pygmalion's love outraged and disappointed the passionate longings of her creator.

When we reached Shoreham, we found that a number of people had arrived, and had already become familiar with what must have been to them the very novel amusements of the gardens. Here some young girls in gauzy white, with red roses in their hair and pink gloves on their hands, were practising archery in a reckless fashion, and getting extraordinary compliments from one or two gentlemen who were their attendants whenever chance brought a stray arrow near the target. There a party was playing at croquet, and exhibiting to bystanders a much greater skill in the fine art of flirtation than in sending a ball through the bell. Then there were the quiet walks through snatches of copsewood (with some painted pasteboard figure suddenly staring at you from among the bushes), the greenhouses, the flower-gardens, the lake, and what not, to attract straggling couples. I do not mean here to describe the various amusements that occupied us during the day—a picnic on the lawn being prominent among them; nor yet the performance at the theatre, where Miss Lesley sat in the front of the gallery, and endeavored to keep her numerous gentlemen friends from talking to her while the actors were on the stage. As the people were going out, we happened to get together; and, as chance would have it, we carelessly strolled onwards until we found ourselves in that straggling line of wood which surrounds the lake.

Here we walked up and down in the cool of the beautiful evening, all around us the flutter of green leaves and the stirring of the sweet pure air; and then, when we came to a gap in the trees, we found a pale yellow sky overhead, sharply traced across with lines of cirrus clouds, gleaming like silver on the faint background of gold mist. The young moon was there, too; and Bonnie Lesley turned over all the money in her pocket, for luck's sake.

"You artists don't care to be rich," she said. "You have a world of your own, and you are rich in dreams, and you don't care about us poor folks out here, or what we think is pleasant to have."

"I know what is pleasant to have," I said. "I wish I was rich and beautiful and strong and happy, not for my own sake, but to have the power of conferring favor and pleasure. I see men and women here who have only to smile to confer a favor: you, yourself—you know what pleasure it must give you to be beautiful and bountiful and lovable—to be able to gladden the people around you with a look or a word."

"Do you know what you are saying?" she said, with a laugh of surprise.

It seemed to me that I did not. I was so anxious to show her what I considered the happy position of rich and beautiful persons that I had taken no care to conceal what I thought of herself personally. This I told her frankly.

"You think it is a fine thing to be good-looking and all this that you say? What if you can't please the very people you want to please? Why, if I were to believe the nonsense you talked, I should be able at once to overwhelm you with kindness."

"You do that now," I said, truthfully enough.

"Is what you say true?" she said, turning her large eyes, full of a pretty astonishment, upon me. "Is it really of any concern to you that I should do everything in my power to please you? If I told you now that—that there was nothing I wouldn't do—"

With that she laughed lightly.

"Come," she said, "we are drifting into confessions, and there are sure to be people walking around this way, who would imagine—"

And here she laughed again, and turned away from me, and tripped down the bank to the margin of the lake. Before I knew what she was about, she had jumped into a boat, and, lifting one of the oars, had pushed out from the bank.

"How far would you jump in order to have the pleasure of coming and talking to me?" she said.

"Let the boat stop where it is, and I will jump from the bridge."

"You silly boy, you would break your neck. See, I will be merciful, and you shall break your neck for me another time."

"When I can be of service to you."

"Just so."

She pushed the stern of the boat towards the shore; I got in and took the oars. We paddled about a little—passed under the bridge and out upon the larger lake, which was now growing crimson under the evening sky. Out in the middle of the water we allowed the boat to float idly, and Bonnie Lesley bade me come and sit beside her that she might talk to me.

"Whatever put that strange notion into your head about wishing to be rich and so forth, in order to be able to please people? The only use in riches I see is that they make you independent. For instance, if I had no money, I should have to marry a man who could keep up a house in a certain style; but I shall have a little money, you know, when I come of age, and I can look all around my friends and say to myself, Well, there are one or two who, I think, would like to marry me, but I shall wait until I get desperately fond of some one, and then, if he is as fond of me, I can marry him, even although he is a beggar. Now that is fortunate."

"It would be, for the beggar."

"Why not for me? Surely you have a better opinion of me than to think that I have any sympathy with the common notions about marriage? Oh, I am more romantic than you imagine, and if you would only try me, I mean if you would not misunderstand me. I might— But no matter. Do you remember what Queen Elizabeth wrote in reply to Sir Walter Raleigh's lines about his fearing to rise so far lest he might fall? She was right, too, was she not? Isn't it the business of men to dare, and of women to give?" She uttered these last words in a low voice, with her head bent down.

Inadvertently I took her hand in mine, and she did not withdraw it.

The boat, meanwhile, had drifted back almost to the bridge, and, at this moment, I looked up and saw Hester Burnham standing there alone. Her eyes met mine.

Did I ever tell you what those eyes were like—the large, dark pupils, set in the tender-blue gray, and shaded by long eyelashes—eyes full of a strange, intense life, that was yet tempered by the calm, wise, kind expression of them?

I met that earnest look for a moment, and I withdrew my hand from Bonnie Lesley's fingers. I knew that between me and her, between me and any possibility of such hope and happiness as I had dared to think she suggested, there lay something as wide and as sad as the sea.

CHAPTER XIII.

BURNHAM PARK.

I WAS called from Brighton to see my Uncle Job, who was thought to be dying. It was at his urgent request that I set off immediately after getting the letter; and on the evening of the following day I was approaching the well-known valley down in the heart of Bucks.

How different the place looked now! The fields and meadows were laden with the bountiful summer produce; and the great beech-woods that lay along the successive hills were smothered in thick leafage. I entered these woods as the pheasants were getting to roost, and as the wide plain that stretched over to Oxfordshire was beginning to fade into a blue mist. Just above the horizon, however, lay a splendid sunset—the sun himself being down, and the clouds above gathering into a large, luminous fan-shell of gold. Along the horizon lay a swathe of dark purple, broken by one gleaming line of blood-red, forming, as it were, the base of the great shell; and then above that came the circled lines of gold, dying into a faint green overhead. By the time I reached my uncle's up-lying farm these lines had changed into a dull crimson, and the wooded western country was growing dark.

When I went inside, my mother and father were with my uncle. At his desire, they left the room, that I might go in and see old Job Ives alone. My mother kissed me as usual; but I noticed that my father shook hands with me ceremoniously, and strove to be formal and polite. Could the man's reverence for my mother go further than that? He looked upon me as a gentleman, because I was her son, and he seemed to think it his duty to her that he should be respectful towards me. I scarcely dared quarrel with this feeling (absurd as it was in its demonstrations towards myself), for I recognized the great love and affection from which it sprang. If my mother's marriage was a *mésalliance*, it was the happiest ever made in the world; and I know two people at least, who never regretted it.

My Uncle Job was down with fever, and a very ghastly spectacle he presented—his grizzly beard, his pale face, and cropped hair.

"Shut the dower, Ted," said he.

I shut it.

"Are we all aloan?"

"Yes."

"I suppose I be goin' to die?"

"I hope not, Uncle Job," I said.

"Now, Ted," he said, rather querulously, but in a low, gasping voice, "I have always 'ad a great respect for you as boy and mahn; you've always bin so fair and honest; and doan't you be goin' now to talk that darned nonsense about a man bein' afeard to die, and thinkin' what's a comin' to 'im. I tell ye, Ted, as you get so infernal weak and listless that ye doan't care whether ye die or no; and if I be agoin' to die, I'm darned if I care. I want none o' your pahrsons to frighten me wi' ghost-stories, as if I wur a babby; and I want no 'umbug on my tombstone, if they gie me one. The tombstones be nice things, bain't they?—saäyin' as how folks are grieved 'cause their friends are gone to heverlastin' 'appiness! It makes me think, when I see their grief is honest, that they are either darned jealous o' their friends gettin' the 'appiness first, or that they're not so sure about it as they pretend. And if ye look around, Ted, at the haverage goin's-on o' people, it's no wonder folks should ha' some doubt about everybody goin' to 'eaven. What I says is, I've done my duty by the fahrm and by my relations, and I bain't afeard o' nothin'. Though I do hope them wuts 'll turn out right."

Here my mother entered to give Job his periodical dose of quinine, or some such medicine. He muttered a word or two about his wishing to be let die in peace; but he took the medicine, and only cursed once and feebly about the taste of it. So soon as my mother was gone, he recommenced his chance observations on his having done his duty, a point he insisted on. Whence Uncle Job had borrowed his notions of duty was a puzzle. He recognized no authority beyond his own idea of what he ought to have done, and he looked for no recompense. He had done his duty, and he knew it, and wished to be let alone by parsons.

"Sure we be aloan, Ted?" he murmured.

"Yes."

"D'ye know why I sent for ye?"

"No."

"It was to tell ye somethin' I never told to *them.* I didn't want to have the pahrson a-botherin' about me, and all the darned idiots in the place talkin' lies about my convarsion; but I wanted you to come, for I'd something to tell ye, and I bain't so weak as not to be able to—"

Here Uncle Job ceased, and lay still for some seconds. His eyes were half shut, and he seemed to be thinking about something. What was the confession which this old heathen was about to make? The villagers would have believed any evil of Job Ives; for they knew that he said bitter things about parsons, and sneered at their church-going, and walked about on Sunday morning in his oldest clothes, with a clay pipe in his mouth. Not the old Major himself, who had refused to be buried in consecrated ground, would have been so readily accredited with evil doings. Indeed, more or less vaguely, they suspected Job Ives to be capable of any crime—except one. Even in Great Missenden I scarcely believe there was a man who would have dared to say that my uncle was secretly a Roman Catholic.

"That darned doctor," he said, "makes believe as he knows what's the mahtter wi' me; but he knows no more nor I know. It's their business to make believe. I remember as there was a feller—a professor he called hisself—came down to Missenden to explain things to us poor hidiots in the country, and he gave a lecture. D'ye know what he wanted us to believe?—why, that the water as rises in a pump is made to rise by the pressure of the air. Darn his eyes!—does the air press on my hand now? But you see, Ted, they've to explain it somehow, them professors; and one reason's as good's another."

Here the old pagan's ghastly face grinned, as if to say that Job Ives, even on his death-bed, was a match for any number of learned impostors.

"But you were going to tell me something," I suggested.

I knew I was no great hand at administering spiritual consolation; but if the old man had something to confess, or had even some religious difficulty to propound, I was anxious to make his last hours as peaceful as possible.

"Ay, ay, I doan't forget," he said, slowly. "Take out your pencil, and write down the name of Stephen Catlin."

He added a frightful oath as he uttered the name. It was no doctrinal point, clearly, on which he wished to have his doubts resolved.

I did as he bade me.

"Ted, that man Stephen Catlin wur my friend, and he ruined the girl as I wanted to marry."

A complete transformation had suddenly come over the old man. As he uttered the words, he struggled to raise himself on the bed, his face became whiter than ever, and his eyes actually gleamed with passion. His voice, too, that seemed to come from the grave, was shrill and harsh, and his whole frame trembled.

"I say as he took her awaäy from me, when we wur livin' in Datchet, and she over in Windsor. She wur to have married me, Ted, and I caught them walkin' together one night, and we had a fight—and, thank God! thank God! I felled him down, Ted—I felled him down—and he laid at her feet, and never spoke a word—"

He laughed, and the laugh had a hollow sound as it died down in his throat.

"I didn't knoaw then," he continued, sinking back on the pillow, "as he didn't mean fairly by her, or I should ha' killed him theär. It wur a bad day for her when she met him. She and I were very comfortable then—we used to walk along the banks o' the river in the evenin's, or under the trees in Windsor Park; and she wur a sweet, pure thing, Ted, as ever stepped, wi' a fine, plump cheek, and a pretty, soft eye. But I think she wur afeard o' me, for I never went to church wi' her on the Sundays; and *he*—that's how he got acquaint wi' her. It's a pretty likin' I've had for churches, chapels, and pahrsons since then. Howsever, when the worst came to the worst, and the poor lass had to go to London for shame o' people talkin' of her, he packs his traps and cuts for Australia. Would you believe it, Ted? And every one on us expectin' him to marry her. *But I could go to hell, Ted, if only to see him theär.*"

He rested himself awhile, for the terrible excitement under which he had been laboring had made him gasp for breath.

"You're younger than us about here, Ted. You'll live to come across them two—stay, put down her name, Katie Dormer—she's in London, and the last I heard of her was that she wur in service. She's, mayhap, gray-haired now."

I was about to write down her name, when he said, angrily—

"No, not on the same bit o' paper—on another bit o' paper: d—n him!"

This I did.

"I've made a will, Ted, and there's fifty pounds for Katie Dormer. You'll advertise for her; and you'll tell her, when you find her, as it's from old Job Ives."

"If she's alive, and in London, I'll find her out," I said.

My uncle stretched out his lean, hairy arm, and feebly shook my hand.

"As for him," he said, with that fierce light again coming into his eyes, "if ever he come back to England, and if you meet him, Ted, kill him, my brave lad, kill him dead! If you had a sister, wouldn't you kill the mahn as ruined her? And Katie Dormer was fit to have been the sister of—of—"

He lay back with a sigh.

"Open the dower, and tell my brother and his wife to come in," he said, in a little time.

I called them in.

"I feel wonderful better," he said, with a grin on the haggard, unshaven face—"I feel wonderful better. I bain't dead yet, Tom; and mayhap I'll cheat ye all. Howsever I want to tell ye as I've made a will, and in case them darned lawyers make believe as they've found a mare's nest in it, I'll tell ye what I mean by it, and you'll all three stick to it."

"Never mind about the will, Job," said my mother. "Lie still, and get better, and then we'll talk about it."

"Do ye wahnt me to come back as a ghost to talk about it, do ye? Happen as ghosts doan't talk anythin' so sensible when they come back—they talk darned nonsense to old women, and raise pianners! Fancy old Job Ives playin' on the pianner—what darned queer tunes my ghost 'll make if they bother me!"

"Oh, Job, don't talk like that!" said my mother, almost frightened.

But there was a ghastly grin on old Job's haggard face, and he said—

"Ain't it 'ard as I'll have to wear one suit o' clothes forever in the next world—them old things as is hanging up there—and in a year or two's time I'll be out o' the fahshion. And the people 'll say, when I begin on the accordion, 'Poor old Job Ives, 'e never could wear good clothes even when he wur alive, and now he's a reg'lar guy.'"

"Job, have you nothing else to think about?" said my mother, urgently, who was horrified to see her relative dying in this ungodly mood.

"Yes, I have," said he. "Brother, I've left you and your wife all the stock on the fahrm. I hope you'll take the fahrm, and do your duty by it, as I've done. If them wuts in the ten-acre ud only get some rain, you'll ha' a good crop this year to start wi'; and I hope you and your wife 'll live comfortable. If I'd ha' married a woman like you, Susan, I'd ha' lived a different life mayhap; but I've done my duty, as I say, and no one 'll deny it. Brother, don't you forget old Betsy Kinch; she wur a good friend to our father, and she'll look to you when quarter-day comes round. And you'll be able to afford her, besides, a trifle o' taters, or butter, or the like—"

My father took Uncle Job's hand, and pressed it.

"You're a good man, Job, and you've been a kind-hearted man since you wur a boy."

"As for Ted," said my uncle, "I've a matter o' eighteen 'undred pounds in the bank, and I've left it to 'im. You won't think that 'ard on you, Tom? You know, he's no' like us. Look at him—"

"I know, I know," said my father. "It's him as has to complain o' me; I should ha' started him in life; but how could I?"

"Why, father, you gave me a good education: what more does any one want than that?"

"Your mother did," said he.

"Make a good use o' the money, Ted," continued my uncle. "It isn't much; but it's a good nest-egg; and you may make us all proud o' ye yet. D—n it, I'm a-talkin' as if I wurn't dyin'."

"And neither are you," I said; "if you would only keep still and quiet, you'd get all right again."

With that he turned away his face from us, and lay perfectly silent. My father and I slipped out of the room, leaving my mother by the bedside.

"What a wonderful energy there is in him!" I said to my

father. "His system is at its very lowest, and yet you hear how he talks."

"Ay, there's fire there," said my father, sitting down in a great wooden chair in the kitchen—"there's fire in him yet; and I shouldn't wonder if he'd cheat the doctor. If he does, he has to thank your mother, Ted. She has watched him and tended him as if it wur you."

My father seemed to be struck by the notion that my mother should care so much for one of his family.

"There's a good woman, Ted," he said, thoughtfully; it's but a hard life she has had of it."

"Why do you say that?" I remonstrated. "Did you ever see a woman more contented?"

"But she was brought up to expect mower," he said, shaking his head. "She might have been a gentleman's wife, Ted, riding in her own carriage. What is she—"

"Happy," I said, looking him boldly in the face.

"She deserves to be," he said, rising suddenly, and beginning to walk up and down the wooden floor.

Then he said by and by—

"Was it about Katie Dormer he wanted to see you, Ted?"

"Yes," I answered, with some surprise; for Job had said it was a secret.

"I thought so," said my father; "I thought so. Your mother would have it as he was wantin' somebody to talk to him about religion, and didn't like to ask us about here, lest we should speak about it to the neighbors. But I thought it was Katie Dormer he wanted to talk about. So he told you the whole story?"

"Yes."

"Ah, he was never the same man after that happened. It turned his life round and round for him, and he got sour and cantankerous, and bitter in his speech wi' the people about. But he wur a good man for all that—I wish there wur more like him."

"And the man—?"

"Catlin? I heard as he had come back a rich man, and had started as a builder in Highbury somewhere, with a wagonette and a pair o' horses, and the like. It wur well for him as he got off for Australia afore my brother Job laid hands on him."

Here one of the servants came in for a minute or so, and inter rupted our conversation. When she had left, my father continued—

"So Job is still thinkin' o' that girl. I dunnow if he's done aught but think of her these twenty-five yurs and more. But what d'ye say, Ted, to get your mother to go home? She wun't go home for me, and she'll make herself bad by sittin' up night after night. You take her home, and I'll wait here to-night. In the mornin' she can come over again from Burnham."

I was going into the room, when he said—

"Mind you don't tell him as you heard me speak o' Catlin—for he doesn't know as he's back in London."

"All right," I said.

I went into the room gently, that I might not disturb my uncle. He was not asleep, however; and so soon as he saw me he signified that I was to sit down by his side.

"You woan't forget about them two?" he said, in a faint whisper.

"No," I said.

"Fifty pounds for *her;* death, and hell afterwards, for him! If I could only see him drownin', Ted, from the side of a river, me with a rope, him lookin' at me!"

A wicked laugh came over the gaunt, gray face; and then my uncle seemed to recover his spirits, and said aloud—

"I bain't agoin' to die, Ted; I be goin' to live, so as you may paint my pictur. Then you'll put a date on it, and people 'll know as I was in the fashion. What your mother wun't believe, Ted, is this—that folks have to wear in the next world what they wore in this—or how could you recognize their ghosts?"

"Job, pray don't talk any more about that!" entreated my mother, who was evidently being "talked at" by her hardened brother-in-law.

"What I says is, as it's 'ard they should make me walk about the next world wi' my old green shootin'-coat and corduroy breeches, and never gie me a chance o' changin' the cut—"

"You've told me all that before," she said, "and you are only harming yourself by talking."

"You want me to say as I'm darned sorry for my life, and as I beg the pahrson to forgive me for not goin' to church," he said, with a sneer. "I'm none o' your sweet-tongued sort, Susan. You'll teach old Job Ives to sing hallelujahs when you teach a jay

F

to talk French. Pahrsons! bah! Tell ye what, Ted, if ye kep' a lot o' pahrsons in a greenhouse, and manured 'em and let 'em develop, they'd grow into mealy-mouthed women."

"And what would the women grow into, Uncle Job?"

"Why, wi' plenty o' heat and damp, you'd see 'em beginnin' to sprout claws, and meyow, like cats. That's what all women would do, except one, Ted—*her*."

And he looked at my mother.

But nothing would persuade her to go home this evening, although it seemed clear to all of us, the doctor included, that Uncle Job was gaining ground. And as the doctor had promised to sleep at the farm-house that night, after seeing another of his patients, there was no room for me, and so I set off to walk over to Burnham, with a promise to return in the morning.

Somehow the reckless talk and manner of my uncle had given me the impression that he was not so dangerously ill as they had imagined. Could a man die whose whole energy was bent upon gibing at parsons, thinking over an old love-story, and making jokes about his prospects in the next world? When I got out into the clear night-air, it seemed as if I had come down into Buckinghamshire on a pleasant excursion, and that I ought to enjoy the opportunity.

Shall I confess here—since this is a book of confessions—that the gay life which had for a little while fascinated me at Brighton had begun to grow, to me, dull, heartless, and hopeless? It even destroyed the keen pleasure I felt in being near the sea. It was only at times that there wandered into that atmosphere that was sickly with the scent of wines and of ladies' finery a reminiscence of the far-off waves; and that vague suggestion stirred pulses that had grown apathetic. I began to long even for London, and the delight of labor, and the hopefulness and satisfaction of well-spent time. If I went down to Brighton again, I resolved to take my picture thither, and work at it, so that I should have some right to enjoy a chance hour of rest by the shore, out of sight of people, alone by the sea.

As I walked along the dark road, recognizing this wood or clump of trees or house that had been familiar to me in the old time, I became glad that the fashionable life with which I had no sort of sympathy was wholly cut off and separated from me. I was free to dream and dress and bend my steps just as I pleased.

Even Bonnie Lesley seemed now something distant; and when I tried to call up her features, and paint them on the dark background of the gloom in front of me, I could only summon up a vague shape, that scarcely awakened interest. But then I thought of her low and tender words on that evening at Shoreham; and my heart beat rapidly.

It was a lovely night. There was no moon visible, for it lay down in the south behind a great thin veil of cloud that stretched up and over the sky in successive cirrus lines. Singularly enough, these fleecy stretches of cloud were so transparent that you could see there was moonlight lying on the other side—a sea of light rippling in upon a breadth of ribbed and gleaming silver sand. But where the clouds grew still thinner, up in the north, they lay in long streaks across the deep blue, like the white hair of some Scandinavian god, blown by the polar winds. The rest of the sky was dark and still; and there was not sufficient moonlight falling through the curdled clouds to lighten up the landscape; so that the strangest effect was produced by those auroral-looking gleams of tremulous white fire that stretched across the dark vault overhead.

Very dark, too, were the avenues of tall Spanish chestnuts that led up to Burnham House; but nearer the House, the open park grew lighter, and at times the moonlight threw a slight shadow from the old and rounded oaks. There was a faint mist hovering about the foot of these trees that made the various objects around wear a spectral look. It was a long time since I had seen Burnham House; and now the gray front of it seemed strangely beautiful. In my early days the place had been associated with errands, and birthday presents, and what not, that gave it a wholly modern and prosaic character; but now it looked legendary and old and picturesque. Fancy this ancient house, in which the leaders of the Commonwealth, sitting deep into the night, with their leathern doublets and top-boots still on them, had planned their daring schemes and written out their despatches—the stately and venerable building that was full of memorials of great personages who had lived there—which seemed to belong to another century and another order of people; the noble and striking figures whom history paints—fancy this old place belonging to a young English girl, who was familiar with Brighton, rode in the Row, and read the *Times!*

I was startled by a singular noise behind me, and, looking around, found beside me a young horse that had come playfully cantering up, and now stood within a yard of the iron railing on which I sat. I rubbed his nose with a cane I had (all the young men of that day wore a cane as part of their attire)—he threw up his head, trotted off, and then came back again. Finally, by dint of various manœuvres, I managed to get near enough to seize hold of his mane and jump on his back.

"Come," I said, "you shall pay for the fright you gave me."

Such, however, was not his intention. He tossed up his head; he shot down his fore-legs, and kicked out his hind ones; he pranced and swerved, and tried all his tricks, with no avail. This, at least, I had learned in my boyhood—to cling with my knees to a horse's bare back, so that he might as well have tried to shake off a leech; and at length this particular animal gave in, and started into a good round gallop along that part of the park in which he had been turned out to graze.

The excitement of this wild night-ride grew into a sort of madness. The moonlight had come out more strongly, and it seemed to me that it was weaving strange shapes and figures of the mist that lay around the trees. Such a mild and beautiful night, in this old English park, should have produced English fairies and sprites; Puck should have been peeping from among the branches of the oaks; the fair Titania and her magic train should have been coming sedately over the sward, with the jealous Oberon down there in the brushwood to see her pass. But with the sound of horses' hoofs throbbing in the stillness, there was something German, wild, legendary about the place. The figures in the mist seemed to be tall shapes that grinned maliciously, and waved their shadowy garments as they gathered together and chattered in the moonlight. But could any one of them catch me on this strong young beast, that seemed to be possessed by the madness of the hour? My hand was twisted in his mane; my cap had fallen off, and I felt the wind rushing through my lifted hair. I laughed aloud in defiance as we tore past the grinning figures.

Then, just beside me, I heard a sudden shriek, so shrill and sudden that it seemed like a death-scream. I saw that I had ridden around the park and back again, almost to the gate of the modern wing of Burnham House. I tried to stop my excited steed; but the brute paid no attention. So I managed to slide down and get clear of him without a kick; and then hastily ran back to the spot at which I had heard the scream.

There was something lying on the ground—it was a white face. When I got near I was horrified to find that it was Miss Burnham who lay there, quite motionless and pale, the dark shawl she had been wearing thrown back and revealing the deathlike features. I knew not what to do. If I ran to the House for water, what might happen in the interim? I wished to lift her up, and ask her if she were hurt; but I dared not. I took her hand; and somehow I was obliged to let it fall again—the mere touch of it by my fingers seemed a sort of desecration.

With what intense relief I saw that she was coming round again! When her dazed eyes caught sight of me, she uttered a slight cry, and shuddered so that I thought she was like to faint again. But by and by a strange look came into the eyes, and she was about to speak when I asked her hurriedly if she had been hurt.

"It is you, really, then?" she said, and she glanced in a frightened way all around her.

"I hope you are not hurt," I said. "It was a foolish trick of mine—and I thought when I heard some one scream that—"

She shuddered slightly, and then attempted to rise. I was forced to offer her my hand, and afterwards my arm, as I saw she was rather unsteady when she rose. For a little time she availed herself of this assistance; then she withdrew her hand and said coldly—

"You need not come any farther."

"But you have not told me if you are hurt, Miss Burnham."

"No, I was only frightened. I should not have been out so late—I suppose it is past eleven—but the night was so beautiful; and then when I saw you galloping up, with your hair streaming—"

She smiled faintly.

"I am more than sorry," I said. "I did not know you had returned from Brighton; and I am sure I did not expect to meet any one in the park, or I should not have done anything so foolish. I hope you will forgive me for the alarm I have caused you."

By this time we had nearly reached the shrubbery that surrounds the back gate of Burnham House. I heard the sound of footsteps on the gravel; and then I heard some one crying—

"Hettie, Hettie, where are you?"

It was Mr. Alfred Burnham's voice.

My companion murmured some words of thanks, bowed slightly, and walked towards the House. I wandered up and down the park in the moonlight until I found my cap, and then went home. There was a note lying on the table from Bonnie Lesley. She wanted to know the name of the man in Brighton to whom I had given her fan to be mended.

CHAPTER XIV.

THE LADIES' GARDEN.

Old Job Ives apparently got much better; and I prepared to return to London. On the morning of my intended departure I received a message from Burnham House, to the effect that Miss Hester wished to see me for a few minutes. Accordingly I went over to the House. Since our memorable adventure in Burnham Park, I had met her several times when she was out riding. Sometimes she was accompanied by old Stephen, the groom; sometimes by Colonel Burnham; but more frequently by her cousin, Mr. Alfred.

A very handsome pair these two looked now, as they rode along the leafy lanes that intersect the Burnham valley. They were no longer boy and girl, but man and woman; and it was understood among the neighbors that they would in time become husband and wife.

"And a good thing, too," they added, "for that yaller-faced young mahn as has spent all the years of 'is life a-doin' nothin' ony waitin' for ur."

When I went into the House, he and she were playing billiards in the old hall. Burnham House was divided into the ancient historical building, all the rooms of which were preserved intact, and a new wing which had been built by Miss Hester's father, for the better accommodation of visitors. The latter rooms had never been properly finished; but they were used by the family, who preferred them to the old, damp, musty chambers of the House proper. This venerable hall was about eighty feet by forty-five, and had a narrow gallery running around the walls, with a frontage of wondrously carved oak. The balustrades of the staircase going up to this gallery were also of carved wood, of singular design and rare execution. In front of the gallery, at the head of the hall, was a pair of huge antlers, and immediately underneath the Burnham arms; on the walls surrounding the gallery hung a series of large and gloomy family portraits, many of them by celebrated masters, and one or two of them the originals of well-known engravings; while on the walls underneath the gallery—and especially over the great fireplace—were ranged all manner of rusty muskets, daggers, swords, pistols, and cross-bows. Down here in a corner was the chest that contained Oliver Cromwell's Bible; there, in a window-recess, were displayed a sword and belt which Elizabeth had presented to one of the old Burnhams on visiting the House—everywhere the look of antiquity that the successive holders and owners of the place had religiously preserved. In the midst of all this a modern billiard-table, and a bright young English lady making flukes.

"Good-morning," said Burnham carelessly, trying to make a simple carom and missing it—it was clear that his opponent was not betting. "Wonder you never came over before."

The ease of his manner was, I presume, intended to show that he had forgotten that little incident about the weight of the stone.

"I wished to ask your advice, Mr. Ives, about the pillars in the drawing-room," said Miss Burnham; "I hope you will forgive my breaking in upon your time. Will you come this way and look at them?"

There was no effort of any kind in *her* speech; nothing but a quiet, self-possessed, matter-of-fact directness, which was neither forbiddingly cold on the one hand, nor awkwardly familiar on the other. I professed myself willing to do whatever I could, and so she led the way through a narrow stone corridor which opened out on what was called the Ladies' Garden. Her cousin remained behind.

She was a little woman, you know; but she wore a rather long train, and she walked with a grace that was queenly in its every motion. And when she got out into the sunlight, and turned her face towards me, she looked as fresh and bright and sweet as a wild strawberry—one of those tiny, sweet, wild berries that you catch in the early morning, with sunlight on its fresh color and sweetness in its heart. I suppose anybody looking at her from a distance would at once have called her dark and small; but when you came near, and saw the fresh young life that was in the charming face, with its handsome features and its pretty forehead, and the strange, wise kindliness that lit up those eyes of which I have many a time spoken—when you saw the perfect symmetry of her form and the perfect grace that seemed to accompany her every movement—even if the small pale fingers were only pulling a rose-leaf in two—you began to dream dreams about this slight and young English girl, and wonder whether there lay not under that calm exterior great and even tragic possibilities of character. She was fit to have lived in the olden days, you would have deemed—in the days when great deeds of self-sacrifice and heroism were oftentimes demanded from our gentle English dames and their gentler daughters. It was so easy to imagine her grown into a noble and perfect woman, that, as you thought of her future being linked to that of such a creature as he whom she had just left, it was impossible not to grow sad at heart.

"I understand you and Mr. Heatherleigh work together when you are in town?" she asked.

"Yes," I said.

"Then perhaps you could tell me whether he and you together would care to come down here and put a few sketches—or even some ornamentation merely—in the panelling of those pillars."

The wing which her father had built (and which he had nearly ruined himself in building) had been made to front this Ladies' Garden, so that it might not interfere with the original look of the house as seen from the great avenue. She walked over to one of the French windows, opened it, and stepped into the drawing-room. I followed, but I knew the spacious and handsomely ornamented apartment well, and also the pillars which she wished Heatherleigh to decorate.

"It would be difficult to ornament these pillars in keeping with the rest of the room," I said; "they ought to have pictures."

"That is exactly what I wish," she said. "Most drawing-rooms look narrow and formal from the absence of pictures. I was thinking chiefly of the winter time; and then it would be so pleasant, when one is shut up indoors in the long evenings, to have just beside you a view of some great distance. The pictures should be faint and thin and light, with long perspectives, which would make you forget that you were shut up in a room."

"Then you don't want merely decorative pictures?"

"No. I should like to have pictures as real-looking as stereo scopic views, but still so light as not to be too prominent in the room."

"Leave that to Heatherleigh, then," I said, "and let him follow his own fancy. You should see the smoking-room he painted for Lord Westbournecroft—two summers ago. The room juts out from the house like a conservatory; and on three sides there are alternating panels and windows, with pictures on the panels and transparent flowers on the windows. The flowers you only see during the day; the pictures when the place is lit up at night."

"Miss Lesley told me he had done something of the kind, or I should not have asked," she said. "Now can you tell me what it would probably cost to have them done?"

"I can only tell you that he was asked by Lord Westbournecroft to fix his own terms, and he said five guineas a-day; but he received some considerable present over and above that when he left."

"And you," she said, with some little embarrassment—"you will come?"

"On one condition," I said, calmly.

"And that?"

"Is that you will deign to accept as a gift whatever I may be able to do."

Her cheek flushed, and she bent her eyes on the ground.

"I cannot do that," she said; "you have no right to expect me. Besides, it is absurd. If Mr. Heatherleigh accepts payment for what he does, why should not you—"

She did not finish the sentence.

"Why should I not take money from you, you would say. Well, I'd rather not—it is merely a notion or whim I have."

She looked at me for a moment with those grave, earnest eyes; and I imagined that she knew why I would sooner have cut my right hand off than take money—a second time—from her. I dared to think that she would accept my offer, and thanks were already on my tongue, when she said, coldly—

"I am sorry, then, that I must give up thinking about this pro posal at present. I am much obliged to you, however."

Here Alfred Burnham came along the corridor, whistling.

She stood for a moment or two in apparent indecision, as though she expected me to rescind my resolution. That was impossible.

"Shall I write to Mr. Heatherleigh," I asked, "and say that you wish to see him when he returns?"

"Pray don't," she said, in the same courteously distant manner; "I shall think over the matter first. Perhaps I may find some less troublesome way of getting the pillars finished."

So we bowed to each other, and said "good-morning," and I withdrew. Alfred Burnham came through the corridor with me, and said—apparently because he fancied he ought to say something—

"Won't you stay, and have a game at billiards?"

"No, thank you," I said, turning my back on Burnham House, and wondering when I should see it again.

CHAPTER XV.

THE LAST OF UNCLE JOB.

I HASTENED down into the valley, and up and over the hill again, towards my uncle's farm, that I might bid the old man good-bye. Even if Hester Burnham refused to give me my revenge by becoming my debtor, there was plenty of other work before me. I resolved to go no more to Brighton, and its idle atmosphere. Polly Whistler had promised to help me, and I was able now to pay her for her assistance. But the story about what this work was, and what hand she had in it, will come in its proper time.

I found, on reaching the farm, the whole household in consternation. My uncle had suffered a severe relapse, and was now delirious. The doctor had been sent for, but he had gone to Steeple Heyford, and might not return until night. My mother was glad to get me into the house, as my father had had to leave early in the morning to attend to some part of his duties.

"Your uncle has done nothing all night but talk about you and Catlin, and poor Katie Dormer," said my mother. "Oh,

Ted, it's a fearful thing to think of his condition. I think he is getting worse; but he only swears if I talk about getting Mr. Joyce to see him, and says such dreadful things about religion, and his soul, and the next world. I hope he doesn't know what he is saying."

If that was likely to be a saving clause, Job had certainly the benefit of it, for he was murmuring incoherent nonsense when I entered the room. He either imagined or pretended to imagine that I was the devil, addressed me in his grim saturnine fashion, and asked me if I had prepared sufficient room for the rest of the Missenden and Burnham people who were likely to follow him.

"I bain't a bad sort," he said, apologetically, "although my sister-in-law, a rare good woman, said as I wur sure to come to you at last. And 'ere I am; and I'm darned if I'm a darned bit afeard o' you, or one of your darned crew."

"Oh! Job!" cried my mother, ready to burst into tears.

"Why, don't you know me?" I said. "I'm no more the devil than you are. Don't you know me, Uncle Job?"

"Whisper—a secret," he said, softly.

I bent down to him, and he said under his breath—

"No, you're not the devil, but you'll darned soon be one of his friends."

With that he laughed out shrill and loud, in a way to make one shudder. Then he lay for a long time, and when he next spoke he seemed quite sensible, but for a peculiar look that occasionally appeared in his deep-set eyes.

"Ted, you know the story as I told you about Katie Dormer? It's fur away back now—in a mist like—and it seems as if I had never know'd her. But you'll find her out, and give her the money, and tell her as how old Job Ives had a kind word for her to the last."

"Get well, and find her out for yourself," I said.

"None o' your darned lies," he said with a scowl; "I bain't a fool, be I? You say as I'll get well—yeäs, very like! Hillo! is it you, Ted? I thought 'twur one o' them darned neighbors as are tryin' to save poor old Job Ives's soul—d—n 'em! But doan't you go for destroyin' the Church, Ted, all because some precious clever fellows think as they can do without it. They can't. It's ony the fear o' the next world as keeps the ignorant, superstitious, darned hidiots straight, and if ye don't frighten them wi' hell—"

"Job!" cried my mother to the grinning old heathen, "do you know what you're saying?"

The anxious little woman was beside herself to know how to arrest his rambling tongue, and alter the current of his unruly thoughts.

"You're a good woman, Susan," he growled, turning away from us both—"a rare good woman, but a darned fool."

My mother begged me to stay with her, and so I loitered about the house the whole day, sometimes in the room, sometimes out in the back garden. My father looked in once or twice, but he had some important business on hand, and could not finally stay and relieve my mother until the evening.

It was a dull and dreary day for everybody concerned; my mother was anxious to hear all about my new ways of life, and it was to her alone that I ever revealed any of my ambitious dreams. I could see that the little woman was pleased to hear of these projects; and her tender, thougthful eyes grew dim with tears, as she hoped, whatever befell me, that I might have as happy a life as she had had. I did not tell her the part of my vague dreams of the future that referred to herself; and yet sometimes I fancied that she guessed my secret wish.

I told her of all the various people I had met. Singularly enough, she seemed to prefer that I should keep among my artistic friends, instead of prosecuting the chance acquaintanceships I had made in that fashionable world into which I had been casually introduced. With what I said of Bonnie Lesley she seemed particularly pleased.

"I fancy, from what you say, that she must be a girl of a wayward or original character, who does not quite feel herself at home among these fashionable people. Her kindness to you shows how independent she is in her choice of friends, and she must be very good-hearted. Then what you say about her being so handsome is all the more credit to her, as it is a wonder she has not been spoiled. What age is she?"

"She must be about as old as I am."

"Then she is older than Hester Burnham?"

"Yes."

"They are friends, you say?"

"Acquaintances, at least."

"It is singular that Miss Hester has never spoken to me about her, as she and I have long chats about nearly everybody she knows. Ah, Ted, your friend Miss Lesley may be all that you say, but she is no better-hearted a girl, nor prettier, than Hester Burnham."

"They are so unlike each other that you cannot compare them," I said. "Miss Burnham is perhaps bound by her position to be more circumspect and reticent than Bonnie Lesley, as we call her. Besides, I know Bonnie Lesley very well, and I scarcely know Miss Burnham at all."

"No, you and she are not the friends you used to be when you were children."

"How could you expect it? I can tell you I was sufficiently embarrassed when I was forced to be in the same room with Miss Burnham in London. If the people who asked us both to their house knew our relative positions *here*, wouldn't they laugh."

And my mother laughed, too, and blushed as if she were still nineteen, and had just been accused of running away from the parsonage to marry a good-hearted and handsome young keeper.

Night had fallen when the doctor drove up in his dog-cart. The trap and horse—the latter a rather mettlesome cob—were left in the charge of a lad, and the doctor walked into the kitchen, where my father and I stood. My mother came out of the room, and seemed in a state of great emotion. The doctor went into the bedroom, which was on the same floor; but my mother did not accompany him.

"What's the matter, Sue?" said my father.

"He's been talking about that girl fit to break any one's heart," she said, with tears in her eyes; "I never thought he could be so fond of any one. And now he imagines that they are going to be married, and he has been talking to her as if she were there; and when the doctor's dog-cart drove up, he said it was the carriage come to take him to church, where she was waiting for him."

At this moment the doctor appeared.

"He is very excited, and we must get him soothed at any cost," he said. "Nothing will do for him but that I must go up-stairs to his old bedroom and bring him down a picture which he says is behind some books. Mrs. Ives, will you give me a candle? Mr. Ives, will you go in beside him for a moment?"

My mother herself took the candle to show the doctor up the narrow wooden stairs; while my father passed through the kitchen, and went into my uncle's room. A second afterwards—and all this had occurred within a minute—I noticed a figure dart across the yard towards the dog-cart. Something made me rush out to see what this could mean, and there I saw my Uncle Job trying to persuade the bewildered lad who had charge of the dog-cart to go away, and give the horse up to him. I ran forward and seized him by the arm. He shook me off, and swore horribly. He tried to get up on the dog-cart; I caught him by the neck and shoulders and pulled him down by main force.

"Would you make me late for church, you darned hound!" screamed my uncle, aiming a blow at my face.

I warded off the blow, and closed with him again. But twenty men could not have held him down. He struggled up into the dog-cart, caught hold of the reins in the darkness, and the fool of a boy jumped back from the head of the horse, that was now excited with the noise. At the same moment my father, in great consternation, came running across the yard, and shouted out for God's sake to catch hold of his brother.

I saw in a moment how it had happened. My uncle, possessed by the illusion that he was about to be married, had cunningly employed a *ruse* to get the doctor out of the way, had hurriedly donned a pair of trousers and a coat, stepped out of the window and ran across the yard. My father, on entering and finding the bed empty, had probably been too bewildered to notice the open window, and very likely wasted some seconds in looking under the bed or tables.

However, there was not an instant to lose now. I ran forward to the horse's head, and was knocked down the same moment. When I rose (one of the wheels just grazing my elbow) I saw that my father had scrambled up behind, and was endeavoring to catch at the reins. The horse was now wild; and as he backed the dog-cart with a terrific crash against the stone-wall of the farm-yard, the doctor appeared.

"Give him his head!" he shouted. "Give him his head for a bit, or he'll be the death of the whole of you."

But the responsibility no longer rested with my father. My

uncle had again wrested the reins from him, and the horse sprang forward.

"Job, for God's sake, give me the reins!" cried my father, who still stood up behind.

"Doan't you hear the church bells ringing?" shouted my uncle, hoarsely. "I can hear 'em plain, all the way up the hill; and she's waiting—she's waiting—she's waiting."

By this time he had driven the horse into a narrow path that led from the farm-yard across my uncle's fields, and down the hill, passing the deep dell of which you have heard him speak. The path was narrow and rugged, for it was only used for the farm-carts, and the doctor and I, running after the slight vehicle, could see it swaying from side to side, as it fell into deep ruts, and was dragged out again by the half-maddened horse.

"Yes, Job, yes," we heard my father say, imploringly, "we know she's waiting, but let me drive—there's a good fellow! Job, old man, give me the reins!"

But again he lashed the horse, and then he waved his whip triumphantly in the air. There was just enough light for us to see his spare figure, that looked tall and gaunt in the vague darkness, standing erect in front of the dog-cart, while he waved his arm and cried—

"No man but me shall drive! No man but myself! For doan't ye hear the church bells down there—I can hear 'em ringing, ringing, ringing—in the air, all around, up in the sky too—and she's waiting; I tell you, she's waiting! she's waiting!"

He laughed out shrilly and clear.

"If we don't stop the horse, they are both dead men!" cried the doctor; but it was hard to keep up with the dog-cart in this dark lane, at the pace the horse was going.

For they had now got on the breast of the hill, where there was no bank on either side of the rough path. I heard my father making more desperate efforts to restrain his brother, while Job was shouting more wildly and shrilly than ever about the church bells "ringing, ringing, ringing"—then there was a fearful crash, prolonged for a couple of seconds, a hoarse groan or two, then silence and darkness.

That terrible stillness! I stood on the edge of the deep cleft in the hill-side alone—for I had outstripped the doctor—and it seemed to me as if the darkness was throbbing with points of fire.

During that moment of paralyzed hesitation the clouds parted, and there was a pale gleam of moonlight thrown along the circular side of the dell. But down in the hollow there was only gloom, and the dreadful silence that hung over the fate of two men.

My uncle had formerly ploughed up the bottom and the other side of the dell; but the side that I now proceeded to descend was covered with patches of brier growing among the rough inequalities of the chalk. I scrambled down among these weeds, dreading every moment to touch a living form, and yet possessed by a vague horror that it might *not* be alive. I heard the doctor following me. The first object I stumbled on was the wheel of the dog-cart, and then I trod on the leg of the horse. The animal was quite motionless.

"Father!" I cried, making a wild effort to break this frightful silence, "where are you?"

There was no answer.

"Stay," said the doctor, "until I see if I have a light with me."

But the moonlight was now so full and strong above that the pale reflection of it down here was sufficient to guide our steps. We had not long to search. My father and my uncle lay within half-a-dozen yards of each other. Neither stirred as we approached. The doctor knelt down for a moment by the side of Uncle Job, and took his hand in his; then he came over to where I was trying to lift up the helpless body of my father.

"Who is to go back to your mother?" he said—and his voice seemed to me distant and strange and unrecognizable. "They are both quite dead."

CHAPTER XVI.

IN LONDON AGAIN.

WHAT a good friend Hester Burnham was to my mother during that terrible time. The wonderful, wise way in which the girl crept into her confidence, opened the fountains of her grief with a tender sympathy, and then wiled her away into thinking of practical necessities and future plans, was beyond comprehension, as it was beyond all praise. Where had this young creature been educated into a large and heartfelt sympathy with human sorrow? Where had she been taught her kindly, matronly ways, that were not the ways of an inexperienced girl? And who had lent to those eyes which were meant to bewitch and steal the hearts of men that grave and beautiful compassion which seemed to transfigure the face of the girl, and make one regard her as something more than woman?

My mother and she had always been friends, but during this time it seemed to me that no two human beings were ever so closely drawn together as these two were. On the day of the funeral, my mother and she came to the small old church of Burnham to hear the service read, and Hester Burnham sat in the same pew with my mother, and held her hand in hers the whole time. They stood at a little distance off, and watched the lowering of the two coffins into the grave; and then they went away by themselves—whither, I know not.

My mother could not remain in the place, so I decided upon taking her with me up to London. Fortunately, the man whose farm lay adjacent to that of my uncle was not only anxious to take up the lease, but was willing to purchase the entire stock of the farm. I had a lawyer sent down from London; the necessary valuations made, and the transfer of the farm was complete. The proceeds of the sale—somewhere about £2500, were invested on mortgage for my mother, along with a few hundred pounds that my father had saved up, through much economy, for her whom he so dearly loved. My own small fortune of £1800 was invested in a similar way.

These matters being settled, we left the quiet Buckinghamshire valley, and came up to London. There being no use in taking a house for us two solitary creatures, I engaged some furnished rooms in a house that looked over upon Primrose-hill—a situation that pleased my mother much. She protested against the expense of the rooms, however, until I pointed out to her that our income did not consist exclusively of the interest on these investments. Still, she begged me to be cautious, and was nearly out of her senses when Polly Whistler and I, laying our heads together, invented a new style of decoration for her neck and the upper part of her dress, and had the same composed of rather luxurious materials. She positively blushed when she arrayed herself in these things, and Polly said she looked like Mary Queen of Scots become respectable.

Polly frequently came to see us. My mother was inclined to be afraid of her at first. Polly's blunt and ready talk, her rather masculine wit, and the careless manner in which she snapped her fingers at a good many social observances, were calculated to impress the mind of the simple countrywoman with the notion that this young lady was rather a dangerous person. The very first evening she came to see us, our talk had wandered somehow into reminiscences of old dramas. Incidentally Polly remarked, quite calmly—

"Ah, in those days actresses wore clothes."

"Don't they now?" said my mother, simply.

Polly laughed; and, when she had left, my mother asked with some concern what sort of strange young woman that was, who made very odd remarks, and was so carelessly easy in her manner. By and by, when they got to know each other better, my mother became rather fond of the girl and her wild speeches and pranks; but there was never at this time perfect intercommunion between them.

Bright and clever as she was, Polly had not a grain of *finesse* in her composition. Doubtless the principal reason that she came to see us so often was that she found in our house a refuge from the annoyances of her own home; but several times it seemed to me that she came merely because she wanted to hear of Owen Heatherleigh. She never had the skill to hide her interest in him, nor the address to conceal the satisfaction she felt in hearing him spoken of. Many a girl would have assumed a fine air of carelessness, and made believe to mention his name accidentally; but Polly, in a hesitating way, and generally with her eyes cast down, used to ask me how Mr. Heatherleigh was, and how he was going on with his work.

This was one point on which an astonishing change had come over Heatherleigh. He had returned from Brighton before his holiday was out; and he had no sooner come back to his lodgings in Granby Street than he set to work in quite an unusual way to get his pictures forward. The transformation surprised me all the more that I knew he had not spent the whole of the money he had earned before going down to Brighton. There was even an expression of purpose on his face that I had never previously noticed. He gave up his indolent lounging, his wanderings about Regent's Park, his lazy forenoons in an easy-chair with Ueberweg's "Logik" or Spencer's "Social Statics" before his eyes. He even dressed himself with a trifle more care, although he had subsided into utter Bohemianism of habit.

One evening Heatherleigh was sitting with me, smoking and chatting. My mother, having a slight headache, had retired early; and we two were left by ourselves. She had scarcely gone, when a maid-servant came to the door and announced Miss Whistler. Polly walked lightly in, expecting to see my mother; but when her eyes rested on Heatherleigh she involuntarily retreated a step, and stood for a moment silent and embarrassed. He had risen from his chair at the same moment, and was about to advance when he noticed her confusion, and paused irresolutely, while I think he looked as confused and vexed as she did.

"Mrs. Ives is not at home?" she said to me.

With that Heatherleigh had come forward, and she shook hands with him formally and coldly.

"She has gone up-stairs. Won't you come in and sit down, Polly?"

"I only ran up in passing," she said, hurriedly. "I will call some other evening. Good-bye."

So she went out. Heatherleigh had stood in the middle of the room, without saying a word. The moment she had left, however, he instantly opened the door and went after her.

"Polly," I heard him say, almost roughly, "don't be stupid.

Come back at once, and let us have all this settled—let me understand what you mean by it."

She came back quite submissively, he having his hand on her arm.

"Come, Ted," he said, "you know more about it than I do. Get her to tell me what the matter is—why she should fly from me as if I were an ogre. What *is* the matter, Polly—have I offended you?"

"No."

"Have you anything to find fault with me for?"

"No."

"Why, then, are we not friends as we used to be?" he said, with some wonder in his eyes.

I saw this was becoming very painful for the girl, and I said—

"Polly can't tell you, Heatherleigh; but I will—only you might know it yourself. You remember the night Mrs. Whistler came up to your studio? She talked a lot of nonsense; and Polly won't understand that both you and I knew it was nonsense."

"Is that all, Polly?" he asked.

"No," she said, in a low voice. "I don't care whether you believe what she said of me or not. But you were good enough to make me a sort of acquaintance of yours, you know; and after you have seen what—what my mother is, I shouldn't like to continue—"

"What absurdity, Polly!" he said, going forward and seizing her hand in spite of her herself. "Ted hinted something like that to me, and I scarcely believed him. Why should your mother interfere to break up our very pleasant friendship? Why, the evenings that we three have spent together, when I look back on them, seem to me about the happiest portion of my life. And neither of you two ever looked very miserable. I say, what has your mother to do with it? She was excited—and—and said some things—which—"

"My mother was drunk," said the girl, in a hard voice, drawing away her hand from his, "and she insulted me before you, and she insulted you. She would insult you again if she saw you. If she knew that I went up to your studio, to sit to you, she would haunt the place, and persecute me and annoy you. Do you wonder that I do not wish to be beholden to you for forbearance shown to her? I liked to meet you both well enough when I was independent of you; but now your acquaintance would be a sort of charity. Is that plain enough? Oh, you don't know what my mother would do. Last night she wanted money—I had none. She said if I did not get her money she would go down and demand it from Mr. Layton; and she went and put on her bonnet. *What* was I to do? I took my brooch that old Mr. Herbert gave me when he left for Italy, and went out, and—and pawned it."

The girl burst into tears.

"My God, that this should be!" muttered Heatherleigh between his teeth.

I took Polly by the shoulders, and drew her into a chair, and untied her bonnet.

"You sha'n't leave this house this night," I said, "until we come to some better arrangement. We will have a bit of supper, in the old way, you know, and a talk over matters; and surely we shall be able to devise some means of giving you your liberty."

"Well," said Polly, brightening up, "I am safe here, for she doesn't know your address. That is why I come to your house so often. But how are you going to give me my escape?"

"We'll see about supper first," said I.

The small maid-servant was called up and interrogated about the contents of the larder. Eventually a very presentable little supper was placed on the table, and then I produced a bottle of champagne.

"You are destroying the simple and appropriate character of our suppers of old," said Heatherleigh.

"But on this occasion it is with a purpose, which you shall soon learn."

Don't imagine, however, that I had started an expensive wine-cellar out of our modest income. Including everything, I suppose our annual receipts amounted to about £250, and at that time, when there were fewer champagnes sent to the English market, a man who, on an income of £250 a year, offered you champagne, might reasonably have been asked to present to your friends the cost of a post-mortem examination. My champagne came to me through a picture-dealer, who owed me a small sum for a picture, and who, having had to seize *his* customer's goods in payment for this and other pictures, paid me in kind.

So we sat down to the supper-table, and got on very comfortably, although Polly would not drink more than half a glass of wine. I suppose she wished to show that she had not inherited the tastes of her mother; but the poor girl need not have imagined that we wanted any proof. However, the tiny quantity was just sufficient to brighten up her spirits.

"Is your mother a Londoner?" asked Heatherleigh, of Polly.

"No; she came from Greenwich to London."

"Has she friends there now?"

"Yes, of a sort."

"Suppose I offered her a sovereign a week to go and live there, would she go and leave you unmolested here?"

"And pray," said Polly, proudly, "in what way would you have me explain to my friends that you were supporting my mother?"

This was a poser; although I fancy Heatherleigh, under his breath, expressed a wish about her friends that was very uncharitable.

"I don't know," said Heatherleigh, awkwardly. "I didn't mean that I should pay her directly. If you could make some such arrangement with her, I should help you, at least, to make up what you want."

"I don't think you know what you are saying," said Polly, with her cheeks flushed. "You are offering me money."

"You're as bad as Ted!" said Heatherleigh, impatiently. "You're worse, for I can't bully you into common-sense, as I can him. Here are we three people sitting together, professing to be friends with each other. If I don't mistake, we have precious few friends elsewhere. We have no rich relations to turn to, even if we cared to turn to them. We have no great desire, I suppose, beyond being able to live a comfortable life, and help each other, if we can. Why should we not help each other? When you are not in want of anything, you say, 'Oh, how pleasant it is to have friends you can rely on in time of need!' Then the time of need comes, and you say, 'No, your help looks too much like charity.' Come, Polly, be reasonable. The money you need for this purpose is a mere trifle; it is impossible I could miss it. On the other hand, look at the happiness the sense of freedom will add to your life. Look at the many pleasant evenings, like this, which we might all have together."

I did not add my solicitations to his, because I knew she would not consent.

"I ought not to leave my mother, for one thing," she said.

This was but a poor excuse; and he saw that it was an excuse.

"You are ruining your mother," he said, impetuously. "You have yielded to her so that she does what she likes. There is no control being exercised over her. Now, down among people she knew, she might be induced to start well, and continue well. There must be some pride in her which would make her keep herself straight before her neighbors. You are doing her harm, instead of good, at present, besides destroying your own life for no purpose whatever. Come, won't you accept this trifling help?"

"No."

"Why? There must be some other reason."

"Well, there is," she said, provoked into frankness, and yet appearing terribly confused. "Don't you see that men can give money to each other; but it is different between a woman and a man—especially when—when they are not in the same position?"

The girl's cheeks were burning; and the story that her manner conveyed was so clear and palpable that I could not understand his not perceiving it.

He was puzzled, at least; and he saw that it would be unadvisable to press the subject just then.

"At all events," he said, with a shrug, "if you must be hunted about, we can still meet here, unless Ted becomes too much of a gentleman to care about harboring us waifs."

She looked up at him with some surprise. The cool way in which he had proposed that they two should meet there was in itself peculiar. Heatherleigh seemed to be in a fog, and was blundering about at random.

"Yes," said Polly, "Mrs. Ives has been very kind in asking me to come here. But I must go now—it must be nearly eleven."

"First, though," I said, "you must see what I have got to show you. Didn't I say that I had a design upon you? I have dazed the intellect of my critics with wine; I have bribed them with meat and with drink; and now—I will show them my picture."

CHAPTER XVII.

KILMENY.

Do you know the legend of Freir, the sun-god, who, looking from the heights of Hlidskialf over all the world, let his eyes fall upon Jotunheim, the land of the giants, and there saw the maiden Gerda, near the house of Gymir, her father? She was so fair and comely that the white beauty of her arms caused the seas to shimmer in light; and Freir went home sick at heart for love of her. Then he called to him his servant Skirnir, and told him all his woes; and Skirnir, demanding from him his swift horse, that could bear him through flames, and his magical sword, set out for Jotunheim, to carry the message of his master's love. Gymir's house he finds guarded by furious bloodhounds, and by a keeper, who asks Skirnir if he is near death or already dead. But the beautiful Gerda wonders what the strange noises portend, and sends her maiden to invite the messenger in and give him of the soft mead. Skirnir tells the story of his master's pain; offers her presents, and threatens her with divers troubles if she refuse; whereupon Gymir's godlike daughter inclines a gracious ear, and promises to wed the son of Niördr after nine nights have passed.

This was the story I thought of, when I strolled around the Serpentine one misty evening, wondering what subject I should take for a picture. You know, the German commentators have got strange meanings out of this mystic story of the Elder Edda; and Freir, according to them, being the sun-god, and the maiden Gerda the auroral light whose beauty caused the seas to shine, might not the messenger be the pale dawn, come to woo her in the ghostly regions of Jotunheim? But the subject was too big and vague; and I gave it up in despair.

Then I bethought me of an old ballad, in which a king's daughter is claimed by the skipper of a vessel as his reward for steering her father and his knights safely through a storm. But how to paint the mist of sea-foam around the girl and her lover

—how to fill the picture with the blackness of the north wind and the motion of rain and wave and cloud—with here and there a fear-stricken face—with the scornful laugh of the skipper, and the clinging, terrified love of his bride? That, too, I gave up. I was too familiar with the moods of the sea to dare the attempt at painting them.

Yet I instinctively turned to the North for the subject I wanted—to the region of wind and mist, of legendary murmurs that still reach us, full of a passionate and tragic pathos. Should it be the story of young Aikin and the Lady Margaret? or of how Gil Morice, with the yellow hair, was slain? or of how young Hynde Horn stole his bride? or of how the Earl of Mar's daughter was carried off by her lover? One or two of these I did try, to no purpose. The result was bare and tawdry—wanting that very glamour and vagueness which fascinate one in the old legends. Their strong and powerful colors appear to us, as it were, through a mist of rain; you know that the Earl of Mar's daughter wears a glowing scarlet cloak, but the color of it glimmers from the other side of this veil, and the beauty of her face is almost without outline.

At last, my erratic and ambitious notions had to make a compromise with my disproportionate skill; and I chose as a subject the simple figure of Kilmeny, when she came home "late, late in the gloaming."

Need I say how many times I attempted to put upon canvas some faint reflection of the strange and mystic beauty of the poem? After innumerable trials, I found that I was beginning with too great an effort. In my anxiety to have something wistful and wonderful about Kilmeny's face, I was forgetting that the very beauty of the conception lay in its wavering, uncertain, shadowy character. To have painted her with an aureole of light around her face would have made Kilmeny a fairy, not a wonder-stricken girl, who had come home "to see the friends she had left in her own countrye." The magic of Kilmeny's presence, that charmed all things around her, was not the magic of a necromancer nor the witchery of a wild spirit. For

> . . . "Oh, her beauty was fair to see,
> But still and steadfast was her ee;
> Such beauty bard may never declare,
> For there was no pride nor passion there;

> And the soft desire of maiden's een
> In that mild face could never be seen."

With such a conception before him, how could any mortal man be satisfied by any possible transference of it into pigments? Besides, I was struggling with innumerable other difficulties, which it would be tedious to mention. Only he who has striven to effect some artistic work with an insufficient acquaintance with technical means can understand what I suffered then.

However, I resolved to finish a sketch of the picture first; and here at once I found some freedom. I was not so afraid of the result; and in time I produced a sort of rough draft of what I hoped the picture would be. It was this sketch which I now brought in to show Heatherleigh and Polly Whistler. My gayety had been only feigned. I was as frightened to show them this rude effort as though I had been an apprentice to Michael Angelo, and had finished my first commission. I brought down my easel with it, placed the picture, and stepped back to Polly's side, not daring to utter a word, even of apology.

She looked at it for a moment, and then she placed her hand on my arm.

"Oh, Ted! did you do that?" she said, in a low voice.

I drank in those words; for what they implied was music to me. Yet she stood there, looking strangely at the picture; and I could not help, even then, daring to hope that some other one, whom I had often thought of in painting the picture, would look at it with the same expression that was now visible in Polly's kindly eyes.

"It is like a dream," she said, slowly, "and yet not a dream, for it makes one feel cold. Where did you see that strange face, Ted?"

"I know," said Heatherleigh, curtly.

He looked at the picture for a long time, and then he said, rather absently—

"You must not work for me any more, Ted."

"Why?"

"Because you have beaten me in the race. Or, rather, there was no race: I gave up *that* notion long ago."

There are some compliments you can laugh off; this was not one of them. There was a certain sadness in Heatherleigh's tone that showed he was thinking of his own career, and of its hopeless future. I think he knew he could never be a great artist; but it was seldom, indeed, that this conviction seemed to weigh upon him.

"I did not think you capable of work like that," he said. "You must waste no more of your time in my manufactory. You must make way for yourself. I will get this picture sold for you."

"I don't wish to sell it. I mean to paint from it a larger picture for—"

"The Academy? Yes; I thought so. Well, you will make an enormous blunder if you try to elaborate a subject like that. I know you will. Let the picture stand as it is—sell it to some private gentleman—and get the loan of it again for the Academy. Don't you think so, Polly?"

"If he touches it he will spoil it. But where did you get that face, Ted?"

"I know," said Heatherleigh, again.

"She doesn't live in Hampstead Road?" said Polly, with a smile. "If she does, I may shut up *my* shop."

"No, she doesn't live in Hampstead Road," he said, "and she is not likely to become a rival of yours, Polly. Perhaps, if you saw herself, you would say that a good deal of that strange, dream-like look is Ted's own creation. And yet she is very pretty—the Kilmeny I speak of."

"You both know her?" cried Polly, with a sudden inspiration. "Why, it must be Bonnie Lesley!"

"No," said Heatherleigh, dryly; and there was nothing further said upon that point.

Yet I was greatly dismayed and vexed that he should see a likeness which I had vainly striven to convince myself did not exist. I have long ago been forgiven by the original of my Kilmeny for having travestied her upon canvas; and the matter is of small importance now; but this I must say, that I never dreamed of copying her perfect features when I sketched the picture. I thought of the most beautiful creature I knew; and her face and eyes, unconsciously to myself, began to grow out of the canvas. Heatherleigh's recognition was the first token I received that others were likely to accuse me of attempting what I never consciously would have dared to attempt.

"I must go," said Polly, at length. "No, neither of you shall come with me. I do not wish to be prevented from seeing you again."

So she went off alone. But she had scarcely got out of the house when Heatherleigh rose and took his hat.

"We must see that she gets home safe, Ted. Let's follow her at a distance."

This we did; nor was Polly ever aware of our dogging her footsteps all the way home. When she had finally disappeared, Heatherleigh seemed to breathe more freely, and he said, as we turned away—

"There is a very good girl, if ever one lived."

"True for you," said I.

"We *must* find some means of getting her out of the clutches of that wretched woman. It is unbearable that a girl like her should suffer such martyrdom; and as for her notions of filial duty, she must abandon what is romance or folly or madness."

"She has no notions of the kind," said I. "The girl has too much common-sense to think that she *ought* to waste her life in living with an irreclaimable old idiot, who only behaves the worse because of her daughter's forbearance and kindness."

"Then why did she refuse to accept my offer?"

"How should I know?"

Of course, I did know; but I could scarcely persuade myself that he was not assuming ignorance in order to fish for confirmation of his suspicions. For some time we walked on in silence, until we had got near the tall railings of Regent's Park again. It was a clear starlight night.

"Heatherleigh," said I, "I should be sorry to give up working with you, as you suggested—perhaps by way of compliment—so long as I can be of any service to you. You know how I am indebted to you. I never hope to repay you; but I should consider it rather despicable of me to fly off from our bargain the moment I saw I might better myself somewhat."

"But there is another reason," said he. "First and foremost, if you can paint pictures like that Kilmeny it would be monstrous that you should waste your time in drudgery. I tell you, Lewison could get you a dozen men to-morrow who would buy the picture eagerly."

"Do you think any one would recognize the likeness that you recognized?"

"Certainly."

"Then I must alter the face before any one else sees it."

"You'll be a fool if you do. However, here is the other reason why you should hive off. I was selfishly glad of your assistance, because it allowed me to have plenty of ease and laziness. *Now*, I mean to go in for making some little sum of money to keep by me, and I shall work as much as I can, and get as much money as I can for the work. You understand?"

"I am heartily glad to hear it."

"Well, you see," he continued, apologetically, "there is no saying what might happen to a fellow like me, quite unprepared for any emergency. I might want to assist a friend in distress, or I might take some whim in my head that needed money; and where should I be?"

"Quite true."

"Besides, I have been living a purposeless sort of life—an aimless, lotos-eating, hedgehog sort of existence, that is pleasant enough at the time, but not very satisfactory to look back upon."

"That is also true."

"So I mean to pull myself together a bit, and see what I can do. Mind you, I have no intention of satisfying any ambition. That has been knocked out of me long ago. When I cut my family, and threw myself upon the world to fight my own way, I fancied that I had in me that which would make me richer in the end. I fancied that I could cope with all these crushing conditions that hem in a poor man, who has no parental fortune to back him, and no rich relations to take him by the arm, and lead him into good society, and forward his interests and chances in life. I was going to do for myself what other men get done for them. I was going to fight the world unaided and single-handed. Now I made two mistakes. In the first place, it was a blunder to think I could do so, even if I had had the powers I fancied I possessed; and the notion that I had them was a second blunder. You see, I wanted to open the big oyster *without* a knife. I failed. I did my best; but when I found my best was ludicrously inadequate, I did not become misanthropic. I took the matter quietly; and in a short time had acquired sufficient wisdom to laugh at my own folly. I am not going to engage the world any more. Society and its conditions are too strong for me. I give in. Perhaps I have no great ambition now to figure as an important person at swell houses, in the park, at conversaziones, and so forth. Perhaps I don't care to compete for the favor of elderly ladies, or young ones either, with this poor lad whose father has left him a small brain, a title, and an encumbered estate, or that equally dull lad whose father has left him £20,000 a year, and the sentiments and sympathies of a hostler. I am very well satisfied with my ill-fortune. But this notion of mine, which I mention to you, is only a precaution to keep my present position safe for me. That is all. If you limit your aims sufficiently, you can always be successful; and I think I shall be able to get the little nest-egg I want."

"I know you will," I said.

We had reached the door of my lodgings. As I stood on the steps, and shook hands with him, I said—

"After all, I think I must tell you a secret which you ought to have discovered for yourself. Do you know why Polly would never go near you after that scene with her mother?"

"Well, I couldn't understand the reasons she and you advanced."

"Do you know why she wanted to go away when she saw you were here to-night?"

"No."

"Or why she refused to accept the money?"

"No."

"Because, then, as I believe, the girl is as deeply in love with you as ever a girl was with a man. There, you may think over that at your leisure. Good-night!"

His back was turned to the lamplight, so that I could not see what expression his face bore. But he did not speak a word: and so I left him, and went inside.

CHAPTER XVIII.

THE WHITE DOVES.

"THAT wur a rare good shot, sir, that wur. You couldn't ha' gone nearer her without 'itting of her. Look at the turnip-blades thear, where she wur a sitting, all riddled wi' the shot."

Heatherleigh and I looked over the hedge, and saw before us, standing in the middle of a field of turnips, a very big and stout farmer, who was mopping a roseate face with a red pocket-handkerchief, while he grumbled out his wrath over some annoyance. This was Mr. Stephen Toomer, who had taken my uncle's farm, and was now engaged in shooting over it. Toomer was a tall and corpulent man, with a thick neck, a bullet head, a quick temper, and a round, jolly red face, which had two black beads of eyes, and was surmounted by short-cropped black hair. He was a stupid, well-meaning, irascible man, who was very fond of shooting, and could not shoot a bit. My uncle, when angry at Toomer's missing some easy shot, used to say to him—

"I'm darned if you ain't the biggest fool I know. Why doan't ye let the shootin' over your farm to some mahn as 'll hit something, and you go and fire off your powder and shot at butterflies and bees? They'd do ye quite as well, and you might kill some on 'em sometimes."

Toomer was accompanied on this occasion by his bailiff, who also acted as his gamekeeper, and told a hundred lies an hour in order to excuse his master's missing everything in the shape of partridge, hare, or rabbit that came in his way. The fabulous flakes of fur he found about the turnip-blades, the imaginary feathers that came floating down from the tail of a pheasant that was thirty yards out of shot before Toomer fired, the fictitious "warmers" that perfectly untouched partridges were supposed to carry away with them, did credit to old Kinch's imagination and wit. But when his master, in one of his rare fits of generosity, offered some neighbor a day's shooting, Kinch made up for his flattery by discharging himself of all his accumulated sarcasm upon the new-comer. *Then* there were no flakes of fur or feathers found. On the contrary, the new-comer had "never gone a-nigh 'em." "What wur the use o' shooting at birds i' the next parish?" "Why, that hare wur through the 'edge afore ye fired;" and so on.

"Ah, how be ye, Mahster Ives?" said Stephen Toomer, coming over to the hedge to shake hands with me, while he nodded familiarly to Heatherleigh.

"Pretty well. My friend and I have come down here for a week or two—"

"For the shootin'?" he said, quickly, obviously fearing that we were going to disturb his interesting and bloodless pastime by demanding permission to accompany him.

"No, not at all. We want you, though, to let us have the occupation of the Major's house."

"Law, you doan't mean thaht!" he said, opening his eyes.

"Yes we do, if you don't mind."

Toomer had inherited the guardianship of the haunted house; and he was not the sort of man to think of interfering with its ghostly immunity from occupants.

"I mind! Of course I don't mind; but ye cahn't mean to stay in that 'ouse? Why not come up 'ere and stay in your own uncle's 'ouse, as you wur accustomed to? I'll make ye as comfortable as may be. Folks say as you are a painter like, and mayhap—"

"That's it. My friend and I want one or two big empty rooms, with plenty of light in them—just like those down at the Major's. We've come up to see if Mrs. Toomer could kindly spare us a couple of mattresses—to be laid on the floor, you know—and a chair or two, and a table. If she will oblige us so far, we have engaged old Mother Ilsley to come and make our breakfast for us—"

"*She* woan't stay in that 'ouse!" said Toomer, decisively.

"No; she will go back to Missenden at night. You see, we want a house that is nearer Burnham than this is (thanking you for the offer), and besides we are curious to know whether these stories about the place are true."

Toomer looked from one to the other of us, and then found refuge in calling for his bailiff, to whom he explained the proposal, with many an ominous shake of the head.

"If ye do mean it," said he at last, speaking despondently, as if we were already the victims of our rashness, "my missus 'll do what she can to make the pläace comfortable; but I 'ope as ye'll both think better on it, and not make light o' things as 'ave puzzled older 'eads than yourn."

"It's a temptin' o' Providence," said Kinch, solemnly. "Not as Mr. Toomer or me ud believe in ghost-stories and all thaht 'ere nonsense—"

"Certainly not," said the master, with some dignity.

"But there's things around as we doan't see and we doan't understand, and I be for lettin' 'em alone, I be."

"Quite right, too," said the master, who was glad to have this wholesome argument urged in his defence.

"Then you'll let us have these things? Thank you. And perhaps you'd kindly send with them some old gun or other, just that we may have a shot at any stray visitor, you understand? I don't know what sort of pointer is best for ghosts—"

"Your poor uncle wur a very bold mahn in talking about them things; *but he never went nigh that 'ouse after nightfall*," said Toomer, significantly. "He wur afeared o' nothin'—"

"And he's found out 'is mistake," edged in Kinch, spitefully.

"I say, he wur afeared o' nothin', and why didn't he go a-nigh that 'ouse arter nightfall—that's what I wahnt to know? Howsever, you'll get the bits o' things, and I'll send ye down the gun as Kinch uses for them sparrers that hev been hawful this yur. They're the mischievousest things, them sparrers. I'm thinkin' it would puzzle the pahrson, for all he says, to find out what they were made for."

"Mother Ilsley will come over and see about these things you have so kindly promised us. Meanwhile, we're going on to Burnham House."

"To visit Miss Hester, belike?"

"No. To do some work at the House."

"Eh! I be rare glad to 'ear it," said Stephen. "It's what I've allays said to my missus, as there wur one thing wrong about Burnham 'Ouse; and that's the color of the front, as you see it from the havenue. It's too yallow, that's what I say—a deal too yallow; and I be glad to 'ear as you and your friend 'ave come down to freshen the pläace up a bit; and I do hope as you'll alter that yallow."

"We mean to paint the inside of the House first," said Heatherleigh, gravely.

"Well and good; well and good," said Mr. Toomer. "I doan't pretend to know any mahn's business but my own; but what I says is as the front's too yallow, and I'll hold by thabt—"

"I've no doubt it is," said Heatherleigh.

"And I 'ope as you and Mahster Ives 'll put on another color."

"We'll do our best. Good-morning!"

We *had* come down to paint some portions of Burnham House, although we did not mean to commence, as Stephen Toomer suggested, by whitewashing the front walls. Miss Burnham had gone up to town and seen Heatherleigh about the panelling of the pillars, and had arranged with him to have them filled with appropriate subjects. Heatherleigh, in his new-born zeal for work, had gladly accepted the commission, and also undertook to secure my co-operation. The reader may remember that I had professed myself willing to do what I could in that way, on certain terms. I received a brief note from Miss Burnham, saying she hoped I would accompany Mr. Heatherleigh, and do part of the work, on any terms I chose to name. The latter words were underlined; and I went down into Buckinghamshire rejoicing.

"What a fine country it is about here!" said Heatherleigh, as we descended the hill, after leaving Toomer pottering among his turnips, and got into the valley that lies underneath Burnham. "It was a good notion to take that haunted house, as we ought to have an occasional holiday for sketching. But what on earth did you want with a gun?"

"Lest some tramps should hear of our being there, and prowl about the place to steal. I don't suppose there is a lock or bolt or bar in the house; but when they know we have a gun in the room, they will be chary of coming near."

"I thought, perhaps, you meant to have a shot at the evil spirits."

"You never see them; you only hear them. You will hear the sound of wheels being driven up to the house in the middle of the night; and if you open the door suddenly you will hear bursts of laughter all around, mocking you for your trouble. Sometimes it is the sound of a horseman galloping past that you hear, though where the horseman gallops to is a mystery, as the place is surrounded by trees. Sometimes the people have seen a black dog dashing past, without making any noise. Sometimes it is a woman singing a song, apparently hushing a baby to sleep; and sometimes it is the deep voice of men, cursing at each other. But whenever you attempt to surprise them there is instant silence, and then the strange laughter all around in the air."

"Comfortable, exceedingly."

"Even the tramps who go about are afraid to use the empty rooms, into which they could easily get. But here we are at Burnham; and what do you think of that for a view?"

We were in front of the broad and stately avenue that led up between giant rows of Spanish chestnuts to the front of Burnham House. As we ascended the avenue the mullioned windows of the gray old building became plainer, the spire of the small church was visible through the trees, and behind us lay a long prospect down the valley and up over the hills, which lay steeped in the soft, warm glow of autumn sunlight. There was an autumn haze, too, lying over the olive-green of the distant woods, and round about the great trunks of the trees near at hand—a soft, thin, gray veil that caused the yellow stubble-fields, the red fallow, the far-off brown-green beech-woods, and the gray-and-white chalk hills to become faint and visionary in the heat, rendering their various hues pale and ethereal, and laying, as it were, a gossamer-net of frail and fairy-like texture over the still, beautiful landscape. The glory of Buckinghamshire is its beech-woods, that assume, later in autumn, an indescribable intensity of color; but it seems to me that they should be seen with this silvery harvest haze hanging over them, through which the distant hills, covered with these forests of beeches, actually shimmer in pale rose-color and gold.

We went up to Burnham; and the lady of Burnham—how slight and small she looked in front of the big house!—was standing on the steps, and came forward to meet us.

"How wrong of you," she said to Heatherleigh, with a bright smile, "not to let me know when you were coming, and I should have sent over for you."

With that she came over and shook hands with me, saying simply,

"I am very glad you have come."

Heatherleigh explained to her that we had stopped at Wycombe on the previous evening in order to enjoy the walk over on that morning; and that our traps would be sent over from that ancient town some time during the day.

"Your rooms have been prepared for you; and Madame Laboureau has done you the honor of gathering some flowers for you with her own hand. Her husband was an artist."

Madame Laboureau—an elderly small French lady who had accompanied Miss Burnham on her return from France, and been her official companion ever since—now came forward, and begged to know, with many expressions of dramatic sympathy, how my mother bore her loss, and how she was reconciling herself to London.

"But, with your permission," said Heatherleigh to Miss Burnham, "we mean to stay at some empty house near here, which we understand is occasionally favored by ghostly visitors. Pray don't look alarmed — we shall be very comfortable, a worthy farmer having promised to give us all the furniture we need, and we have already engaged a housekeeper."

"You mean the Major's house?"

"Yes."

"That is too absurd. You will die of cold and hunger down there. Madame Laboureau and I have done everything we could think of to make you comfortable—"

"You are very kind, indeed—"

"And I have asked down several of your friends to lighten the dulness of your stay—the Lewisons, Mr. Morell, Miss Lesley—"

"Really your kindness, Miss Burnham, will make us play the traitor to our own compact, I fear. But in the mean time you will allow us to follow out our whim for at least a few nights. I am really anxious to say that I have slept in a haunted house; and then, if we *should* see something—"

"Well, what then?"

"Look at the honor and glory of being allowed to publish a report of it. We should get Morell to write an article about it; and we should be positive heroes for a couple of months."

"It is an heroic undertaking," she said. "You will have to brave a good deal, even if you see no ghosts. But at least you will follow my advice so far as to dine with us this evening; and I will meanwhile send over some people to see that the place is made more comfortable than you are likely to find it. Mr. Ives, you are at the bottom of this—will you urge your friend to accept the compromise?"

"We accept with pleasure," I said, "and Madame Laboureau will be a witness that our appointment with the spirits is only postponed until night."

The bright, quick little Frenchwoman shook her head gravely, and there was a solemn look in her gray eyes.

"It is not right you laugh. They say, 'Il n'y a que les morts qui ne reviennent pas.' Hm! They do not know. If you live in my country—la Bretagne, Monsieur—you get to hear of these things. We know of these stories—we used to gather them—and we used to speak them to each other in the long evenings—c'est un passe-temps comme un autre!"

She addressed these latter words to Miss Burnham (to whom she always spoke in French), and shrugged her small shoulders as if to let us understand that she did not believe *all* such legends.

"But you yourself, Madame," said I, "have you ever seen any ghosts?"

"No," she replied, simply. "They are not so many now, since the Revolution. Once we used to have plenty of stories about them. But the Revolution has altered all that."

"Come, Madame," said Miss Burnham; "perhaps the gentlemen will go inside and rest themselves after their walk."

"I should like to see whether the panels have been properly prepared," said Heatherleigh.

"I think I can assure you of that. Madame is also an artist, and she has superintended the work."

"Oui, ma chère," said Madame to Miss Burnham, as they entered the house; "je consacre mes loisirs à la peinture; et tu—à la bienfaisance."

They went with us into the drawing-room, and there we held a consultation over the adornment of the pillars. I was not aware that Miss Burnham knew so much about artistic matters, nor that she took so much interest in them as was evidenced by her bright and intelligent talk with Heatherleigh. At length our plan of operations was decided upon, and then the two ladies left us. I had accidentally learned that Colonel Burnham, and a niece of his, by his wife's side, were staying in the house.

It was late in the afternoon when our traps arrived from Wycombe. Almost at the same time the party from London made their appearance, and there was just time for all of us to dress for dinner. Going down to a sort of reception-room—the drawing-room being shut up for the present—I asked Heatherleigh if he thought we should be accommodated with a side-table.

"I don't know," he said. "I believe comic singers, at some great houses, come in with dessert, having dined in another room. But then we are not able to amuse the company, even in that way. However, if we have to sit behind the screen, Morell shall come with us. Being an author, it is his place."

This Mr. Morell was a gentleman who moved in very good circles, and was much thought of as a wit. There was a vagueness about his sources of income. He had chambers in the Albany, rode a good horse in the Park, belonged to a first-class club, and was known to contribute smart articles on fashionable subjects (particularly the *demi-monde*) to one or two newspapers. He was a magnificent diner-out; the end of the season found him as fresh as a lark, with his stock of stories (for dinner and after-dinner) not half exhausted. His acquaintance with titled persons was enormous. He got his cigars through a duke; and never made a purchase in wine without consulting a marquis. He was a middle-aged, stout, bright-looking man, with a resemblance, in the contour of his face, to Tom Moore; he sang and played exquisitely; he conversed and paid compliments, sat a horse, and handled a breech-loader all with the same consummate ease; and he borrowed money from every one of his acquaintances with the most charming air in the world.

When we went down-stairs, we found him alone in the room, seated at the piano, and rattling off some light and rapid selections from "Dinorah."

He immediately stopped and sprang from the stool.

"My dear fellow, how do you do—how do you do? And you, Mr. Ives—a little bird has whispered to me something about a certain picture. Ah, well! perhaps it is a secret—no harm done—and so you have come to help us to scatter destruction among the Burnham pheasants? I say" (here his voice dropped to a confidential undertone), "is it any good down here? You know a woman lets her preserves run to the devil—somebody might make a joke out of that, but no matter—and doesn't care if she gets enough out of them for her own table, and to send to her friends."

"I don't know how the Burnham woods are," said Heatherleigh; "Ives can tell you something about them, but he and I have come down on business merely."

"The deuce you have!"

"And we are going to tear ourselves away from your society every evening, in order to sleep in a haunted house."

"A haunted house! Oh! damme! I must join your party. I never did such a thing in my life—should like above all things to coquet with a spirit, and draw pentagrams on the floor, you know, and that sort of thing."

"No, no," said Heatherleigh; "too many would spoil the game, and frighten them off. If we can inveigle them into a performance, depend upon it you shall have the full benefit of it, and be able to thrill London with a description."

"Ah! I'm in bad odor, just now, with my literary friends. I was imprudent enough to write an article on the morality of paying one's debts, and—would you believe it?—every editor I sent it to took it for a personal insult! Upon my soul, there wasn't an editor in London would print it.—Oh! Miss Lesley," he instantly added, as Bonnie Lesley came into the room, radiant in white silk, that glimmered through gauzy folds, with a bunch of blue forget-me-nots in her yellow hair, "do you know what awaits you down here? These gentlemen have discovered a haunted house, and mean to engage the spirits to appear for your amusement. There is something so much finer in getting ghosts that are private property—kept on the premises, as it were—than in paying a guinea a-head to have your grandmother's name misspelled on a piece of paper."

I had not seen her since we were together at Brighton, and it seemed to me as if she had brought away something of the sea with her, in the blue of her eyes.

The other people now appeared in ones and twos, among them Mr. Alfred Burnham, who had not made his appearance before. Dinner was announced, and an orderly procession of couples passed along the corridor and into the dining-room, which was brilliantly lit. It was my good-fortune to find myself seated by the side of Madame Laboureau. Colonel Burnham had taken in his niece, but Heatherleigh, sitting next her, turned from his own partner, and talked, in his quiet, half-humorous fashion, to Miss Burnham during the whole time. Mr. Morell had brought in

Bonnie Lesley, and was already on the best of terms with her, telling her funny anecdotes about all sorts of celebrities in town, describing to her the absurdities of the new play, ridiculing the newest fashions. She appeared to be very much delighted. She paid him the most devoted attention, although she received with the same amount of amused interest his good stories and his dull ones, his quips and his relapses into sober earnest.

"You are a great friend of that young lady," said Madame Laboureau, with a smile. She had been watching the direction my eyes had taken.

"Yes, she has been good enough to take me in hand."

"Ah! you must not speak in that tone. You think she flirts? No. It is only her good-nature, that makes her to amuse people. Or perhaps—eh?—she wants to make you jealous?"

"It would be too great a compliment, Madame Laboureau."

"Ah, well!" said the old lady, with a sigh. "There are ladies—there are gentlemen—who you cannot understand. They do not wish to annoy others, they do not wish to be inconstant, or to receive all friends with the like favor, but they cannot help it. It is their nature. It is dangerous to fall in love with them, for they never fall quite in love; if they do, they forget next day, when a new friend comes. They do not try to act wrong; they only cannot help liking novelty, liking the excitation of new falling in love. Perhaps they like better the falling in love rather than the being in love. Is it not so?"

"I think you are quite right," I said; and, indeed, I have often thought of Madame's shrewd phrase, "*they like the falling in love better than the being in love*," as explaining a good many of the odd pranks and love miseries which happen in one's circle of friends.

But I added—

"I hope you are not talking of Miss Lesley?"

"Not at all, not at all. I speak of a particular kind of nature. You may meet it, perhaps not. And I know many ladies are blamed for coquetting, when they cannot help it. They cannot help being pleased with new attentions. I should explain so much better if I spoke in French, but I do not like to speak French, except to Miss Hester."

"Won't you extend the same favor to me? You will speak to me in French, and I shall answer you in English. Is not that the best arrangement for giving both freedom?"

And this she did. She chatted away with great volubility, and no one could have failed to be delighted with her pert sayings and her touches of literary adornment, and the little personal coquetries of her manner. Yet I listened to it all as if it were a dream, and I don't know what sort of answers I made to her. What I did hear, clear and sharp, was the conversation between Bonnie Lesley and her companion. Do what I would, I could not help hearing it, and, although I persistently kept my eyes away, I fancied I could see her face, and the smile on it, and the amused wonder of her big eyes.

"I am the happiest man upon earth," he said to her. "Every pleasure I enjoy I look upon as a bit of luck. Fancy how happy a criminal who has been condemned to death, and been reprieved, must feel all his life after. Every glass of beer he drinks is a pleasure he had forfeited. So it is in my case—"

"Oh, have you been reprieved?" said Miss Lesley.

"Well, it is about the same thing. My mother-in-law lived two years in my house, and I didn't murder her."

I fancy this elaborate witticism had done duty on many an occasion. At all events, it rather failed in this instance; as Miss Lesley merely said, "Oh, indeed!" with a half-puzzled look on her face.

Sometimes, too, I heard Hester Burnham's voice through the various hum of talk. Occasionally I caught sight of her face and her eyes; and it seemed as if Kilmeny were sitting there, pure and calm and beautiful, scarcely comprehending the Babel of sounds around her.

To tell the truth—and are not these a series of very unromantic confessions?—I was very savage during that dinner—with what I hardly knew. Irritated, discontented, impatient, I waited for the close of it; and I was heartily glad when the ladies rose.

"Que nous allons nous ennuyer, enfant!" said Madame Laboureau, with a little laugh, to Hester Burnham, as they passed from the room.

Mr. Morell shut the door, and returned to the table.

"What a charming old lady that Madame—"

"Laboureau."

"Madame Laboureau is. You never see Englishwomen preserve that sprightliness of manner in their old age. They get apathetic and corpulent and commonplace—"

"Englishwomen grow fat on the *h*'s they swallow," said Heatherleigh.

"And if there ever was a county of *h*-droppers, Bucks is that county," said Morell. "The feats of jugglery the people about here perform with their *h*'s are astounding. Now what do you say, Colonel Burnham, to our changing our coats and going outside for a cigar? I fancy there are no deep drinkers among us."

"Or into the billiard-room?" said Mr. Alfred Burnham. "There are pool-balls, if you're not particular about the cues."

No one seemed to care about this disinterested proposal on the part of Mr. Burnham.

"Or what do you say," suggested Heatherleigh, "to our going into the drawing-room, and postponing our smoking until the ladies have gone up-stairs? In any case, Ives and I are going off presently."

This latter course was agreed upon; and after a little time we went into the drawing-room. Mrs. Lewison was singing; the other ladies were crowded into a corner, on sofas and chairs and cushions, listening to some ghost-story that Madame Laboureau was telling them. It seems the conversation had turned upon the Major's house, and Madame, who had begged to be allowed to speak in French, had trotted out many of her Breton reminiscences. When we entered the room, she was saying that a much more extraordinary occurrence than that she had just related had happened to herself. We prayed her to tell the story.

"Will the gentlemen also permit me to speak my own tongue —I have too much constraint in English?"

She crossed her thin, small, brown hands on her knees, and began the story.

"Il y a de cela bien longtemps. J'étais jeune encore, et soit dit en passant très-jolie"—with which she looked archly at Bonnie Lesley, and smiled. "Nous habitions à cette époque le nord de la Bretagne, et j'avais alors une demi-sœur dangereusement malade—tellement malade que nous craignions à tout moment de la perdre. Pour ma part j'avais passé deux jours et deux nuits auprès d'elle, lorsque, oppressée par l'air malsain de la chambre, je profitai d'un instant où ma demi-sœur sommeillait. Je me rendis au jardin. Le temps était magnifique. Un superbe clair de lune argentait les objets, une brise légère agitait les arbres, et un rossignol caché dans un bosquet faisait entendre ses jolis accents. Mais je parle trop vite—me comprenez-vous bien, messieurs et mesdames?"

The little gesture with which she accompanied the question was admirable. She was acting the *raconteuse.* The measured gravity of her voice, the formal introduction of the moonlight and the nightingale, the apologetic look with which she urged the question, were all parts of an excellent and delicately finished performance.

"Je me promenais," she continued, "respirant le doux parfum des roses. Voilà que soudain je vois apparaitre une nuée de colombes, blanches comme neige. Elles voltigent silencieuses, et me saisissent d'effroi. Tout d'un coup elles s'abattent sur la fenêtre, et s'envolent de nouveau—"

She lifted her hands, her eyes were fixed on vacancy, as if she saw there the white doves wheeling around the window of her foster-sister's room.

"—Les rideaux de la chambre s'agitent. La fenêtre s'ouvre, et se referme. Un long et profond soupir se fait entendre, et tout disparaît. Épouvantée, éperdue, me trainant avec peine, je rentre, et tremblante je me dirige vers la chambre de la malade. . . . Ma sœur était morte!"

The old lady's face was quite pale; and she had so vividly impressed on her hearers the reality of the details of the story—the flying of the white doves around the invalid's window—their silent disappearance—her hurried and trembling rush to the sick-room—and the discovery of her sister's death—that for a second or two after she had finished no one spoke.

"Voilà, certes, une bien curieuse histoire, madame," said I at last, "mais la fatigue agissant sur votre imagination explique peut-être l'étrange hallucination dont vous étiez l'objet."

"Was it, then, an hallucination, monsieur?" she said, looking up, with reproof in her eyes.

The silence now being broken, it was curious to notice the different ways in which the listeners had received the story.

"What a singular thing!" said Miss Lesley, with a smile, and a look of wonder on her face. "It would make a pretty picture, would it not?"

"*Sie kann auch gut auf schneiden,*" said Morell, in an undertone, to Heatherleigh—a remark which I did not understand, my acquaintance with Continental slang being very limited then.

"Yes," responded Heatherleigh, "she is a magnificent actress."

"Capital!" said Alfred Burnham, when the narrative was ended. From that, and the accompanying laugh, I concluded that he had not understood the story, and had fancied it was probably a joke.

Hester Burnham said nothing; but, long after the others had ceased talking of it, I saw that her eyes were very wistful and strange in their expression, and that she sat rather apart and silent.

We remained perhaps about half an hour in the drawing-room. During that time Miss Lesley did the most she could to make her extreme condescension to Mr. Morell visible to the rest of the guests. She played an accompaniment for a song which he sang very well indeed. Then he and she sang a duet together. She even devoted a few minutes to Heatherleigh, and was very gracious to him.

"Now," she said, coming over to him, "you must settle all our doubts about Madame Laboureau's story. Is it, or is it not, too improbable to be true?"

"You should never doubt the truth of a good, wild, absurd story, Miss Lesley," said he. "We want all the improbable, miraculous, supernatural material we can get, if only to vary the commonplaceness of life. Don't you think so? I think the human race should enter into a compact to believe that all wild stories (except those of the *Levant Herald*) are true. However, won't you sing for me, before I go, my favorite song—you know?"

"Oh, I'm tired of it," she said, turning away with an air of petulance, and not so much as giving a word to me, who sat by Heatherleigh, and had not spoken to her since the dispersal of the Brighton circle.

"Is that a lesson for you?" said Heatherleigh.

"That she should not speak to me?"

"Yes."

"She has a right to please herself in her choice of companions, surely?"

"Yes, and to throw them off when she has done with them. But I confess she puzzles me in your case. She does not seem angry with you, and she ought to be, if my notion of the matter is right."

"I don't know what you mean," I said, "but I have no doubt whatever that your notion is entirely wrong. For you, who see the best side of every one's nature, are invariably unjust to her, and to her alone."

CHAPTER XIX.

THE HAUNTED HOUSE.

We were a sufficiently gay party as we left Burnham that night in quest of ghosts. Morell had insisted on at least walking over with us, in order to have a cigar by the way.

"But how are you to find your road back?" said Heatherleigh, as we issued into the cool night-air.

"We'll see about that," he replied, carelessly.

He was evidently bent on sharing the adventure.

"You are not ashamed to leave your charming partner," said Heatherleigh.

"Miss Lesley?" he said. "Oh, a charming girl. But, I say, you know, if one were to see her at a distance—if one had not spoken to her—I think it would occur to one to ask whether she were *cocotte* or *cocodette*. No offence—I only mean her general appearance, such as a stranger might see it. Problem for a young man—whether a *cocotte* or a *cocodette* will ruin him the faster.

Here he began to sing an abominable parody of Heine's "Du hast Diamanten und Perlen;" little snatches of which were continually crossing the rather wild and desultory current of our talk during the remainder of the journey.

It was a lovely night, the moonlight throwing long shadows from the Burnham chestnuts and oaks upon the broad avenue leading down to the valley. Far up on the hills the woods lay dusky and silent; while here and there a chalky field gleamed white among the darker patches of turnip or potato that covered the long, rounded slopes. I was glad to get away from the big house that lay behind us—high up there, among the dark trees, with a red glimmer in its lower windows, and the moonlight falling on its pale front. I was more and more getting to believe that there was something wrong in my manner of life—that I ought not to go among these people, who led me into wild dreams and bitter disappointments. I was glad to be outside—in the free air—and with only men for my companions. Luckily more jovial companions could not have been found. We startled the calm solitudes of Burnham with some rather imperfectly executed madrigals; nor did Morell cease his gay, rapid talk until we had passed up the long narrow path through the shrubbery and stood before the Major's house.

"It is a ghostly looking place," said he, looking at the low, flat house, with its projecting bay-windows, its curious veranda, and the crumbling white walls which gleamed in the light of the moon.

"By Jove, I have forgotten the key!" said Heatherleigh.

"But there is no necessity for a key in getting into the Major's house," said I, throwing up one of the windows, and jumping into the room.

I was astounded by what I saw there. Instead of a bare, empty chamber, with bits of plaster about the floor, and cobwebs obscuring the window-panes, I found that the place had been carefully swept out—there were a table, some chairs, a sofa, a lamp, and a couple of candles, etc., etc., making the place quite habitable. When I had struck a match, I found a note addressed to me lying on the table. It ran as follows:

"Dear Sir,—The things as Miss Burnham have sent over are in the cubbard in the all, the key over the door. My compliments, and hope you will send for anything you want and be very welcome.

"Sarah Toomer."

We went to the "cubbard in the all," and there a wonderful display met us of bottles, glasses, knives and forks, a cruet-stand, plates, a cold pie, a ham, some bread, etc.

"What a thoughtful little woman it is!" cried Heatherleigh. "Why, I declare, here is a box of cigars!"

"And this is positively Mumm—and here is some seltzer!" exclaimed Morell. "Does your gentle friend smoke, also, that she knows the only champagne that should accompany a cigar? Such kindness overpowers me. It would be the depth of ingratitude not to pay our respects to these good things: what do you say?"

So we formed a triumphal procession back to the sitting-room, carrying with us, like the figures in an Egyptian bass-relief, all manner of glasses, bottles, and what not, including the cigars.

"Now this *is* what I enjoy in the country," said Morell. "That old colonel, I swear, has gone to bed to dream of shooting partridges, and he will get up somewhere in the middle of the night, and start without breakfast, and bother the birds so that one sha'n't have a shot all the day after."

"It is a curious thing," said I, "but you never do any good partridge-shooting if you go out too early."

"It is a blunder," said Morell, "which I never commit. I'm for having my sport comfortably. I am not a slave to shooting, and I positively loathe and abhor the weariness of fishing. Motto for an angler's club: '*The fishing for the day is the evil thereof.*' Do you fish, Heatherleigh?"

"No," said Heatherleigh, who was cutting the wire of one of the bottles.

By this time the candles and lamp were lit, and we sat down to our cigars. But the light of the candles was not strong enough wholly to overcome the light of the moon, which came in through the large open bay-window, and painted squares of pale white on the wooden floor.

"Is that a gun in the corner?" asked Morell.

"Yes."

"What did you get that for?"

"Merely to keep about the house so that tramps mayn't be tempted to break in upon us during the night, there being but few bars about the place. But I see Toomer has stupidly loaded it and capped it."

"You didn't get it to shoot at the ghosts?"

"You may have a shot if you like when they come."

"Here's to their coming!" he cried, lifting a glass of seething wine. "And here's to the good little lady, with the pretty eyes, who sent us this feast; and here's to the partridges of the neighborhood, and to the Colonel, and to Miss Lesley—

'Du hast meine Uhr und Kette,
Ruinirt mein Porte-monnaie—'

By the way, has Colonel Burnham any money?"

"Precious little," said Heatherleigh.

"His son?"

"Not a rap."

"Oh, then he'll the more easily get into heaven—that must be his consolation. It must be a comfort to many people not to be rich."

"I fancy young Burnham would rather take the riches and chance the rest," said Heatherleigh. "You know if rich men can't get into heaven, they can get into the House of Commons, and most of them don't seem disgusted with the compromise."

"Burnham would rather go on the turf than enter either," said I, "if you only give him the funds."

Morell nodded his head sagaciously.

"A little cousinly feeling, eh? That's why he hangs about the place; but surely the girl won't have him?"

"Why?" said I; "he is handsome, and well-mannered towards women, has as much brains as most idle men of his class, and—"

"And therefore she ought to marry him!" said Morell, gayly. "Ah, well, perhaps you are right. When my poor wife was alive, she used to try to get me to believe that women had some sort of romance in them, but now— I suppose they are what we have made them; and that the whole lot of us are a set of selfish, mean, interested wretches. Here's to the better disposition of the next age!—

'Und hast mich in den Rinnstein geworfen,
Mein Liebchen, ich sage ade!'"

"Don't sing that song while you are talking of anybody over at Burnham," I besought of him.

"My dear sir, there was no reference whatever to anybody at Burnham or elsewhere. I am just in such a mood at present that I could go on chatting or singing for hours, without the faintest notion of coherency, which is always an offensive necessity. I feel myself free from all trammels. I don't need to be logical or grammatical. I get glimpses of fine fancies and suggestions—from myself and those around me, and I have not to stop to weigh their business-value. It is only the next day that the fine, clear, crystalline thought thaws and resolves itself into a newspaper article—"

"Where you disguise yourself in phrases," said Heatherleigh, "and hide yourself, like a cuttle-fish, in a cloud of ink."

"I tell you," said Morell, his voice increasing in volume, "that with a good cigar in my lips, and some cool wine near me, I imagine poems that would startle some of you, if I could only jot them down. I have not the trick of rhyme—that is the difference between me and some whom I am delighted to honor. I sometimes fancy myself writing a poem—

Ah, sweetest, how chill is the morning air!
Is it your last kiss that is on my lips?
How pale you are and you tremble, but your small fingers are warm,
And your eyes are full of love.
The morning mist is full of the yellow sunlight, cold and chill,
But there are dreams in your eyes, and stories of all that is over—"

He recited these lines as if he were really in a state of bewildered exaltation; then he burst out laughing, and fell to singing his abominable "Du hast meine Uhr und Kette."

Presently, however, he had returned to his normal condition of indifference; and Heatherleigh and he were discussing the origin of conscience, Morell's crude notions on the subject being just the sort of incentive that was needed to provoke Heatherleigh into entering upon those humorous, thoughtful monologues which were to me a constant source of delight. But that I might tire my reader, I should dearly like to insert here what I could recollect of some one of these inimitable discourses, which were the very reflex of Heatherleigh's nature.

However, I went outside to breathe the fresh air, and also to reflect on one or two events of the evening. Was I angry or jealous that Miss Lesley had so openly disavowed our former intimacy? Surely I had no right to be either. In descending from her high estate to confer the favor of her speech and friendship upon me, she had probably obeyed a thoughtless whim, which was now forgotten. If I had ever been tempted to dream foolish dreams of the future through this intimacy, it was not her fault—it was the fault of my inexperience of the manners of good society. I had taken as meaning something what really meant nothing. Yet I could not help regarding her with a certain cold distrust; and I was very loth to think of going over to Burnham next morning, to undergo the humiliation of her too ostentatious neglect. I wished that I had not undertaken to assist Heatherleigh. I was again being thrown among those people with whom I had no real sympathy. It was not by mixing with them that I was to work out my redemption from the thraldom of Weavle:

and I began to long for my small room overlooking Regent's Park —for the close, hard work, and the joyous feeling, and the bright hopes attending thereon.

How lovely the night was! It seemed too beautiful for the country. That pure, calm moonlight should have fallen on a green, breaking sea, and a long, curved bay, with distant rocks jutting out here and there into the water. It was a night on which fairies might have been seen hovering over the sand—on which, listening intently, you might have heard the mermaiden singing sadly for her lover of Colonsay. Even as it was—a soft moonlit night in harvest, down in the leafy heart of Bucks—it was very beautiful, and perhaps a trifle sad, in that it suggested the sea.

I had wandered some little distance from the house, through the shrubbery, thinking of far other things than ghosts. It was the ghosts of half-suggested pictures that crowded before my eyes, and the ghosts of half-forgotten snatches of old madrigals that hummed about my ears. As I passed on I came to the side of the road, from which I was separated by a tall hawthorn hedge. Through this dark mass of stems and leaves it seemed to me that I could see two or three figures passing along, making, so far as I could hear, not the least sound. I stood and watched.

Through the shrubbery I saw that they had left the road, and were proceeding up the path, under a dark avenue of lime-trees, towards the house. I could not make out the number of the black shadows, but there was one figure clothed entirely in white. They passed along quite noiselessly; and as noiselessly I followed. Suddenly I heard a strange laugh—low, and yet strange and unearthly. At the same moment the white figure—the figure of a woman—glided rapidly across the lawn and was lost in the trees opposite. I drew nearer. The laugh was heard again from among the trees; and again the white figure darted across the lawn in front of the house, retreating behind some tall larches that stood at the end of the shrubbery. While, however, the figure was invisible to those inside the house (supposing that they had been attracted to the window by the noise), it was fully visible to me; and, as I drew yet nearer, it seemed that the outline of the head and shoulders, shown clear in the moonlight, was quite familiar. In a moment the truth flashed upon me. This was Bonnie Lesley, who had dressed herself up as a ghost for the purpose of frightening us, and who had persuaded some of her friends to accompany her. They, I now saw, were secreted behind various bushes, evidently waiting for the entertainment. I crept up along the side of the shrubbery, fancying it would be a fair retort to frighten them; and then I saw that Hester Burnham stood alone, and nearest of all to the window, behind two large laurels which were not overburdened with leaves. The moonlight being at her back, she was probably not considering that, from the shadow of the room, if either Heatherleigh or Morell came to the window, she would be more seen than seeing. Indeed, I felt sure that the dark outline of her figure must be clearly visible behind the sparsely covered branches, and that she would assuredly reveal the trick.

Again the white figure laughed. I now recognized Bonnie Lesley's voice, as she ran across the lawn.

There was no one as yet at the window. The two men inside were apparently so deep in metaphysics that they had heard nothing.

Should I utter a wild shriek and startle the ghost-makers themselves? I was not half-a-dozen yards from Miss Burnham's place of concealment.

I saw that Bonnie Lesley and a gentleman whom I took to be Mr. Alfred Burnham were at the other side of the lawn, gathering together small stones from the gravelled walk; and in a few seconds Bonnie Lesley threw a handful of them at the window. But the window was open, and so the gravel rattled in upon the wooden floor. With that she noiselessly glided across the lawn and into the bushes.

"Did you see that?" I heard Morell exclaim, apparently in consternation. "It was a woman. Where is Ives?"

"Gone up-stairs to bed, I suppose," said Heatherleigh.

Heatherleigh went around the passage and appeared at the door; Morell was still standing at the window. Then I saw the latter disappear for a second, and the next moment I saw in the moonlight the pale gleam of the gun-barrel. It was pointed at the bush behind which stood Hester Burnham. I was paralyzed. I tried to cry, and could not. I staggered forward, caught her arm, and drove her from the place where she stood. At the same moment I received a terrible blow, and sank to the earth, with a frightful noise in my ears, and a sensation as if the sea were breaking over me.

CHAPTER XX.

SOME REVELATIONS.

I AWAKE in a strange room, in a dusky light that scarce reveals the objects around me. Surely some one came close to the bedside, and bent over me for a moment, and touched my forehead with her lips, and then glided out of the room. But I can see nothing and hear nothing for the din that is in my ears—resembling the rustling of innumerable leaves—and the mist that is before my eyes. I feel tired, also, and weak and drowsy.

The doctor comes into the room. I have not seen him since my father and uncle were buried on the same morning. I connect his face with all that terrible time, and wonder whether I, too, am dying. It seems as if it would be an easy thing to die—just the sinking into a quiet sleep, with plenty of sweet, deep rest.

The doctor appears a little surprised, takes my hand, and says he is glad I am so much better.

"Where am I?"

"Why, in the Major's cottage. In a day or two we shall have you removed to Burnham."

"But—but what is the matter? Has anybody been sent to tell Mr. Weavle that I couldn't come—"

"Mr. Weavle?" said the doctor.

Then I begin to recollect myself. I must have been dreaming about Weavle. I am no longer a slave to Weavle or to anybody. I can go where I like—do what I like. But why this bed and the doctor? I further recollect; and then I beg the doctor to tell me all that occurred that night when I saw the gun pointed at Hester Burnham.

"But first tell me who went out of the room just now, before you came in?"

"Why, no one. You have been so soundly asleep for some time that your mother went down-stairs for a little while to get something to eat."

"There was no one else up here?"

"No. I dare say you were a little confused when you awoke, you know, and may have fancied you saw some one."

"Ah, I dare say."

And yet I thought that some one came and touched my forehead with her lips; and, in my utter prostration and nervous weakness, I wished that she would come and kiss me once more, that I might fall asleep and die.

"How long have I been ill?"

"Only a few days. You have been a little feverish, you know; but the ball has been extracted—"

"A ball, was it?"

"Yes. That idiot Toomer put a ball and a sixpence into the barrel; and that bigger idiot of a friend of yours must needs go and fire it. Lucky for you that it caught your watch first, or you wouldn't have been speaking now."

"I hear wheels—who is that?"

"Miss Burnham going home, I think. She has been here the best part of the day with your mother. I suppose you know you saved that young lady's life by very nearly losing your own?"

"Doctor, I wish I was able to laugh. Miss Burnham once gave me half a crown in charity, and for many a year I have been trying to get some way of paying it to her back again. Have I paid it back now?"

"You shouldn't talk in that way of her," said the doctor, gravely and kindly; "she is all gratitude towards you. Indeed, I told her she was doing her best to kill herself in return—sittin' up when there was no need for it, and cryin' when there was no need for it, and generally conducting herself like a precious young fool. But she has been of great assistance to your mother. She has sat up when there *was* need for it—sat on this very chair half the night through, and, in spite of her wilfulness, showin' an amount of wise common-sense and helpfulness that fairly astonished me, though I knew her pretty well. So you mustn't say hard things of her—"

"Did I?"

"Well, you spoke bitterly, you know—and—and when you were a little feverish, you know, you said some things of her then that made her cry as if her heart would break. These are tales out of school, you know, and if I tell them to you, it is that you mayn't think she is at all ungrateful to you for what you've done and suffered for her. She has been here pretty well night and day; and the whole lot of 'em have been just about as anxious, and a pretty to-do I've had to keep them from botherin' up here. But there's only your mother and herself have the sense for a sick-room, that's the fact. Now, have I told you everything? Is your mind perfectly at rest? For it's only rest that is required now to bring you round, and you must have a good dose of it. No exciting interviews with young ladies, you know; no attempts to soothe Mr. Morell's protestations of remorse—nothing but quiet and rest. Get well; and tackle them afterwards."

All this, said in his low, quiet, kind voice, was so gentle and soothing, that in a few moments thereafter I again fell asleep.

Next morning I found that the doctor had absolutely forbidden every one, except my mother, to see me for several days. I thought this a very hard provision, but had to admit the prudence of it. However, I received all manner of messages from every one around, and sent them back replies. Indeed, I lay and imagined the various interviews I should have with each of them; and promised to myself the satisfaction of again making friends with Bonnie Lesley.

As it happened, she was the first who was permitted to see me. At the end of these few days it was proposed that I should be removed to Burnham House; but this I objected to so strenuously that the project dropped. There was no urgent reason for such a removal. Thanks to the kindness of Mrs. Toomer and Miss Burnham, the cottage we had taken possession of was furnished with every convenience. My mother slept in the room which had been intended for Heatherleigh; and a bed had also been fitted up for the maid-servant from Burnham House who attended her. Heatherleigh had taken up his quarters at Burnham House; and was, at my request, going on with the whole of the panellings. The accident which had happened was a sad damper upon both his work and the sports of the other guests; but so soon as it became definitely certain that my recovery was only a question of time, a more cheerful tone got abroad, and things went on as usual in the quiet valley.

"Ted," said my mother, with a laugh, "I have a visitor for you."

"Who is it?"

"The most beautiful lady in the world."

"Is it Miss Lesley?"

"It is a young princess out of a story-book, dressed all in white and blue and silver, and she wears a white hat and a white feather above her long yellow hair. Shall I bid her come in?"

My mother's description was correct. When Bonnie Lesley came into the room, she did look like a princess out of a story-book. And she came over and took my hand, and was for accusing herself of all that had happened, when I stopped her.

"It was a mischance," I said, "for which nobody is responsible. It was my carelessness that was chiefly to blame, in leaving the gun about after I saw it was loaded."

"But there is more than that for which I must ask your forgiveness—"

Here she glanced towards my mother. I suppose women understand these mute appeals better than men: in a minute or two she made some excuse for leaving the room and went downstairs.

"I have to ask your forgiveness for my conduct over at Burnham that evening—you know what I mean. When I ran forward and saw you lying on the ground, I fancied you were dead, and the thought that I should never have the chance of explaining—of begging you to pardon me—"

"That is all over. Don't say anything more about it."

"But I must. You don't know what it meant; and yet, when I saw you lying on the ground, I resolved that if ever I had the chance I would confess everything—"

She seemed very much distressed. The whole affair was a mystery to me; yet I had grown so accustomed to see things in a kind of mental fog that I was not surprised. Perhaps, after all, she was not there? Perhaps this beautiful vision was in reality a vision? But again she began speaking—in a rapid, confused, painful way.

"I must tell you everything now—then you can judge whether we shall ever meet on the old terms. Long ago Mr. Heatherleigh said something of me that hurt me much. I needn't tell you what led him to say it; but he said—not to me, of course, but to a friend of mine—that I was incapable of sincere affection, that I was by nature frivolous and light, and unable to feel deeply; that any man of a strong and sensitive nature would turn from me as soon as he 'found me out,' and a great deal like that. I cannot explain it exactly; but you know what he meant."

I nodded; wondering, at the same time, what had led to this strange conduct on the part of Heatherleigh, and wondering whether I should ever get to the bottom of the mystery.

"I was deeply mortified, and very angry. Just then you became acquainted with Mr. Heatherleigh. He took a great liking to you, and kept praising you to everybody—I suppose because you were in many things very like himself. It was then — oh! how can I ever tell you!"

She buried her face in her hands. After a few minutes' silence she continued, evidently forcing herself to speak.

"I thought it would show him how much he was mistaken if you and I were to become great friends; and I—I even determined to revenge myself upon him by—by flirting with you. . . . You will despise me; I deserve it; I despise myself; and I don't know how I am able to tell you all this, but that I made a vow that night to confess everything to you, and beg your pardon. Well, we did become great friends, did we not?"

I nodded again.

"And I—I confess that I was many a time sorry that it was not in earnest, and many a time ashamed that I was deceiving you. Sometimes I thought I was not deceiving you, and that I meant it all; and, then again, it seemed so shameful, for you were always so honest with me, and kind. Very well: you didn't fall in love with me, did you?"

There was a smile and a blush on her face as she spoke; but she kept her eyes fixed on the ground.

"I was very near," I said, rather sadly.

It seemed as if the old world was all fading away now, with the dreams that were its chief inhabitants. I could see it as a thing apart, cut off from me, and slowly receding. I think every man experiences at times flashes and spasms of consciousness, that suddenly reveal to him his position and his relation with the circumstances around him. These glimpses of self-revelation show him how he has altered in a few years—how he has grown, without being aware of it almost, so much more healthful, or rich, or poor, or famous, or sad. As this girl sat and spoke to me, the old panorama was unrolled, and I saw all the stages of our acquaintanceship as so many pictures. I was regarding myself in the light of her revelations.

"Are you angry with me?" she asked.

"Not at all."

"You didn't fall in love with me, and I was vexed. On that evening at Burnham, I thought I should at least provoke you into being jealous; and so I flirted with Mr. Morell, so that you must have noticed it. I must have been mad. I can scarcely believe myself when I look back over all these things, and see how shamefully and cruelly I behaved. I was terrified beyond measure at the result of my proposal to play at ghosts. I thought it was a judgment—"

"It must have been a judgment," said Heatherleigh, afterwards, when I told him of this conversation, "*for it fell on the wrong person.*"

"When I went back to Burnham—none of us got home till the gray of the morning—I lay awake for hours, thinking what I could do to atone for all my folly and cruelty; and I made up my mind that, on the very first opportunity, I would confess everything to you. I have done it—I have debased myself in your eyes—I have humiliated myself—"

Suddenly, and to my great surprise, she buried her face in the end of the pillow next her, and burst into tears. I was amazed beyond belief; as I had never seen Bonnie Lesley give way to any violent emotion whatever. Indeed I had really begun to doubt her possession of any great sensitiveness; and then to think that one so beautiful and graceful should have been moved in this way on my account! Yet I looked on the exhibition, I confess, as a sort of phenomenon. She had herself shattered that old world of foolish hopes, and severed the frail cord that bound us, so widely separated from each other, together; and now it was with more curiosity than sympathy that I saw her so strangely affected. I can recall that, through the languor produced by my weakness, I lazily contemplated the pictorial effect of her attitude—the bowed head, the covered face, and masses of yellow hair.

At this moment my mother re-entered the room. The beautiful penitent hastily raised her head and endeavored to conceal her tears.

"Will you take a biscuit and a little wine, Miss Lesley, before you go?" said my mother.

This was merely an invitation to leave.

"Yes, thank you," she said.

She rose, and, as she bade me good-bye, she stooped down and said—

"Will you forgive me *every*thing?"

"Everything."

"And we shall be better friends than before, I think?"

"I hope so."

With that she left; and I spent the rest of the day in dreaming over the strange story she had told me, and in recalling all the old scenes and circumstances. Certainly, many a peculiar feature in our past relations became clear. I remembered, especially, the manner in which, on the top of Lewes Castle, she had questioned me about my possessing the same tastes and disposition as Heatherleigh, and also the strange fashion in which she endeavored to arrive at my impression of her character. I certainly had not imagined her to possess so much self-consciousness as she had exhibited, and sensitiveness to criticism. She was evidently proud, and capable of some persistence in her notion of revenging herself.

But the wound that had prompted her to attempt this revenge was still a mystery. What reason had Heatherleigh to depart from his usual courtesy of bearing to make an attack upon a girl who was, if not a friend of his, a friend of his friend? Ordinarily, Heatherleigh was most generous in his interpretation of people's conduct; given to seeing the best side of their nature; slow to express an unfavorable opinion; and invariably considerate and respectful, even chivalric, towards women. Why had he gone out of his way to sneer at a girl for lack of those qualities which no effort on her part could have acquired—that is to say, presuming that his strictures were true, which I wholly declined to believe? Young as I was, I had even then observed that there is no more common charge brought against a woman than that of emptiness of heart and fickleness of disposition, and the charge is generally preferred by a rejected suitor.

Next morning Mr. Morell came up. I had to stop his protestations of regret also.

"Look here," I said, "do you regard as a joke the getting a ball through your left arm and shoulder, and the slitting of your ear with a sixpence?"

"Certainly not."

"Well, it is fast becoming a comedy. Everybody insists on being the only responsible party; and, instead of fighting it out among yourselves, you come and appeal to me. Sit down, and tell me what you have done among the Burnham stubbles."

"Oh, but, damme, you must let me tell you how awfully sorry I am—"

"I won't."

"There never was such a beastly idiot—"

"All right."

"—without knowing what was in the gun, to think of only frightening whoever it might be—"

"Very well. I'm tired of hearing about it. How many brace did you kill next day?"

"Well, I'll tell you. None of us shot next day. We mooned about the place as if it were Sunday. Next day the same, until Alfred Burnham proposed billiards; and the brute won twenty-five pounds from me, confound him. Then we all played pool: Heatherleigh, the Colonel, he, and I; but it was only a shilling the game and threepenny lives, and Burnham did not play so well. I was going to remark that all men are honest where their interests are not concerned; but it wouldn't be appropriate, would it? You can't cheat much at billiards."

"You don't suppose Alfred Burnham would cheat?"

"I never suppose anything about so remarkably dark a horse. To continue. Miss Burnham was over here night and day; the other ladies had buried themselves, and we only saw them in the evening, at dinner. On the third day the ball was extracted from your shoulder, and the doctors told us you would get on all right. Then we resolved to go out shooting."

"Did Heatherleigh go with you?"

"No, he has been working hard at those pictures. When I went to open my gun-case, I almost felt sick as I saw the two long barrels. I declare to you, I trembled when I took the gun in my hand; and when we began walking down those turnips beyond Burnham Common, I felt certain I should kill somebody through my nervousness. We had scarcely got inside the gate when up got a hare—what the devil it was doing out in the path, I don't know—almost at my feet. I put up the gun, and, damme, I couldn't pull the trigger. The Colonel waited for a second, in surprise; and then up went his gun and over rolled the hare. The wind brought a puff of the smoke my way, and I pretty nearly got sick again. You know what it is to smell bad tobacco in the morning, when you have been making a night of it, and smoking four times as many cigars as were good for you. Well, on we went; I wishing that I had the moral courage to fling the infernal breech-loader over a hedge and walk home. Every time I shot, I expected to hear a cry and a heavy tumble on the ground. I declare to you it was purgatory. I didn't know what I was doing. I fired at the Colonel's birds. I let a whole covey of partridges go past within fifteen yards of me, untouched. I missed a hare that was caught in the hedge and stuck there for a couple of seconds—"

"You fired straight enough when you fired at me."

"Yes, idiot that I was. Well, we went into old Toomer's to have some bread and cheese and beer. Mrs. Toomer kindly presided at the table. I was so thoroughly upset and dazed that I considerably astonished that stout person.

"'How glad you must be to get into the country, now the worry and confusion of the season is over,' said I.

"Probably she stared; but I did not notice.

"'I presume you were a great deal out,' I continued. 'Do you go much to the opera?'

"You know Mrs. Toomer has rather a rosy face; but when I turned to look at her she was positively scarlet with rage and indignation. She thought I was chaffing her about her being a rustic. I declare I never thought who she was; but, knowing there was a woman near whom I ought to talk to, I talked the ordinary nonsense you would talk to anybody. I made her every apology; and told some monstrous lie about having believed that she had just come down from London. I fancy she did not believe me; and I wonder she did not complain to her husband about my impertinence."

I could see the germ in this brief sketch of many a fine story for Morell's friends; and, actually, a long time after, being at a certain club, I heard a man say—

"Oh, did you hear that devilish good story young Brooks told here last night? He had it from some writing-fellow—about a swell trying to get into conversation with a farmer's wife, and talking to her about the Row, and the opera, and the new style of bouquet-fans. It was as good as a play: shouldn't wonder if the fellow who told Brooks put it in a play."

"I was very much amused by old Toomer," continued Morell; and just as he spoke, who should appear at the door but Stephen Toomer himself, accompanied by Heatherleigh.

"How be ye, Mahster Ives, how be ye? I be rare glad to hear you are getting all right again; and as we couldn't find the missus down-stairs—"

"Of course you came up," said Morell. "But we are too many for a sick-room, so I'm off; besides I was to meet the Colonel and his party at eleven, and it is now half-past."

"Where are you going shooting to-day?" I asked.

"I was to meet them a little beyond Hare Wood."

"Then you are coming back to drive the wood?"

"I suppose so."

"Very well. You get as near as you can to the upper side of the dell that lies in the northeast corner. The place is full of hares, and they all make for that corner, to get over to Coney-bank Wood. Get yourself into a good place, and they will run just in front of you, either up the lane or around the hedge-side of the dell."

"Come, that is unfair," said Heatherleigh. "If you were to give those wrinkles to me, who can only sit on a bank in the twilight and pot a rabbit when it comes out to sit on its hind-legs, and wash its face with its fore-paws—"

"And that bain't easy, ayther," said Mr. Toomer. "Lor, 'ow quick they be in catchin' sight o' the gun! You come up to my fahrm, and I'll show ye a dozen rahbbits a runnin' out and in o' their 'oles, and I'll bet the coöt off my back that ye sha'n't 'ave one o' them. What do you say, Mahster Ives?"

"Not unless you get into a sheep-trough, with a sheaf of corn to hide your head, and lie there for half an hour."

"And fall asleep, mayhap, like the mahn as stole the pig. D'ye know that story, Mahster Heatherleigh? It wur one o' my grand-fäther's."

"No, let us hear it, Mr. Toomer."

"This mahn was took up for stealin' the pig, and it wur found on him—leastways in the bahg he had over his bahck. 'Please your worship,' says he, 'I never stole that 'ere pig.' ''Ow did you come to 'ave it in your bahg?' said his worship. 'Please your worship, the rale truth is I wur very tired, and I went into this mahn's pig-sty with my bahg, and I lay down, as it might be, to rest mysel'. I fell asleep, your worship, and I suppose when I wur asleep this ere dahmned pig got into the bahg. I never knowed it wur there till the constable he found it wur there.' "

Mr. Toomer recited this story with profound solemnity, as if it were a collect he had been asked to repeat. He looked remarkably uncomfortable while telling the tale; and the moment it was finished he pretended to be vastly taken with a picture of London—a sheet out of some illustrated paper—which Heatherleigh had nailed up on the wall.

"What uncommon sharp folks they be in Lunnon, to be sure," Toomer remarked, meditatively. "When I wur thear five yur ago, I had just left the yard where the bus stopped, and I went to buy a pennorth o' happles from an old creetur as was sellin' them on the side o' the street. 'You're a Buckinghamshire mahn, ain't ye?' says she. ''Ow did you find that out, missus?' said I. 'Why, doan't I know every one on you Buckinghamshire folk by your *be's?*' says she, with a grin. But I don't hold by Lunnon."

"No?" said Heatherleigh. "Why that, Mr. Toomer?"

"I doan't know. I know as I doan't like the plääce. I reckleet well when I got on the top o' the coach again, and when we wur a-coming out by Notting-'ill, and when I began to smell the fields again by Hacton and Healing, I turns to old Joe—he wur the driver then, and wur a great man for thinkin' hisself a real Lunnoner—'Talk o' your furrin parts, Joe,' says I, 'but gie me Hold England!' "

"What did he say, Mr. Toomer?"

"He wur a poor creature, was Joe Barton, and couldn't understand what I meant. He said as Lunnon was in Hengland too; as if there wur a man alive as didn't know that Lunnon was in England. He wur a sour-minded mahn, Joe Barton, and 'ud catch you up literal-like. Yet he wur somethin' of a scholar, wur Joe; and they tell me as he wur able to pint out the way to a French gentleman as come down into these parts."

"Good-bye, everybody," said Morell. "I'm glad you didn't put me in for manslaughter, Ives. I hope you'll soon be well again."

And we heard him go down the stairs and out past the front of the house, humming—

"Du hast meine Uhr und Kette,
Ruinirt mein Porte-monnaie."

Toomer seemed anxious to go, too, and yet appeared not to know how to get out. He began to study London again; then he suddenly seemed to remember that his hat was on the table, and might as well be on the chair. Finally he burst into speech in a tone so solemn that it startled both Heatherleigh and myself.

"I allays said it, and say it now, as it's fur too yallow."

He looked hard at Heatherleigh.

"I beg your pardon, Mr. Toomer—"

"If there's one thing as I've said to my missus again and again, it's thaht; and I hold to it—as the front is too yallow—"

"Oh, the front of Burnham House!"

"Exahctly!" said Mr. Toomer, with a broad and happy smile on his blooming face; "bain't I right, Mahster Heatherleigh?"

"Well, yes, I fancy it would do to be a shade grayer."

"Ah, look at that now!" said Mr. Toomer, turning to me with a triumphant laugh. "Look at that now! Haven't I allays said as it wur too yallow; and when I say a thing, I hold to it. Lor bless ye, women cahn't understand them things. There's some things, as I say to my missus, outside of a woman's comprehension; and we're not to fight agin the Almighty, and break down the barrier as he has plaäced between them and hus. What I've allays said—and I hold to it—is as woman is shallow."

He looked from one to the other of us; and then fixed his eyes for a few seconds on the picture of London.

"What do *you* say, Mahster Heatherleigh?" he continued, returning suddenly from the picture. "Bain't I right? I say nothin' agin women—as fur as they go. They be very good—*as fur as they go.* But I do say, Mahster Heatherleigh, as they're shallow."

The eagerness with which he courted assent displayed itself all over his fine, broad, bucolic English face.

"They haven't the masculine force of intellect, have they, Mr. Toomer?" said Heatherleigh.

"Didn't I say so!" exclaimed Toomer, beaming with delight, and turning to me. "Didn't I say as they wur poor creeturs, and most uncommon shallow! Bless ye, a woman has as little steady common-sense in her as—as—as a stone steeple!"

I suppose Mr. Toomer borrowed this illustration from the picture of London, on which his eyes were again fixed. However, after having sat a little time in profound silence, he thought of a wonderful joke about turnips, fired it off, and under cover of the smoke made his exit.

"Now," said Heatherleigh, "you must tell me what you have been doing to Bonnie Lesley?"

"I? Nothing."

"She was talking of you last evening in a way that surprised me. I grew to fancy that you had conferred a soul upon her—Undine fashion. I confess I began to have remorse of conscience; for I have had throughout a very ugly theory of her relations with you—"

"And your theory was quite correct," said I. "It is only now that I can understand all the loose hints you used to throw out—hints that made me remarkably angry. Indeed, Heatherleigh, I will tell you the truth—I fancied Miss Lesley had refused you, or done you some sort of injury, and that you were revenging yourself by dropping these suggestions."

"That *was* turning the tables!" cried Heatherleigh, with a hearty laugh. "Why, do you think I'd have said anything about the poor girl but to open your eyes and save you from a possible catastrophe? I don't blame people for their nature. How can they help it? What is it Burns says of 'Bonnie Lesley?'—'Nature made her what she is;' and as she is not responsible, she cannot be blamed. Only I ventured to take precautions, that you, through your ignorance of what she is, might not suffer; and in return you thought me guilty of a mean revenge, whereas the truth is—"

Here he stopped abruptly; I looked hard at him, but he turned his eyes the other way.

"There is no use in going further into the story of what is over and gone; but how did you come to know that my theory was correct?"

"Because she came here yesterday, and confessed everything, and seemed heartily sorry and ashamed of herself—"

"And what does she propose to do by way of atonement?" asked Heatherleigh, with a peculiar smile.

"I don't see that she has anything to atone for. What harm has she done to me?"

"Yet I shouldn't wonder," he said, musingly, "if, in her new fit of penitence, she were to coax you to fall in love with her in earnest. Now don't flare up in that hasty fashion of yours. Look at the thing calmly. I say nothing against the girl whatever: she has a rare notion of doing what is right, only she does it self-consciously, and with an obvious effort. She forces herself to be magnanimous in spite of her nature, which is narrow. She considers what is good and generous and noble—in short, what she ought to do in order to please other people and raise herself in their estimation—then she makes an effort and does it. This effort to be thought well of is the only thing which seems to stir her at all. But for that, one would think she had no more mind or judgment or sensitiveness than a butterfly. She is as cold as a sheet of glass to all other impressions; but if you touch her self-esteem, you wound her to the quick."

"It is the old story," I said. "You interpret every one's disposition with kindliness, except hers. I don't ask you what you have done to her, but what has she done to you, that you should be so savage with her?"

"I don't think I am dealing savagely with her. I only gave you my honest impression of her character—which may be quite wrong. I began to believe myself that it was wrong, when she spoke to me of you last evening. I could scarcely credit that it was Bonnie Lesley who spoke to me, and she must have seen something of this, for she said, 'When once you form your judgment of people, I suppose you never alter it?'"

"And what did you answer?"

"Some ordinary compliment, which rather vexed her. Let us see what her penitence leads to, Ted, before saying anything further."

"By the way," I said, "I wish you to do me a great service."

"I will," he said, "if it is not connected with her. But I decline entirely—"

"It has nothing to do with her. You remember my telling you how I buried a half-crown in a dell many years ago?"

"Yes."

"I want you to go this afternoon and dig it up. You will easily find it. Ask one of the keepers to show you Squirrel Dell

Down in the hollow there is a tall ash-tree; and the stone I put over the half-crown is only a yard or so from the foot of the trunk. Very likely it is grown over with weeds or hidden by the bushes, and you may have to scrape about a little. But if you can't find it, get one of the keepers and tell him I will give him a sovereign if the half-crown is found, and we shall have it before the morning."

"What do you want to do with it, Ted?" said he.

"Miss Barnham is coming over here to-morrow morning, and I mean to give it to her."

CHAPTER XXI.

QUITS.

I HAVE said something of the strange flashes of consciousness which suddenly reveal to a man his position. They resemble those glimpses of half-forgotten actions and words which a man who has been drinking too much wine after dinner recalls the next morning, and by which he can instantaneously picture certain events of the evening before which had wholly escaped his memory. It now occurred to me as passing strange that, after an interval of only a few years, I should be able to lie in bed from day to day, and do nothing, without running up a fearful amount of debt and earning the accumulated growls of Weavle. What a blessed thing was this freedom, this independence, which the possession of a little money gave! It seemed very strange that, instead of having to work wearily and economize painfully, one had only to remain still, and let the mysterious agent out-of-doors go silently on, multiplying sovereigns, and supplying us with as many as our small needs required.

Was I not now as independent as the people whom I used to envy in the Row? That evening I walked around the Serpentine, with eighty pounds clasped in my hand, I was proud enough; and yet I knew not how long the money, even if I were to claim it, would last. Now I had a machine for coining money; and it went on day and night, day and night, turning out that small flow of sovereigns. We had to spare. If I saw a poor wretch wanting his dinner, could I not give him five shillings and make him happy? Walking along the London streets, I should have in my pocket the possibility of rejoicing the heart of any wretched beggar or starving child or needy seamstress whom I met. While in London, I had scarcely realized all this to myself. Here, in the still depths of Bucks, I had time to scan my own position, the great changes that had so naturally and easily fallen over my life, the great good-fortune for which I ought to be so thankful. And I thought that when I returned to London I should exercise my power, and go about the streets like a special Providence, armed with half-crowns.

During these fits of reflection I arrived at another resolution. It became clear to me that I should never emancipate myself wholly from the depressing and constraining influences of my youth unless I got quite away, at least for a time, from England and all the old associations. I was free (except in dreams) from the tyranny of Weavle; but I was still bound hard and fast by certain notions which seemed to me peculiarly of English growth. I was more a gamekeeper's son than an independent human being to the people around me—a small sort of prodigy, who had so far raised himself above what ought to have been his lot. Now I wanted to go into some other country—should it be America, where the free fight of humanity is at its frankest?—to assert myself as a man among men. To break asunder the old influences, to engage in the grand levelling process of competition, and actually discover for myself my own value—that was the purpose I now formed in these long days at Burnham, with the breath of the winter already telling on the autumn air.

Naturally, I began to chafe against the necessity which confined me to bed, much as Heatherleigh counselled patience, and pointed out that I ought to wait to see what effect my "Kilmeny" might have in the Academy.

"Do you think, then," said I, "that it is sure to be admitted?"

"Certain," he said, decisively; "just as certain as that everybody will recognize the likeness."

"I hope not," I said.

"Why?"

There was no particular answer to the question; although the notion of this picture being hung on the Academy walls, and looked at by many people whom I knew, provoked several strange suggestions.

But before telling the fate of "Kilmeny," I must say a word about the visit which Hester Burnham and Madame Laboureau paid me.

Heatherleigh had, without much difficulty, found the old, discolored coin which I had buried in the dell years before. I looked at it with many peculiar emotions, and with some faint reflex of the feeling which prompted me to wreak my wrath on an unoffending piece of silver. I remembered again the bitter humiliation I suffered when Miss Hester offered to take back the money, and when I found myself unable to give it to her. We had become more intimate since then; but I dared never revert to this subject. Indeed, the mere thought of it at any time was sufficient to break down the frail bridge of acquaintanceship that had been, with much uncertainty and diffidence, established between us. With more of years, of judgment, and reflection, I might have treasured that poor coin as the witness to the existence in the world of at least one true, kind heart: as it was, I hated it, and wished that I could bury it in oblivion, even as I had buried it in Squirrel Dell, with all the bitter recollections of that memorable day.

When Hester Burnham came into the room, she was very pale, and there was that strange glow in her dark gray-blue eyes that testified to the presence of some strong emotion. Very pale she was, and beautiful; and the look of her face had a tenderness in it which was obviously febrile, uncertain, ready to break into tears. Yet the quiet little woman, with that wonderful grace and carriage of hers, came over and timidly took my hand. I think she spoke a good deal in a low, tremulous voice, but I only vaguely knew its purport. There was something so extraordinarily sweet in the voice that you were glad to listen to the music of it without harkening to the words. You could so easily read the emotions that the thrilling, low, soft tones expressed, that you forgot to think of words and sentences. The delight of hearing her speak seemed to blind one to the sense of what she said; and yet you found afterwards that you had followed her all through her pretty entreaties, her protestations, her tenderly expressed wishes. I should like to have shut my eyes, and lain and listened to that strangely sweet voice forever.

Madame Laboureau speedily broke the spell with her bright,

quick chatter, and her dramatic expressions of profound sympathy. Of course, I was in her eyes a wonderful creature—a hero. I had saved Miss Hester's life. I had been severely wounded in doing so. I might have been killed—

"That would have been more romantic," I said, interrupting her, "and a more appropriate end to the adventure, wouldn't it? As it stands, the play has lasted too long already; and you can't expect to have people wait to see a fifth act that extends over several months, and is played in a sick-room."

"But it is too serious for a play," she said, shaking her head, "though I am glad to see you improving yourself much. You must keep still, and have no excitations—then you may much sooner be sound again. And when you can Miss Hester hopes you will come up to Burnham and make perfect your—your guérison there. The room is all prepared—it is better than this old house."

"I am sure I am much obliged to Miss Burnham, and to you, Madame," I said; "but as soon as I can move, I must go back to London."

"You will not think of that!" said Miss Burnham, suddenly.

She had been sitting quite silent, still apparently a little pale and excited, and with her eyes fixed on the floor. Now she looked up, with surprise visible in them.

"The winter exhibitions will be open shortly. If I have been able to do nothing myself, I must see what others have been doing."

"But you have one picture?" she said, turning her eyes upon me.

I dared not meet that glance, lest there should be a question in it. I said to her—

"Yes, I have a picture that Heatherleigh thinks might do without further finishing. If I cannot work between this and then, I may send it as it is, to take its chance of the Academy. But who told you of it?"

"Mr. Morell; and he thinks it will make a great impression."

"He may think so," I said, "for he hasn't seen it."

"Oh, he has *not* seen it?" she asked, quickly.

"No."

"Mais c'est un véritable prodige, ce monsieur," said Madame. "He knows everything, everybody; he has been everywhere; he can do anything, except play the German music. Oh! he plays Beethoven as if it was Gung'l, and Mozart as if it was Offenbach.

I cannot bear him then; but at other times he is charming. And your Bonnie Lesley thinks so, does she not?"

Madame appealed to her companion, who did not answer.

"Mr. Morell may be able to speak of the picture without having seen it," said I; "but if he had exercised his miraculous powers of vision before firing through a certain tree—"

"That is a mystery!" exclaimed Madame, decisively. "Did he think the gun was not loaded? Did he fire only to frighten whoever was playing tricks? Or did he believe in the spirits, and fire at them? I have never been able to comprehend, so rapid he talks on that subject. He is so anxious to explain, he is to me unintelligible. And he goes back to town to-morrow."

"He does?"

"Yes; he says he cannot bear to remain here, after the accident. And soon we shall have all our party broken away, and be alone again; and so it would be quiet for you if you come to Burnham—"

Here my mother, who had been over to Great Missenden, came up-stairs, and was at once attacked by Madame Laboureau on the subject of my removal to Burnham House. Sheltered by their brisk talk, Miss Hester stole over to my side, and said, with her eyes cast down—

"I hope you will come to Burnham. There is so little that I can do to show you how grateful I am—how impossible it is for me to say—"

"You need say nothing," I said to her. "Do you remember, a good many years ago, your making me your debtor to the extent of half a crown?"

She raised her eyes suddenly, and there was reproach there, with a touch of pain and even of indignation.

"You bring that up again," she said bitterly. "Is the mistake of a girl, of a child, to last through a lifetime? You know how that misadventure has made strangers of us all this time; but I thought you had at last allowed it to be forgotten. You revive it now to pain me—perhaps to insult me. It is not fair—I do not deserve it—"

"Do you think it was for that purpose I revived the old story?" I said, looking at her. "When, not knowing what I did, I took the money you gave me, I carried it over to Burnham, and buried it there in the ground. When you offered to take it back again,

I could not give it to you; and I was too proud to take it to you afterwards. It has lain there until yesterday; but I have it in my hand now; and I have it that I may give it back to you, if you will take it."

"You want to make me altogether your debtor," she said, with a strange, sad smile, as she took the tarnished silver coin, and looked at it wistfully. "I am not so proud as you are, I think."

She opened her purse, and took the accursed bit of money, and laid it—almost tenderly, I fancied—in the crimson silk. As she left, she stealthily pressed my hand, and both of us knew from that moment that henceforth we were nearer to each other.

CHAPTER XXII.

A WILD GUESS.

"I AM not so proud as you are, I think." The phrase lingered long with me in these dull days, while I waited and wearied for the coming time of action. For already I smelt the wintry air—the cold, misty flavor in the atmosphere that tells of the close, dark winter, the long nights and hard work. The glorious Buckinghamshire autumn slipped by me unnoticed. I saw none of the glare of color that, as I knew, lay along the far beech-woods, while the red sunsets burned over the stripped harvest-fields and the brown ploughed lands. I saw none of the gradual change from olive green to the glowing gold and crimson that make these hills a wonder; for, when I was able to go out, the time of hoar-frost, and morning mist, and cold coppery sunlight had arrived, and the day was sluggish and heartless and short. All the more I hungered for the life and activity of London—for the joyous gas-lamps, and the quick stir of labor, the comfort of warm rooms, and the intense pleasure of work well done. Every one had gone from Burnham House now, except Miss Hester and her small, bright French friend and companion. Morell had speedily left, and had sent me many a chatty, vivacious letter, and many a journal, foreign and domestic; Bonnie Lesley and the Lewisons were again at Regent's Park; Heatherleigh had finished the panels, and had returned to assiduous labor in Granby Street; Alfred Burnham had gone I knew not where—his father likewise. Only Miss Hester lingered here, and wandered about the still, cold park, or rode down the rimy lanes in the morning air, when the scarlet hips and the ruddy haws were frosted with white, and when the struggling sun had just managed to melt the hoar-frost on the spiders' webs, and change them to strings of incrusted, gleaming jewels. Red and crisp were the leaves that still hung on the trees, while those that lay rotting in the damp woods were orange and brown and black. The tall, broad brackens, too, that had a few weeks ago turned from a dark green to a pale gold, were getting sombre and limp; while everywhere in the woods frosted berries came to be visible along the bare, leafless stalks of bramble and dog-rose, of rowan and elder and white-thorn. It was a cold, cheerless time out here for any one who was not after the pheasants of Burnham woods, or the hares that lay out on the hill-sides; and it often seemed to me, looking down the cold, still valley, with the yellow, wintry sunshine glimmering along the dull fields and the voiceless farmsteads, that I could hear the low, hurried throb of London life, and the murmur of its innumerable wheels.

At length the time arrived when I was able to undertake the journey. I wished to say good-bye to Hester Burnham, and while I was still debating whether to venture upon walking across to Burnham House, she and Madame Laboureau made their appearance. They had made several calls of a like nature before, and were aware that I purposed going to London, but both of them seemed surprised when I now informed them that I should leave next day.

"You ought not to go yet," said Miss Hester, quietly, her eyes turned the other way.

"You will not allow it, Mrs. Ives, will you?" said Madame.

By and by, however, when they saw that our departure had already been settled, they were anxious that they should help a little towards our comfortable travelling.

"Did you mean to go up by the coach, or by the train from Wycombe?" asked Miss Hester, of my mother.

"We thought there would be less jolting by the coach, and there is a cab ordered to come over from Missenden to-morrow morning for us."

"But the coach goes very early, does it not?" asked Madame.

"Seven."

"And you leave here—"

"About six."

"Mon Dieu! In the dark of a winter morning! Is that proper travelling for an invalid?"

"I hope, Mrs. Ives," said Miss Burnham, "that you will let me send a carriage for you. It will be so much better that you should start at any hour you please, and go all the way in one vehicle, without the bother of changing. Besides the jolting, you will have the draughts and discomfort of both the cab and the Missenden coach; while, on the other hand, if you let me send a carriage for you, you may make a leisurely day's journey of it, and Cracknell may come down again the next day, or the day after."

"I could not think of such a thing, Miss Hester," said my mother, who knew how seldom that luxury had been indulged in even by the Burnhams themselves since the opening of the railway.

"Then I must appeal to you," said Hester Burnham, turning to me, with her frank eyes.

Why, her manner had something of a challenge in it. Her regard seemed to say, "Two months ago you and I buried the old feud between us, and promised to be friends. Show that it is so." I accepted the challenge, and replied to her frank look—

"Sha'n't you want the carriage or the horses for a day or two?"

"Certainly not. I never drive now; I always ride."

"Then, since you are so kind, we shall be very glad to accept your offer. Only, I hope we are not disturbing your arrangements in any way."

You would have thought, from her bright, quick look of gratitude, that I had conferred a favor on her; but it was only her pleasure at seeing that I understood the implied challenge she had thrown down.

Next morning, about ten o'clock, just as the sun was beginning to thaw the gray and frosty roughness of the morning, the carriage was driven up the avenue of bare limes to the Major's door. I was surprised to see Miss Hester and Madame Laboureau alight.

"You must have got up as early as we intended to do," said I.

"We wished to see you off," said she, simply; and then she turned to my mother to say that, as the hostelries between Burnham and London were mainly of a dubious kind, she had sent with the carriage something in the way of luncheon. This, as we afterwards found, was a modest way of representing the wonderful preparations she had caused to be made for us. A very good friend of mine is accustomed to point out the curious fact that men who never ride a horse, or expect to ride a horse, are in the habit of carrying about with them for years an instrument, attached to their pocket-knife, for picking stones out of a horse's hoof. There was something of the same extravagant forethought in the arrangements which Hester Burnham had made about our day's journey to London, which might have been meant, so far as they were concerned, for a week's travelling in Norway; and yet who could even make fun over these incongruities of a great thoughtfulness and kindness! When I did venture to suggest, during the journey, that Miss Hester might have added to our stores a coffee-grinding machine, a patent percolator, and a spirit-lamp, my mother seemed much hurt, and remarked that we could not have been better provided for had we been princes. It was, however, my first essay in travelling *à la mode de prince;* and I had to learn that even royalty must submit to conditions.

"Au revoir—bon voyage!" said Madame, as the carriage door was closed.

"We shall see you in London, shall we not?" said Hester Burnham, looking to my mother; then she said good-bye to me, in her simple, direct fashion, and we drove off.

As we gained the main road near Missenden, I put my head out of the carriage window and looked along the spacious valley towards Burnham. Far up on the opposite heights, near the margin of Coney-bank Wood, where the morning sun was shimmering palely along the hill, I saw two figures. I think they were standing and looking back. I waved a handkerchief to them; and one of them—presumably Madame—fluttered something white in return. That was the last I saw of Hester Burnham for many a day.

There was more of hard study than of ambitious effort for me during the remainder of that winter. I attended a certain life-class, where models, of no very intellectual type of beauty, of both sexes, and of various degrees of costume, stood on the raised platform, or sat, on cold nights, upon a warm stove, to be roughly outlined and colored by the busy young men who sat in a semi-circle before them. The room was not a large one, and the glare of gas, with the stove which was necessary to keep alive the (when clad) thinly clad models, rendered the atmosphere a not particularly healthy one. Indeed, what with that, and other studies which I could not help myself following, I felt that I was just hovering on the verge of my slowly accumulating strength, and that some caution was necessary to prevent a collapse and catastrophe.

Despite the entreaties of Heatherleigh and Polly Whistler, I sometimes fell to working a little at the "Kilmeny," as it seemed impossible to me that a picture with so little real labor in it could be worth much. But at length I resolved to leave it as it stood, and let it take its chance. Many of my fellow-students, and of Heatherleigh's maturer artistic friends, had seen it, and were sufficiently hopeful. But artists are singularly devoid of the vice of meaningless flattery when called upon to judge, *ex officio*, of the work of a friend. They talk of your weak points with an incorrigible frankness, while pointing out quite as frankly what they consider the strong points of the work. On the whole, I was fairly satisfied with its chance of acceptance; although inwardly I chafed at not being able, through want of experience in manipulation, to make it what I saw it ought to be.

Under Heatherleigh's auspices I had become a member of the Sumner Society—a society of artists who held, and still hold, a little half-private, half-public exhibition of their pictures prior to their being sent to the Academy. "Kilmeny," having been properly framed and labelled, was left at the rooms of the society, and as the evening drew near when the exhibition was to come off, I waited with a burning anxiety to see how it would look hung up on a wall, among other pictures painted by men of renown. I got so to fear this ordeal, that I could scarcely muster up courage to accompany Heatherleigh on the night of the display.

We went first to a tavern in Oxford Street, near the corner of Regent Street, which was then much frequented, as a chop-house, by members of the society. Here we found a goodly company of artists—always distinguishable by the preponderance of velveteen coats, which seem to hit the artistic fancy as powerfully as seal-skin waistcoats appeal to the journalistic taste—engaged in the different phases of dining, drinking, and smoking. A bronzed, intelligent, manly looking lot of men they were, with their slovenly dress, their quick jest, their hearty laugh. More than any other men, I think, artists enjoy the means by which they make their bread; and they bring back from the country with them, along with good spirits and a capital appetite, a rare fund of good stories and jokes, and bits of character observation. The shop, it is true, is a little too much with them; but when they get out of that, there are no such men for boon companions —their intellect quickened by much seeing, their habit of life eminently sociable and enjoyable. But they are better company to others than to themselves; for the long evenings, devoted chiefly to talk, at last get to the end of a man's jokes and stories. It used to be the pride of the Summers to defy any outsider to tell them a new story; but that proficiency was purchased dearly by the dearth of novelty among themselves. Now and again a man did introduce a fresh anecdote; and then it was accurately measured, judged, and laid on the shelf. I should like to write a good deal about the frank fellowship, the unworldliness, the rough, practical, healthy joyousness of artistic society in general; but all that has been described by abler pens than mine—by men who, being entirely outside of it and unconnected with it, could better appreciate its peculiarities than I.

Certainly there was no want of talk, for several of the men now met for the first time after their summer and autumn wanderings. There were stories of eccentric farmers' wives in Sussex, of adventures in the Ross-shire glens, of fishing-nights off the Devon coast. But the grand current of the talk, of course, set in towards the forthcoming Academy, and there were plenty of hazardous prophecies and strenuous opinions about the great works which were known to be yet on the easel. One or two of those present had not finished their pictures—were actually fighting against time during these last few days—and were, one could fancy, less noisy and joyous than their companions who had their labors consummated and off their minds.

Shortly after eight o'clock, a general movement was made to the chambers, situated in the neighborhood, in which the temporary exhibition was to be held. They were two long, narrow rooms, which were ordinarily used for drawing-classes, and from the dusky corners and gloomy shelves which were not covered by the new pictures there glimmered out fragments of plaster casts —a bust of Jupiter with marked lines of spider-webs about it, the ubiquitous disk-thrower, the broken-armed and reclining Theseus, the wavy-haired and calm-browed Venus of Milo, with here and there an arm or a leg finely shaded with dust. Down the middle of the two long rooms went a double screen, on which pictures were also hung, the passage between it and the walls being so narrow that anything like rapid circulation on the part of those who now entered the place was clearly impossible.

Heatherleigh seemed not to look out for his own pictures at all. When our eyes had got accustomed to the glare of the gas and the gilt frames, he carefully glanced around the walls.

"It is not in this room, at all events," he said.

"Do you mean 'Kilmeny?'"

"Yes," said he, struggling through the crowd that had already wedged itself into the narrow apertures.

We had just got to the door dividing the two chambers when Heatherleigh, looking far over the heads before him, exclaimed—

"By Jove, it '*shines* where it stands!'"

A moment after I caught sight of "Kilmeny," and started as if I had seen a ghost. For now there could be no doubt of the likeness of which Heatherleigh had spoken. I had tried to blind myself to the fact; and, in the solitude of my own room, I had gazed at the face until I had convinced myself that it was not that other face. But here the picture seemed beyond any thwarted interpretation. It stood up there, at the head of the room—scarcely veiled by the mist of yellow light through which I saw it—as a definite witness, and looked down upon me, as I fancied, accusingly. I moved nearer. There were some men round it, and they were criticising the picture freely. Heatherleigh called out to one of them, and this had the effect of announcing our approach, so that I fortunately missed hearing what they said. Now, out of mere modesty, a man may not stare at his own picture in an exhibition-room; and I was forced to turn away. Yet it seemed to me that the eyes of it followed me with a mute reproach. It was no longer Kilmeny. It was a beautiful, sweet face that I was familiar with, and it said, "Why have you put me up here, among all these people?" The unconscious wonder of Kilmeny's eyes was gone. There was no more unearthly lustre in them; but the wise, sweet look of the face that I knew; and I felt ashamed of the profanation.

"Why," said Heatherleigh, "you don't seem proud of the place you have got, or of the notice they are taking of the picture. It holds its own, I can tell you."

"I wish I could whitewash it," said I; "I never saw that likeness until now."

"You must have been blind, then. But here is a man coming towards us who is competent to speak on the subject. He is some sort of a half-cousin of hers—Mr. Webb."

"The Webb who is member for Gosworth—who married the Earl of ——'s daughter?"

"Yes. He and Lady Louisa used to be great patrons of mine, until, I think, they were disgusted because I was not anxious to become famous under their tutelage."

Mr. Webb was a tall, thin man, with a gray, careworn face, sunken gray eyes, a black wig, and an eye-glass which he kept nervously twitching about. He spoke in a hasty, confused manner, and had an odd fashion of not looking at you until he had got out the last word of the sentence, and then he glanced up as if to drive the sentence home. When I had been introduced to him, and when he had studied the picture for some considerable time, he muttered to himself, "Very good—very good—very good;" and then he turned sharply to me, with his eyes glancing towards his boots—

"Did she sit for this likeness?"

"No."

"Striking likeness—very striking likeness. Have you sold the picture?"

"No," said I. "Nor do I mean to sell it, if it is as clearly a likeness as you say."

This time he did look up, and fixed his sunken gray eyes on me in a curious way, as he said, slowly—

"May I venture to ask why you have taken that resolution?"

"Why, merely that I have no right to sell a portrait of anybody without his or her consent. Surely that is a sufficient reason. I did not know it was so much of a likeness until I was informed of it—or I should not have sent it here even."

"That is quite right—very right," he said; "but your objection to sell it—if otherwise you would sell it—does not apply to me. You may call it a family picture. But it is not as a likeness that I wish to have it. What do you say—what do you say? Perhaps we ought to have a little talk over it, if you don't mind the trouble. Let me see. Shall you be passing the House any time to-morrow?"

"I will keep any appointment you like to make," said I.

"I shall be down to-morrow about two. From that to four or five I shall be at your service."

With that he passed on to the other pictures.

"I congratulate you," said Heatherleigh. "I suppose you fancy that eccentric gentleman, who looks like a broken-down banker, is the victim of a good-natured whim. If you do, you make a mistake. With these few seconds looking over your picture, he could tell you more about it now than you know yourself. He has spent his life in studying and buying pictures, all over Europe, and, though he enjoys extending a little patronage now and again, like other men, he does not buy bad pictures out of charity. Take what you can get from him for your picture; for you may be sure he won't give you more than its value. Who knows but that he and Lady Louisa may take you up, and become your patrons, as in the old days? They were good enough to patronize me a little; but they found that I had little ambition; that I was lazy; that, when I went down to Clarges Castle, in Hants, I used to disappear for hours when I was most wanted, and be found smoking a pipe in a conservatory."

"Had they put up a tight rope for you across the lawn, or how were you expected to amuse your patrons?"

"Don't you make a mistake," said Heatherleigh; "the good graces, well-intentioned, of rich people are not to be despised. You should value the friendship of a rich man, not because he is rich, but because his being rich is a proof of the disinterestedness of his friendship. There! that sounds like a proverb; but it is common-sense."

Heatherleigh was rather in the habit of uttering maxims of this kind. Once, down at Brighton, Mr. Alfred Burnham got into a very bad temper with the billiard-marker at his hotel. There was no doubt about it, the marker had been trying on a bit of sharp practice, and lied about it; whereupon Alfred Burnham fell to cursing and swearing at him. The marker appealed to Heatherleigh, who listened attentively, and tried to smooth down the matter, when Burnham exclaimed—

"By Jove, Heatherleigh, you speak to a billiard-marker as if he were a gentleman!"

Whereupon Heatherleigh replied, with a sharp look in his eye—

"I speak courteously to a billiard-marker, not because *he* is a gentleman, but because *I* am."

Mr. Barnham pretended not to hear that remark, and made a very pretty losing-hazard, without, however, having previously touched either of the other balls.

When all the pictures had been gone over again and again, commented on, criticised, and their future chances canvassed, there was a general disposition towards pipes and beer. Those who could extemporize a seat or stool of any kind, did so; while those who were too tightly wedged in to move, struggled to open their coats, and get at their tobacco. Heatherleigh and one or two more of us got into a safe corner, and monopolized a small platform, whither was speedily brought one of the large jugs of ale that were now being introduced. In a remarkably short space of time the atmosphere had thickened, so that the blazing gas-lights were palpably pale. A dense blue atmosphere hung over the place, and the thicker it grew the louder grew the Babel of voices —with hurried jests, and scraps of welcome, and bits of criticism flying about, attacking the ear from all points, and leaving the brain somewhat bewildered. In our secluded corner, however, a choice company had assembled; one of them, a burly gentleman, in a velveteen coat and immense water-proof leggings, declaring that gallons of beer were useless in slaking his thirst, now that the Royal Academicians had made a drunkard of him.

"But why the Academicians?" said Heatherleigh.

"That was the very natural question Lady Osborne asked me last week," said he, with a laugh; "and I told her simply: 'I go to the Academy exhibitions every year as a duty; and of course I look out for the Academicians' works first. Well, of late I have found them so confoundedly bad that I had to go out after looking at each picture for a glass of brandy. I have been forced to become a drunkard in order to keep my stomach steady.'"

"I hope you didn't tell her ladyship the story in these words?" said one.

"More's the pity," said he, with a shrug. "Women would suffer a good deal less—I mean, they wouldn't so often be the victims of an idiotic delicacy—if, with them, language didn't stop at their necks and begin again at their ankles."

But if the Academy had taught him to drink brandy, he seemed to take very kindly to beer, as they all did, until the place got to be, as one of them said, "like Noah's ark in a thunder-storm, with all the animals roaring and kicking."

One man proposed to play pitch and toss as a quiet and intellectual amusement; another exclaimed that he was sick of it; a third retorted that one got sick of playing at pitch and toss only in crossing the Channel; a fourth blundered about the initials of two artists named Brown, and Heatherleigh consoled him by asking how the recording angel was likely to distinguish among the Welsh Joneses; another was deep in philosophy, maintained that a man must worship something, and that a man who cut himself off from all dogmatic religions must take to the worship of woman; Heatherleigh inquired of him if he meant that irreligious men went in for the woman of Babylon; a newspaper man, again, was describing a tenantry dinner he had been at in Kent, and swearing it was a capital one, by Gunter! while here and there were serious dissertations on the future of the new school, coupled with the question when England would gain the least bit of recognition in Continental galleries.

Heatherleigh had no fewer than four pictures on the walls, and he had other two in his studio, all of which he purposed sending into the Academy.

"Why not make it eight," I asked of him, "and be an R. A. in number, if not in name?"

"I am afraid eight would goad the hangmen into fury, and they might turn again and rend me. But I might sell one or two of the pictures that are here before then, and these I shall not send in."

Had they been cheeses he could not have treated the question in a more matter-of-fact way. Indeed, there was no concealing the fact that Heatherleigh regarded the Academy as a good sales-room, and looked forward to any reputation he might gain by his new pictures chiefly so far as that affected their price. He was far too honest a man to seek to hide these views of his; and he explained them with a simplicity which admitted of no argument. I noticed, also, that of late he had considerably increased his prices. Formerly he had been accustomed to treat the dealers who came about him in rather a cavalier fashion, bantering them, and so on; but he generally ended by letting the picture go for whatever they offered, and often, as I saw, much beneath its value.

"My getting seventy pounds instead of fifty for a picture won't better the quality of my bottled ale, will it?" he asked.

"No," I said; "but it might secure your being able to get bottled ale in those times when you may be unable to work."

"You mean that I ought to lay up for a rainy day?"

"Yes."

"I daren't begin, Ted; for I know the consequences. A man who has just what money he wants, with the chance of getting a little more by a little extra work, is in a happy position; but the man who saves ever so little pledges himself to a draining system. He is never satisfied with what he has saved. Its ignominious smallness haunts him, and drives him to unnecessary work, and unnecessary economies. God forbid that I should become avaricious, with my eyes open, Ted!"

"You talk nonsense," I said. "There is no reason why you should become avaricious. But when you have an extra ten-pound or twenty-pound note, why not put it into a drawer or into a bank, rather than invent some useless extravagance, as you do now, simply to get rid of it?"

"Then the ten-pound note would look shabby. I should say to myself, 'I must get a hundred pounds, instead of eighty, for this picture from Solomons.' Solomons comes up. We have talked about eighty pounds; I demand a hundred. Solomons is disgusted, begins to worry and bargain and deprecate and beseech. Inwardly I cry to myself, 'Good God! am I become a cheesemonger, that I must make my living thus?' Ultimately Solomons gives me ninety pounds; and I never see him afterwards without grudging him the ten pounds, and I never see my small savings without thinking, with a pang, that they ought to be ten pounds more. My dear boy, I don't see why a man should wilfully make his life a burden to him. When the rainy day does come, I shall know at least that I have enjoyed the sunshine. I don't envy the men who sit indoors all their life, disconsolately patching an umbrella."

Doubtless he meant all this when he said it; for, in theory, it was an exact reflex of his actual life. But my friend was much too wise a man to hanker after consistency, the stolid virtue of the Philister. Without a word as to what had led him to see the error of his ways, he changed his whole manner of living. I have already spoken of his increased activity, which at length developed into downright hard work. And now he demanded the highest price for his work that he was likely to get. The dealers were astonished to find the old, easy, profitable method of making a bargain no longer possible. They did not go off in a rage, as one might have expected; for Heatherleigh's pictures sold readily. He had a happy quickness in the selection of good subjects; he had a great power of dramatic and forcible grouping and treatment; and the workmanship of his pictures, though mannered, was invariably clever, striking, and much above that of nine tenths of the pictures the dealers sold.

At this little exhibition Mr. Solomons was present — a stout, good-looking man, much resembling in appearance and manner a Frankfort merchant, with a ruddy face, black and curly hair, a Jewish set of features, a seal-skin waistcoat, and a thick gold chain. He wore a ring on his forefinger, and spoke with a slightly German accent.

He was smoking a cigar when he came along and sat down by Heatherleigh.

"Have you sold any of these pictures of yours, Mr. Heatherleigh?"

"Not one, worshipful sir."

"I don't think you had any of them begun when I called at your place last. You must have lost no time over them."

"Do you mean to offer me thirty pounds less than their worth because you have discovered marks of haste?"

"I have not made you an offer at all yet—"

"And mayn't, you would say? Don't. Is this a time for buying and selling, Mr. Solomons? We are disposed to be generous to-night. It is unsafe to make bargains with the fumes of tobacco in the brain."

"Ah, Mr. Heatherleigh, I can remember when you treated us poor dealers in a different way—"

"And what return did you ever give me—except that box of cigars, and I admit they were of the best. But you know, Mr. Solomons, cigars are of no use to us poor devils; they disappear too quickly. Cigars were made for kings and picture-dealers."

"I don't know how kings are faring," said Mr. Solomons, "but I know it is a hard time for picture-dealers. People *won't* buy pictures. The state of business in the city is frightful, and it tells upon us directly. We *can't* sell a picture."

"What a merciful arrangement of Providence it is that a man who can't sell a picture is at least at liberty to buy one! But haven't you always been saying the same thing, any time these thirty years, Mr. Solomons? It is only a habit you have got into. You know, you will see a professional beggar, in the hottest day in summer, shivering with cold, and drawing his rags about him, simply out of habit."

"It is an ominous comparison, Mr. Heatherleigh. But there's no saying what may befall one, if one has to come between the artists and the public, submitting to the wit of the one and the indifference of the other—"

"While pocketing the money of both. But I am ashamed of you, Mr. Solomons, to hear you talk in that way, considering the harvest that surrounds you on every side. You look like a farmer standing in the middle of his sheaves, and cursing at Providence. However, I forgive you—"

"Thank you," said Mr. Solomons, with a sneer, indicative of a possible change in his temper.

"And, although this is not a time for buying and selling, as I said, what would you be disposed to give for that 'Kilmeny,' which is the work of my friend here? Mr. Ives—Mr. Solomons."

"How do you do, sir? I rather like that picture; there is a freshness about it which might attract a purchaser. Yet the subject is not a popular one, you know. Well, let me see, I shouldn't mind venturing fifty pounds upon it."

Heatherleigh burst into a fit of laughter.

"Why I will give him £100 for it myself, on the chance of making fifty per cent. by the bargain."

"Oh," said Mr. Solomons, coldly, "you think you will get £150 for that picture?"

"Yes."

"Then I wish you may get it," said Mr. Solomons, rising and walking off, apparently in high dudgeon.

"If impudence could withstand powder and shot," said Heatherleigh, "the seed of Abraham would by this time have changed the world into a big Judea. But don't imagine that he is much offended. Solomons never quarrels with his bread and butter; and that is the position in which we stand to him at present."

"There is something unnatural, it appears to me," I said, "in having the relations of dealer and artist reversed in that way. The dealer ought to be the patron; you, the artist, ought to be humble and grateful—"

"So I was at one time," said Heatherleigh. "Nor do I think that I took any advantage when I got the upper hand. I have let them off very easily—that is, hitherto. Now I mean to wake them up—"

"Why?"

"Because I have grown avaricious."

"Why have you grown avaricious?"

"Because I am getting old," he said, with a laugh.

On our way home (I had already remained out much longer than an invalid ought to have done), we talked more of this and of other matters, as we went up by Regent's Park, in the cold, clear night.

"I suppose," said Heatherleigh, "that if you had been left to yourself, without the advantage of my sage counsel and experience, you would have given the picture to Solomons for fifty pounds?"

"No, nor for £500 either," I said.

"But why?"

"Fancy a Frankfort Jew becoming the owner of—"

"Of a portrait of Hester Burnham."

"Exactly."

We walked on for some time in silence; and I suppose Heatherleigh had been running over all sorts of absurd deductions in his mind, for he said, just as we were nearing home—

"I once was very nearly thinking that Bonnie Lesley had fallen in love with you, but now I begin to think that you have fallen in love with Hester Burnham. The situation would be very romantic—but, for you, very uncomfortable, just at this particular time of day."

CHAPTER XXIII.

MY PATRON.

Next morning Polly Whistler came up to see us, and she had no sooner entered the room, breathless and excited, with a fine color in her pretty cheeks and gladness in her bright eyes, than she cried out—

"Oh, Ted, do you know that I have met three different people this morning whose first talk was about your picture! They are all astonished—you are going to turn the Academy upside down —and I declare, when I met the last of the three, and heard what he had to say, I was near crying for fair happiness. You know I've a great deal to do with it, Ted—I—I beg your pardon—"

"If you call me Mr. Ives again, Polly, as you did when I came back from Bucks, I shall order you out for instant execution."

"Because I begged of you not to alter it; and I knew what they would say of it—"

"And you helped me with it all through, Polly. It is too true. I must give up to you three fourths of all the honor and glory—"

"Though I could not understand, even at the time, how you managed to finish it, painting from me, without putting a trace of me into it. Mr. Heatherleigh says you will only be able to paint one face all your life—"

"Isn't it worth giving up a lifetime to paint, Polly?"

"Perhaps it is, but that wouldn't pay. But really, Ted, I'm very, very, very glad, and I hope I'm the very first to wish you joy, for our old acquaintance' sake, you know."

And the kind-hearted girl grew almost serious with the earnestness of her congratulations.

You would scarcely have known Polly now, so much had she changed during the past eighteen months. The old frank manner was still there, with the bright smile, the ready tongue, and fearless speech; but Polly had grown suddenly genteel in her dress. In the old days, it must be admitted, she had a trick of running to and from her home, wearing, to save trouble, the shawl in which she had 'sat' to this or the other artist—that is to say, when the shawl belonged to her own considerable stock of properties. I have met her in Granby Street, running home in the dusk, with the most wonderful articles of attire on her back; and not unfrequently with her shawl wrapped around her head in place of a bonnet. Now all that was over. Under my mother's tutelage and millinery aid, Polly dressed like a young lady—very plainly, it is true, but very neatly. Her own mother had at length been prevailed upon to go to Greenwich, on a pension granted her by her daughter; and Polly's spirits, never of the lowest, were now remarkably high in consequence. Nor did her efforts at self-improvement stop with her change of attire. My mother had taken a great fancy to the girl, and was instructing her in all manner of delicate housewifely arts. There never was a more willing pupil, there has seldom been a cleverer one. Quick in the "uptake," as the Scotch say, she was nimble with her fingers, and untiring in her perseverance. My mother was delighted with the duties of instructress, as most women are; and, not content with teaching Polly the secrets of womanly lore, she took to giving her lessons in French. My mother's pronunciation was not very good—how many years was it since she, a clergyman's daughter, had acquired the language?—but it was good enough for Polly, who soon began to be able to read French with tolerable ease. In other directions her efforts at self-improvement were equally strenuous and successful; and it must be remembered that her acquirements were immediately tested by the ready conversation she held with all the people who surrounded her. The information possessed by artists is, as a rule, remarkably many-sided; and as Polly did not hesitate for a moment in revealing the bent of her studies—especially in literature—she had the benefit of a good deal of extempore and suggestive criticism from the ready-witted and intelligent men with whom she passed most of her forenoons.

Some people would say that a girl of quick and sensitive nature, aiming at self-culture, should, as a preliminary step, have relinquished this calling by which she got her living. That was a point which never occurred to either her or my mother. These two simple-minded women were too pure and innocent to see anything wrong in a girl suffering her portrait to be daily painted, especially as her patrons were a small number of men who were well known to her and to each other. Indeed, Polly, with her bright ways and her clever speech, was the common friend of that small community, and there was not one of them who would not have directly and courageously broken the law of his country in order to administer a conclusive thrashing to any stranger who should dare to insult her. To every one it seemed a matter of course that she should remain in her old calling, except to Heatherleigh.

"It is a shame that a girl like that should be a model," he said to me, one evening, after a fit of gloomy meditation.

"Why, what harm does it do her?"

"No harm, truly. The girl could walk through anything, and consort with any kind of people, and yet preserve that fine freshness of character which springs from her fearless honesty."

"If that is so, why should she throw aside an occupation which is not arduous, which is well paid, and which she seems to enjoy?"

"Well, it seems a shame that she should be called a model, when you know what sort of women bear the same name."

"But that principle would make every calling in life dishonorable. Should a man be ashamed to be called a lawyer because there are some lawyers who are scoundrels? Should a woman be ashamed to be called a woman because there are many women who are drunken, perverted, and vicious?"

Heatherleigh did not answer, but he kicked away his landlady's cat from the fender (ordinarily, it was granted every liberty in the room, including the inspection of his breakfast-table), and sucked his wooden pipe fiercely.

However, Polly knew nothing of this discussion, and remained as she had been, perfectly satisfied with herself, and her friends, and her manner of living. I never saw a more contented or happy creature.

Towards the appointed hour I made my way down to Westminster, and to the House of Commons. When I arrived, the bell had just rung for a division, and the nondescript loungers who were hanging about were ignominiously swept into the corridor, to study the ill-lighted frescos. When the stir was over, and communication again established, I sent in my card to Mr. Webb, and in a few minutes he came out, hastily apologizing, in a nervous sort of way, for his having been detained. I accompanied him along another corridor and down some steps, until we arrived at a dingy and melancholy apartment, with small windows fronting, but not allowing you to look out on, the river, which he said was the smoking-room. In the partial dusk of this gloomy chamber one or two men, far apart and silent, sat and smoked disconsolately over a newspaper, there being nothing to disturb the silence beyond the muffled throbbing of the steamboat-paddles outside.

"I need not ask you if you smoke—let me give you a cigar," said Mr. Webb, as we sat down. "You must have consumed many a pipe over your 'Kilmeny.'"

"There is not much work in the picture," I said; "but it was painted under great disadvantages. I am merely an apprentice as yet, and, simply through my want of technical education, have to spend hours over what an experienced man would do in a few minutes."

"I understand," he said, "and I had some thought of speaking to you upon the point. I should say it was most important for you to get some such practical education, under a competent master, just at this period of your career, before you settle down into a mannerism which may keep you crude and unfinished all your life. I have been much interested in your picture; and I should not offer you the advice if I did not think you were improvable."

This he said with a slight smile; but most of his hesitating speech had been pointed at the corner of the table before us, and had been given out in sharp, quick, detached phrases.

"Where have you studied?"

"Nowhere, except under Heatherleigh. Then I have been a pretty constant attender at our life-class—"

"Ah, I know. May I ask if you have any sort of plans for the future?"

"None, except a wish to get wholly out of England for a time, that I may get away from certain influences I dislike, and—and—and, generally speaking, find my level."

"That is good, very good," he said, abruptly, "but vague. Don't think me impertinent if I ask further—do you depend on painting for a living?"

"Not wholly. I have a small income; but if I left England, I should have to leave pretty nearly the whole of it for my mother."

"You will find living abroad very cheap. What do you say to Munich? It is the cheapest town in Germany. It is the richest in point of art-treasures. Every facility is given you for study; and I have an excellent friend, Professor Kunzen, whose name you may have heard of in connection with the discussion about the Nibelungen frescos. Kunzen has some students; and an introduction from me would give you at once an instructor and a friend."

To leave England had long been a dream of mine, but now that it was put bluntly and practically before me, I involuntarily hesitated. To leave England, and live so long in a foreign land that the old places should grow strange to me—that, coming back, I should look at the great chestnuts of the avenue at Burnham, and scarcely know them again!

"You can turn the project over in your mind," he said; "it is worth your attention, and I shall be glad to give you any little assistance I can. You may depend on Kunzen. But to our present business. You said you had not sold 'Kilmeny?'"

"I have not sold it yet."

"You do not mean to keep by your resolution not to sell it?"

"Well," said I, "I will tell you frankly how the matter stands. You judge by my being here that I am willing to sell the picture; but I have come mainly because you were good enough to ask me. I would rather not sell the picture. Don't imagine I say so to tempt you to offer me a big price. I would rather not sell it, for the reason that I told you. On the other hand, I want the money, as I have been earning nothing for some months, through an accident I suffered."

"Good heavens!" he exclaimed, suddenly glancing at my arm, which was in a sling, "was it you who got shot instead of Hester—"

"Not instead of Miss Burnham," I said, "for the ball might not have hit her at all; but there is no mistake about my having been shot."

"This is extraordinary—very extraordinary," he said.

I saw him finger the card, which he still held in his hand. He had evidently forgotten my name, and was anxious to refresh his memory, but politeness prevented his doing so, and so I was probably Mr. Gyves or Mr. Jervis to him for the time being.

"Very extraordinary. My dear sir, we owe very much to you. I beg you will forgive my not having noticed the similarity of the name, which is perfectly familiar to me—"

What a good-natured fib that was!

"—And I hope our acquaintanceship will not cease with this matter of business. How stupid of Heatherleigh not to tell me! However, I must consider the picture mine; and you shall put your own price upon it—"

"Pardon me," I said, "we are still discussing business. Heatherleigh told me you knew the value of a picture better than any man of his acquaintance. I know nothing of it, and so—"

"And so I must make the offer? Good, I will give you £150 for the picture."

I looked at him with amazement. There was on his face none of that bland look of patronage with which a man generally exhibits his generosity. Indeed, the cold gray face was quite businesslike and calm.

"I am much obliged to you, Mr. Webb," I said, very much inclined to laugh, "but I would rather not be paid by you for having pushed your cousin out of danger."

"Good heavens!" he said, "how can you imagine such a thing! On my soul and honor, I would have bidden that sum for it at a public sale, partly, of course, because it is so quaint a transfiguration of Hester's face. If you think the price too high, name your own, but I tell you that you wrong yourself in taking less."

"Suppose it is exhibited at the Royal Academy, will you give me whatever is offered for it by anybody?"

"I will give you £20 more than the highest offer. Is it a bargain?"

"Yes."

"And I hope that our acquaintanceship will not terminate with this matter of business. Lady Louisa will be delighted, I am sure, to make your acquaintance."

So we parted, and I got out again into the roar of Westminster. In all that hurrying crowd of people, there was no one who suffered such pangs of remorse and shame as I did at that moment. I suppose when we are too well off we exaggerate minor causes of worry until we reach the common level of discontent; or it may be that some people are morbidly sensitive on particular points; but, at all events, I had no sooner got out of that dull smoking-room than I felt wretched and guilty. I had sold my honor for a mess of pottage. I had gone down to meet Mr. Webb in an irresolute frame of mind, tempted both ways, and yet hoping I should cling to the right side. I had succumbed to the temptation, and, through the dusk of the afternoon, my eyes seemed to wander up to that exhibition-room where "Kilmeny" stood, and looked out upon me with reproach in her mystic face.

I envied the jolly policemen who were cracking jokes with each other at the corner of Parliament Street, and the burly omnibus drivers with their ready fun, and the honest men and women who were going home, after a good day's labor, to their comfortable chimney-corners. Finally, I walked straight up to the exhibition-rooms.

Most of the pictures had been left there, so that the owners might send them directly on to the Royal Academy. I had

"Kilmeny" taken down and put into a cab; then I drove home and carried the picture up-stairs to my own room.

What should I do? On the one hand £150, or some approximate sum, would be an opportune nest-egg to leave with my mother, if I were to go to Germany. Then, if this little girl with the wondering face were to get into the Academy Exhibition, would not people talk of her, and might not the critics be kind to a beginner, and deal charitably with a first effort? That was a sore temptation. I sat and imagined all the possible scenes that might arise with this "Kilmeny" of mine, whom I had grown to love, hanging on the Academy walls. Would not Bonnie Lesley come, and let her beautiful large eyes light on it, and would she not say something generous about it? My mother, too, would see it and be glad. Perhaps—but I dare not think of Hester Burnham walking up to this picture, and reading all the tell-tale meaning of it.

It was a pretty dream—far more fascinating than any one can imagine who has not labored carefully and lovingly over a work of art, and then sees it ready to be sent abroad for recognition, with all the halo of possible success about it. And what if it should be successful—if people should praise it?

I turned and looked at the calm, strange face; and now the likeness seemed startling. It was Hester Burnham who stood there, with the calm, kindly eyes; and she seemed to say, "I have been with you many a still and silent day, in this very room, and we had got to know each other. We were friends. And now you would make money by the results of this intimacy; and you would have people talk of me, and idle crowds stare at me."

"Never with my will," said I, aloud.

I caught up a penknife that was lying on the table—I was in too great a hurry to answer this mute reproach to think of taking the picture from the back of the frame—and ran the keen edge through the canvas, up both sides, and across both ends, leaving only a narrow strip adhering to the frame. Then I rolled up the picture and put it in a drawer, and sat down in the dusk, cold, trembling, and contented.

The dusk deepened and grew dark. But before my eyes there came a series of lambent visions—all the bitter suggestions of what might have been. Bitter enough it was to look at these things; and yet I felt a certain austere sense of satisfaction with myself which was indeed a sort of grim happiness.

I was withdrawn from these reveries by the sound of voices. Polly and Heatherleigh had both chanced to visit us that evening, within a few minutes of each other. So I went down to meet them, bold and comfortable.

"What is the matter with you, Ted?" said my mother; "you are ghastly white."

"It is joy, mother; I have been offered £150 for the picture."

"A hundred and fifty!" said Polly, with her eyes widely open. "Mayn't I see it now?—you know it was not quite finished when I last saw it."

"It is down in the Sumner Exhibition-rooms," said Heatherleigh.

"No," said my mother, "it is up-stairs. I saw Ted bring it in this afternoon."

"Then I must see it," cried Polly. "Shall I go up, or will you bring it down?"

Determined that Heatherleigh should meanwhile know nothing of what had happened, I told Polly to come up-stairs with me. I lit a lamp, and went with her. When we entered the room I went forward to the table, and lifted the frame, with its margin of canvas.

"There, Polly, what do you think of 'Kilmeny' now?"

She looked at it for a moment in blank wonder, and then a sudden expression of alarm came into her eyes.

"Oh, Ted, what have you done?" she cried.

I sat down in the dimly lighted room, before the empty frame, and told her the whole history of the case. I explained, as well as I could, the necessity which had driven me to abandon all the hopes I had formed about "Kilmeny." When I had finished I looked up, a little surprised that Polly had nothing to say, either by way of agreement or condemnation. I found that the girl had buried her face in her hands, and I fancied she was crying.

CHAPTER XXIV.

THE ROYAL ACADEMY.

Once the thing definitely done and disposed of, I was much more contented. I bore with equanimity the silent reproach of my mother, and the fiercer indignation of Heatherleigh.

"You deserve to be hanged," he said. "I never saw such accursed pride in any one. You were not born a duke."

"Don't you know," said I, "that Miss Burnham and I made up our old misunderstanding, and became almost friends down there? And what if I had gone and publicly exhibited her, and sold her portrait, and tried to gain a reputation through the sweetness of her face?"

"Confound it!" was all he said. Then he added, "I fancied we were going into the Academy together—that we should celebrate the varnishing day together—that we should run the gauntlet of the critics together. I expected great things from the picture. I had told people about it. I expected more from it than ever I told you, because I wanted the reception it was sure to get to be a surprise to you. But you have always been like that—morbidly sensitive, wayward, extravagant. Did you never think of Bonnie Lesley coming to see it?"

"Of course I did. I have enjoyed in imagination all sorts of visits and all sorts of praises, which I should never have enjoyed in reality. But that is not the question, Heatherleigh. You talk as if I had had any option in the matter. I tell you that, rather than have sold Miss Burnham's portrait to that Jew, as you suggested, I would let him pull my teeth out one by one."

"That would have been reversing the order of nature. It was the Christians who pulled the Jews' teeth out, in accordance with the spirit of the New Testament. Why, do you know who proposed to be a purchaser?"

"Who?"

"Bonnie Lesley herself. She told me privately that she meant to offer you, without your knowing her name, a handsome sum, in order to give you confidence in yourself. She says you will never be an artist until you gain some artificial belief in yourself."

"What did you answer?"

"Only what I have said to yourself—that there is nothing to equal your modesty except your pride."

I pointed out to them all, however, that there was no use crying over spilled milk; and I looked forward with anxiety to the opening of the Academy Exhibition merely for the sake of Heatherleigh. Before the varnishing day arrived he had already ascertained that four of his pictures were hung—a very tolerable number for a man who had never cultivated the acquaintance of the Academicians. On the morning of the varnishing day he called upon me.

"I want you to come down with me."

"They won't let me in: I am not an exhibitor."

"Worse luck," said he; "but I think I can arrange about it."

So I agreed to accompany him. There would be no mortification in being turned away, as there would have been had I been a rejected contributor.

On our way down, he said—

"Did you cut your picture all to pieces?"

"No, certainly not."

"What do you mean to do with it?"

"Keep it for myself as a portrait. I am going to Germany soon: I shall take it with me."

"Why should you take a portrait of Hester Burnham with you?"

"I hope to take portraits of all my friends with me."

"Then I suppose you have asked Bonnie Lesley for her portrait?"

"Well, no; but I mean to do so."

"Why don't you thank me for reminding you?"

He smiled as he said this, and yet I did not care to inquire what he meant, for my thoughts were running on this great collection of pictures we were going to see, where my poor "Kilmeny," I fondly thought, might perhaps have had a place.

The Academy Exhibition was then in the National Gallery. I ascended the broad stone steps without much hope of being able to gain admission. Heatherleigh went up to the man who was passing people in, and I fancied there was a quiet look of intelligence on his face. He nodded to Heatherleigh. There was scarcely a word said, and in a second or two I found myself inside the entrance-hall.

"Have you brought no colors with you?" said Heatherleigh.

"No; why?"

"I should have let you touch up one or two of my pictures, to pass the time."

"I thought you never went through the farce of touching up or varnishing in the rooms?"

"Neither do I; but it might amuse you."

So we went up-stairs. In the first room there were two of Heatherleigh's pictures; one had an excellent place; the other was "floored," and in a corner.

"That leaves me in an equable frame of mind," he said, "so far as this room is concerned. Ha! what is this I see! They *have* given me a good place!"

He was passing through the door as he uttered these words. I could only look vaguely into the next room. There were several artists lounging about, one or two of them pretending to touch up their pictures; and one gentleman, mounted on very high steps, was carefully varnishing a remarkably small work which, it was evident, was never likely to be seen by anybody after his own eyes were withdrawn.

Heatherleigh turned to me.

"I am going to blindfold you, and lead you up to my 'Lady Teazle,' that you may be astonished—"

But it was too late. There, at the head of the room, from out of the wilderness of brilliant colors and gold frames, looked the calm face of "Kilmeny!" The wall seemed to dance before my eyes; the yellow frames became a misty spider's-web of gold, the delicate lines crossing and interweaving; and Kilmeny looked like a phantom amid these bewildering, moving splatches of color. It was like one of those half-conscious dreams in which you see the face of one who is dead, or as good as dead to you, and you quite well know that it is impossible the beautiful face should be so near you. I walked up to the picture in a kind of stupor; and met the gaze of the eyes that I knew. The picture did not melt into mist. I looked round about it, and the other pictures were stable.

"You are lucky," said a strange voice at my shoulder, and,

turning, I saw one of my companions of the life-class, a man who had just returned from Brittany. "Your first picture in the Academy, isn't it?"

"Yes," I said, with some fear that I was lying; and that "Kilmeny" would suddenly vanish, and be replaced by the real picture which ought to be there.

"Don't look so scared," said Heatherleigh. "It isn't a ghost, although many people will fancy that Kilmeny, with her wonderful face, has just come out of the land of spirits, with a cloud of impalpable dreams around her. Don't you think so, Jackson? It is the most visionary face that I have ever seen painted. Would you believe that Ives wanted to keep it at home—nay, had kept it at home, and that it is here against his will?"

With that he turned to me.

"Ted, your mother and I did it. She found the picture out; I carried it off and put it in another frame—I'll trouble you for £6 10*s.* when I come to pay Weavle's bill—and here you are. You won't be such a fool as to carry off the picture now—indeed, you dare not, for the Academicians would have your life. And look at the place they have given you—it is as good as a notice in the *Times.*"

Now it seemed to me that the man on the top of the tall steps was a great friend of mine. I hoped his picture was well-painted; I compassionated him in that it had been "skied;" I trusted he had pictures elsewhere. The other men, too, about the rooms—did they not suddenly assume a kindly expression? I was now a fellow-laborer of theirs; whereas, when I entered the place, I was an outcast and a stranger. I hoped they had all painted good pictures; that the public would be kind to them all; that they were all "on the line." Yet it was clear from many of their faces that it was possible to be above or below the line, and still be happy.

"What do you say, then?" asked Heatherleigh, a little timidly.

"Now it is done, I am glad you have done it."

"And I promise to tell Hester Burnham all about it, and that it was my doing."

"Yes, I suppose she will come here," I said, absently, for I fancied I could see her walk up to the picture.

"Undoubtedly. And Bonnie Lesley is coming to buy 'Kilmeny.' I have told her so much about it that she is jealous; and

I fancy, so soon as she has acquired possession of the picture, she will cut it to pieces more effectually than you did."

"She will have some difficulty in becoming the owner, as I promised to give it to Mr. Webb, if it got into the Academy, for £20 beyond what anybody might offer for it."

"It would be no bad plan, then, to get Bonnie Lesley to offer £500 for it. Of course you must take off a few pounds in consideration of the picture having been reduced in size by a couple of inches. Ted, my boy, I consider myself your best friend, and hereby invite myself to dine with you at Greenwich, now that the whitebait have come in."

We had a walk around the rooms; but I fancied the eyes of Kilmeny followed me, and they were not quite so reproachful as they had been.

"Now that I am in for it," said I to Heatherleigh, "I shall make the best or the worst of it. Could you get to know when Miss Burnham is likely to visit the exhibition?"

"I will try. What then?"

"I should like to come here, and watch her from a little distance, and see how she takes it."

"Ah, you wish to see the flush of pride and pleasure on her face?"

"No," I said, gravely enough—for it seemed to me that the temporary triumph of showing off my poor picture was but a trifle compared with other and life-long considerations—"I want to see if she understands why the picture is there, or if she misapprehends it altogether, and so is likely to raise another barrier between us, far more insuperable than the other, never to be removed. What if she were to think, even for a moment, that I had used her face to further my own ambition—that I had dared to demean her before all these people—do you think such a thought could ever be effaced from between us? And I should read it in her eyes in a moment!"

"Ted," said Heatherleigh, kindly, "that girl is more womanly and wise than you fancy. She will understand it, and she will understand you, without any interference of mine."

"And I ask of you not to mention the matter to her. It will be a test of confidence between us."

"So be it," he said; "but I fear you set too great store upon her interpretation of your motives."

CHAPTER XXV.

LEB' WOHL!

It was some little time before Hester Burnham came into town, and I waited with some impatience for her visit to the Academy. In the mean time the gracious eyes of Kilmeny had softened all the critics' hearts, and they talked of her in a way that filled me with gratitude. For somehow I fancied that, in praising her, they were praising that other Kilmeny, who still lingered among the Burnham woods, and I treasured up every scrap of criticism that had a word to say about the tenderness of her face or the wonder of her eyes.

I can remember the first criticism that appeared on the picture. Heatherleigh and I were seated in that dining-place near the top of Regent Street in which the members of the Sumner Society used to congregate. We were all alert in scanning the newspapers at this time (a few days after the opening of the exhibition) to see what our fate was to be. Heatherleigh had been attentively reading one of the morning-papers for some time, when, without a word, he handed it over to me.

"Kilmeny" was the first word I saw; and then, as I read on, it seemed to me as though there were behind the gray paper and type a kind and earnest face that I was not familiar with, and that nevertheless seemed to be filled with a grave and friendly interest. Is there any gratitude like the gratitude of a young artist to the first critic who speaks well of him, and lends him the wings of encouragement and hope? To my knowledge I have never seen this invisible friend who spoke so warmly and confidently about my first tentative effort; yet I have never forgotten the desire I experienced to know him and thank him, and how I came to fancy that, if I saw him anywhere, I should instantly recognize him.

Other writers, no less generous, spoke in a similar strain, until "Kilmeny" came to be looked on as one of the features of the exhibition. Could I wonder at it? It was a face, seen anywhere, that all men must worship; and the glamour of Kilmeny's eyes blinded them to the imperfections of my handiwork.

Of course, there was great joy in our small circle; and it was no uncommon thing for Polly to appear before we had sat down to breakfast, flourishing a newspaper in her hand. How she managed to get a look over all the papers published in London, at such an early hour, I never could make out; but one thing was certain, she never missed the least mention of Kilmeny's name.

I met Bonnie Lesley at the Lewisons' several times. We were on very intimate terms now; our past relations, and her confession, singularly enough, not having left a trace of restraint in her manner towards me.

We were very good friends, as I said; and I may hereafter say something of a notable excursion we made together to Richmond. Meanwhile, she had written to Hester Burnham to ask when she was coming to town.

"What a pity it is that Hester won't take a house in town, like other people," said Miss Lesley.

"If you got accustomed to living at Burnham, you would understand why she does not," I said.

"I suppose she is waiting for Mr. Alfred to take the house for her."

"I suppose so."

"It seems a pity," said Bonnie Lesley, musingly; "but you often see people who seem to have marriages made for them. They come in a natural sort of way, and you never think of avoiding them. I don't believe Hester cares much for her cousin, and yet you will see that she will drift into a marriage with him, quite involuntarily."

"Very likely."

"Indeed, I fancy she would marry him now, if he cared to ask her."

"Why doesn't he?"

"Well," she said, with a pretty smile, "it would be a *little* too apparent just now that she would have to support him. I dare say he is waiting to get some sort of position or commission, by way of excuse."

Then she added—

"Did I tell you she was coming to town on Monday? One advantage of her not having a house in London is that I get more of her when she comes. She will stay here; and on Tuesday, I should think, we shall go to the Academy. Will you meet us there?"

"I am afraid I can't promise."

"She knows all about the picture, you understand, and how all London is talking of her portrait."

"Did you tell her it was her portrait?" I asked, with a sudden qualm.

"Certainly—her portrait, more or less. But what was it Mr. Heatherleigh said about its being Hester clad in dreams? It is more that than a portrait."

Early on the Tuesday morning I went down to the front of the National Gallery, and walked up and down the east side of Trafalgar Square, waiting to see Mr. Lewison's brougham arrive. It was nearly twelve o'clock when I saw the easily recognized pair of chestnuts and the dark-green carriage coming along from the west. Still keeping some distance off, I saw the occupants get out—Bonnie Lesley, Mr. Lewison, Mrs. Lewison, and Hester Burnham. I saw her go up the broad steps—the small, graceful, queenly figure, and the long, floating, dark-brown hair causing her to look like the princess of one of the old Danish ballads—with Bonnie Lesley, in her brilliant costume of blue and white, at her side. Then they went inside, and were lost from sight.

I slunk into the place. The crowd was dense; but I made my way to the corner of the room in which "Kilmeny" was hung, that I might see how she would walk up to the picture and look at it. I was barely in time; for they had gone straight thither. I could see Bonnie Lesley laughing merrily; and there was on Hester Burnham's face a confused, timid smile. They approached the picture. The smile died away from her face. In its stead there was a strange, wistful look, as one might look at one's portrait of many years ago; and just at that moment I caught the wonderful likeness between the weirdness of Kilmeny's eyes and her own. It was imagination, doubtless; but it seemed to me as if the living Kilmeny stood there, with the wonders of the other world upon her, a vision among men.

"Nae smile was seen on Kilmeny's face;
As still was her look, and as still was her ee,
As the stillness that sleeps on the emeraut lea,
Or the mist that sleeps on a waveless sea."

In the middle of the dense, chattering mass of people she stood, and it seemed as though the breath of heaven still clung about her, and made an impassable barrier around her, separating her from the crowd. I could not stand there any more. I went forward to her suddenly, and took her hand. She looked up, in a bewildered sort of way, and then a faint blush sprang to her face.

"You are not vexed that this should be here?" I said.

She glanced into my eyes for a moment—with a look that I shall never forget—and then she said, slowly, and in a voice so low that no one around could hear—

"I thank you."

With that Bonnie Lesley came forward and protested blithely there should be no quarrelling—and so forth, and so forth. I escaped from them out into the open air, and walked I knew not whither, with a new life tingling within me. I walked on blindly. The man who has never been so keenly happy as to be unable to remain at rest has never known the extreme of happiness. There was not in London a drunker man than I was at that moment.

Hester Barnham remained in town some three weeks. I never saw her during this time. I dared not go near the house; and by some means or other managed to evade Mrs. Lewison's repeated invitations. I was engaged in preparing for my going abroad, and was busy.

Yet the autumn was approaching before I was ready to start. Mr. Webb, who had become the owner of "Kilmeny," had crowned his many friendly acts by arranging that I should not only join Professor Kunzen's pupils, but also board in the Professor's house. And when everything was ready, and all my plans of operations sketched out, I privately slipped away down into Buckinghamshire, to bid good-bye to the woods of Barnham.

It is worth while, I think, for a man to become an artist that he may learn to perceive the picturesqueness of a dull and windy day. Summer as it was, the broad plains and far hills of Bucks looked strangely forlorn; and there was a wild picturesqueness about the masses of flying gray cloud, and the sombre hedges, and the dark oaks that were clearly and gloomily marked against the pale sky. The Barnham valley, stretching up from Missenden, looked like one of those intense, low-toned French landscapes, in which you seem to perceive the blowing of a bleak and blustering wind. But, although I wandered all about the familiar places during this long and desolate day, I dared not go near Burnham.

It was night when I went up there—a dark night, with no stars visible. A cold wind came over the hills, and you could hear the rustle of innumerable trees in the darkness. Any one less acquainted with the road would have had a hard fight to avoid the hedges; but I knew every step of the way, and at length found myself in the great avenue leading up to Burnham House.

There was no sight or sound discernible around the solitary building—only the murmur of the wind through the cedars and the beeches. Nor was there any light in the windows; for the family lived in the more modern part of the house, which was not visible from the front. But it was on this space in front of the house that Hester Burnham and I used to play, many a year ago, when we were children; and it was here I used to wait for her until I saw her bright face at the window above.

If the window would but open now! Here, in the darkness, might not one speak freely and boldly, and say good-bye as it ought to be said? If the window were but open, and Kilmeny there, listening! I could almost imagine that she was actually there at this moment, and I looked up in the darkness, and whispered—

"Listen, before I go! Let me tell you, now, when it won't matter. I have loved you always; I shall love you always. You cannot prevent me loving you. I have loved you since ever I was able to look into your eyes; and I must love you to the end. Now, good-bye, and may God guard you, my very dearest, and keep you safe from harm."

There was no sound in reply but the rustle of the leaves. The great front of the house remained still and silent, the windows cold and dark. So I turned away from Burnham, and from my love; and nothing seemed to say good-bye, except it were the tall and ghostly trees, as the cold wind of the night blew through them.

CHAPTER XXVI.

THE VILLA LORENZ.

"GOOD-MORNING, Mr. Sun! How do you do this morning, and how have you slept? I hope you are going to bring us a bright and pretty day; for the Herr Papaken, and the Frau Mamaken, and Annele and I are all going out for a walk in the Englischer Garten. Good-morning, Mr. Linden-tree! And how have you slept? You—handsome old man that you are—you must not think of turning yellow yet. Good-morning, Messieurs et Mesdames Sparrows! I shall have some crumbs for you presently."

I became drowsily aware that the soft and pretty German I heard came from the lips of little Lena Kunzen, who had just thrown her casements open, to let the sunlight into her small chamber, which was apparently next to mine. I jumped out of bed, and found the morning well advanced, a golden flood of light falling over the smooth pastures and stately trees of the English garden, and on the branch of the Isar that runs through and around and about them.

The Königin Strasse of Munich is, as you may know, a long and quiet street that leads down from the Hofgarten and skirts the Englischer Garten, the handsome trees of which it fronts. Here dwelt the Herr Professor Kunzen, his kindly, commonplace wife, and his wicked and witching little daughter. Anybody who is familiar with the sort of houses in the suburbs of Leipsic, or Berlin, or Baden, will know what the Villa Lorenz was like—a large, square, white house, with white casements outside all the windows, and with white balconies projecting from the first story, these balconies hung with trailing creepers of various kinds, tumbling in masses of light-green leaves about the white porch. Then a small enclosure in front, with a small white statue, and fountain in the centre, separated from the street by a row of acacias, with here and there a rowan-tree and a sumach, just getting crimson. Behind, a larger garden, with bowers covered with Virginia creepers, and another dirty-white figure and a fountain.

The Professor was a tall, well-made man of about fifty, with a shy, womanish sensitiveness about his ways and manner which did not seem to correspond with his athletic frame and his prodigious pedestrian powers. But it accorded well with his face when you came to know it—when you got to see its emotional softness, and the quick way that a blush would spring to the pale and rather sunken cheek, whenever the Professor had given way to a sudden access of enthusiasm. Such occasions were rare; for he was a very shy man, who did not like to disclose himself. He was full of strong and generous sympathies, the fruit of a remarkably simple and childlike nature; but he had got into such a habit of hiding away his inner feelings, that you would have considered him merely a thoughtful-looking man, timid in manner, and with strong tendencies towards idealism in his dark, soft, deeply intrenched eyes.

His wife was a short, rather dumpy woman, a shrewd and sensible housekeeper, practical in her notions, and very fond of her husband, over whose negligent habits and odd ways she was continually complaining. I think she looked upon him as half-mad; and was thankful he had had the sense to marry a woman capable of looking after him and his house. As for his pictures, she knew nothing of them beyond the price they fetched. She was proud to see his name in the papers, and she behaved with circumspection when great people visited the Villa Lorenz; but she took care to make it understood that she would not talk about art.

"He knows enough for both of us," she used to say, sensibly; "I busy myself with other matters."

Under the circumstances, there could be no great communion between man and wife. The Professor never revealed his solitary enthusiasms to his spouse; and she was satisfied in doing her duty as regarded the wonderful freshness and purity of the linen of the house, and also as regarded the cooking. There were several things she always cooked herself; and her honest face beamed with pleasure if you praised her preserves. The Frau Professor's coffee I have never found equalled anywhere.

Now, how did this strangely assorted couple ever come to have such a daughter as little Lena Kunzen? This small witch, with her short light-brown curls, and her big gray eyes that were full of mischief, was a perpetual torment to her surprised and grieved mother, and a perpetual puzzle to the shy Professor, who used to sit and watch her as if he wondered if this wild creature were really a daughter of his. The fun of it was that both of them loved her to distraction; for, with a kitten's drollery, she had a kitten's captivating ways, and could get atonement at any moment for her mad pranks by a little fondling and coaxing. She was about fifteen, but a perfect child in most respects; and, doubtless, much of her waywardness of manner and habit had arisen from the fact that she had mixed little with strangers, and had been allowed to do pretty much as she liked in her own home. Sometimes, too, the wild, madcap spirit seemed to go right out of her, and she sat mute and pensive, with a look of her father's dreaminess about her eyes. At such times she used to show a strong resemblance to a portrait of a shoemaker's daughter, which you will find in the second room of Stieler's "Portraits of the Most Beautiful Women," in the Festsaalbau. This latter is a face that is unforgetable. It has all the finer characteristics of the intellectual South German face—the broad forehead, the calm, reflective eye, the delicately shaped nose, the short upper lip, and that peculiar deeply cut under lip which one never finds out of Germany. Let me add, here, that my greatest trouble in all my art-studies in Germany was with this type of face. It seems almost impossible for an English artist to escape from painting the self-consciousness which is the obvious characteristic of the finest English female faces. You will find the type of German face of which I speak painted by English artists, and while the features are there, there is superadded that pitiful trick of consciousness which is only not a smirk because the lips are thoughtful. The difficulty is to give the wonderful self-possession and self-regardlessness of such a face, without making it merely commonplace and dull. It is a difficulty; and an Englishman, I fancy, can only get over it by change of climate—by leaving our cold and fogs and bustle for the warmer air and the mellower life of the South. If one of the women whom Raphael painted had been introduced to our life-class as a model, what harsh and coarse interpretations of her would have been the result!

To return to Lena. Her constant companion was a small white goat, which had been given her as a present. It was variously called Anna, Annele, and Aennchen; and its mistress was fond of expressing her love for her favorite by singing—

"Aennchen von Tharau ist, die mir gefällt,
Sie ist mein Leben, mein Gut und mein Geld;
Aennchen von Tharau hat wieder ihr Herz
Auf mich gerichtet in Freud' und in Schmerz;"

and then, at other times, she would sing, to a tune of her own, the plaintive old lines—

"Isch 's Anneli nit do?
S' wird regne, wird schneie,
S' wird 's Anneli g'wiss reue.
Isch 's Anneli nit do?"

By rights, Aennchen von Tharau should have been a gentle and timid creature, so that she and her mistress might have looked like the group of the pretty goatherd and her pet, which is a favorite subject for lithographs. On the contrary, the small white Aennchen was a demon of wickedness; and it was fortunate that her malice was not equalled by her strength. She loved to run at children unawares, taking a mean advantage of them from behind, and tumbling them at the feet of their nurses. Indeed, she had all manner of tricks; which were rather encouraged than repressed by her mistress, who used to shout with laughter when Annele had done something especially naughty. The same spirit appeared to dwell in both; and Lena used to lament bitterly that her goat should be prevented by nature from enjoying the fun of hearing my blunders among the German verbs. Lena was wont to tell her friends that, on the first day I dined there, I had offered her some "Pantoffelnsalat"—an audacious figment, which used to make her laugh till the tears ran down her cheeks.

Lena had a lover. His name was Franz Vogl; and he was one of the Professor's half-dozen pupils. Vogl was not a handsome lover. Nature seemed to have meant him for a comedian—his face having precisely that odd irregularity which nearly every comic actor exhibits. But in every other way Franz was a most desirable sweetheart. He was full of fun; he was immensely good-hearted and kind; he was never out of spirits; and he played the zither in a way that won all hearts to him. I have heard the zither played by many people, but never as Franz Vogl played it. In his hands it became another instrument. It lost all the twanginess of the guitar, and gave forth such wails of passionate feeling—so human-like in the cry—that, when it was all over, the people used to look at Vogl's humorous, commonplace face, and wonder whether he were not a magician.

"Franz, Franz," Lena would often cry, petulantly, "why can't you teach me to play the zither?"

"You will never be able to play the zither, Linele."

He was a Waldshuter, and constantly used the rustic diminutives, and frequently the rustic dialect, he had learned when young.

"But why, why, why, Franz? I don't understand what you say about the thrill at the end of your fingers. Is it electricity?"

"Perhaps it is. At all events, without that, you will never do more with the zither than what most people do—play a jerky sort of music, in the ordinary, staccato fashion."

"And I can see your fingers hovering over the strings, until the cry of the music in the air makes me think of a human voice overhead, and I get almost afraid. Did you see how that dear little Marie Schleiermann cried last night when you were playing the *Chant bohémien?*"

"That was because poor Friedrich Kink used to play it. I was a fool not to remember that."

"But your playing makes me so wretched sometimes that I am near crying, too. Franz, you are conceited, and you won't teach me to play the zither because you will have nobody but yourself make people cry."

"I will teach you the zither, if you like, Linele."

"Oh, yes! To go strum, strum—twang, twang—like old Frau Becher and her guitar. No! I want to be able to make it cry and sob, and then laugh again; I want to do everything; and, oh, my poor Aennchen, I can't do anything."

With which she would clasp Annele around the neck, and pretend to whimper.

I have never seen any man who enjoyed life better than Franz Vogl. It was a part of his simple and joyous nature to be pleased with whatever he happened to be doing, and that in a hearty, happy way which was remarkably infectious. He was never conscious that he was enjoying himself, as Heatherleigh was; nor did he pause to estimate the value of his various enjoyments. He sang for the pleasure of singing; he painted because he liked painting; he enjoyed a conversation with a wagon-driver about the weather and fields, or with a learned doctor about the deluge. He enjoyed sleeping, eating, drinking, walking, and sitting still; and you always found him ready with a joke and a laugh at any time. His father was, in his way, an artist. He had a studio some little distance from Waldshut, and there he got up and painted crucifixes, and those various pictures and decorations which adorn the small way-side shrines of the peasantry. He was also a bit of a sculptor, and had himself, with his own methods, hewn out one or two very passable figures for the same purpose. Furthermore, he had a moderately sized farm; and Franz being the only son, the farm was to fall to him in due course. So his future was pretty well cared for; and Franz took good care to enjoy the present.

He was far more of a musician than a painter. Sitting by himself, over his beloved zither, that was his constant companion morning and evening, he used to improvise in the most wonderful fashion; harmonizing his melodies as he went along, until you lost sight of the mechanical effort, and seemed to hear him speak with this magnificent, many-toned voice. He had a general liking for all the arts, and a tolerable proficiency in several. His pictures were clever, and had a certain novelty of manner about them; but Franz set little store by them, and it was clear he was not going to be a great artist.

"If I had an ambition," he often said to me, "it would be to write a whole series of songs in my native dialect, and set them to music."

"You can't feel the want of a hobby much," I said, "so long as you have your zither."

"No," he said, "I shouldn't get on very well without my zither. 'Öbbis muess me ze triebe ha, sust het me langi Wil.'* I always take my zither with me when I go on my pedestrian excursions. By the way, you will accompany us on our grand autumn excursion?"

"I hope so."

"Down through the Gutach-Thal, and around by the Constance Lake, and then, hey! for a swing through the clear air and the cold sunsets of the Tyrol!"

In the mean time we were busy enough with those opportunities of study which this wonderful city afforded. Every alternate morning we went with the Professor to the Old or the New Pinathothek, and there he, singling out some particular picture, discussed its various characteristics and those of the school to which

* "Etwas muss man zu treiben haben, sonst hat man lange Weile."

it belonged. Occasionally we paid a visit to the grand Nibelungen frescos, not then finished, until Kriemhild and Siegfried, the red-bearded and dark-browed Hagen, Brünhild, and all the other personages of the mighty drama were familiar to us as our own friends. I confess that, at first, I was a trifle disappointed with Kriemhild, the

. . . "schœne magedin,
Daz in allen Landen niht schœners mohte sin;"

and looked upon her face as characterless and wanting in emotional expression. But in time the traditions of English facial painting faded away from me, and I got to understand the stately repose of the women of the old Flemish and German and Italian painters. Then we had our exercises in composition, which were grievous things for exposing one's ignorance of the rough material of art. A solecism or anachronism in costume, for example, was instantly picked out by the somewhat wondering Professor, whose severest reproof was a hint that you must have been misled by some theatrical scene. Of all our little company, I was the most backward in this respect. I knew as little how to deal with such a subject as "Savoyardenkinder auf der Wanderschaft" as with such a one as "Cervantes wird von dem Arnauten Manni als Sklave nach Algier gebracht." When the Professor announced that the subject for the following Monday's sketch would be "Carl I. von England nimmt Abschied von seinen Kindern," he added, with a smile—

"This time, Herr Edward"—so he invariably named me, finding some difficulty in pronouncing "Ives"—"you will have the advantage. You must be familiar with the costumes of your own country."

I don't know that, Herr Professor," said I. "With its present costume, I am."

"The majority of your countrymen are *sans-culottes*—nicht wahr?" said Franz Vogl with a laugh. "However, I suppose Charles I. of England dressed in the French fashion of the time. You English are fond of French importations, are you not?"

"Yes; we could afford, however, to do without some of them—eggs and dramas, for example."

"The chief manufactures of England," said Vogl, "are lords and beggars. But you can't produce kings. Let me see, you haven't had an English king since Edward VI."

"You produce so many here that you can supply the markets of the world with them," I said; "and then they have had the advantage of an economical bringing-up."

"Well, the kings we have sent you, excepting William of Orange, were rather a stupid lot, certainly; but they were a good deal better than the Stuarts."

"They couldn't be worse," I said, "but they tried."

So the days passed peacefully away, in the quiet, white city. Franz and I became great friends; and many a merry walk we had, and many a merry chat in the beer-garden "Zum Tivoli," on the wooden benches, under the great limes, fronting the narrow strip of the Isar that runs around the Englischer Garten. I had a letter from England occasionally; sometimes from Polly Whistler; sometimes from Heatherleigh, who had become a thorn in the side of the dealers; and two letters I had received from Bonnie Lesley, containing abundant gossip about Burnham.

"People have not yet done speaking about 'Kilmeny,'" she added. "When are you going to send us another picture over? And this time, mind, it must be no likeness; or, if a likeness—well, I will say no more. I send you, as you wish, a bit of the great St. John's-wort from the Burnham woods. I wrote for it to Hester, who desires to be remembered to you. But I dare say you have forgotten us all, and are walking every evening with some pretty Fräulein along the long green avenues near the Isar. Or do you buy her gloves in the Maximilian Strasse? Or do you take her to hear Wagner's operas in the Hoftheater; and does she call you 'du' yet? Good-bye. If you are not too much engaged to answer this impertinent note, address me at Burnham, whither I go on Monday next."

When I got such a letter as this, breathing of English life and associations, I used to go out into the "English garden," and lie down on the banks of the Isar, near that great open space of meadow in the middle of the trees. Lying here, with the bulbous spires of the Domkirche shut out from sight, you might imagine yourself in an English park; and I used to try to make myself believe that I was looking over upon the Burnham woods. Very few people entered the garden during the day, and those who did kept to the shaded walks under the lindens and elms. Lying quite alone there, I used to read and re-read those portions of my letters which spoke of Buckinghamshire, until I should scarcely have been surprised had I seen Miss Hester herself come walking over to me from among the trees. For, indeed, my heart was a sort of carrier-pigeon; and the moment I let it loose, it flew straight back to Burnham, and only folded its wings at the feet of my dear mistress.

CHAPTER XXVII.

DAS WANDERLEBEN.

I THANK God for Germany. It was there that I first began to throw off the hideous thrall that had weighed upon my life in England. It was there, properly speaking, that I began to live. Out of that whirl of anxious struggling, with its petty ambitions, its envious competitions, its narrow interests, its bitter fears, that had at one time overawed and, later on, sickened me, I had got into the more beautiful, simple, joyous life of South Germany. Here was no agonized fretting and scrambling after wealth, but a peaceful moderation, and contented enjoyment of small means. Well do I remember the half-conscious blush of enthusiasm that passed over the face of the good Professor, as we stood above the great Gutach-Thal, and looked down upon its green fields, its rushing stream, and the steep sides of the mountains covered with a dense green forest. We had come over from Hausach, and walked along the wonderful valley, on either side the precipitous and wooded hills steeped in a glorious sunlight. From Tryberg we had followed the winding road that leads up the mountain to St. Georgen, and now, as we stood some five thousand feet above the level of the sea, and looked down into the still, vast hollow, a more charming picture of pastoral life could not have been conceived. Far below us, a long wooden wagon, drawn by a couple of oxen, was coming slowly up the hill. By its side were two women, with large white hats and black rosettes, with short petticoats, puffy white sleeves, and bronzed arms bare from the elbow. A young girl was with them, whose profuse light-brown hair hung in two long twisted tails down her back. There were few people now in the fields, for the afternoon sun had begun to glow with a lurid brilliancy on the gleaming scarlet bunches of rowans, a row of which beautiful trees came up all the way from Tryberg. One side of the ravine lay in shadow; along the other the warm light fell on immense stretches of forest that rose up to the pale green sky. Underneath our feet, and yet far above the bottom of the glen, a large hawk sailed in the air, sometimes fluttering for a few seconds, and then poising himself and remaining motionless.

"I will venture to call this the Happy Valley," said the Professor, with a sudden burst of enthusiasm. "Here you will find neither rich people nor poor people; but all have fair labor and moderate means, and a healthy and virtuous life. In England, Herr Edward, you are all too rich or too poor; and your rich are growing rapidly richer, while your poor are growing rapidly poorer. What is your general percentage of pauperism?"

"Twenty-three per cent., I believe."

"Herr Je!" exclaimed the Professor. "Here, I will undertake to say, you will not find three people out of every hundred who are unable to work, and who live upon charity. Is it that your taxes weigh too heavily on the poor; or do you pay too expensively for your kings and their circle; or is your population increasing more rapidly than your trade; or are your poor wasteful and extravagant when they have work, and mean-spirited when they have none?"

"Du!" said Franz, maliciously, addressing one of our small company, by name Silber. "Do you know why the Gutach-Thal has always been a prosperous, contented place?"

"No," said Silber, a heavy-looking, fair young man from the Rhine country, who dressed like a theatrical student, and wore his flaxen hair down to his shoulders.

"Because the people are Protestants. You have not seen a road-side crucifix all the way up from Tryberg."

"Do the crucifixes keep the corn from growing?" growled the practical Silber, who was a good Catholic and an indifferent painter.

We had all sat down by this time. Almost instinctively Franz unslung the case which held his zither, took out the instrument, laid it across his knees, and let his fingers wander for a second or two over the strings. And then he sang, in a careless sort of fashion, the story of Schiller's maiden, who came, like Kilmeny, no one knew whence, into a valley like the one at our feet—

"Sie war nicht in dem Thal geboren,
Man wusste nicht, woher sie kam,
Und schnell war ihre Spur verloren,
Sobald das Mädchen Abschied nahm."

And then he sung a tender farewell to the Gutach-Thal, and greeted it "ein tausend Mal," as we got up and went on our way.

Franz was not much of a singer; but you forgot that in listening to the wonderful tones of the zither. His singing was a sort of excuse for his playing; and what was lacking in his voice was more than made up by the extraordinary, pathetic power of the instrument that he loved so well. Every spare half-hour of this memorable excursion was devoted to the zither; and his stock of music was literally inexhaustible. Above all, however, he preferred the old *Volkslieder* of the Black Forest and the Tyrol; and many a glad evening we spent in remote country inns, with Franz's music as our only speech.

We stayed this night at St. Georgen, on the top of the mountain. There were no other strangers in the solitary inn except a young girl and her father, who were going on next day to Hausach by the *Eilwagen*. She was a pretty sort of girl, with dark hair and eyes, and a mobile, sensitive face. During dinner—we all happened to dine at the same time—Franz became very good friends with the Herr Papa, chiefly by reason of his miraculous flow of stories, which kept the old gentleman laughing from one end of the meal to the other. After dinner, said Franz:

"Does your daughter sing, sir?"

"Oh, yes, she sings a little."

"Will you be so friendly, Fräulein, as to sing a little song, and I will give you an accompaniment? Or will you hear me first? My companions are tired of me and my zither; and I shall be glad to have a new audience."

But we all sat down at the table, when it was cleared, and the candles were lit; then we took out our cigars and pipes, and Franz placed his zither before him.

"Perhaps you can play yourself, Fräulein?" he asked.

"No," she said, with a smile. "We are from Cologne."

"Then our southern songs may be a novelty to you. Do you know 'Es ritt ein Jägersmann über die Flur?'"

"Ach, Gott, yes! But I could hear it a hundred times," she said, softly.

So he sang the pathetic ballad, and the thrilling joy and tenderness and agony that he woke from the strings of the zither seemed to make the song almost a dramatic impersonation. You could see the huntsman riding gayly home, blowing his horn to let his "Herzliebchen" know he was coming. Then his wonder that she was not at the threshold to kiss him—his entrance into the house—no meal ready for him, no wine in his cup; and then his finding his heart's love lying cold and dead among the flowers in the garden. Then, with sharper and bitterer music, how he unbridled his horse for the last time, and set him free; how he took down his gun again from the wall and loaded it with "deadly lead;" and how, with one final, despairing carol of his hunting-song, he "went home to his heart's love."

> "Drauf stimmt er an den Jagdgesang,
> Den lauten und fröhlichen Hörnerklang,
> Trarah! trarah! trarah!
> Und ging zum Herzliebchen heim."

"Sir, you make that instrument speak," said the girl's father; as for her, she sat quite still and silent, but I fancied I could see a slightly tremulous motion of her under lip.

We had the merriest of evenings in this old Gasthaus. The Fräulein's Herr Papa and the Professor were soon deep in a conversation about the Black Forest people; and the Papa, who had been living in Hüfingen, proudly declared that the whole population of the town could produce no more than half-a-dozen paupers—six poor old women, who inhabited the barn-like building bequeathed by Prince Fürstenberg. So we younger ones were left to our singing; and the Fräulein, with the dark eyes and the pretty smile, sang too, in a timid way. We had Dr. Eisenbart, whose wondrous skill could make the blind to walk and the lame to see; we had Herr Oloff, who met with the Erl-king's daughter, and grew deathly white and died; Franz gave us that devil-may-care ditty, "Ich gehe meinen Schlendrian;" and Silber, being from the Rhine-country, could not help singing the "Loreley." When they asked me for an old English ballad, I felt puzzled. Have we any? Scotland is rich in old songs; Ireland has plenty; but England—? So I took refuge in the Tyrol; and sang them the song of the lover who plaited a garland of flowers, and bound his heart in it, and laid it at his sweetheart's feet.

It was a merry evening, and it was a merry morning that followed; for as we crossed the top of the mountain, and looked away down into the south, we saw the sunlight lying on the long, dark-green hills of the Black Forest, and above them, rising faintly in the far horizon, the splendid line of the Bernese Alps. The prospect of this magnificent plain, with its undulating masses of forest, its scattered villages, and its winding river-track, filled us with joy, for it said, "Henceforth you are cut off from cities. You shall wander along by river and valley, by farmstead and village, forgetting the pallid faces and the sluggish ways of the dwellers in towns. Your hunger will grow sharp, your thirst keen, your sleep profound and sweet. Then up again and away in the morning, through the fine cool air!"

Ye gods! how hungry one became in that rare atmosphere! Cold veal, brown bread, and red Tischwein became a feast to us; but when we fell upon a more favored spot, where a good landlady could transform the veal into a luxurious and occult "Falscher Vogel;" and when she produced from her cunning cupboard a bottle of Affenthaler, then we found no words to express our delight.

"Soon," said Franz, "we shall leave the land of the 'Falscher Vogel' for the land of the 'Schnitzel.' We shall see no more of the dark-green forest; beeches and birches will mix with the firs. We are going farther, to fare worse."

His heart clung about the Black Forest, his native country. I think he would fain have darted away from us, and gone down by Donaueschingen and Lenzkirch and St. Blasien to his beloved Waldshut. He was just a trifle sad as we turned our back on the dark-green woods, and entered the valley of the Danube, near where the great river rises, a small spring, in Prince Fürstenberg's garden. But his melancholy did not last long. The day was lovely. On each side of the valley the great mountains were covered with beech, now turning red and yellow, and the sunlight burned along these successive slopes. So we wandered on; and down by Thalmühle, in the heart of the hollow, we came upon a small inn, that had a bowling-alley in the garden.

"Who will challenge me?" said the Professor, with a laugh.

"I will," replied Silber, who had lived in Mainz, and fancied he knew how to hit the front pin at the proper angle.

We called for some beer: the Professor threw off his coat, and took up one of the large balls. He kept his long legs rather apart, balancing himself; and then, without moving a foot, he lowered his right arm, and with a rapid sweep sent the ball spinning up the alley. There was a rumble and a crash, and the whole nine pins were lying in a confused heap.

"Silber pays for the beer," remarked Franz, with a laugh.

And so it turned out. The Professor had not forgotten his skill since his student days; and Silber had but a poor chance against that powerful arm, the lithe and supple frame, and dark, sure eye. It is needless to say that Franz accompanied the performance with some music; and the landlord, who had come with the beer, hung about and stared at the musician, as the latter "made the zither speak."

We lingered some little while in this beautiful valley, making such sketches and studies as were thought desirable. Then on again, with Franz singing his doggerel verse—

"Ich bin der Graf von Freischütz,
Der so gern hinter 'm Ofen sitzt,
Der Tag und Nacht marschirt,
Hunger leidet und halb verfriert."

We left the course of the young Danube and drew southward towards the infancy of the mightier Rhine, entering upon that wide plain which, between Engen and Singen, is studded with huge volcanic peaks, rising abruptly from the level soil. How did the old nobles build their spacious strongholds on the summit of these perpendicular peaks—the splendid Hohenhöwen, Hohentwiel, Hohenstaffeln, Hohenkrähen? Did the peasantry fly away from the neighborhood in which such a whim had overtaken their lord, or did they meekly submit to it, and spend their toilsome days in dragging huge blocks of masonry up the sharp and rugged cones? At all events, the ruins of the castles still stand there, miracles of human labor and perseverance, far surpassing those on the Rhine. And all the country about seemed still and quiet around these memorials of ancient power. The fields that stretched for miles around the foot of the isolated peaks were as silent as the great Raubvogel that spread its wings and hung motionless in the air, spying for some fluttering bird or creeping thing in the valley beneath. But here, also, there was peace and comfort; and we had a good laugh over the sorrows of the only man we found in the district who seemed to complain.

This was a stone-breaker—an old man, with bleared, wistful eyes, that had a strange, innocent look of surprise in them. I cannot express in words the feeling which this old man's look gave one; but it seemed somehow the half-frightened, half-pitiful glance of a boy that was busy with some appointed task, and raised his head apprehensively as his master approached. There was something very touching in this queer look, which appeared to say that the man had been doing his best all his life, and hoped he was doing right.

Of course, Franz began to talk to him; and we, who could only gather odd words and sentences, understood enough to see that the man's whole life and interest were confined to his occupation. He spoke of the different kinds of stones as if they were sly fellows who had to be cunningly treated; and, as he spoke about a very good kind of stone, there was a half-comical grin on his face, as if he had said—

"We can get on very well with that merry little devil of a stone. He is easy to break; he lies well on the roads. Ah! he is a good helper to us, that funny little stone."

Then his face fell again, and he turned to his work, and said, with a sigh—

"D' Welt word alle Tag schleachter—s' ist en böse Zit für üs arme Lüt, dia so alt sind."

And then he murmured something about his poor pay and his struggle with the world. But it turned out that he made a florin a day; and Franz was immensely tickled by the affected sorrows of a stone-breaker who could make only 10*s.* a week; some of my readers may fancy that a poor wage for a working-man; but consider that, whereas in England the working-man's beer costs him fivepence a quart, in Germany it costs a penny; that a penny in Germany will get a pound of bread, for which in England he pays twopence; and that most articles required by the working-man are to be got in the latter proportion. Why, the people who chop wood in the by-streets of Munich can make a florin and a half per day, or 15*s.* a week.

It was towards dusk on a lovely evening that we drew near to

Constance, and the long lake shone a light crimson under the sunset. Far down in the southeast a cold, blue mist had gathered along its shores and under the great, purple masses of the Tyrolese Alps, that seemed to encircle the horizon; but here at hand, under the white town, the still, clear waters lay with scarcely a ripple on their surface to break the splendid glow of color. Overhead the last flush of the sunset struck along the golden bars of cloud and then died out in the pale green of the east; while the distant mountains had a touch of red along their peaks, where the great shoulders rose out of the pale mist. So still was the lake! And as the evening deepened, the keen colors faded out, and the white mist came up and lay all over the breadth of the water; while the orange lights of Constance began to twinkle in the dusk, and a small steamer in the harbor ran up its colored lamps.

We had letters awaiting us. A long epistle from Heatherleigh I shall give presently; but I may insert here the brief note which Lena Kunzen sent her lover. Franz was deeply disgusted by it, as he had been expecting a tender and affectionate letter. He showed it to me, with a rueful countenance. It ran in this fashion:

"MÜNCHEN, *Tuesday*.

"Fräulein Annele von Tharau presents her compliments to Herr Franz, and hopes he is a good boy. She is quite well, and in good spirits; was out for a walk in the Englischer Garten this morning, and accidentally ran against a little Scotchman, who was dressed in the peculiar costume of his country. The little Scotchman tumbled and cried. The Frau Mütterlein was for cuffing Annele; but she was saved from that indignity. Hopes the Herr Papa is well. Will be glad to hear from the honorable company of travellers, and thinks that a hat such as is worn by the young ladies of Innsbruck might become Fräulein Lena well, and be a pretty present, if Herr Franz is also of that opinion. Fräulein Annele commends herself."

"She is a little devil of a girl," said Franz, disconsolately.

CHAPTER XXVIII.

FATHER AND SON.

"My dear Ted, it is to you alone that I can write fully of all that has befallen me during the past few days. If we could only go out now, in the dusk of the evening, and have one of our old saunters around the Serpentine, with the yellow lamps burning in the gray, and courting couples regarding warily our approach! But then it rains at present, and you—you lucky dog—are down in the clear South, where night is like day, and the stars, I dare be sworn, are shining over the Bodensee. Hang you!

"A week ago I got a letter from home. It was the first time that I had seen my father's handwriting or the familiar crest for many years.

"'Come,' said I to myself, 'are we all about to become sensible, and is the world getting to an end?'

"You remember that I told you how I parted from my family when I was young. The cause of that parting I cannot help feeling as bitterly now as then; and yet, what is the use of it? What is the use of keeping up old grudges? But there are some things a man cannot forget.

"Pride helped to widen the breach. It is a fault that runs in our family, and a good deal of it has run my way. There is only one person I know who, in that direction, is a bigger fool than myself; and that's you. However, to cut the matter short, my father told me that he was coming up to town in a day or two, and would call upon me. I was surprised, but contented.

"He came up one forenoon, looking just as he used to look, but a trifle grayer. He was stiff and cold in his manner, as though he would have it known that he had not come as a suppliant. He looked with some contempt around my studio, and then fixed his eyes on the table, where some beer and tobacco stood.

"'Will you put that pipe and the ashes away? The smell is abominable.'

"I carried them into my bedroom, and put them on the mantel-piece. Then I returned. It was an affecting meeting between a father and son who had not seen each other for something like nine years, was it not? And yet, I declare to you, Ted, there seemed to hover between me and him an almost invisible shape, tender and delicate and beautiful; and I felt all the bitterness of the old irreparable wrong rising within me. Call me what you like—unnatural, insensate: there the feeling was, and how could I make believe to be friendly? At the very moment, too, I knew that my darling in heaven, if she could have interposed between us, would have besought our reconciliation. I felt that also. But when a man's wife has been insulted, does the husband care for the pleading of the frightened face that would fain come between?

"'I am sorry to see you in such a place,' he said, looking around.

"'I am very comfortable,' said I.

"He sat down.

"'This unhappy estrangement has lasted long enough between us.'

"'I think it has, sir.'

"'I am glad you think so. You have doubtless seen more of the world since you took that step which—which—"

"'Which I don't regret having taken,' said I.

"'Let us talk sensibly. Let us understand each other,' he continued. 'There is no use in recalling what is over and gone. There were—hem!—faults on both sides, I dare say. You must see now that it would have been most imprudent of you to have married—'

"'I thought we were to forget those things, for form's sake,' I said, feeling my cheek flush. 'But since you have recalled them, let me tell you that I shall never forget them—that the more I see of the world, the more despicable and cowardly seems the conduct of you and yours to that poor girl. Do you fancy I did not marry her because of the underhand ways you took to prevent the marriage? God knows it was for a far different reason; but not the less do I remember what you tried to do at that time, and the memory of it has gone on bearing heavy interest ever since.'

"I am sorry I said this, Ted. For what was the use of saying it? I should have let the thing go; and then my father might have had the satisfaction of thinking that he and I were likely to get back to our old terms. But you who know me, know that that is impossible in this world. I hope I do not bear my father any ill-will. I should like to do anything in my power to please him. But there is no man living whom I am so anxious to avoid.

"'Confound it,' he said, 'let all that alone. Let us talk sensibly, like two men of the world. You are no longer a boy. You know the advantages of a good name, of a position, money, and its comforts. I am willing to make a bargain with you—to let by-gones be by-gones, and that you should come back home again, and take up your proper place in the house.'

"For a moment I thought with an involuntary shudder of having to meet this man's face every day—recalling another face! Then I reflected that, after all, I was his son, and owed him a certain duty.

"'Very well, sir,' I said; 'I have no objection to go and live in your house. Of course, I have my profession, which I should like to follow—'

"'As an amusement,' he interposed, hastily.

"'Very well,' said I; 'I am not artist-mad, as I used to be.'

"Even as I gave in this half-adhesion to his proposal, a startling thought suggested itself—What if I should only go home to be again placed in an attitude of antagonism to all my relatives? Did my father think of this at the same moment?

"'There is another subject I want to drop you a hint about, that may make your return to us more attractive. Of course you must marry some day or other. Now it has occurred to us that there is a certain young lady, a neighbor of ours, who would prove a suitable wife—that is, of course, of *course*, if you were to become fond of each other. God forbid there should be any money-marriage between you, without affection. I am proud to say that our family does not need that method of increasing its fortune; it can stand by itself. But at the same time, the young lady is young, not bad-looking, and they say she has never even thought of anybody, while the junction of the Whitby lands with ours—'

"'Oh, you mean Miss Whitby?'

"'Exactly. I hope you have nothing to say against the girl?'

"'Nothing. On the contrary, she was a charming creature, in

pinafores, when I last had the pleasure of her acquaintance. And so you make my marrying Miss Whitby the condition of my returning home?'

"'How can you dream of such a thing?" he said, earnestly enough. 'You do not know that the match would be agreeable to the young lady. No. I merely suggested it as a very desirable thing; and I don't see what is to interfere with such an arrangement. The girl is a most amiable girl, according to all accounts; and the marriage would be a most sensible one. My dear boy, you are now well up in years—'

"'Yes, sir; and I have acquired very fixed notions as to what it is worth one's while to live for. Oddly enough, these notions, that have been growing upon me, are rather romantic. I was much more prosaic at twenty. Then I had a profound admiration for great wealth, and had a curious sort of belief that if I could get vast sums of money, I should be able to drink proportionately large quantities of champagne, and so forth, and so forth. I have no longer any ambition that way. I should like to have a lot of money, on account of the security it gives one in accepting certain responsibilities; but I have grown sceptical about its supreme power. The older I get, the more romantic I get, and the more absurd become my notions of what it is that is alone of value in life. Now, if you were to offer me the marquisate of Westminster on condition of my marrying Miss Whitby, I should find no difficulty in saying No.'

"'What do you mean? Have you anything to say against the girl?'

"'Nothing. But I shall prevent your wasting more time by telling you how the case stands. A good many years ago you practically turned me out of your house because I wanted to marry a girl who was poor. If I went back with you now, I might very soon find myself in the same position again—'

"'Be reasonable!' cried my father. 'Or are you saying that out of revenge?'

"'Certainly not,' I answered. 'During these few years I have grown so accustomed to my independent ways and narrow means that I had forgotten any wish to find myself in another condition. I was—I am—quite content, and quite ready to abide as I am. It may be those books you used to dislike, or it may be my own stupidity; but I am quite content. I have also thought of marrying; and, if I marry, I shall marry a girl who is even poorer than myself.'

"'Good God! are you mad?' exclaimed my father.

"'I hope not. I have not asked her to marry me—she may want to marry somebody else, for aught I know. She is an honest woman; she has a bright, affectionate, amiable nature—just the sort of nature to sweeten a poor man's life and make it pleasant to him; and she is a good deal prettier than Miss Whitby, I dare say, though that is not of so much consequence to a middle-aged man. If she will marry me, I shall look forward with confidence to having a pleasant and intelligent companion—one who has known poverty, and can brave it—one who is not afraid of the chances of life—in short, a good, pure, honest, affectionate girl, with not a taint of fashionable ways or self-regarding notions about her.'

"'But who is she?—what is she?'

"'Well, sir, she is at present a model.'

"I confess to you, Ted, that I had been looking forward to the surprise of this declaration as a good joke (are you surprised, too, old man?), and was inclined to be highly amused by my father's consternation. But it suddenly occurred to me that in his resentment he might say something *about her* that I should have to remember forever; and so I hastily added—

"'Don't be alarmed, sir. Nothing may come of it. In the first place, I shall not marry until I have enough money to make a small provision for my wife. I have already saved up £800—I heard that you sunk more than that on the north farm last year—and I am working hard to increase the amount. It is only, as yet, a dream of mine—a fancy that I like to speculate upon; and it has at least added a good deal of interest to my work.'

"'And so,' continued my father, slowly, 'you actually contemplate marrying a model—a woman—'

"'Pardon me, sir,' I broke in, 'but if you will reflect that you are talking about her who *may* be my wife, you will see that it might be as well to say nothing hastily. Like most outsiders, you may have mistaken notions about models—I don't know; but, at all events, it is premature to trouble yourself about the matter. I suppose, too, there won't be much use, in the face of such a possibility, in our talking further about that arrangement you proposed?'

"With that he broke forth suddenly—

"'What? Do you think, sir, I shall let you bring a shameless woman into my house—a woman who allows herself to—'

"'Stop!' I said. 'We are no longer father and son, but two men. You turned me out of your house: shall I turn you out of mine? By heavens! if you utter another word against that girl, you shall have to choose between the stair and the window!'

"The old story, Ted—the old story—hasty words and angry passions, to be remembered and regretted for many a day. But who should appear in the room at this moment but Polly herself. She did not come in. She stood at the open door, her hand on the handle, her face white as death. We had been speaking sufficiently loud; she had heard everything as she came up the stairs. What her most unexpected errand had been, I cannot tell; but the coincidence was terrible.

"Look back over the minute account I have written. You will see that her name was never mentioned. But in the sharp crisis neither she nor I remembered that: we both took everything for granted. I went forward to her, and said, firmly—

"'Come in, Polly. It is better you should hear this out.'

"There was that wild, pitiful, scared look on her face that she wore the evening she heard her drunken mother's ravings. I was overwhelmed with pity for her, and also with that ghastly consciousness of powerlessness to retrieve what is past redemption that crushes a man sometimes.

"'I have heard quite enough,' she said, with a strange calmness; 'and I came in to let you know that I heard it.'

"'It is the second time you have been insulted in this room,' I said, 'and, please Heaven, it shall be the last. The first time it was your mother; now it is my father. We have got rid of the one; now let us settle with the other, and put the matter beyond interference. It is rather odd that people should have to talk so of their parents, isn't it? But it happens sometimes. And so—'

"'And so,' said my father, 'this is the young lady you mean to marry. I am sorry, miss, that you heard what was said; but —but—'

"'But it was better I should,' said Polly, quite calmly; 'because, you see, I can remove this misunderstanding between you. I do not know what you want your son to do; but I beg you to believe that I shall be no hindrance to it, for I will never be his wife.'

"Then she went to the door, pale and self-possessed. I thought of stopping her; but what would have been the good? My father and I were left alone.

"'Well, sir, are you satisfied?' he asked, coldly.

"'I shall be when you leave the house,' I answered.

"'Then you still persist in your determination to marry a girl whose profession must at least put her under the ban of suspicion?'

"But the thought of the poor girl going out, with that burning sense of shame around her, into the lonely streets, recalled me to my senses. I snatched a cap, left my father standing there, and hurried after her.

"The arrangement you made when you left has proved a comfortable one; she has been living ever since with your mother; and the two seemed very fond of each other. Of course, I could not go up there so often as I did when you were at home; but I visited the small household occasionally, and each time had another opportunity of noticing Polly's obedient and daughter-like ways, and your mother's affection for her. I guessed that she would go straight there on leaving Granby Street; and I hastened around to your house by the route I fancied she would take. I saw nothing of her on the way. When I got to the house I asked for your mother; and I was shown up to the parlor, which was empty. In a little while your mother came into the room, and I could see by the expression of her face that she knew everything, and that she was much vexed and disturbed.

"'Polly has told you,' I said.

"'Yes,' she answered; 'you cannot fancy how bitterly your father's words have wounded her. You know how she has been schooling herself—learning things—and taking every opportunity of self-improvement. Whether she had any purpose in all this is more than I can say; but now she is cast down utterly, and wounded far more deeply than you can imagine. I have appealed to her self-respect; but she has been so deeply humiliated that she is quite prostrated. There is another thing, also. She blames herself for having opened the door, and she is covered with shame to think that she should have taken it for granted that you and your father were speaking of her.'

"'But we *were* speaking of her: and she must have known it. What is to be done to relieve the poor girl's sufferings? I know how sensitive she is; and how she must feel all this vexing nonsense. Tell her I wish to see her, only for a minute.'

"'If you were to see her now, in her present mood, you would make the thing irrevocable,' said your mother. 'It may be so as it is.'

"'What do you mean?'

"'I know Polly very well—better than you do. Under her happy and good-natured ways there lies a firm will; and if she were to resolve at this moment that she will never see you again, she would keep her word. Be advised: leave her to herself. I will do what I can to help you—that is, if you think you will be happier in marrying her than in becoming a rich man.'

"Your mother said this with a peculiar smile, Ted, that made her face look lovely, and yet a trifle sad. Does she know that you told me her story?

"'If you marry her,' she added, gravely and kindly, 'you will get a true wife, tender-hearted and honest, whom you will be always able to trust, who will be the same to you in good or in bad circumstances. And you will get a wife who will look up to you, and give you her love as the only thing she can offer you. I must not advise you to do it, Mr. Heatherleigh. There may be great inducements on the other side; and there are people who, in your position, would be ruined by such a marriage. But you are no longer a very young man. You know what you have to expect in life. You must make your choice.'

"'My choice is made—was made long ago; and I shall rely upon your aid,' I said, very gratefully.

"When I got out into the open air, Ted, it seemed to have been all a mistake or a dream. I asked myself if it was possible that people should permit themselves to be so deeply vexed—should, perhaps, alter all their plans in life—in consequence of half-a-dozen words. Why, all the circumstances of the world were just as they were an hour before. London had got a little nearer its dinner-time, that was all. Yet these half-dozen impalpable words had knocked our lives completely off their ordinary axes; and were likely to interfere with the future in a very remarkable fashion. I fancied if I could have got hold of Polly, and shown her the absurdity of vexing herself about two or three insignificant words, resolvable into their original letters, she would have been willing to send them into this alphabetic chaos, and pay them no further attention. These words had altered neither her nor me, nor anything: why heed them? They had not even altered to the extent of an apple the stall of that old woman at the corner to whom you gave the five shillings when you sold your picture. Yet with women words are powerful.

"Nor have I been able to see her since. She was to have given me some sittings for a picture I have just begun, yet she has never made her appearance. So far as I can learn she has sat to nobody since that unlucky forenoon. I can't get a glimpse of her. I have called twice to see your mother; and, on both occasions, Polly, who was in the house, declined coming down.

"You will say this is very absurd, and so it is. But I am getting to be somewhat uneasy, especially as your mother looks rather grave over the matter. She says Polly's deep hurt is far from being healed, and that the girl says, quite calmly and fixedly, that, whatever my resolutions may be as regards my father and myself, nothing will interfere with her determination. Your mother, I suppose, has been pleading my cause, and Polly only replies—

"'I have still some self-respect left. It is not necessary that I should marry anybody, least of all into a family where I should be despised.'

"If she would only let me see her for a few minutes, I think I could reason her out of this deplorable resolution. Where is *my* family, I should like to know? In the mean while the perplexity of the position harasses me. I cannot work, and I cannot remain idle; I cannot even read. I have tried to cut my anxiety to pieces by analysis, but I have no sooner got to the end of some chapter on the influence of the mental emotions on the vital functions, than I fling the confounded book aside, and wonder whether I shall ever get to see Polly. Even Marcus Aurelius, whom I used to look upon as a charm against all the evils of life, goads me into fury. Many a time have I looked from that calm and lofty pinnacle of philosophy, whence all human ills become beautiful objects of contemplation, but then they were the ills of other people that I was contemplating. 'All that is from the gods is full of providence,' says the emperor, but it may also be full of pain

"One thing I have resolved upon. If ever I get the chance, I shall marry Polly out of hand, and thereafter there will be no question of divided interests. Let me know what you think of the whole matter.

"I have selfishly reserved this long letter for my own affairs, and I can only add a line to say with what anxiety your friends here look forward to your next work. Tell we how your studies, so far, have moulded your intentions. Your sympathies are wholly Northern, I think;—I shall never forget your scornful and unfair contrast between the Nibelungenlied and the writings of poor Chateaubriand. You are always unjust to France and the French, while your strong natural bent for Northern simplicity, naturalness, and rough, untrained emotions leads you to overrate what is crude in art. Munich, however, is a city of eclecticism, and you will probably have your sympathies widened. When you get back to Munich, I wish you would send me a minute description of whatever of Wohlgemuth's work you can find. I am curious, and a little sceptical, about Dürer's obligations to him.

"Farewell! I will address a brief note to you at Innsbruck."

So here was the story out at last. I was not much surprised by Heatherleigh's announcement. It was easy to guess that something very important must have occurred to effect such a complete change in his notions and habits as he had recently exhibited. The Heatherleigh of this later period was very unlike, in many things, the easy-going, indolent Heatherleigh of other years, who used to lounge about in his roughly epicurean fashion; at times sharply interrupting his Bohemian life by fits of splendor and extravagance. It was easy to guess that Heatherleigh meant to do something with the money which he was now so industriously hoarding; for the notion of Heatherleigh hoarding money for his own use or satisfaction was too preposterous to be entertained for a moment.

Nor could there be much doubt about the way in which Polly would otherwise have regarded his proposal. I fancied she had read his secret, and was as busily, though with far greater shyness and closeness, preparing for the marriage, as he himself. I saw in these various efforts at self-improvement she was so laboriously making, so many honest and praiseworthy efforts to make herself more worthy of the man whom she loved. My mother took care never to hint anything of the kind. She praised Polly's industry, and to us, when Polly was absent, she was never tired of eulogizing the girl's sweetness of temper, and general brightness and cleverness.

"She is one in a thousand," she used to say. "Who could have expected to find a girl brought up all her life in London so winning in her fearless, simple ways? She has the cleverness of the town, and the natural frankness and good-nature of the country, and whoever marries her will marry a good, honest woman."

It did seem hard that these two, so cunningly preparing for a long, life partnership—laying in stores, as it were, wherewith to furnish their nest when the happy spring-time came—should thus be separated. But I knew Polly's extreme sensitiveness, and her indomitable firmness, and I was a good deal less surprised than apprehensive in reading Heatherleigh's story of what had happened.

Her position was by far the more painful of the two. I could imagine the poor girl brooding over the cruel wound that had been dealt to her self-respect, and resolving that there was but one way in which she could clear herself in her own eyes. It was a cruel method of repelling an unjust accusation, whichever way she resolved. I knew that she must be suffering with all the keenness of pain that accompanies a deeply sensitive nature; and when I went up-stairs to bed that night, and looked out and saw, above the misty waters of the Constance lake, the far constellations of the northern heavens, I fancied those cold stars were shining down upon the huddled darkness of London, and I knew that they saw few more unhappy faces there than the pleasant one that Heatherleigh loved.

CHAPTER XXIX.

THE SONG OF WÖLUNDUR.

"You see," remarked the Professor, "it is our only German lake; and therefore we are very proud of it. And is it not a noble lake?"

He might well say so. We were standing on a little height outside the town—the huddled white houses, spires, and boats of

Constance on our right—and there before us lay the long lake, an intense pale blue, so clear and still that the square-sailed little boats, which caught the sunlight on their yellow canvas, seemed to hang in mid-air. Out into this blue ran wooded promontories; the green bays between, with their occasional villa, being faintly mirrored in the smooth water. And then, far beyond the jutting points of Romanshorn and Friedrichshafen, overlooking the lake, and yet appearing strangely distant in the white haze of the morning sunlight, the grand range of the Vorarlberg mountains, with the jagged Kurfirsten and the snow-flecked Sentis down in the south.

We remained in the neighborhood of Constance for three days, filling our portfolios with sketches. Certainly there was no lack of material; for the autumn was now wearing on, and the mists that hung about the lake and the mountains in the morning, or gathered over in the evening, produced a constant series of new effects. Vogl was a lover of mist. He used to describe the strange white clouds that sometimes hang over the dark firs of the Black Forest, even when the morning sunlight is lying yellow on the valleys, and falling here and there into the wet woods. He used to describe the wonderful stillness of the forest under this white canopy, that just touches the tops of the dark trees, leaving a sort of twilight underneath, where the air is moist and laden with resinous odors; how you go in among the moss and brackens that are heavy with dew, expecting at every footfall to startle a wild-eyed roe; and how the clouds slowly gather themselves together and draw upwards to the hill-tops, as if they were covering the stealthy flight of Diana, when she has left Endymion, "pale with her last kiss," to waken in the cold morning freshness.

"I paid Lena out for her impudence," said Vogl to me privately, as we sailed down the lake to Bregenz.

"How?"

"I wrote her a short note in the broadest Black Forest dialect, and she will puzzle over it for days. It is even worse when written than when spoken. What would you make of this, for example?"

He put a bit of paper on his zither-case, resting it on the paddle-box, and wrote—"Ech woas es nit, wenn i ka Zagarta kuma, darno will der's saga, wegem Schoppa biatza, i kinnt jetzt che kuma, aber i ha nit der Wiel, du häschmer au scho en mänga G'falle than."*

"It is a very good conundrum," I said, "but I give it up. And I don't envy you when you come to read the answer that Lena will send you."

"Nothing keeps Lena a quiet and good little girl like the zither. So soon as she gets away from the charm of it, she is wild, impudent, untractable. But she will make a good little wife, will Lenele, when we grow old enough to marry."

"What does the Herr Professor say about it?"

"He does not care. I suppose he does not know that we are sweethearts. Yet he knows that she writes to me, and I to her; and that we go out together always."

"And the Frau Mamma?"

"Oh, she is a good, homely woman. She has friends in Waldshut, and they know that my father is pretty well off. The Mütterlein will make no objection."

"And the Fräulein Caroline herself?"

"I am puzzled," said Franz, with a comic look of bewilderment. "Lena is a Will-o'-the-wisp. I can't catch her. She won't talk seriously. But being sweethearts with her is very pleasant, and if she won't marry me, I can't help it. If she marries anybody else, I must take to singing all the heart-broken songs; but I sha'n't break my own heart for all that. I was not made for it, *lieber Freund*," he added, gayly; "love affairs will never interfere with my liking for 'Falscher Vogel,' stewed apples, and red wine."

"Yet you could support the character of the heart-broken lover so well—you could fly away from the sound of the mill-wheel and become a minstrel, and wander up and down the world, singing from house to house."

"Ah," said he, "when I hear the song of the broken ring, I begin to fancy there is some truth in all that business of love and despair."

I looked at the zither-case; I knew he could not help turning his hand to it. Only speak of songs, and Franz mechanically be-

* Which, in ordinary German, would be something like this: "Ich weiss es nicht, wenn ich auf Besuch kommen kann; dann will ich dir's sagen, wegen dem Kittel flicken. Ich könnte jetzt schon kommen, aber ich habe keine Zeit; du hast mir auch schon manchen Gefallen gethan."

gan to undo the leather strap, and pull out the zither, and touch the strings. This time he played the pretty Tyrolese waltz that Donizetti has introduced into "La Figlia del Reggimento," and then the music somehow led him into the old Tyrolese song that I have already mentioned—

> "Herzig's Schatzerl, lass dich herzen,
> Ich vergeh' vor Liebesschmerzen,
> Und du weisst es ja zu wohl
> Dass ich dich ewig lieben soll!"

He sang it almost to himself; and the simple pathetic melody was mingled with the sound of the paddle-wheels, as we churned our way through the blue waters down to Bregenz.

All during this beautiful time I was haunted in a way that is scarcely expressible in words by the imagined presence of Hester Burnham. Quite in spite of myself, I kept continually picturing her as she would appear if some miracle were to bring her into the same boat or the same hotel. Then would follow long imaginary talks with her; and visions of the wonder of her eyes and the delight of her face as something especially beautiful came in our way. I got to look at everything just as if she were by my side; and I judged of it as she would be likely to judge of it. Now, when I look back upon this journey, it seems as if the whole of it were imbued with her presence. I cannot think of that steamboat on the lake without seeming to see there a small figure, dressed in black, with a certain graceful and queenly carriage about it, with a strange honesty and tenderness in the eyes, and a calm, wistful beauty in the dark clear face. Indeed, so deep-rooted had this habit become, that I should not have been in the least surprised had I in reality encountered her. So far as the influence of her presence was concerned, she was actually there, with me, wherever I went. I began to forget that it could only be by a sort of miracle that we should meet. I came down-stairs in the morning, half expecting to hear her voice at the breakfast-table; and then I used to feel a kind of accepted disappointment in seeing that the room was empty. When I saw at any distance a girlish figure dressed something like an English lady, it was with a secret hope that I drew nearer. Why was it so impossible we should meet? Why should she not come this way for her autumn tour; and then, some morning, as I go down and into the large bare apartment, with its long table and rows of cups and napkins, lo! standing at the window, with her face half-hidden in the light, the lady of many dreams?

What shall I do? Why, you know, we are in Germany now! England and its coldness, its harsh ways and cruel thoughts, are gone from us. This is the home of the old romances; and the breath of this land tells you even now that a woman's love is something better than money, and better worth striving for. I go forward to her. I say, "Hester, I dared not tell you in England that I loved you: here, in Germany, I must tell you. Will you give me your love in return for mine? Will you be my wife, and let us go away together, our backs upon England, into the green valleys of the Tyrol? We are free here; and I think we love each other very dearly." I can see a look of heaven in her eyes. She puts her hand upon mine, light as the touch of a rose-leaf, and says, with that strange smile of hers, "We do love each other: why should we not always be together?"

Ach, Gott! These were the pictures that hovered before my eyes during all this journey. Strange, too, that in these day-dreams she always appeared alone. I never granted for a moment the presence of any one else. And doubtless the small girlish figure seemed rather solitary at this time—the only mistress of the great house at Burnham, with no near relations, with few companions, and leading all by herself a quiet country life, attending to her duties, with apparently no wish to alter the current of her existence. That small lady was a striking figure to me; and the great woods of Burnham, and the loneliness of the Burnham valley, made her individuality, her solitariness, all the more vivid and distinct.

My constant thought was, if I could only meet her here, apart from all the old associations that separated us in England, I would venture everything upon one effort to win her. Differences of social position may be something in the west of London; but they are nothing in front of the lonely mountains of the Vorarlberg, or even at the common breakfast-table of a remote Tyrolese inn.

Nor was there any bitterness in the thought that these dreams were delusions. In England they would have been very bitter—the aspirations after a happiness too clearly impossible. But here in Germany I had grown bold. It was no longer impossible—this beautiful, though distant dream, that ringed the vague future with a band of burnished gold. Delusive, doubtless, in the mean time; but who could tell what the coming years might bring forth? And as I looked forward to them in this spirit—a spirit that had grown strong and hopeful with much joyous living—I was not curious to ask which of the pale years should be singled out from its fellows to be smitten with the radiance of the dawn. It would come in good time; and it always lay ahead.

That evening I heard, but indirectly, from England, the Professor having had some letters forwarded from Munich, among them one from Mr. Webb. We were now in the brisk little town of Bregenz, which lies at the southern end of the lake, under the shadow of the rocky and wooded hills above; and we had caught our first glimpse of the picturesque costume of the Tyrol. As we walked along to the inn, we overtook a smart, dark-faced little woman, who was slowly driving home her cows—those beautiful little animals, with large mild eyes, and pretty dun-gray hides, which one meets everywhere among the Tyrolese valleys.

"What sort of skin is that hat made of?" I asked, looking at a large beehive-looking thing she wore, which had a shining, deep-brown color, like the skin of a bear.

"Shall I ask her?" said Franz, gayly.

"Yes."

"Fräulein," he said, going up to her and gallantly taking off his hat, "a Mr. Englishman wants to know what sort of skin your pretty hat is made of."

The little woman turned upon him, sharp as a needle.

"Not of an ass's skin, so you've no concern with it," she said, with a look of courageous anger.

Silber burst into a loud guffaw; but Franz was not much taken aback.

"It was a compliment, Fräulein, to your fine wool; and you shouldn't be so snappish with strangers."

"You shouldn't be so ready with your jokes, Mr. Englishman."

"Lieber Himmel! she takes me for an Englishman!" said Franz. "Why? I haven't offered her money for a cup of water; nor has she seen me laughing at the costume of a priest or a nun."

But the small Tyrolese woman went away in high dudgeon; and doubtless treasures a grudge against the English nation until this day.

In the evening, after dinner, when we had gathered around the fire, the Professor pulled Mr. Webb's letter out of his pocket, and said slyly—

"Gentlemen, it is always good, when one of our small company earns praises, that the rest should know it. I propose to translate into German for you a letter I have received from an English gentleman respecting a picture that has been done by one of us, and that has made a stir even in so unimpressionable a country as England."

The letter was about "Kilmeny," and need not be further noticed here. Neither the Professor nor my fellow-students had heard of this picture; and I had to answer many questions about it. Franz was too curious about the lady of whom Mr. Webb incidentally spoke, as having suggested the face; and there was nothing for it but to tell Franz to be less curious. So he only murmured under his breath—

"Die Dame, die ich liebe, nenn' ich nicht,"

and made a wry face at Silber, who was puffing his large student's pipe, and thoughtfully passing his fingers through his long yellow hair.

"My friend in England," continued the Professor, "sends you very good wishes, and hopes you will let him know what you mean to paint next, when our present trip is over. Have you thought of a subject?"

"Yes."

"Then tell us about it."

"With pleasure, if it is of the least interest to you. It is merely the story of Wölundur—the *Völundarkvidha*."

"My remembrance of those old sagas is very faint now," said the Professor. "Pray tell us the story."

"Yes," said Silber, "tell us the story altogether, for I don't know one of them."

"Very well," said I; "but I cannot vouch for the accuracy of my memory."

So I told them the story in this wise:

"There were three brothers, sons of the King of Finland, named Slagfidr, Egil, and Wölundur. They went away over the ice, on a hunting expedition, and they came to Wolfsthal, and there they built houses. Near to Wolfsthal is the Wolfssee, and early one morning they found near the borders of the lake three maidens, who were spinning flax. Two were the daughters of King Lödwer; but the third, who was called Alhwit (All-white), was the daughter of Kiar von Walland. The three brothers took the three maidens home with them; Slagfidr and Egil marrying the king's daughters, while the maiden Alhwit became the wife of Wölundur.

"Now Wölundur had more knowledge of all the arts than any other man; and he made many beautiful gold bracelets, and hung them up in his house. But after they had spent seven winters together, the three sisters fled away 'in search of their fate;' and, while Slagfidr and Egil went to seek their wives, Wölundur remained at home, fashioning his cunning bracelets and rings, and waiting for his young wife to come back to him.

"All this became known to Nidudr, the King of Sweden; and when he heard that Wölundur lived alone in the Wolfsthal, he took some men with him and went there by night, and bound Wölundur while he was asleep, and stole his sword and a beautiful gold ring. When Wölundur missed the ring, he thought that Alhwit had taken it with her. The sword King Nidudr kept to himself, and the ring he gave to his brown-lovely (*braunschöne*) daughter Bödwild.

"But the queen said, 'When he sees the sword and the ring, Wölundur's mouth will water, and his eyes will burn.'

"'Wild glüh'n die Augen
Dem gleissenden Wurm.'

"And she bade her husband go and cut the sinews of the hero's knees, and place him in an island, so that he might not wreak vengeance upon them. And this was done; and the king put him into a smithy, where he was kept making jewels and treasures for the royal household. Then Wölundur saw that the king wore the sword that had belonged to him, and he saw that Bödwild wore the red gold ring of his beloved Alhwit; and he swore to be revenged, for he fancied they had murdered his young wife.

"The king's sons, two boys, came playing near the smithy, and Wölundur seized upon them, and hewed their heads off. Then the maiden Bödwild came, and she brought the red ring of Wölundur's beloved that he might mend it. Then he said he would mend it, and the king's daughter sat down in a chair, and he cunningly gave her mead to drink, so that she slept.

"'Wohl mir,' sprach Wölundur,
'Wär' ich auf den Sehnen,
Die mir Nidudurs
Männer nahmen.'

"Bödwild went home, weeping bitterly over the fierce wrong that had been done to her; but Wölundur went into the open air and laughed aloud. And the king came to him, and asked where were his two boys. 'Swear to me first,' says Wölundur, 'that you have not killed my bride.' Wölundur tells the king that he has cut his sons' heads off; that he has rimmed the skulls with silver for a present to the king; that he has changed the eyes into jewels for the false wife of the king; that he has made of the teeth breast-jewels for the king's daughter. But the heaviest blow of his vengeance is to come; for the king bids them bring his brown-lovely, ring-incrusted daughter, and demands of her if she sat an hour with Wölundur in the island. And Bödwild answers very sorrowfully—

"'Wahr ist das, Nidudur,
Was man dir sagte:
Ich sass mit Wölundur
Zusammen im Holm
Hätte nie sein sollen!'"

"I remember the story," said the Professor. "It is a terrible one. And what scene do you propose to take?"

"That of the island smithy, with the maimed hero, dark and revengeful, looking at his wife's ring, which the king's daughter brings to him."

"It is a grand position," said Franz; "and I would have the king's daughter looking young and beautiful, and innocent of the crime."

"Then people will ask why she should suffer for the wickedness of her father and mother," said Siller.

"Let them ask!" said Franz. "We don't say who is right and who is wrong. We tell the story of old and hard times, in which a man's family was a part of his wealth, and you robbed him that way as soon as any other, if you wanted to be revenged."

"That is very well said—very good," remarked the Professor. "You tell the story, and let the audience sympathize with whom it pleases. The most prominent figure of a picture or a drama is not necessarily the hero. I think the subject is a good one, if treated carefully. But it must be neither sentimental nor melodramatic. What do you say, Franz—shall we make the subject a class-subject, and give Herr Edward the benefit of all our suggestions?"

"Capital!" said Franz. "And then, after we have done what we can for him in the way of helping the composition, we must get the proper models for him. I have them in my eye just now."

"Who are they?"

"Why, our good friend Silber will stand for Wölundur, and one might hope to gain the kind assistance of Fräulein Riedel—"

"I beg you will not mention Fräulein Riedel's name," said Silber, with a sudden and angry flush.

"No offence," said Franz, with a provoking calmness; "I was not aware you were so much interested in the lady."

"I am not interested."

"Who is the Fräulein Riedel?" asked the Professor, apparently to smooth the matter down.

"Herr Professor," observed Franz, "the Fräulein Riedel is—a lady. I hope one may be permitted to say so, even in the presence of my good friend Silber."

The Professor laughed heartily, and the matter dropped. This Fräulein Riedel was a young lady who played and sang in the burlesques and operettas of the Volkstheater in Munich—a theatre which the Professor was not likely to visit. Silber maintained hotly that many a worse singer and actress appeared as *prima donna* in the Hoftheater; and that some day the Fräulein would sing there too.

"She knows the whole of the part of Rezia in 'Oberon,'" he used to say proudly; "for I have been permitted to hear her sing it; and I doubt not she is equally familiar with the rest of your *grand* operas. But I believe you only affect to despise Offenbach, because he is new, and French."

There was really some romance in connection with this affair. Silber had fallen desperately in love with the Fräulein when he first saw her, in some small town near the Rhine, play the heroine of our English farce "The Rough Diamond," which Alexander Bergen has translated. "Ein ungeschliffener Diamant" was too much for the young student, who never forgot "Margaretha von Immergrün's" black eyes and hair. Three years passed, and he had almost forgotten Fräulein Riedel, when whom should he see walking along the Karlsplatz, in Munich, but the same girl who had struck his fancy as the young Baroness von Immergrün. He followed her—all the way to the Volkstheater, where he saw her enter. He looked at the bill—Fräulein Riedel was announced to appear in an operetta that evening. Silber went, and renewed his thrall. By and by he managed to get acquainted with her; and he was beside himself with joy when she allowed him to present her with a bracelet. One day he ventured to propose a walk, and she kindly consented. They crossed the Maximilian Bridge and passed along the leafy avenues of the "new pleasure grounds" on the banks of the Isar; then they went down by Brunnthal, and again crossed the river by the wooden bridge which abuts on the Tivoli gardens. Now, as it happened, Franz and I, who had been dragged by Silber many times to the theatre to look at Fräulein Riedel, happened to be sitting under the Tivoli trees, with some beer on the small table before us.

"Du Himmel!" exclaimed Franz, "there is Silber, with his Schätzchen of the Volkstheater!"

And so it was. Silber saw us, gave us a grave bow, and passed sedately on. How proud he looked! It was from this time that he cultivated more and more the student appearance—wearing his fair hair long and smooth, sporting blue caps with prodigious gold tassels, smoking preposterous pipes, talking metaphysics, of which he did not even know the terminology, and drinking beer in quantities that disagreed with him.

"Silber is a vast and uncommon humbug," Franz used to say; "but that little girl with the black eyes believes in him."

I think she was quite a respectable little woman, and did her best to keep him from drinking useless quantities of beer—a feat he never sought to perform, except that he might boast of it to her. She was evidently impressed by his assuming the character of the careless, happy, brave, and withal lovable student who figures on the stage. Why could she, familiar with acting, not see that this stupendous ass was only acting? That was always a mystery to Franz and me; for we did not believe that the Fräulein was actually in love with him.

"How many glasses of beer have you drunk, Silber?" Franz used to ask.

"Five."

"Is that all?"

"Yes."

"Fräulein Riedel will despise you."

"Himmel sapperment!" Silber would growl; as much as to say, "Another word and I challenge you, *ohne Mützen, ohne Secundanten.*"

"I will make you a proposal."

"Well?"

"Pay for three more glasses of beer. I drink them. Then you go to Fräulein Riedel, and say, 'Admire me: I have drunk eight glasses of beer!'"

With which Silber used to become furious, and declare that if we were in Heidelberg Franz would not be so bold.

I could forgive Silber everything except his singing. Of course, he fancied that he ought to sing the "Burschenlieder," to support the character; and he used to sing the jovial and jolly student-songs with an affected swagger which was at once ludicrous and irritating. One could not help being amused by Silber's peculiar method of leering at the humorous passages, nor vexed to hear the fine and manly songs burlesqued by this poor, conceited wind-bag. Kotzebue's "Bundeslied" was one of his favorites, as was also the universal "Gaudeamus igitur," which Franz used to alter in this way—

"Gaudeamus igitur,
Juvenes dum sumus,
Post jucundam juventutem,
Per molestam senectutem,
Nos habebit conjux."

A sorer trial, however, was Silber at love-songs; for his voice had an odd habit of contradicting the theatrical expression of rapture he endeavored to throw into his face. With great good humor, Franz used to play accompaniments whenever Silber would sing; and it was certainly a queer conjunction to hear the sensitive, thrilling, beautiful music of the zither hovering around and about poor Silber's quavering voice. Silber had a notion of learning to play the zither himself; but seemed not to be quite sure whether it would befit the character he ordinarily assumed. Yet, with all his weaknesses and affectations, the lad had some good points about him, or how could that black-eyed little actress have smiled upon his uncouthness?

CHAPTER XXX.

NEWS FROM ENGLAND.

Was it love, or was it the keen air of the Tyrol, that awoke all those wild enthusiasms which now, as I look back, I can see clustering around our happy journey through the mountain land?

"Why," I said to myself, "should I return to those old dead times for a story? Why not take our modern life, which is as full of love and tragic misery as any time before it, and seize the hearts of men with some noble tale of suffering or courage or heroism? And what is the message which I should take home to my countrymen from this rarer atmosphere, in which the finer aspirations of human nature flourish—what but that love is better than wealth, and that a true heart is of more value than big estates?"

The message was not nearly so startling as I fancied. Many a man has preached it without being much attended to; many a man has found out its truth when, after spending a lifetime in growing rich, he looks back, and sees in the past a young face full of love and the pain of parting, and wonders whether less money and more of the love that he threw away might not have made his life happier.

"Why are you always so silent in the morning?" asked Franz, as we left Bregenz. "You are visited by grand flashes of silence, in which you seem to sink into your breeches-pockets. You are practically dead. You see nothing and hear nothing, unless you are listening inside your brain to some music that a girl sang to you in England. Is that true?"

"Yes; I can hear her singing sometimes," I said.

We had turned our back on the lake, that was half hidden under the thick white mist, and were now skirting the base of the rocky and wooded mountains that encircle the Tyrol, preparatory to our crossing the giant chain of the Arlberg. The busy Tyrolese were already abroad in their fields and meadows, where the small, meek, large-eyed cattle browsed. As we ascended, the air became rarer, the sun broke through the mist, and lit up for us the immense range of the Appenzeller Alps, that were here and there dusted with snow.

"What is the color of her eyes?" said Franz, insidiously.

"They are like the sea," I said—"of all colors, in different moods. But they are generally dark and clear and calm."

Franz unsuccessfully endeavored to push his inquiries further.

"Tell me," he said, "what she is like altogether, and I will write a song about her in Tyrolese."

"A song has been written about her already."

"By whom?"

"Schiller. She is the beautiful and wonderful maiden who came down into the valley, no one knew whence."

"You are, then, in love with a phantom?"

"Yes, Franz; I am indeed in love with a phantom."

I could almost have believed then that Hester Burnham had come down the valley before us, even as Schiller's maiden did; for by reason of constantly looking at things, and fancying what she would think of them, I came to regard them as having already acquired from her some touch of fascination. Would it ever happen that I should bring her this very route? Should we hire a carriage at Bregenz, drive out from the brisk little town, along the level road through Dornbirn, with its quaint houses, and Hohenembs with its Jewish-featured people—on to Feldkirch and the lovely valley of the Ill—past Bludenz, with the mountains getting higher, and the valley more rugged—then down the Klosterthal, to rest in the evening in the old inn at Dalaas, with a warm and well-lit room, and casements opening to show us the moonlight shimmering along the pale white glaciers of the mountains under which the little village lies? Would it ever be my great joy to wrap up the little figure cosily in her carriage, and see that she was snug and warm as we drove through the cold mountain air? Should I be able to look in her eyes as I drew the shawl tighter under the small chin, to keep the white little neck comfortable and close and safe? Fancy going through this beautiful country — away from towns and strangers, and the formal obligations of society; her only duty being to look and charm the very air around her, mine but to wait upon my dainty little queen, and beg the mountain-wind to be gentle with her hair. Of these sweet dreams the deadliest poison of misery is made.

The Tyrol was for me henceforth and forever saturated with memories and thoughts and suggestions of Hester Burnham. The reader, who may have gone through this charming country, and enjoyed its simple ways, its homely meals, its clear air, and its splendid lines of snow-hills, will perhaps scarcely understand how a small lady, secreted among the leaves of Buckinghamshire, could have changed the character of a whole country, and permeated its gigantic mountains, its green fields, its gray, rushing rivers, its very sunshine, with the subtle influence of her presence. The sunshine was different there. A month later, dwelling among the dull white houses of Munich, I used to wonder if there were any sunshine like the sunshine of the Tyrol, and whether she and I might ever see it together.

As ill-luck would have it, there was no sunshine for the Professor's party in crossing the Arlberg. On the contrary, we found our way to the summit of the mountain in dense clouds of mist and rain, that concealed from us the precipices under our feet, and prevented our looking either to the right hand or to the left. It had been raining all night, too; and the mountain torrents, swollen and muddy, dashed down the channels they had cleared for themselves with a noise that was all the more impressive that we could only now and again catch glimpses of the masses of foaming, tumbling gray water. Sometimes the mist became so thick that we could just see the posts stuck along the edge of the road, to prevent carriages from going over; while, on the other hand, there was a faint green hue appearing through the vapor, which we took to be the wet side of the hill glimmering behind the fog.

There was only one water-proof coat among us, and that we voted over to the Professor. So we walked on.

"I take it," observed the Professor, drawing up his spare figure, seemingly in defiance of the rain that dashed about his face and trickled down his nose—"I take it that all imaginative art has sprung from the mountain districts of the world—that the human mind has been awakened to the conception of music, poetry, and painting by the solitude of mountains. Yet you will find that the men who have caught the imaginative width and power of the hills into their nature have gone down into the plains—into the towns and cities, perhaps—to seek the calm of artistic expression. All the great artists of Italy have been born beneath the spell of the Apennines; and then they have gone into Florence, or Rome, or Milan, as the case may be, and they have put the free inspiration of the hills into their work—".

"But, Herr Professor, Michael Angelo was not born among the mountains, and he had the most powerful imagination of them all," objected Franz, who was at this moment a wretched spectacle.

"Learn, sir," said the Professor, "never to destroy a theory with a fact. Yet, tell me, where was Michael Angelo born?"

"At Arezzo," replied Silber, like a good boy.

"And Arezzo," continued the Professor, "if not among the hills, is only a few miles off. It is no farther from the great backbone of the Apennines than is Urbino, on the other side, where Raphael grew up under their shadow. Why, you ought to be able to tell, without knowing where he was born, that Michael Angelo was no dweller in the plains. Look at his 'Moses'—there is the majesty of a great mountain in that figure—that is the only thing by which you can characterize the force and the grandeur of it."

"I know," said Franz, ruefully, as he shook his dripping sleeves, "that there isn't much in a day like this to stir one's imagination—unless it is the prospect of a fire and some cognac at the end of the journey."

"It is the wild contrast of atmospheric conditions," continued the Professor, "that impresses one who is brought up among the hills with the strong life and intensity of nature. There is no mild sameness always around him. There are great forces at work, a constant motion, and the vivid, startling presentation of change. Look around you just now. It is a world of eddying mist and fog, with pitiless rain, and the sound of hurrying waters sweeping down below us, unseen. But suppose a great wind were to arise right ahead, and come blowing along the mountain-tops, and clear away the fog and the rain—suppose, when we were in dejection and despair, this great wind were to come, and all at once we saw before us the valley glittering with rain-drops in the sun, the warm, gleaming light all around us, and the wonderful, intense blue overhead, should we not have the power and the beauty of the sunlight impressed upon us as it never was before? Then the simple peasant, reaching up his hands to the warmth and the sun, and thinking that heaven has suddenly come near, must needs sing aloud, as if he were a bird, to the blue sky; and the man who has the heart of a painter in him is amazed by the intensity of the colors of the world around him, and forgets the vision never! He will not try to reproduce this wonder of light—he may despair of his colors; but all these intense, vivid impressions of change and majesty and calm and beauty that he receives among the hills remain a power within him; and when, in his studio, down in some great town, he tries to picture to himself the grandeur of an heroic figure or the purity and sweetness of a woman's face, his memory of the wonders of the mountains will lend him his ideal. Did you ever, any of you, see Pordenone's 'Santa Giustina,' which is in the Belvedere at Vienna? I tell you that to look once at that woman's face—to get a glimpse of its surpassing and gracious sweetness, its perfect serenity and repose—it were worth while to walk from here to the Kaiserstadt with bare feet!"

The Professor was very gruff and silent for some time thereafter. He had been surprised into an enthusiasm, and there was nothing he more disliked. His singular bashfulness invariably produced a strong reaction; and when once he had recovered possession of himself, I fancy he used to brood over what he had been saying, and look upon himself as having played the fool. He used to blush like a girl, too, after these outbursts; but on this occasion he was safe from scrutiny by reason of the tall collar of the water-proof coat.

"I know," said Franz, "that all our fine old melodies have come to us from the hills—from the Tyrol, from the Thüringer Wald, from the Riesengebirge, and the Saxon Highlands."

"You ought to sing one now, or we shall all be getting downhearted," said Silber. "We don't know how many miles it is yet to Landeck, and the rain will not cease to-day."

"But it will cease to-morrow, or some other morrow," said Franz, gayly. "You ought to look forward to the snug inn at Landeck—the warm stoves, a schnitzel, wine, a pipe, and sleep—all of which luxuries lie ahead. I have the picture before me.

A large room, long tables, one of them covered with a white cloth; a green stove, very warm, two candles, some matches—"

"A zither," I added.

"And a picture of the patron saint of brewers, the king Gambrinus—a jolly person in blue and red robes, holding a foaming jug of beer in his hand, and honored by these highly ingenious lines—

"'Gambrinus, in Flandern und Brabant,
Ein König über Leut' und Land,
Aus Malz und Hopfen hat gelehrt
Zu brauen Bier gar lobenswerth,
Drum ist er in der Brauer Orden
Ihr oberster Patron geworden;
Wo gibt's ein ander Handwerk mehr,
Das sich kann rühmen solcher Ehr?'"

"It is not in the Tyrol, Mr. Franz," said the Professor, "that you should be surprised to find a man at once brewer and king. Remember Andreas Hofer."

Which, of course, set Franz into singing "Zu Mantua in Banden," with its touching words and rather commonplace music.

At Landeck there was more awaiting us than food and warmth, desirable and welcome as these were. The Professor had had another packet of letters forwarded; and among them was one for me. By the handwriting on the envelope, I saw it was from Bonnie Lesley.

"Will she tell me anything about Hester Burnham?" I thought. "Will she at least write the name, that I may carry it about with me?"

The first words in the letter (and it was curious to read her successive statements without seeing her pretty looks of wonder accompanying them) were these—"Hester was with me the whole day yesterday; she is living with some friends at Notting Hill. I hope I am betraying no confidence in telling you something about her. I will tell you; and you shall send me in your next letter a promise of secrecy. Briefly, then, Hester is a little fool, and is about to make herself wretched for life. Of course, you know why. Alfred Burnham, I must tell you, in the first place, has come to *awful grief;* and, as far as I can understand these matters, has taken advantage of poor Hester's kindliness—weakness, I call it—and has landed her *in extreme difficulties.* I should not be surprised if she had to sell Burnham."

To sell Burnham! Was it, then, reserved for this quiet little girl, so prudent and considerate in all her ways, to let the old house go away from the family that had owned it for many centuries? What had she done that the pain and the shame of this sacrifice should fall upon her? It is recorded in history that one of the Burnhams was shorn of three parts of the then extensive family estates (the alternative being that he should lose his right hand) for striking the Black Prince a blow on the face. That was the first step to narrow the means of the Burnhams; and now the last of the family, a girl, was to give up the final relic of their ancient power.

"Alfred Burnham," continued the letter, "has become penitent, and vows that the only thing to save him from ruin is for Hester to marry him. Perhaps he speaks the truth, and hopes to recover himself by the proceeds of the sale of Burnham; but he has persuaded Hester that it is his moral reformation she is bound to accomplish. Now you know what an unselfish little puss she is, although you can't see that *as we women see it.* She is so far removed from the ordinary jealousies of the drawing-room, for example, that she will insist on other people singing her best songs; and she will go about in her mouse-like way, making everybody display their best points while keeping herself in the background. Do you think she could turn a cat out of a chair she wanted to sit in? Well, you know, all this is very pretty, and it makes one fond of the sly little woman, but there is a limit to it. And she has taken it into her small head that it is her duty to reform her cousin *by marrying him!* Did you ever hear of such a thing?"

Yes, I had heard of it often. And I had seen cases in which pure and good women allowed themselves to suffer, through some such theory of duty and self-renunciation, the most cruel and revolting usage at the hands of men who only grew the more debased by being accustomed to presume on their great unselfishness.

"I acknowledge," continued my correspondent, "that Hester has some spirit, and has a quiet, determined, managing way with her that many people don't perceive, although they obey it. But what effect would that have on a man like Alfred Burnham, who would, I am sure, leave Burnham and its present mistress to themselves (that is, if the former should not be sold), and be off to enjoy the pecuniary results of the marriage in freedom. Meanwhile, poor Hester is in a pitiable state of apprehension and indecision. She fancies she should marry him; and yet she shrinks from it. You know, she is not given to much crying or hysterical nonsense; but yesterday, when she sat in this room, and spoke to me in her low, frank voice about these things, I saw tears slowly fill her eyes and stealthily trickle down her cheek. I put my arms around her neck and hid her face, and let her cry to her heart's content, and then I gave her a hearty scolding. She was very much shocked by the way in which I spoke of her precious cousin; but I had the satisfaction of seeing that it had at least awoke her alarm. She went away without having said anything in particular. I am to see her in a day or two.

"Tell me what you think of the *complication*. Is it likely that Alfred Burnham would be anxious to marry Hester at once, if it is true that these monetary affairs will necessitate the sale of Burnham? Of course the place would fetch a large sum, and there might be a handsome balance left, worthy of that gentleman's consideration; but somehow, from what Hester said, I have a suspicion that this terrible collapse on the part of Alfred may be only a *ruse*. In any case, he holds her securities for a considerable amount; for she told me of the altercation she had had with her trustees, lawyers, and what not, about the matter.

"'Besides,' said I to Hester, 'suppose you were capable of reforming your cousin, don't you reflect that, in sacrificing yourself (as you assuredly would), you are also sacrificing some other man whom you might have made happy?'

"'I have never given any man the right to think of me in that way,' she said, a little proudly.

"'My dear,' said I, with the calmness of superior wisdom, 'that is a right which men assume without its being given them. Now, on your honor, is there no man whom you suspect of loving you?'

"'The question is too absurd,' she said, hastily, and turned away under some pretence or other.

"But for the first time I saw in her eyes, that are generally so honest and clear that they look through you, a sort of troubled concealment. Can you read me my riddle, Mr. Foreigner, and tell me who is going to carry off the lady of Burnham? You see I have not given in yet to Hester's folly, but I shall have a hard fight with her, I am afraid, before I can make her change her mind."

There was nothing else of any importance in the letter, except that, curiously enough, the envelope contained a slip of paper with a few words, and a "*glückliche Reise!*" from Mr. Morell. How came this enclosure there?

CHAPTER XXXI.

BONNIE LESLEY'S METAPHOR.

The long journey through cold and rain, and the late dinner that followed, made our party rather sleepy that evening. The Professor subsided into a soft slumber, which Franz would not break by taking out his zither. Indeed the whole of us were in a comatose state, and had just sufficient energy to keep our cigars from going out, so that I had plenty of time to think over the contents of Bonnie Lesley's long letter. The friendly confidence therein displayed, and the concluding hint it contained, were chiefly, I fancy, the result of an excursion which she and I had made to Richmond, and which put our relations on a much more intimate footing than they had ever hitherto been. The history of that excursion was a curious one. When I went up to London after recovering from the accident down in Buckinghamshire, I expected that Bonnie Lesley would be much embarrassed when we met. The reader may remember the peculiar confession which the beautiful penitent made. For a woman to tell you that she has been trying to make you fall in love with her, in order to revenge herself on somebody else, and in order to prove to this third person that she was worth falling in love with, is rather a startling revelation. Under ordinary circumstances, you could not help despising the woman who could act in this fashion, however ashamed of herself she professed to be. At least, you would expect that this sense of shame would hang about her for some little time, and put some constraint on her manner.

With Bonnie Lesley nothing of the kind happened. When I met her in London, she comported herself as if nothing had occurred.

"Is it true," I asked myself, thoroughly amazed, "what Heatherleigh says—that she has no soul? Is she incapable of feeling shame, or any other emotion whatever?"

I looked back over our long friendship; and she seemed to have been always the same. I began to see, however, in many of her words and actions which I could remember, a sort of self-conscious effort to reach sensitiveness, as if she thought it her duty to be emotionally struck by such and such a picture, or view, or person. She wanted to be what she could not be. She saw this emotional faculty in other women, and strove to attain it without success. Yet she counterfeited it sometimes with an earnest hypocrisy which was less of a vice than a virtue. The only time I ever saw her genuinely moved was when she made my sick-room down in Bucks her confessional; yet now, a month or two afterwards, she met me as if she had never been there.

I was rejoiced to find her so little embarrassed. It was better to sink that old time, with its foolish notions. So I, too, met Bonnie Lesley as if nothing had occurred, and we succeeded so well in dropping into the ordinary relations of friends that she confided to me a great secret, and asked my co-operation.

"The day after to-morrow," she said, "I am going down to see Mr. Lewison's three little nieces—great friends of mine—who are at school in Richmond. I often go down to see them; and they are good enough to call me Auntie Canary, because, I suppose, I have yellow hair. I don't know any other reason. Well, it is no great fun for the poor little things to be asked to a formal luncheon with the schoolmistress and me; and I have determined this time to go down early, get them a holiday, and take them to dine at the Star and Garter. Fancy their delight. But nobody here must know anything about it, until they find it out afterwards; and so I am going to ask you to write and make the proper arrangements for us at the hotel—do you see?"

"Yes," said I. "But a far simpler way would be to let me go with you."

"I am going alone," she said, doubtfully, but with a puzzled laugh in her eyes.

"I shall go alone, too; and meet you there."

Even now she looked surprised and pleased, although I know she had anticipated the offer.

"There is no reason why you shouldn't come up to Mr. Lewison's, and drive down with me in the brougham," she said; "but it would add a little mystery and romance, wouldn't it, if you did meet us down there?"

"Then that is settled," said I. "You go down and get your nieces out. I accidentally meet you at the gate of Richmond Park, above the hotel, at one o'clock. I am delighted to see you—"

"Well, I hope so," she said.

"—And your young charges also. I accompany you on your walk, and instruct them in the differences between the roe, fallow, and red deer. Perhaps we have time to walk down by Ham House and the river. Then the sight of Richmond Hill recalls to me that the children must be getting hungry; and I invite you all to dine with me at the hotel, which we can see in the distance."

"But, at present, it looks as if I were inviting you to dine with me," she said, with a touch of fun in her eyes.

"No," I said, "that is not proper. Shall it be one o'clock?"

"Yes, one," she said.

It was in the middle of summer, but a light wind, blowing over the wooded country through which the Thames slowly winds, cooled the sun's heat, and sent flakes of white cloud gently across the intense blue overhead. There was a mid-day haze clinging about the horizon; and even here, among the rugged oaks and undulating slopes of Richmond Park, there was a sleepiness and silence that seemed to weigh on the large, mild eyes of the deer. Warm and still, too, lay the woods along the river, showing every shade of green, until in the remote west they turned into a faint purplish-gray. The haze hid Windsor; and so the beautiful wooded valley seemed to lose itself in the white of the horizon.

Bonnie Lesley was punctual. Shortly before one o'clock I caught a glimpse of a figure, far down the road, that actually shone in the sunlight. Even at that distance I could see that she wore her favorite color—a pale blue silk dress, with a white shawl over it so thin that the blue shone through, and a remarkably small and glossy white hat, with a pert blue feather in it. I supposed that she had, as usual, either a bunch of blue forget-me-nots or a white rose in her yellow hair, and that she wore some strings of large white beads around her neck. She had a white parasol, also, with a gleam of blue around the edge.

There were three children around her, clearly all talking to her at once, and coming along in that half-skipping, half-jumping fashion indicative of juvenile excitement. I could hear their voices a long way off.

I was very much surprised and delighted to see her, of course; and was formally introduced to her young friends. Two of them were fair and ordinary-looking young misses, but the third one was a little Brownie, with large, mischievous brown eyes, and soft brown hair. Anything to approach the impudence, the cleverness, and the winning, fascinating ways of this little miss I have never seen. Although the youngest, she was the spokeswoman for her sisters, and did not a little to shock them by the audacity of her fun. During the whole day, it was "Oh, Ethel! how can you?" or, "Oh, Ethel, I *do* wonder what has come over you!" Ethel remarked that she preferred the company of gentlemen to that of ladies; so she took my arm, and we walked on in advance of the others.

She began to tell me of her schoolmates, and their friends, and her friends. She mimicked this one's pompous manner, and that one's gruff voice, and then gave an admirable imitation of her music-mistress.

"She never does rap our knuckles, you know, with a pencil, when we make a mistake; but she pretends to do it, and then laughs—so—and thinks it is funny. She always sings, too, when she counts; and, oh dear! she can't sing a bit, and it is so dreadful! She tries to follow the music with her 'one, two, three, four; one, two, three, four;' and she does it out of time and leads you wrong. Now how *could* you help yourself if you had a music-mistress like that?"

"I should ask her not to sing."

Ethel burst out laughing.

"That is all you know about school! My stars! she would box your ears, and then send you home. There's the French mistress, too—she's another caution—I beg your pardon—I must say 'fright.' Lottie White's brother—oh, such a wicked boy he is! —told Lottie to ask Madame if she would translate the name of a play, 'Love's Last Shift,' into 'La dernière chemise de l'amour?' and Madame's rage was awful. She is pale and dark, and has a moustache, and I think she says very naughty things sometimes, when she is angry, under her breath. You should hear her when she comes into the class-room at eleven. She says to us all, 'Good-morning, my dear children' (she says it in French, but I sha'n't let you hear my pronunciation); 'I hope you will be good children to-day, and profit by your lessons.' Lottie White's brother says that is her grace before meat."

"Do you like French, Ethel?"

"No; I am afraid it will broaden my nose if I go on with it. And Lottie White's brother says the French are a weak sort of people, for they can't say *no* without using two words."

"Lottie White's brother seems to say a good many things. Do you see him often?"

"That is a secret," said Ethel, with a comic shyness. "I am not going to tell tales out of school."

"Will you come and dine with me at the hotel over there?"

"Oh, with pleasure!" she said, with a mock courtesy.

"Do you think you could persuade your sisters and your aunt to come also?"

"That isn't material, is it?" she said, looking up.

"But it would be so much better—so much jollier to have them all with us."

"Then I will ask them."

She stopped and turned to the others.

"Ladies and gentlemen," she said, with admirable gravity, "we invite you to dinner. You needn't change your dress; there will be no ceremony; and no papas and mammas to interfere at dessert."

"You forget me, Ethel," said Bonnie Lesley.

"Oh, we can always coax Auntie Canary into good-humor by saying she has pretty hair."

"Oh, Ethel!" said her elder sisters, in a breath.

So it was arranged that we should proceed at once to dinner. There were but few people in the large dining-room; and when the three small ladies and their aunt had left their hats and superfluous articles of attire up-stairs, we secured a table at the spacious bay-window which looked out upon the garden and the far sunlit landscape beyond.

"Oh, how *very* jolly!" cried Ethel, as she plumped herself down in a big, soft chair. "I wish Auntie Canary was our mamma, and would take us to live in hotels always. Wouldn't it be jolly to live always in hotels, and have everything you ask for, and no schoolmistresses or lessons?"

"When you are grown-up, Ethel," said Bonnie Lesley, "you will be able to live always in hotels if you please."

"But I mayn't like it then," said Ethel, with precocious philosophy.

The majority of voices carried the day in favor of sparkling Carlowitz; Ethel wisely observing, however, that she would rather drink no wine at dinner, and have a glass of port at dessert.

"It is the proper time for wine, isn't it, Auntie? And you know I'm very, very fond of port wine; it is because I was christened in it, and so I must always like it."

I was about to ask her the meaning of this remark, which I did not understand, when a sharp rattle was heard on the window, which made the children jump. I looked out and saw on the window-sill a small blue tom-tit, that was bleeding at the bill and lying quite motionless. We raised the window and brought the unlucky little bird inside, but it was just dying. Ethel took it before its heart ceased to beat, and while there was yet a dumb frightened stare in its small bright eyes; and she folded her hands around it and kept it close into her bosom, to see if she could revive it. I saw her big brown eyes fill with tears when it became clear that the bird was dead; and it was some little time before the natural gayety of the children recovered from the shock.

"Birds don't go to heaven when they die," said Ethel, contemplatively. "The best they can expect is to be stuffed and put in a glass case."

"Don't you think, Ethel," I asked, "that the tom-tit saw your aunt from the outside, and killed itself on purpose that she might wear it on her hat?"

"It's Auntie Canary, not Auntie Tom-tit," said Ethel, rather irrelevantly, but with the effect of making her sisters scream with laughter.

The young ones were in no hurry with their dinner, and they lingered quite as long over dessert. Ethel had now become quite possessed with excitement, and was making small speeches, and acting, and mimicking all manner of people, to the alarm of her sisters.

"Oh, Ethel," they cried, "you must be mad."

"So you said when I called Mr. Templeton a parson. But he is a parson, for a clergyman is a parson, isn't he, Mr. Ives?"

"Yes; I think so."

"And he comes into a room like this—mincing and treading on his toes, and he peers—*so*—through his blue spectacles, and he bows—*so*—over the hand of the lady he goes up to; and he always holds his cup between his finger and thumb—*so*—and says, 'I am so pleased to see yah this evening'—just as he drawls in the pulpit 'Ah Fathah which aht in heaven—'"

"Ethel!" said Miss Lesley, sharply; and Ethel's sisters looked inexpressibly shocked.

For a moment or two Ethel's countenance fell; but she was presently in her old mood again, and gayly narrating how Lottie White's brother had thrown some lucifer-matches on the stage when he was admitted, along with the other relatives of the school-girls, to see a French comedy performed by the young ladies.

"But do you know what Mrs. Graham is particularly angry about just now, Auntie?" she said.

"No," said Auntie, with wondering eyes.

"Well, you must know, ladies and gentlemen, that in the spring we had a gardener. He was a very nice person, for he used last autumn to smuggle us all kinds of fruit, and we paid him with our pocket-money, when we had any. Well, Mrs. Graham told him he must leave, and gave him a month's notice. So Mr. Gardener dug, and dug, and dug; and made squares and diamonds and lozenges; and filled them all with seed, and put bits of stick in, with names written on them. Do you know how much money Mrs. Graham gave him for seed for the kitchen and the flower garden?"

"No."

"Nearly £5. Wasn't it a lot? Well, after the gardener had gone, we waited to see the flowers come up in the squares and diamonds; and we knew what to expect as the earliest, for he had written all the names of the flowers on the sticks. But first one thing didn't come up, and then another thing didn't come up, until everybody knows now that he never sowed any seed at all. Wasn't it a capital joke, Auntie?"

"It was no joke, Ethel: it was dishonesty," said Bonnie Lesley.

"But it may be a joke as well, mayn't it?"

Then, with the air of a young princess, she asked one of the waiters to tell her what o'clock it was.

"Five minutes to four, miss," he said.

"Oh, fancy, fancy!" she cried, with a gesture of delight—

"fancy, ladies and gentlemen, our having been three hours at dinner! Did ever any one hear of the like? And I have had—oh, how many kinds of fruit and sweets!"

"A great deal too many, Ethel," said the elder of her sisters, severely.

"Then I shall be ill to-morrow morning, I suppose. But you know, Emmy, that that is all nonsense. We *don't* get ill after eating heaps of jellies and sweets and fruit; and it is only the old people who say so to frighten us. I suppose they don't like them, and they envy us our liking them."

"Ethel!" said Miss Lesley, reprovingly, "you're becoming rude: don't you know I am your elder?"

"Oh, Auntie Canary, you've hair like a fairy!" said Ethel, with wicked merriment in her brown eyes, and with a burst of laughter which was sufficiently infectious.

I think they would readily have stayed there all the evening; and it was with some evident reluctance that Ethel accompanied her sisters up-stairs to prepare for going back to school. When we arrived there, we found Mr. Lewison's brougham already waiting; and Bonnie Lesley only stayed a few minutes to say good-bye to the schoolmistress.

Then she came out. As I handed her into the carriage, I said—

"Won't you offer to drive me up to town?"

For a second there was a puzzled and surprised look in her eyes; then I saw an inadvertent glance towards the solemn person, in a green coat, brass buttons, and black cockade, who stood at the door; and then she said, suddenly—

"Yes, with pleasure. Do come. And you will go on and see Mr. Lewison, won't you?"

"That," said I, when the grave person had shut the door, and received his instructions, "is a matter we can settle afterwards."

It was a ladies' brougham. No one had ever smoked in it. On the contrary, the dark-green lining and cushions were saturated with various scents; and in one of the leathern pouches there was placed a flask purporting to have come from one of the fifty Farinas of Cologne. Now one of Bonnie Lesley's weaknesses was a love of powerful perfumes; and on this mild summer evening she not only insisted on having both the windows up, but she took down this bottle (how singular it is that all these Farinas write in the same fashion!) and splashed about the contents until the atmosphere was suffocating.

"Do you wish us, then," I asked, "to die of the fumes of spirits of wine? Charcoal would be preferable."

"Do you think so?" she asked, with a wondering little laugh. "If it were possible to die of eau-de-cologne, I should choose that death. You, being a man, would of course choose to be drowned in a butt of claret."

This led us on to talk of a tragic circumstance that was interesting newspaper-readers at the time. A young man, of good family, happened to fall in love with a governess who lived in his father's house, a pretty young girl who unfortunately was equally in love with him. The young man insisted on marrying this girl; the father threatened him with the usual penalties if he did; and the governess was ordered to leave. On the day before she was to go the father was sitting in the drawing-room, at the end of which was a conservatory opening into the garden. His son and the governess came into this conservatory, and sat down beside a small table, on which some wine and glasses had been left. The father, probably wanting to see how the two lovers would behave, sat still and looked through the glass doors. Standing with his back to him, the son apparently poured something into two glasses, giving one of them to the girl. With surprise, he saw them both stand up, clasp each other's hand, and with the left hand raise the glasses to their lips. "It is a lover's parting," he thought. The next moment the girl sank into the chair behind her, and the young man fell heavily back on the stone floor. The father rushed to the conservatory, opened the doors, and was immediately struck by the powerful odor of almonds that was in the air. Both of the lovers were dead.

The circumstance naturally produced a profound sensation, and most people, while deprecating in a conventional fashion the rashness of the suicide, sympathized with the two unfortunates, and were inclined to look upon the deed as rather heroic.

"I suppose you, too, think it was very heroic," I said to Bonnie Lesley, "this devoted love, and constancy, and resolution?"

"Well," she said, "I think it is fine in these days to meet some such story as this, to show you that love is still possible, and that it is capable of triumphing over the worldly and selfish notions that are common."

"Do you know," I said, "that the story of Edward A—— and that young girl produces quite the contrary impression upon me? I look upon it as the worst symptom I know of the degraded sentiment of the present time. Why did he kill himself and her? Not for the sake of their love, but on account of his father's threat. His real theory was, 'I love this girl, and wish to marry her. But if I do I must become poor, and give up society. So, rather than lose the luxuries to which I have been accustomed, I will kill myself and the girl also.' Confess, now, that he was an abject sneak, instead of a hero!"

"Well," she said, doubtingly, with a smile, "there is something in what you say. But unless he had loved the girl very much—"

"I say he loved his social position more. Look at the circumstances. Here are two young people, with average health, who have fallen in love. They have youth, hope, a good circulation, and faith in each other. What more would they like? The world is before them. People with far less stock-in-trade have encountered the conditions of life, got to understand them, and managed to live very comfortably. Poverty is as yet an unknown experience for them: they have not that excuse for going to extremes. But the man is so great a coward that he distrusts his capacity to exist without his father's help. He fears to take the chance of the future which hundreds of thousands of men and women, far from heroic, annually take; and so he says, 'Life without my horses, cigars, and wine would be worse than death; and, therefore, Bessy dear, we must die.' Such is the product of the sentiment of England in the nineteenth century!"

"You have converted me," she said. "I think he was a contemptible coward, and the only pity is that the girl was killed as well."

"So, Mr. Edward," she continued presently, in a lighter tone, "you have suddenly taken a strong opinion on the point that differences of social station should not interfere with love-marriages. Does your theory hold both ways—for instance, when the woman is rich or well-born, and the man is poor?"

"No, it does not."

"Oh, you think a woman who is rich should not marry a man who is poor?"

"What is the use of laying down arbitrary laws, when every case is dissimilar, when—"

"Don't be angry. Let us take one case. The lady is well-born, tender-hearted, tolerably rich, and has a pretty considerable pride in her ancestry. The lover has no family-tree, and little money; but he has all manner of manly and lovable qualities that win the lady's liking and admiration. Now, ought they to marry?"

"Not in England; particularly if she has a lot of friends and relatives."

"A decisive judgment," she said, smiling; "still you leave me a loop-hole of escape. They may marry out of England. Then you don't see any real obstacle to their union, so far as they themselves are concerned?"

"How can there be?"

"Forgive me for saying it, but you stare at such a notion as if there were something ghastly in it. Yet it is natural that, wherever she goes, the girl will retain much of the opinions she has caught in our English atmosphere, and may even at times show the awkwardness of over-striving to convince the man that he is her equal."

"Then they ought not to marry, if such is her character. It depends wholly on that. If she is honest and earnest in loving the man, there will be no question of awkwardness, no embarrassment between them; and so far from striving to make him her equal, she will look up to him as her natural superior."

"And do you really think," she asked, slowly, "that there is one woman in England capable of all this?"

"Plenty," I answered.

"Why," she said, with a look of pleased astonishment, "your splendid belief in women is quite catching. Do you know that, when I hear you talk so, I feel that I could go and be a heroine such as you imagine? I do, indeed; but then I should probably feel myself badly qualified for the part afterwards, and regret that I had undertaken it. Still, I like to hear you talk so; for we women cannot be so very bad if one or two men think of us like that. I suppose," she added, turning her eyes upon me, "that you don't know of any two people who could try such an experiment as that we described?"

"I? How should I?"

"I do."

"Indeed."

"Yes; and, strangely enough, I am the friend of both of them. Yet I don't think they will ever marry."

"Why?"

"Because," she said, slowly, "the man is proud, and the woman is sensitive and reserved. The one will not speak, and the other cannot make advances; and so they allow the chance to slip by, and other circumstances will arise. The woman will be led into marrying some one else; and the man will break his heart slowly in work that has lost interest for him."

"You don't give me any suggestion," she said, rather petulantly, after a while. "What have you to say about these two?"

"Oh, nothing. They are probably unfitted for each other, or they would have come to an understanding long ago."

"Now that is just the point I meant to arrive at," she said. "What is it that prevents their coming to an understanding? You've seen two drops of water on a table lie perfectly still and quiet, although they are within an eighth of an inch of each other. But if you put the least thing between them—if you draw one of them a little way with the point of a needle, there is a splendid rush, and you can't tell the one from the other. I am the mutual friend of these two people—"

"And you would perform the office of the friendly needle?"

"Precisely. I owe a debt of gratitude to the one, and a debt of contrition to the other; what if I paid both off by one grand stroke of mediation?"

"Taking it for granted that both of them would thank you—that, in other words, both of them love each other. It is taking too much for granted, Miss Lesley."

"But at least there could be no harm in my attempting it, and seeing how far it would be acceptable to both."

"You mean," said I, calmly, "that you intend to pave the way for a marriage between Miss Burnham and myself."

She started visibly when I thus dragged her from the ambush of metaphor.

"You frighten me," she said, "when you speak in that cold and bitter way, as if you were suffering greatly, and still laughed at your sufferings. What is it you see between you and her?"

Yes, indeed: what was it that kept hovering between me and Hester Burnham—blotting out the beautiful lines of her features and the lustre of her eyes, so that I could see them no more—

what but the face of Weavle and the memory of those early years?

* * * * * * *

The Professor awoke with a snore.

"I have slept," he said.

"We have all been asleep," said Franz, "except Mr. Edward, who has been sitting and dreaming of England, with an open letter in his hand. Were the dreams pleasant?"

"Yes," I said. "They were about Richmond, in England, and a summer-day I spent there."

"Ah, I dined there once," said the Professor, "with several of your great men. I was surprised to find that they ate much and spoke little. But that was of no consequence to me, as I could find nobody who could speak French with ease, and so I was helpless."

Silber went to the window, and uttered a shout of joy.

"The rain is over; the night is fine. Herr Professor, we shall have a beautiful day to-morrow."

So we departed to our several rooms. Mine was next to that of Franz; and I could hear him singing of Schiller's wonderful maiden who came down into the valley in the spring-time. How did it fare, I thought, with that tender-hearted girl who was then among the dark trees of Burnham? At least, the same sky was over our heads, and, though we might never see each other on the voyage, we were still travelling towards the same far bourne.

CHAPTER XXXII.

INNSBRUCK.

Silber was right in his conjecture. Never was there a lovelier morning than that on which we started from Landeck to wander down the picturesque valley of the Inn to Imst. We had gradually ascended for a day or two, until even the valleys were high above the level of the sea; and the rarity of the mountain-air had its natural effect upon our spirits. Then the beauty of the country—the swollen, rushing gray waters of the Inn sweeping down the spacious chasm, the warm sunlight lying on the small farmhouses, the fronts of which were covered with yellow maize hung out to dry, the flocks of goats on the hill-sides, the great masses of berberry-bushes covered with scarlet wax-like berries, and all around the magnificent hills, with the splendid peaks of the Tschürgant and Sonnenspitz hemming in the end of the valley.

Much wilder and more solitary was the great valley which we entered after leaving Imst. Here the mountains showed a peculiar, soft, olive-green hue up to the very snow-line; and when the sun fell on these far masses of hills, the olive-green became warm and dark, like velvet in firelight. Round the base of the mountains stretched large forests, here and there broken by a patch of gray, where a mountain-torrent had cleared a passage for itself down to the Inn, bringing masses of *débris* with it. It was Sunday, too; and in some small village, shining yellow with hung-up maize, you would hear the crack of the rifle echoing along the hills, Sunday, after service, being the favorite time for the Tyroler's practising. Occasionally we met a sturdy peasant marching along with his huge weapon in its cumbrous water-proof covering, wondering, probably, how many kreutzer-points he was likely to make. The women, having come from the small village church, were in their finest attire, and stared curiously at us as they returned Franz's "*Grüss Gott!*" while the young lasses, in their braided bodices, short petticoats, and peculiar hats, had a sly look at Silber, whose student-appearance they doubtless admired extremely.

"Do you know that chamois is to be had here for sixpence per pound?" said Franz, "so we need not scruple to ask for it in the inns."

We remained a few days at Silz, exploring the Oetzthal and filling our portfolios with sketches; and we soon got accustomed to eating chamois. Indeed, chamois-flesh much more nearly resembles in flavor roe-deer venison than the flesh of the goat—a dainty we occasionally met with, but failed to appreciate. From Silz we passed along the splendid Oberinnthal, with its masses of gray limestone mountains, flecked with snow, the needle-peaks of the Selrain lying down in the south. Towards sunset we drew near Innsbruck; and I shall never forget the strange appearance which presented itself to us near Zirl. The sun had sunk behind the Tschürgant, far in the west; and all around us the limestone mountains were darkening in their gray, the sky above having changed from red and gold to a pale, chilly green. All at once, as we looked up and over the dark mountains on our left, we saw an immense cone of fire, still and cold. The wonderful gleam of this snow-peak, which, rising into the pallid and dusky twilight, caught the last light of the sun, had an extraordinary effect; it seemed as if the dark ridge of mountains in front alone separated us from a world on fire on the other side.

"Do not look at that any more," said the Professor, "or it will turn red, and then gray, and then purple. Come away now; and as long as you live you will be able to see in your mind that wonderful peak of yellow fire standing all by itself in the twilight."

Then we passed underneath the Martinswand, where, as you may know, the Emperor Maximilian, chasing a chamois, rolled down a precipice, and clung to a projecting rock. No one could reach him; but the priest of the neighborhood got up a procession, raised the host, gave the Emperor absolution, and implored divine succor; whereupon an angel, in the guise of a chamois-hunter, appeared and saved the Emperor, to the great glory of the Church.

"Now," said the Professor, "the story of the Emperor's peril and deliverance seems to be well authenticated; and I take it that he was rescued by a chamois-hunter—probably one of his attendants. I should like to know how they smuggled this poor man out of the road in order to persuade the people that it was an angel who saved the Emperor's life."

"Very likely they murdered him for the good of the Church," remarked Franz.

"It is clear," said the Professor, "that he could not have been ennobled, or presented with a piece of land in his native valley, for either would have contradicted the story of the angel. He could not have remained in the character of an angel at Maximilian's court, or in custody of a farm; for we don't naturalize angels, even in legends."

"They may have given him a post in the army," said Franz; "and very likely he would live to a good old age, and hear the story of the miraculous deliverance so often that he would come to believe it himself. But there is something highly humorous in the notion of the worthy priest, while the Emperor was hanging on to a rock, getting up a religious procession and going through ceremonies at the foot of the place, instead of sending people with ropes. I wonder if Maximilian swore at them; and whether he felt inclined to hang the lot of them after he came down?"

"I admire your efforts at historical criticism," said Silber. "You are supplementing one legend with half a dozen others; and the result is that you miss the points of divergence, and end in vapor."

This, I take leave to say, is perhaps the most idiotic remark ever made; but Silber delivered it in an impressive and thoughtful manner, as befitted a man who knew something of Heidelberg, metaphysics, and beer. Franz looked at Silber, expecting him to laugh; but when he saw that Silber was in earnest, he took to whistling; and so we went on.

The dark and narrow streets of the capital of the Tyrol were glittering with gas-lamps as we crossed the broad bridge and entered the town. We made our way to our appointed resting-place, and for the first time for some weeks found ourselves surrounded with the luxuries of a hotel. There were still a few tourists in Innsbruck, chiefly American; but there were one or two English, and it was with a strange sensation that I heard my native language spoken again. We dined at the table-d'hôte that evening; and I can believe that the English family who sat opposite us looked with some wonder and a little contempt upon our peculiar travelling-dress. Indeed, with that airy confidence which distinguishes our countrymen abroad, the father and eldest son made some observations which, to put Franz in a good-humor, I translated to him. He laughed heartily, and looked so pointedly at our opposite neighbors that they spoke less loudly thereafter.

There was no letter from Heatherleigh. What had occurred to interfere with his writing? We had a walk, after dinner, through the low archways and along the narrow thoroughfares of the town, and then we retired to rest, somewhat tired after our long ramble.

Next morning we went to have a look at the environs of Innsbruck, and made our way up to the hill on which the Schloss Amras is built. From the tower of this castle we had an excellent view of the great and elevated plain through which runs the Inn, cutting Innsbruck in two on its way. So lofty is this plain that the mountains which surround it have their snow-line singularly low; so that the visitor, looking at them on a warm autumn-day, is struck by the notion that he can easily walk up the side of one of those huge masses of limestone and find himself walking upon snow. The Martinswand now seemed to block up the entrance to the Oberinnthal, through which we had come on the previous afternoon; and lying on this side, just looking down on the plain, and on the many steeples of Innsbruck, were the gray and misty bulks of the Solstein, Brandjoch, Seegruben, Rumer Joch, and Spech-Kor, with here and there a small cluster of houses near their base, whence rose a pale blue smoke into the morning sunlight.

"What," said Franz, "if that wonderful fire-peak we saw last night was the Solstein over there; and what if the mountain got its name because it catches the evening light like that?"

"Nothing more probable," said the Professor. "The great Solstein lies just behind the Martinswand."

"And is 9300 feet high," said Silber, who had been bothering the peasantry all the way along with questions.

We went through the quaint old castle, and Franz was permitted to play an air on the chamber-organ that once belonged to Philippine Welser. The instrument was in fair tune, and the result sufficiently good. What honest workmen they must have had in those times! Fancy how one of our gorgeous piano-fortes—all carved wood, and satin, and polish—will sound four hundred years hence.

That evening we went to the theatre; the Professor, however, remaining at the hotel; and, as luck would have it, the piece to be played was Benedix's "Mathilde; oder, ein deutsches Frauenherz," the hero of which is a poor artist. We had a box for three florins; although Silber pointed out that the manager, wishing to make his theatre a means of education, had offered all students tickets at reduced rates. "Für die Herren Studierenden sind Parterre-Billets à 25 Kr. beim Herrn Universitäts-Pedell Hofer zu haben." Silber fancied he ought to have the same privilege as the university students, and evidently thought he would rather be in the pit among the soldiers and the scholars than in the boxes with the comfortable and Philistinic *bourgeoisie*.

It was a hard ordeal for the piece that it should have been criticised by a band of young artists, who, just fresh from a long journey, were practical in their notions and courageous in their hopes. Franz was most unmercifully severe upon poor Berthold Arnau, the artist, who is in love with a rich merchant's daughter; who has grand dreams, and is tortured by distrust of his own capacity; who makes love to Mathilde secretly, and then tamely submits to be turned out of the house, with shame and contumely, when his love is discovered.

"What a fool of an artist!" cried Franz, with infinite contempt. "What is the use of his crying, 'I feel it; I feel the power within me; and then it dies away, and I am in despair!' Instead of vaporing to a girl, why doesn't he sit down and take out his palette?"

Further on, when Mathilde has left her father's house and married Berthold, who is now grown rich and prosperous, the father offers to be reconciled, and the offer is repulsed.

"A fool again," cried Franz. "A real artist would look with indifference upon all these things. He would not remember a bygone grudge against a stupid old merchant for all these years. He would say, 'Here is my hand, old gentleman, if it is of any use to you; but go away now, for I have my pictures to look after.' He ought to be above the opinions or insults of a Philister—*nicht wahr*, Silber?"

Silber started.

"Yes," he said, "it is a very good piece."

"I have it," said Franz in a whisper. "Don't you think that Mathilde there, with her black eyes and hair, is something like Fräulein Riedel?"

There was certainly some resemblance between Fräulein Anschütz (to whom I beg to pay a passing compliment), of the Innsbruck Nationaltheater, and Fräulein Riedel, of the Munich Volkstheater.

"Silber is trying hard to imagine himself in Munich, and that the little Riedel is before him. Will he cry presently? No; he has drank no beer this evening."

Silber, however, applauded most boisterously at the end of each effective scene in which Mathilde appeared—so much so that Mathilde inadvertently glanced up at our box.

"She thanks you, Silber," said Franz; "wouldn't you give your ears now for a bouquet?"

"She acts remarkably well," said Silber, hotly.

"That is no reason why you should bite my head off," said Franz. "All I know is that her stage husband is a prig, and should have been a lackey rather than an artist. Yet Fels is not a bad actor; and I have seen many worse than Herr Ströhl. I will drink their very good health, and yours, Silber, and that of a young lady who rather resembles Fräulein Anschütz, when we go out."

"Ah, you think she *does* resemble Fräulein Riedel?" said Silber, eagerly.

"You do, at least; for I don't believe you know anything of the piece. Now what is the name of Mathilde's brother?"

"Stuff!" said Silber, turning angrily away.

When Mathilde had at length effected a reconciliation between her husband and her father by means of her "deutsches Frauenherz," we left the theatre, and proceeded on a prowl through the town, visiting such places of amusement as were still open for the benefit of the soldiers. Now we entered a gayly-lit beer-garden, again we heard a little music, and so forth, until Franz, who was beyond the ameliorating and controlling influences of his zither, and who had drank a little more wine than was necessary, began to wax warm about political matters, and generally expressed his readiness to fight any man or woman born in the whole of the Tyrolese capital. But the fit did not last long; for presently he was off into the dark streets again, singing somewhat loudly the mad carnival song—

"Alle Vögele singet so hell,
Bis am Samstig z' Obed;
Alle Meideli hättet mi gern,
O! wie bin i ploget.
Narro!
Hidele, hädele, hinterm Städtele
Hät en Bettelmann Hochzit;
Es giget e Musle, 's tanzet e Länsle,
Es schlägt en Igele Trumme;
Alle Thierle wo Wädeli hond,*
Sollet zur Hochzit kumme!
Narro!"

When we got home to the hotel we found the Professor and an American gentleman busily discussing the merits of the various Continental galleries; the American speaking French fluently, and with very little intonation.

We did not stay long in Innsbruck; there being little (beyond

* "Alle Thierchen, die Schwänze haben,
Sollen zur Hochzeit kommen."

some picturesque street-views) worthy of an artist's attention in the place. We followed the course of the Inn to Jenbach; and there we turned sharply to the left, ascending the main street of the steep little village, and following the road that leads up and over the hills to the Achensee. What a strangely solitary lake this is, lying high among the mountains; and how beautiful were its clear blue waters as we first caught a sight of them, with the sunlight lying over the wooded slopes that descend almost perpendicularly to the shore, while a slight wind was causing the keen blue surface to ripple in lines of light. Our road wound along the right bank of the lake, under the craggy rocks, with their thick brushwood and ferns; but we met no carriages on this narrow path, for a bridge had broken down some two days before on this side of Scholastica. The perfect stillness of the lake and of the solitary mountains was quite unbroken; and the warm sunlight seemed to have hushed the animal and insect life of the woods into peace. Near the other side of the lake we could see a woman pulling a small boat; but no sound was heard, as the prow slowly divided the brilliant plain of blue.

When we got up to this broken bridge we found a carriage and a pair of horses which had been hired by a party of English ladies at Jenbach. Not one of the ladies could speak German; and they stood on the road, having descended from the carriage, blankly staring at the broken planks of the bridge, and at the two or three swarthy men who were driving in new piles. Their coachman was doing his best (by much shouting) to let them know that there was no help for it—back they must go to Jenbach. When I explained the position of affairs to them, they poured torrents of sarcasm and abuse upon the stupidity of the peasants who had not sent on word of the accident to that village.

"The workmen," I told them, "say that for three florins they will patch the bridge together and take your carriage over."

After a good deal of bargaining, they agreed to pay the three florins; but the head-workman was seized with a fit of honesty, and admitted it would be of no use, as there was another bridge broken just beyond Scholastica.

"This is a pretty country," said one of the ladies, with a sneer.

"There seems to be nothing left for you to do but to return," I said; "so I shall wish you good-day and a pleasant journey."

"Oh no! pray don't leave us without telling these men that—that—"

But there was nothing to tell them. Abuse of the Tyrol and the Tyrolese generally was a communication which it was quite unnecessary to make to the poor bridge-makers, who had again betaken themselves to their labors.

"May I ask where you were going to?"

"To Munich, of course. Here is our contract, written in French, made with that rascal in Jenbach, who *knew* the bridge was broken down."

The speaker was one of those tall, solitary-looking ladies who are constantly seen in Continental hotels, and who go wandering about Europe with a charming belief in the omnipotence of the English tongue, and a fine contempt for the manners and customs of the people whom they deign to visit.

"Then you must go back to Jenbach, and proceed from thence by rail to Rosenheim and Munich; or you can wait at Jenbach until the bridge is ready, probably by Monday next."

So saying, we went on our way, and saw them no more. But I do not envy the innkeeper at Jenbach when they returned to him—that is, if he could understand either French or English.

CHAPTER XXXIII.

HEATHERLEIGH'S FEAT.

Once more in the quiet and white Königin Strasse, fronting the yellowing trees of the Englischer Garten. Munich looked quite homely when we returned to it. But I went into its formal and stately streets without much hope of meeting there any welcome faces, such as I used to look for in leaving London to get down into the heart of Burnham. Nevertheless, it was a sort of home; and we were glad to see again the familiar features of the Odeon-platz and the Maximilian Strasse.

The good Professor returned with a sigh to his labors and his domestic routine. His homely wife kissed him dutifully, in a quiet, affectionate way, and then began to tell him, in an injured tone, of the interference of the Herren Polizei about something or other. The Professor listened meekly, and then suggested that we should have a little chocolate.

Lena was, for a wonder, gracious, Franz having brought her a very pretty brooch from Innsbruck. Instead of being impudent and coquettish, she was shy and demure; and I think if Franz had taken advantage of her whim of complaisance to ask her for a tiny kiss, she would not have minded much.

"You have been working hard, Mr. Frank?" she asked.

"We have all been working hard, Lena," returned her lover.

"You will let me see your sketches, won't you?"

Franz was overjoyed to find Lena caring a pin-point about anything he did; and he promised not only to show her his sketches, but to finish up any she liked, and present them to her.

"You have been very wicked in your letters since I went away, Lena," he said.

"Why, then?" she asked, elevating her eyebrows with a pretty look of wonder.

"You know."

"I know I wrote to you; isn't that enough? You should be glad to have my letters, even if there was nothing but nonsense in them."

"That is just what was in them."

"Oh, indeed!"

This with a pout.

"If I only wrote nonsense, you shall have no more of it."

Franz began to look apprehensive.

"Lena!—"

"Oh, I can only talk nonsense. Very well. But you like my nonsense, don't you, Herr Papaken?"

With that she went and hung around the Herr Papa's neck, and toyed with his neckerchief.

"What is it, Lena?"

"You will be my sweetheart, Papaken, and you won't mind my talking nonsense, will you? Travelling doesn't improve one's temper, does it, Papaken? and people think they have grown wise when they go abroad, and come back savage and intolerable. But you are always the same, Papaken, and I don't want anybody but you."

Franz became angry. He did not like being talked at.

"Herr Professor," said he, "did you ever know a cat that

stroked herself the wrong way in order to have an excuse for scratching you?"

"Oh, I am a cat," said Lena, with a scornful toss of the small and pretty head. "Mr. Frank, you will beg my pardon before I see you again."

And so she left the room, leaving Franz the victim of a deadly remorse. It was all the work of a few careless words; and yet the mischief they had caused was sufficiently portentous to a lover.

"On the very day of our return, too!" he said. "She is no better than a tigress or a Red Indian."

Heatherleigh's letter had been sent to Munich instead of Innsbruck. It ran in this way:

"Dear Ted,—Did you ever try to break the back of a woman's opinion, and find yourself thrashing the air? I think the most vexing thing for a man is to prove triumphantly to a woman that she ought not to believe so-and-so and so-and-so, and find, after all, that the impalpable thing he fancied he had destroyed is as brisk and lively as ever. With a woman you don't care about, it doesn't matter. You leave her in her 'invincible ignorance.' But to find yourself baffled and tortured and vexed by this invisible, insignificant thing called an opinion, when the interests of one you love are concerned, is a grievous thing, not easily to be borne.

"At last I met Polly. I knew I should, sooner or later; for I watched for her whenever I had the time. It was yesterday forenoon, and I was going around by Gloucester Gate. She saw me at some distance off, and tried to avoid me; but that was of no use. When I went up and spoke to her, she was very much excited; and her excitement took the form of a prodigious freezing constraint, that made her look like a frightened wild bird, lying still, but watching how to escape from your hand.

"'Polly,' said I, 'we didn't use to meet like this?'

"'It is all the greater pity we should meet like this now,' she said hurriedly. 'But it can't be helped, Mr. Heatherleigh; and if you'll be good enough—'

"'To go away and leave you, Polly?' I said. 'No; I don't mean to do anything of the kind. And all this *can* be helped.'

"So I went on to tell her what nonsense her recent conduct had been; and how foolish she was to regard what my father had said. This was evidently a sore point with the poor girl; for you may recollect she was driven by her strong pride and indignation to take it for granted, without my mentioning her name, that it was she I meant to marry. No girl would like to be entrapped into such a confession, and with her I could see that the reflection was excessively painful. But then I urged upon her the necessity of sinking all these considerations, every consideration except one—that here were we two, almost alone in London, and that the best thing we could do was to marry, and keep our own counsel, and let our exceedingly respected relatives, on both sides, pass such comments as their lively wit might suggest.

"You may fancy this a very matter-of-fact way of putting it. But then I had to treat the sensitive malady of poor Polly in a somewhat heroic fashion, and assume a mastery that I did not feel. What were my sensations? Here was I—a man drawing on towards middle-life, looking upon myself as a sort of widower, indeed—with few friends, with a liking for domestic quiet and comfort, and with a disposition sufficiently amiable, I hope, to keep on good terms with an affectionate companion; here was she, alone in London, unfriended, with nobody to look to for assistance in case of need. Why shouldn't we two outcasts join our fortunes, and be stronger through mutual help? There never was a marriage more reasonable in point of circumstances; to say nothing of the affection that leads you to think any marriage reasonable.

"All this and more I represented to her; and still found myself fighting with my invisible enemy of an opinion, or determination, or something of the kind that lay behind the unnatural hardness of her look and coldness of her voice. What was I to do? We had got around into the Park, by the trees above the canal; and there was scarcely anybody there at this hour of the forenoon. I preached, I prayed, I begged, all in vain. She was as obdurate as marble. She admitted all my arguments; and then merely said that what I asked was impossible, that she and I never could marry, that we ought to separate then and forever.

"I made one more vexed endeavor to bring her to reason; and then, that not succeeding, I think I was seized with a sort of madness—a long and happy future for both of us seemed to dance before my eyes—I caught her unawares, and, with a laugh that must have sounded like the laugh of a maniac, kissed her.

She turned around, white and angry; and then, seeing that I was laughing in desperation, all her resolve seemed gradually to break away, until at last she laughed too, in her old frank way, and held out both her hands.

"'I cannot help myself, I suppose,' she said.

"Was there ever a courtship like that, Ted, in the open air, in the forenoon, in Regent's Park? Now, when I look back upon it, I ask myself if I was temporarily insane: whether or not, the result remains, and we are both happy.

"'Now,' said I to Polly, 'let me show you that you have not agreed to marry a boy, who will neither know how to work for you, nor master you in your sulky fits, nor make you take good care of your health. I am about to become rich. I have a grand scheme to make our fortune, Polly.'

"'What is it?' she asked.

"'A company that shall produce something out of nothing, and alter the whole of our commercial relations with India and China. This company will contract to buy up on the Monday morning of each week all the sermons which have been preached on the preceding Sunday. From all parts of the kingdom the various MSS. must be sent in and collected in the works of the company at Millwall. That is the first step.'

"'Yes,' she said, very much interested, apparently.

"'These sermons are now taken and put into vast caldrons, which are in communication with all the ordinary apparatus of a distillery. In fact, the sermons are to be distilled; and the product, which is to make our fortune, Polly, is—'

"'What?' she asked.

"'Opium.'

"She looked vexed.

"'You have just done the most serious thing you ever did in your life, and you fall to joking already.'

"'My dear,' said I, 'I propose to have our engagement, and our married life too, a prolonged joke. People make these things serious, because they grow afraid. We shall not grow afraid, you and I; and we will carry on the joke from day to day, until, when we have grown old and white-haired, we shall look back and see that we have spent life pleasantly and enjoyed it rationally. They will tell you it is very wrong to talk confidently about coming happiness, and to be so sure that life is going to be pleasant; but isn't it better than to be continually foreboding evil and making yourself wretched by anticipation? If the evil must come, let it: we sha'n't whimper like children, Polly. In the mean time you and I will take such enjoyment and comfort as we can get; for we shall never be twice young.'

"You, Ted, know what I think about such things; but I preached in this fashion to give my poor, trembling Polly a little courage. She looked happy and comfortable in a quiet, timorous way; and seemed to have grown all at once trustful and docile and affectionate. Immediately, too, she instituted a sort of right of property in me, and timidly begged of me to promise never to go out any more at night with my throat bare—a thing she used always to protest against. Her remembrance of it just at this moment made me laugh heartily, and she looked a little self-conscious and shy, as if I had taken advantage of her confidence. There was something so odd in the notion that there was now a little woman to see that I must not catch cold or otherwise harm myself, that I felt myself vastly exalted in my own estimation, and ready to look down with a wonderful compassion on you poor fellows who are fighting the world all by yourselves.

"Do I rave? Am I sane? I scarcely know. Your mother tries to make the affair wear a serious aspect, and fails wholly. I cannot get frightened at the notion of taking a house. A parish-clerk is not an awful creature to me, as he ought to be. The cares of furniture sit lightly upon me; for I know that Polly and I won't break our hearts if a saucepan is wanting, or there happen to be no salt-spoons with the breakfast-service. I have no heavy sense of responsibility whatever; and I ask myself whether my want of anxiety is a proof that I am not fitted to encounter the solemnities of a married life. Gray hairs will come soon enough, Ted; and I don't look out for them every morning in the glass."

The rest of the letter contained lots of gossip about our old companions in the neighborhood of Fitzroy Square, and their doings. But through all the letter there breathed the same audacious trust and gladness that showed how Heatherleigh's life had been stirred by these new experiences. Yet even in his joy there was the same wise and kindly spirit that had drawn me towards him in his indolent bachelor days.

Two days later came a letter from Polly herself. She hinted timidly that Mr. Heatherleigh had told me what had occurred;

and then began to talk of other things in a practical, constrained sort of fashion. But again and again she returned inadvertently to Heatherleigh, and his doings and prospects, and spoke of him with a pride which she did her best to conceal. Polly used to have a pretty correct notion of Heatherleigh's capacity as an artist—indeed, he had frankly told her the limits within which he knew he should always work; but now all these things were changed. Mr. Heatherleigh was to wake up from his indolence and do something great. The public were getting tired of the commonplace work of many of the R. A.'s; it was necessary that the august body should get some new blood into it. And Polly enclosed me a cutting from a newspaper, in which a picture of Heatherleigh's was praised in unequivocal terms.

When was I coming home? she asked. I was wanted to make up again the little Bohemian supper-parties that were so comfortable and jolly in the old days. I translated these words into a wish on the part of Polly that I should see her in the full honor and joy of her new position, and that I might share some of her superabundant happiness.

In the mean time there was little chance of my congratulating in person these two who had, in spite of the world and the devil, achieved some measure of happiness amid the discordant interests of life. I feared to go to England. Should I not meet there with the old hopeless feeling, and know that Hester Burnham was as far removed from me as a star might be? Here she was nearer to me. In England I should find her about to marry her pale-faced cousin, with the mean heart and the cold eyes; here I grew bold, and believed such a thing impossible.

So I turned with diligent labor to the picture of Wölundur and the king's daughter in the lonely northern island; and as I worked at it, on those days which were not devoted to class-studies, I knew that she would see it in some far-off time. So the months passed, and the new year came in, and the spring-time, and there was a breath of primroses and sweet violets in the air that seemed to speak of the green hedges and the leafy woods of Barnham.

CHAPTER XXXIV.

AT BURNHAM GATES.

My private studio was my bedroom, and it looked out upon the Königin Strasse and the trees of the "English Garden." While the trees were leafless, and even now when they showed only the young leaves of the spring, you could look over the park-like meadows that lie within the garden, and you could see the few people who occasionally strolled across this open space to the paths under the chestnuts and limes. It was here, somehow or other, that I felt convinced that I should see Hester Burnham. Many and many a time I have looked out of the small window, with almost a definite anticipation of beholding the figure and the dress I knew so well coming out from under the trees. Many a time have I started to observe in the distance some lady who might be she, and wait, with a strange, joyous wonder, to see whether the figure would approach with that dainty and queenly gait which was peculiar to her of all the women in the world. The successive disappearance of these possibilities was scarcely a disappointment, and was certainly not a misery; for I got to connect the English Garden with her so completely that it looked like a bit of friendly Buckinghamshire that had wandered into this foreign land.

Spring came upon us suddenly. One morning I awoke to find a new freshness in the air—a mild, warm gratefulness that seemed filled with the perfume of opening buds. As it happened, Franz and I were invited on that day to be introduced to Fräulein Riedel, that young lady having graciously signified to her lover that she should like to see the two friends of whom he frequently spoke.

We were to meet Silber and her in the Neue Anlagen, just under Haidhausen; and here it was, among the leafy labyrinths of the pleasure-ground, that we encountered the happy pair. The little actress, with the shining black eyes and hair, received us without any show of embarrassment, such as sat upon the concerned and delighted and stupid face of her companion. She walked on with us, and immediately began, in a matter-of-fact way, to ask whether it were difficult to learn English thoroughly, and whether they paid actresses well in England.

"But you don't need to learn English thoroughly, Fräulein," I told her, "to appear on an English stage. We like a marked foreign pronunciation, because it harmonizes with the origin and character of our plays. As to salary, I don't know much about that; but a great many of our actresses wear most expensive jewels, on the stage and off."

"Do you always have your operettas translated into English?"

"Generally."

"What do they pay the principal lady?"

The tone of this conversation did not seem to please poor Silber. He endeavored to divert her attention from such mercenary matters; but she kept firmly to her point, and showed herself a thorough little woman of business. Perhaps Silber was the more annoyed because her talk evidently left him outside of all her plans of the future. She seemed to say that there could be no question of marriage between a not over-rich student and this brisk young actress, who had an eye to lucrative engagements in England.

At length we bade them good-bye, and received, on parting, a kindly invitation to take tea with the Fräulein and her mamma some day on the following week. Franz and I went off towards Brunnthal, and then crossed the Isar and went up by Ludwig's-Walzmühle. The air, as I said, had grown suddenly sweet with the promise of the spring; and there seemed to be a joyous, stirring life in the trees and in the warm, moist ground. I knew what Burnham would be like then; and I could see the green valley before my eyes, steeped in the clear spring sunshine.

"Franz," said I, "will you start with me at six o'clock for England? We shall travel day and night; then I will show you an English valley in spring-time, that is finer than anything you ever read of in an Eastern story; and we shall come straight back again, without anybody in England knowing anything about it."

"You take my breath away—England—six o'clock this evening—and the expense—"

"I invite you to go as my guest. I have become rich to-day. A gentleman in England has heard of this Wolundur picture from the Professor, and I had a letter this morning from him, offering a handsome sum for it. Shall we go at six o'clock, and be back in a week?"

"I have nothing ready for such a journey."

"Why, an old traveller like you should be able to pack up in ten minutes for a voyage to Lebanon."

We walked back to the town. I got him to have some dinner at the "Four Seasons," and this gave him courage. We went over to the Königin Strasse, and bade good-bye to the Professor and his family.

"Why do you look afraid, Linele?" said Franz. "It is only a bit of fun. We shall be back in two or three days."

"You may be drowned," said Lena, with tender and troubled eyes.

"Do you know why we are going? Listen!" said Franz, and he whispered something into Lena's ear.

Lena looked at me, and smiled and nodded.

"Then I will let you go," she said to Franz. "Leb' wohl! Don't be longer than a week, Franz. Ade!"

We started at six. By eleven next morning we were in Cologne. Thence a rapid journey brought us over Brussels to Calais; and at length I heard a fine round English oath, that told me I was in my native land.

We went to the Langham Hotel when we arrived in London, and there Franz speedily became familiar with all the waiters who could speak German.

"I have brought you here," I said, "that you may study American manners and customs, without going to America. Breakfast and dine for a day or two in that big room with the pillars, and you may save yourself the expense of a trip to New York."

"These are not English, then—these pretty girls, with the French fashions, who talk loudly across the table, and have at sixteen the manner of a woman of thirty?"

You will soon see the difference. Perhaps you will prefer the American type."

"If they are all as pretty as these girls I shall have no choice. Surely we have made a mistake, and come to Sachsen, *wo die schönen Mädchen wachsen.* But the Leipsic and Dresden girls are fair."

We spent a day in London, hiring a hansom for the entire

time, and driving about to such places as Franz wished to see. London, I think, was as new and delightful to me as to him. It was so pleasant an experience to be able to understand everything that everybody said, without having to listen particularly; and it was pleasant, also, to feel an easy familiarity with the customs of the place, even while the very streets, that were once so well-known, seemed to have assumed an oddly unaccustomed appearance. Then, on the following day, we got on the top of the Buckinghamshire coach, and drove away from the city bustle and noise.

I was proud of my native county when we saw it, then in all its spring greenery. The young hawthorn was out in the hedges, the chestnut-buds were bursting, the elms were sprinkled over with leaves; and the windy clouds that crossed the blue spring sky gave to the far-off woods and hills a constant motion of shadow and sunlight that created landscapes at every step. We drove down through the old-fashioned villages — Chalfont, with its stream crossing the main road; Amersham, with its broad street and twin rows of quaint, old, red-brick houses; Missenden, with its ancient abbey, and church high up on the hill; and then we found ourselves in the valley that looks up to Burnham.

I took Franz up and over the chalk-hills, and through the woods that were now growing rich with flowers. These were a wonder to him—the wildernesses of wild hyacinth, a lambent blue; the pale, blush-tinted anemone, the pink-veined wood-sorrel, the tiny moschatel, the dark dog's-mercury, the golden celandine; and everywhere the perfume of the sweet violet, clustered among its heart-shaped leaves, along the rabbit-banks and around the roots of the trees. The constant animal life, also—the ruddy squirrel running up the straight stem of a young beech, the disappearance of a rabbit into the brambles of a chalk-dell, the silent flight of a hare across the broad fields to some distant place of safety, the sudden whirr of a cock-pheasant, and the incessant screaming of jays; while all around were the busy tom-tits and thrushes and blackbirds, with a glimpse of a golden-crested wren hopping from bush to bush, or a kestrel hanging high up in the blue, his wings motionless. Over all these, again, the light and motion of a breezy English sky, with cumulus masses of white cloud that chased the sunlight over the Burnham woods, or hid the distant horizon in dark lines of an intense purple.

"That is the house you have told me about," said Franz, as we descended into the valley again, and drew near Burnham. "I recognize it. How fine it looks, with the great avenue and the trees! You said a young lady owned it—who is she?"

I heard the cantering of two horses on the road behind me, and turned.

"Franz!" I cried, "jump into the wood here: she must not see us!"

It was too late. She came along at a good pace on a handsome small horse, followed by old Pritchett on the black cob I had ridden many a time. I pulled my slouched hat over my face; with our heavy German travelling-cloaks it was not likely she would suspect either of us of being English. As she passed, I was aware that she looked at us somewhat curiously; and then she went on. I could look at her with safety as she rode up the soft, elastic turf of the avenue. I saw her once more!—with the clear, white spring sunlight on her cheek and on her brown hair, that the wind lifted and flung about her neck and shoulders. I knew she was there; and yet it seemed I was scarcely more aware of her presence than if it had been a dream. For I had been accustomed to see her in dreams with such a vividness that now, in actual life, she scarcely seemed more real.

And was not this a dream? Our rapid flight from Germany had been so sudden that now I almost feared to turn my eyes, lest I should awake and find myself among the white houses of Munich. Yet surely this was a thoroughly English scene before me—the grand old house, silent amid its great trees, and the young English girl riding up to it, under that windy English sky. You might have fancied it was in the sixteenth century, all this picture; and that presently the gay young lover would appear, singing—

> "Now, Robin, lend to me thy bow,
> Sweet Robin, lend to me thy bow,
> For I must now a hunting with my lady go,
> With my sweet lady go!"

"I am right," exclaimed Franz, suddenly. "I *have* seen her before; it is the face hanging up in your room, in the Professor's house."

"There is nothing to wonder at, is there?" I asked. "I have seen this lady several times—I have spoken to her—"

"And why don't you now go up to the house, and renew your acquaintance with her?"

"Because we are in England, Franz."

So we stood at the white gate and looked up towards Burnham; and I could not go away. When should I ever see it again, and all the trees that I knew? As we lingered there, some one came riding down the avenue. It was Pritchett. I knew the old man could not possibly recognize me, so I still remained there; but when he came down to the gate, he pulled up the cob, and said—

"Beg your pahrdon, gentlemen, but you be furreigners, bain't ye?"

"Yes," I said, "we have just come from Germany."

"Ah, that wur what she said," he muttered to himself. "Miss Burnham's compliments, and if so be as you'd like to go over the house and look at the pictures, you may."

"Will you say to Miss Burnham that we are very much obliged to her, but that we could not think of intruding upon her, since the family is at home?"

"Lor bless ye, the family is only—"

"Herself," he was nearly saying; but probably thinking that such an admission would lessen the grandeur of Burnham in the eyes of the foreigners, he muttered something about our being welcome, if we chose to visit the house, and then rode off.

I translated all this to Franz.

"Such complaisance to foreigners is quite remarkable," he said. "You have no right, I think, to speak of English pride, stiffness, title-worship, and what not, when a grand lady like that goes out of her way to be civil to two wandering German students, whom she finds hanging about her gates."

"But one swallow does not make a summer, Franz."

So we turned away.

"Where are we going now?" said Franz.

"Anywhere you like. If you would rather stay a few days longer in England, and see some of our shipping-towns, I will go with you with pleasure."

"That means," said Franz, with deliberation, "that you came over all the way from Munich to England just to catch one glimpse of that girl's face. Perhaps you will now deny that you are in love with her?"

"Deny it? Oh no. That is the very joke of the position, that I am in love with her. Don't you see what a merry jest it is?"

"I see that you don't laugh much over it," said Franz, bluntly.

"Perhaps not; a few days ago, in Germany, I fancied that I should marry that lady some day. It is a possibility that has hung before me for a long time. Now I see it is no longer a possibility. I was dreaming in Germany: a breath of our English air has woke me out of the trance."

"But why? but why?" said Franz.

"You are a German, and you cannot understand it. One of our statesmen has said that there are two nations in England—the rich and the poor! she belongs to the one, I to the other; and in England for a lady of her position to forget herself, and what is due to her friends— Bah! why speak any more of it?"

"My dear friend," said Franz, "I don't think you can express yourself properly in German yet; for I cannot make any sense out of what you say. You seem to forget the dignity of love and of art. If the girl is worth loving, she will know that any woman, if she had twenty castles, might be proud to marry a true artist. She will think more of him, as he sits with an old coat and oil-stained cuffs before his easel, than of a young dandy smelling like a civet-cat and incrusted with rings, who comes to pay compliments out of an empty brain to her. Suppose she had twenty dozen such castles, she ought to feel proud and honored by having gained the love of a man who may make the next centuries inquire curiously about her, and speak kindly of her for his sake."

"German, all German, my dear Franz," I said. "Translate that into English, and it will become mere bathos."

"To the devil, then, with your beast of a language!" exclaimed Franz. "I should have thought, when you borrowed your speech from all the nations in Europe, you might have got as much as would let you talk common-sense. I was studying your language while you were looking over the gates up to the big house. I found the *mélange* almost intelligible. There was '*fourniture*,' which was French; there was 'mansion,' from the Latin '*mansio*,' I suppose; there was 'park,' which is merely our German '*Park*;' there was '*timber*,' which is an old Icelandic and Danish and—"

"What are you talking about? 'Mansion,' 'park,' 'timber'—where did you see all this?"

"As I tell you, while you were looking up at the house. There are two large bills on the gates."

"On the Burnham gates?"

"Yes."

We had not gone far on our return journey; so we walked back again to see what these bills were. As I had suspected, they were the ordinary advertisements of a firm of auctioneers.

"Burnham is for sale," I said to Franz.

"So the lady took us for two probable purchasers," remarked Franz, ruefully. "That explains her complaisance."

"Do we look like probable purchasers of a house like that?"

Yes, after all these years, Burnham and the old family were to be separated; and the girl who was the last of the race was to be turned out into the world, a wanderer. Here, now, was a splendid opportunity for the hero and lover to step in, buy up the place, and lay it as a gift at his mistress's feet. Among all the young men of England, rich and able to do such a thing, was there not one who would come forward in this romantic fashion, and show that love was not quite gone from among us?

I ought to have been selfishly glad that this catastrophe had brought Hester Burnham so much the nearer to me. But I had been born and bred under the shadow of the antiquity of Burnham, and it seemed to me pitiable that the family should lose its high estate and be cast out among strangers.

We stopped that night at the Red Lion in Missenden, and we found all the talk was about the sale of Burnham. I succeeded in preserving my incognito, and listened to all the rumors and stories which were circulated without restraint about the matter.

"I'm not for sayin'," remarked one old gentleman, who sat in a corner of the parlor, and smoked a long clay—"I'm not for sayin' as anybody's in the wrong."

"I side with you, Muster Clump," remarked another; "but I thinks as it wur a pity Miss Hester should ha' been sent to France. Folks don't stick to the good old English way o' livin' when they come back from France; and though I wouldn't say as it was Miss Hester's doin', I hold as it wur a pity she should ha' been sent to France."

"It wur none o' her doin'," said a third, decisively, "I'll stake my life on't; and I doan't see as any mahn has the right to blame things on France as he doesn't understand."

"Ah, you're a wise mahn, Muster Blaydon," retorted the other, with a sneer, "and so you wur when your good missus axed ye about them pigs o' Mr. Toomer's."

Here there was a subdued laugh all around; and Mr. Blaydon looked disposed to rise and settle the question summarily with his opponent.

"I bain't a dog chasin' of his own tail, leastways, and thinkin' as he's makin' folks laugh. I hold by it as it wur none o' her doin'; and them as talks about France had better show as they've been there by their manners."

"There be more nor Miss Hester in the family," observed the first speaker, sagaciously nodding his head.

"Ah, that there be!" repeated Mr. Blaydon, triumphantly. "There be more nor her, Muster Clump; and it don't seem to me likely as a young lady like that has been meddlin' wi' them lawyers, and gettin' the place into debt. I say wi' you, Muster Clump, there's more o' the name than her; and no mahn will make me believe as it is her fault. Talk o' France! Pah!"

"I'm not goin' to reason wi' any mahn as runs his head agin a stone wall, like a mad bull," remarked the second speaker, with slow virulence; "but what I say is as other folks in the country 'ave stayed at 'ome all their lives, and made theirsels comfortabler and richer than they wur afore, and as it is a suspicious cikmstance—I say, a suspicious cikmstance—as them as has gone to France 'ave come back and found they wur obliged to sell out. I don't reason wi' no mahn; but I see things as lies afore my nose, and I'm no blinder than my neighbors."

"And who is to have the old place, gentlemen?" said the landlord.

"Most like a linen-draper fro' Lunnon," remarked Mr. Clump, contemptuously, "as 'll paint the 'ouse spick-and-span new, and put up boards agin' trespassers—as 'll go out shootin', and hit the dogs instead o' the birds, and pay nothin' to the 'unt—"

"And kill the foxes," said one.

"And contract wi' all the Lunnon tradesmen for what he wants, to save twopence off the pound o' tea."

"Yes, Muster Blaydon," said Mr. Clump, "there's a goodish many o' the gentry as doan't know their dooty—leastways they doan't do it—to the place where they wur born and bred. They mun send to Lunnon for heverythink—even if they want peppermints for church o' Sundays—howiver fur away they be; and all to be in the fashion, and forgettin' as the people around them 'ave rents to pay, and don't grumble when their corn's trodden down by the 'unt. I will say this, as Miss Hester wur good in that way to the folks in this here place; and it's my belief as there'll be a difference when the new howner comes in."

This, indeed, seemed to be the general impression; and there was scarcely one of them there who had not some kindly act to speak of on the part of Hester Burnham.

As I looked along the valley the next morning, it seemed to me that Burnham was about to undergo a great transformation, and be henceforth strange and unfamiliar.

CHAPTER XXXV.

THE DROPPED GLOVE.

On the following afternoon Franz and I were seated at one of the bow-windows of the Langham smoking-room, looking at the people who were driving down Portland Place towards Regent Street, in every description of carriage. Now it was a Cabinet Minister, looking austerely unconscious of the notice he was attracting; now it was a young and pretty *prima donna*, gayly chatting to her husband, and confounding the current rumors about her conjugal unhappiness; now it was a well-known peeress, who had just been attending a meeting of some charitable society; and again it was some poor young girl who had at first figured in a casino, and then been petted and photographed and made much of, until she had come out as a fine lady, and was now coating the primal simplicity of her face with violet-powder, and wearing hired jewels, and looking hard and worn and sad under her new-found wealth and fame.

"Ah, look!" exclaimed Franz, suddenly, "who is that lady with the yellow hair?"

I caught sight of a mail phaeton just turning the corner. The driver, I saw at a glance, was Mr. Morell; and the lady on his left, whose yellow hair had attracted Franz's attention, was no other than Bonnie Lesley.

"That is a lady I have often spoken to you about," I said. "They didn't look in here, did they?"

"Not that I saw," said Franz.

We went to the theatre that evening. When we returned there was a message awaiting us to say that two gentlemen had called, and would call some time later.

Towards twelve we were again in the smoking-room, when Mr. Morell, in full evening-dress, and Heatherleigh, in his ordinary rough-and-ready costume, appeared at the door.

"Ha, ha!" said Morell, "if you didn't see us, we saw you. And now you must explain—"

"We did see you," I said, "and you have more to explain than we have."

"Don't you know, then?" he asked, with some surprise.

"What?"

"You did not get a letter from Miss Lesley, within the past two or three days?"

"Not very likely, since we left Munich nearly a week ago. Let me introduce my friend, and will you be good enough to talk French?"

"If I can," said Morell.

When the introduction had taken place, Heatherleigh explained (allowing Morell to assume a bashfulness which he possessed not) that Bonnie Lesley had written to tell me of her approaching marriage.

"And this is the happy man," he said, putting his hand on Morell's shoulder. "And he has shown his gratitude and good spirits by writing the wickedest reviews he could think of for several weeks past. When he is in a good-humor, he revels in butchery. The other night I went up to his chambers, and found that he had just reviewed several books which were lying on the table. So soon as he saw me he rang for his servant to remove the carcasses, and went into his bedroom to wash his hands."

"You might take a lesson from me, Heatherleigh," he retorted, "and keep your sarcasm for people whom you *don't* know."

"I wish you all manner of joy," I said, "and I must write to Miss Lesley to explain why I did not answer her letter directly."

"Then you don't know anything it contained?" Morell said. "You don't know that Burnham was to be sold?"

"Yes, I knew that. I have seen the announcement."

"Perhaps you know the latest news about it?"

"No."

"There seems a chance of the sale being indefinitely postponed. Only, the house must be let; and I suppose Miss Burnham will live abroad."

"Abroad?"

"I suppose so. I am sorry Miss Lesley is not a blood-relation of that young lady, or I might have the right to administer to Mr. Alfred Burnham a kicking which he much needs. Ah, you don't know anything about it, do you? *Mon brave garçon*, get me something to drink, and, in the words of the drama, I will tell you all."

It was a very pretty story he told me—one with which it is unnecessary to soil these pages. The results of it have already been indicated.

"I will confess," said Heatherleigh, "that I did the old Colonel an injustice. I thought his appearance of simplicity, and his austere and proper conduct, were only a bit of the play, in which he was acting in concert with his son. But it seems clear that the Colonel has come worse off than anybody."

"No, my dear boy," replied Morell, quietly, "the Colonel did not come worst off; for he had nothing to lose. I tried him, before his son did."

"You are modest," said Heatherleigh.

"No, I am repentant. Those days are over. I borrow no more. I am about to become an exemplary husband and citizen; give up all my clubs except one; smoke cigars at thirty shillings; nurse the baby; and pay water-rates. Nevertheless, I *will* ask you for a good cigar, my dear Ives; for the days of renunciation are not yet come."

"And where is Alfred Burnham?" I asked.

"That," remarked Morell, "is a solemn question."

"And the answer is worth money," added Heatherleigh. "If the demand for the gentleman were at all indicative of his value, one might say that Alfred Burnham was somebody worth knowing. But you have not told us yet what brought you over here, just now?"

"You must ask my friend."

"I think," said Franz, speaking in very Teutonic French, "that we came from Munich to England to look over a white gate at a house, and then go back again."

"Was the house called Burnham House, Monsieur Vogl?" asked Heatherleigh.

"I believe it was, sir."

"Then I knew of one man who might have done such a thing; but I did not fancy that Europe held two."

"Be satisfied with the discovery," I said, "and let us talk of something else. I suppose my mother is well; and her young companion, is she also well?"

"Yes," said Heatherleigh, hastily, "they are both well, as you know. But what do you intend doing? What do you mean by living at a hotel when you might be at home?"

"Because we did not wish it to be known that we were in England. We only came over for a day or two, that my friend might have a look at our English wild-flowers in the spring sunshine; and we intended running back immediately. But now I suppose we may as well see everybody properly, and in as little time as possible, and then go back."

This, in effect, was what was forced upon us by our being discovered. We still remained at the Langham for convenience sake; but we spent most of our time in hurriedly visiting people between the hours of Franz's sightseeing. Polly was overjoyed to show herself off as an expectant bride; and yet you could not help being charmed by the odd mixture of humor and frank jollity which accompanied her evident self-satisfaction. My mother, too, seemed to look upon the match as greatly the result of her care in educating Polly; and took every pains to show off the accomplishments which Polly modestly tried to conceal.

Bonnie Lesley I saw twice. On our first meeting, she began the history of her engagement with Mr. Morell in a deprecatory sort of way, as if she felt it necessary to excuse herself to me. I fancied I detected a touch of chagrin in her tone when she saw that I scarcely understood this effort on her part, and was certainly in no great anxiety to remove scruples which I could not comprehend. This odd feeling soon wore off, as she grew confidential in the old fashion; and at last she got to state the relations on which she stood with her intended husband with a candor which would have surprised any one who did not know her as well as I did.

"I think Mr. Heatherleigh was right," she said, carelessly and with much apparent self-satisfaction; "I am not capable of a grand passion—I wish I was; but you can't make yourself do these things; and it is perhaps as well, for it might make one very unhappy. I like Mr. Morell very well. He is good-tempered and clever; he admires me, I know, and thinks I will preside properly at his dinner-table; and that I know I shall do. We get on remarkably well together, and I think we shall be very happy."

"I certainly hope so."

"You may say there is not much romance in all that. But I scarcely see anybody who is romantic around me; and I think we shall be very much like other people. It is *not* a mercenary marriage, either; for he makes only a moderate income, and what I have is no great inducement to a man moving in such circles as he knows. He has expectations, certainly; and I hope we shall be able to meet our friends on equal terms, and not have to be stingy."

Bonnie Lesley had grown much more matter-of-fact in tone since I had first known her, and there was less of pretty wonder in her eyes.

She added, after a pause—

"You see, it is not what you would call a love-match, nor is it a marriage made up for money. It is simply two people who think they can get on comfortably in each other's society, who like each other, and hope to continue to like each other. Upon my word, I think most people marry like that. These wonderful love-affairs only happen between boys and girls, and they never come to anything; for the boy can't marry just then, and the girl ages more rapidly than he, and finds she can't wait for him, and marries somebody else."

"And he has a broken heart for a few weeks, and then turns to his business or profession, and gets older and wiser, and marries a woman much better suited to him in every way, and leads an ordinarily happy life. Didn't you try to give me the first part of that experience?"

"Now, that *is* unkind," she said, "after I told you I was so sorry, and you agreed to forget it."

"I revived it only to tell you how near you were succeeding."

"Was I, indeed?" she said, with a pleased surprise. "Were you very near falling wildly in love with me?"

"Very near, I think—until, one day, while I was sitting beside you, I looked up and saw a face that I knew, in an instant, I had loved all along, without scarcely knowing it."

"I know what you mean," she said, "and your manner was changed to me ever after that day."

Presently she added in another tone—

"I suppose Mr. Heatherleigh will rather laugh at our marriage, and say it is an ordinary social bargain, or something like that."

"I don't think he will do anything of the kind. Won't you tell me now why you constantly fancy he is saying ill-natured things of you, and putting the worst possible construction on everything you do?"

But she would not tell, nor would Heatherleigh ever breathe a word upon the subject; and it was only by haphazard, some eighteen months thereafter, that I was enabled to unravel the mystery. A little fit of very uncalled-for jealousy on the part of Polly was the means of letting me into the secret. From the moment that Polly saw herself the future wife of the man whom of all others she most admired and worshipped, I fancy she was rather given to grudging him his acquaintance with fine folks, and, above all, with fine young ladies. The weakness was a natural one, but Polly knew it was a weakness, and labored to get rid of it; nevertheless she occasionally exhibited little fits of envious depreciation of those who, she fancied, were attracting too much of her husband's attention. Among these she placed Bonnie Lesley, and seemed to dislike that young lady more, I am certain, than circumstances warranted.

"Heatherleigh never liked Bonnie Lesley, you may take my word for it," I said to Polly, after both she and Bonnie Lesley were married.

"I know it," she said, sharply; "for she proposed to him, and he refused her, and she hated him ever after, because he told a mutual friend that she was born without a soul. There!" she added, breaking into a humorous laugh, "I have told you the secret: but I could not help it. Though I think, after that, he ought to have stayed away from the Lewisons' and never seen Bonnie Lesley again, that she might forget it."

"I have no doubt he went there that she might learn to think it of no consequence, and so forget it."

Franz and I remained for yet a few days in England, in order to pay a flying visit to the Cumberland lakes, with which my friend was enchanted. It was perhaps a cruel thing to show that piece of scenery to a man who was going back to Munich.

On the day preceding our departure we were to go up to the Lewisons' to bid them and Miss Lesley good-bye. We went, by appointment, in the morning. Shortly after we arrived, Mr. Lewison, having to go into the city, left; and Mrs. Lewison taking Franz to show him her husband's collection of pictures, I was left alone with Bonnie Lesley.

"What do you think of all that I told you the other day?" she asked. "What do you think of my marriage?"

"I think that you and Mr. Morell will get on very well together; for I fancy you will take pretty much the same views of most things."

"Now that is just it," she said. "Don't you think we should be running a great risk if either of us was nursing a grand romantic passion? Haven't you seen two people married, the one of them very practical, sensible, and matter-of-fact; the other very romantic, and very miserable because he or she can't get the other to be responsive to the sentiment."

"There is no use in saying 'he or she,'" I said. "In such a case, it is always the man who is romantically fond of his wife, and the wife who is matter-of-fact."

"Did you ever see two people married, who were both capable of a grand romantic passion, you know—of heroic sentiment, and picturesque resolves? How would two such people condescend to be bothered by ordinary company? Wouldn't they always be wanting to be in a boat in the moonlight; even although she had a house to look after, and he had—"

The door opened, and Mrs. Lewison and Franz appeared. There was a third figure; and there was something in the look of Bonnie Lesley's face that told me who it was. I knew that the figure was small and dressed in black, and then I turned and looked up, and found the beautiful eyes of Kilmeny there.

What did they say? There was merely an embarrassed surprise in them; and I saw that the meeting, which had been planned by Bonnie Lesley, was as unexpected by Hester Burnham as it had been by me.

She came forward.

"You will forgive me for not recognizing you the other day," she said, in her gentle, honest way. "But why did you not bring your friend up to the house?"

It was impossible, looking at those eyes, to make any sham excuse: she knew why I had avoided seeing her.

"It would have interested him, I dare say; and I suppose he has already told you how much he was delighted with the valley, and all the scenery there, and Burnham?"

"I never knew how pretty the place was until now," she said; and her eyes were wistful and far away.

"Now, young people," said Mrs. Lewison, "I can't let you go down to this picture-exhibition without taking some lunch first."

"But you are coming, are you not, Mrs. Lewison?" I asked.

"Hester will take my place, and look after you all, and bring you back safely. She is already well acquainted with all the mysterious duties of the chaperone and the housekeeper, and is, indeed, the oldest young person I know. Are you not, Hester?"

"A chaperone has only one duty," said Miss Lesley, "and that is to get out of the way, or fall asleep at times; and Hester is always in the way, and never sleeps. She is like a dormouse that lies curled up and small and warm, and all the time is peeping at you with two small bright eyes."

"But then, my dear," said Mrs. Lewison, "it can be of no consequence to you, now, whether your chaperone sleeps or not."

"You mean it can be of no consequence to Mr.—"

But Bonnie Lesley stopped, and laughed and blushed, and Mr. Morell's name was not mentioned.

It was finally arranged that the young ladies should get ready to go out while luncheon was being prepared; and so it was that Franz and I were left alone.

"This is terrible," said he. "I do not know how to take lunch with your English ladies. I shall commit a thousand *gaucheries*."

"Nonsense! Only don't cut up your meat in small pieces to start with, and don't put your knife to your mouth, and don't praise anything unless you are asked. That is all."

Franz did not enjoy his lunch. In the first place, French was a tribulation to him. Then he never dared touch anything, or use any knife, spoon, or fork, until he had seen some one else do so. But he acquitted himself perfectly; and in due time we were in the old, familiar dark-green brougham, and driving rapidly down towards Pall Mall.

It was an exhibition of water-colors that we had arranged to visit. But the exhibition had been open for a long time; and on this particular morning there was not a human being in the place except an old and benevolent-looking gentleman, with white hair, who sat at a table placed in the middle of the room, and calmly read the morning's news. The long room was warm and hushed; the only sound the occasional dropping of a bit of cinder from the grate. The thick carpets dulled your footsteps as you walked across; and there was something in the close, still atmosphere which tempted you, for no particular reason, to talk in a whisper. I wondered that the elderly gentleman who presided over the catalogues had not fallen asleep.

Then we walked straight into dreamland; and found ourselves in all manner of wonderful places—now looking down into some Welsh glen, or fronting the great bridge and the broad stream and the lofty Hradschin of Prague, the city of all cities that I love the most. We had only to move a few inches in order to whisk ourselves across a continent. A slight inclination of the head, and we changed a gray and windy morning into a calm and yellow evening. Here were bits of sea off the Essex coast, cold and pale, and studded with the black hulls of smacks; and here were sunny glimpses of the white houses and green vines of Capri; and here were stretches of dark Scotch moors, lonely and bleak; and warm sunsets down among the Surrey hills; and snow-scenes in the icy wilds of Russia. All these things I saw reflected in Kilmeny's eyes; and I fancied that her face caught a glow from the sunsets, and that the windy coast-scenes seemed to bring a tinge of heightened color to her cheek. We two had wandered up to the top of the room by ourselves, to look at a picture that was marked in the catalogue as "Sunset in the Oberinnthal." This picture was not the grandest performance one could have wished. It was melodramatic in conception, and pretentious in style; yet it was exceedingly like the great valley that stretches along to Innsbruck, and it gave an excellent notion of the intense quiet and solitariness of the place. The sun was down, and while the peaks of the limestone mountains stood bare and red in the pale green sky, down in the valley there lay cold mists, with a few orange points gleaming through the dusk, where a village lay in the valley. There was no other sign of life; everything was as motionless and still as the thin white crescent of the moon that was faintly visible in the glow of the sunset.

"You have just been there," she said.

"Yes. We walked all down the valley, by the road you see there; and it was as still and quiet as you see it, for we came along there in the evening. Don't you think it is a very beautiful valley?"

We had both sat down, opposite the picture, and behind a centre-screen which stood in the middle of the floor. So still was the place, and so completely did this temporary partition cut us off even from our two companions, that it was almost possible to imagine that we were really in the Oberinnthal, under the pale sunset. The eyes of Kilmeny were full of that sunset. They had the strange, dreamlike, distant look that I had often noticed in them—when, if you spoke to her, she seemed to have to recall herself from a trance before she could answer.

"I wish that we two could be there now," I said to her.

I had grown so bold, you see; for it was as if I were talking in a dream, and as if she were far away from me and could hardly hear.

"If you and I could be down there, in that valley, away from England," I said—and I scarcely knew that I was anxious and supplicating as I watched her face—"I would tell you that I loved you dearly; that I have worshipped you from afar off so long, not daring to speak to you; that I have always loved you, ever since I used to watch for you, years ago, coming down from Burnham. And if we were there by ourselves, you would not be angry with me, I think, if I said all that. You might tell me to leave you; but you would grant something to the love that I have for you, and let us part as friends."

Then I knew that her eyes had come back from the picture, and were looking at me earnestly and sadly; and her face was pale.

"You would say that if we were in Germany?" she said, in her low, tender tones.

"And you would believe what I said," I answered, looking into her beautiful face.

"But it is too soon to say it here, in England?"

With that she rose and turned away, so that I could not meet her eyes to learn what she was thinking. But at the same moment I saw her rapidly take off one of her gloves; and somehow, before I knew what had occurred, the pale little token was lying just beside my hand, where she had dropped it.

Then she went, and I remained for a second or two stupefied, and scarcely daring to believe that I was in actual, secret possession of this glove. I rose, stunned with a new, bewildering sense of joy that could find no outlet or expression; and I saw that she had joined Miss Lesley and Franz.

Did they notice how pale she was? Did they notice that one small hand was bare? That, at least, I saw, and my joy was unspeakable; for the little, white hand of my darling told me that the glove I held was real, and mine.

CHAPTER XXXVI.

OUR TRUSTY COUSIN.

"What do you think, then, of England as a place to live in?" I asked of Franz, as we stood on the deck of the Calais boat, and saw the wavering lights of Dover grow momentarily more and more dim in the distance.

"I am not an Englishman," said Franz. "I can't give you a decided opinion about a country, and its people and its politics, from having stayed a week in it."

"Well, you can say whether you would like to remain a year or two in London, for example."

"I could not do it. London seems a nice place for people with plenty of money and plenty of friends. For me, I should probably shoot myself after a month of it. How should I spend my evenings? I could not go to the theatres every night, even if they were better than they seem to be. Your music-halls are the natural resort of your young men who wish to amuse themselves in the evening; and they—"

Franz shrugged his shoulders.

"For my part," he said, "I did not understand the songs. Perhaps they were clever. But I do not see the reason why men and women should applaud and laugh merely because a man comes on the stage in the dress of a dandy. He can sing no more than a cow—the words of the song *may* be good—"

"My dear friend, the wit of the song lies in the color and size of the singer's neckerchief."

"Then the outrageous indecency of the place, with the police stationed as guardians—"

"But there is one where no such indecency is permitted—"

"Why," said Franz, with another shrug, "if decency only means conjuring tricks and ventriloquism, and the efforts of a man to swing chairs with his teeth, indecency is likely to be more popular. No, your London is not to me a lively place. It is too eager and busy, too hurried and too ostentatious. I like your old country towns better; they look as if the people in them were content to live reasonably and peaceably. You—will you live in London or in that valley, when your *Lehrjahre* and *Wanderjahre* are all over?"

"I? When a dozen years of hard work have brought me sufficient money to rent Burnham House, I mean to live there."

"The young lady does not mean to sell it, then?"

"She will never sell it, if she can help it; and I fancy she will only let it until she has got as much money as will enable her to go back there, free from the difficulties in which her cousin entangled her."

"And in the mean time?"

"In the mean time she is going to live abroad—for the sake of cheapness, I suppose."

"Shall we see her in Munich?" said Franz.

"How should I know?"

"She is interested in Munich, at all events," said Franz. "She sent that message to us at the gates of Burnham, just on the chance of our having come from Munich."

"How do you know?"

"She told me yesterday morning, when she came into the room where Madame—your friend with the unpronounceable name—and I were. She recognized me at once. She was very gracious to me, and we had a walk around the pictures; and I became so good friends with her that I wished I could have sat down and played my zither for her. But I saw that I made a blunder."

"How?"

"I was telling her stories, prompted by the different pictures, you know; and I told her by accident of a poor ignorant devil of a painter down in Waldshut who was painting a crucifix, and put 'R. S. V. P.' instead of 'I. N. R. I.' over it. What was there in that? Nothing. But she did not like it, I could see; and I blamed myself for talking freely to one of your English ladies, without knowing their peculiar sensitiveness. Your English-women seem very tender about their religion, and a little too apprehensive, I think, that you may be an enemy, when you are thinking of something quite different."

"But the religion of the country rests with them at present," I said, "and they do right to be vigilant sentinels. Whenever they imagine they see the figure of Irreverence stalking in the distance—"

"They raise a clamor like that which saved the Capitol," said Franz.

I suppose Amphitrite must have heard this remark, and stirred up her husband to revenge her sex; for, as we neared the French coast, the motion of the vessel became much more marked, and Franz, against all persuasion, was fain to take the fatal step of going below. When he reappeared, as the boat was being made fast to the stone walls of Calais pier, the glare of a lamp showed that his face was very white, and there was a general air of helplessness about his person.

"I won't go straight on to Cologne," he said, when he got into the train. "I shall stop the day in Brussels, and go on to-morrow."

"Very well," said I, "and you will give me a little dinner at the Deux Rois."

We spent the day therefore in that most English of all foreign towns, and, having dined at the hostelry aforesaid, were going down to the Théâtre de la Monnaie. In passing through the Avenue de la Reine, which was crowded with people, who walked up and down and stared at each other and the glaring shops, Franz and I found ourselves behind three men who were clearly English in costume and appearance. At the first glance I fancied I recognized the figure of one of them; and as we drew nearer, he turned to look in at a cigar-shop. I saw then that he was a man of about thirty-five, dressed rather ostentatiously, who was more than suspected of being a billiard-sharper when we were at Brighton. At all events, he was politely requested by more than one hotel-manager not to make his appearance again in their billiard-rooms; and it was understood that he received the intimation meekly.

The second of the group was a handsome and healthy-looking

boy of about eighteen, who was neatly and fashionably dressed, and who had an unmistakable look of virgin greenness about his face. He was a gentlemanly-looking lad, and his face gave you the impression that his sisters would probably be remarkably pretty. When he turned, also, to look in at the display of meerschaum-pipes in the tobacconist's window, I caught sight of his other companion. It was Alfred Burnham. He looked twenty years older than when I had seen him last; and there was a hard, hawk-like look about his face that was far from being prepossessing. He was well-dressed, too; but he had lost the swaggering air he used to assume.

What struck me as being very peculiar was the officious complaisance which both these men paid to the boy between them. Alfred Burnham had never, as a rule, striven to make himself very agreeable to the people around him; but now he was trying to look particularly amiable, and was doing his best to ingratiate himself with the young man beside him. So, also, with his friend from Brighton, whose eagerness to be of service was more that of a valet than of a companion.

The object of these favors did not seem quite to relish them. There was a certain coldness in his responses to his amiability; but, all the same, he seemed to assent to a proposition that they made, and the three walked off together.

I told Franz who they were.

"Shall we follow them?" he said. "We may see more with them than in the theatre."

We did follow them, but we had not far to go. They entered a restaurant, went up-stairs and ordered some wine. It was rather a fashionable place; and, as the dining-rooms were down-stairs, this room, with its red-velvet chairs and couches, and its small marble tables, was kept as a coffee and smoking room. It was a large place, and there were two or three people in it, some talking, others smoking and playing dominoes. Franz and I sat down at one of the tables out in the middle of the floor, where there was least light; while we could easily see the other three, who were under the glare of the reflection from the white wall. We could also hear what they said at times, as they seemed to have every confidence in no one but themselves understanding English.

They played dominoes, at five francs the game, and fifty centimes each time a double-six was played. This comparatively harmless form of amusement was proceeded with for some time, while wine was liberally drunk. It was noticeable, however, that, out of mere courtesy, Alfred Burnham kept his young friend's glass constantly filled; and as the latter was smoking what seemed a strong and oily cigar, he drank at the same time a good deal of the sparkling, pale wine that was so generously offered him.

"I have won eight francs," said Burnham, with a laugh. "I must go home now, and carry off my winnings. How much have you won, my lord?"

"Twenty-six or twenty-seven," said the young man, with a louder laugh; and his eyes were now flushed.

"Then I must be the loser," said the oldest of the three, with a resigned air. "Such is luck. Shall we go back to the hotel now, Sir Charles?"

So Mr. Burnham had become Sir Charles Somebody.

"Yes," said Sir Charles, rising, and concealing a yawn; "I feel rather tired."

"Let us make a sweepstakes of our winnings, Sir Charles," said the young man. "I will put my twenty-six francs against your eight, and we will cut for it."

"I could not be guilty of such a piece of robbery," said Burnham, with another laugh. "But if you mean to cut until one of us shall have lost his winnings, let us do it with cards. Here, *garçon!*"

"Oui, m'sieur!"

"Allez, apportez-moi—achetez pour moi un—un—un jeu de cartes anglaises; comprenez-vous? Il faut qu'elles soient neuves."

"Bien, m'sieur!"

Burnham turned to his companions with a sort of apology for his hesitating French, and remarked that it was a pity all the world had not been born in Buckinghamshire.

"You know Bucks?" said the young man, with a vinous delight. "Why, there is no one in the county I don't know. Are you acquainted with the Beckfords?"

"No," replied Alfred Burnham, hastily. "I said Bucks by chance. I know little of the county beyond having ridden through it once or twice. I am from the north."

"From the fens, or the Ridings, or—"

"Westmoreland," said Sir Charles; and then he abruptly changed the subject.

The cards were brought, and some more wine. They cut for francs at first, and Sir Charles won. Then they cut for five francs, in order to get it over the sooner; and fortune kept pretty steady.

"You must let me join," said the person from Brighton. "I can't let you have all the fun to yourselves. Suppose that I, too, have won twenty-five francs; and let us go on cutting until some one has won the whole."

"Agreed," said Sir Charles; and they went on shuffling and cutting the cards.

Now this ingenious game of winning or losing money by cutting for the highest card is a sufficiently fair trial of chances, under ordinary circumstances; but the young gentleman who was thus amusing himself must have been particularly innocent when he did not perceive that the odds were considerably against his winning. He did not seem to reflect on the possibility of his two opponents being in collusion, however; and so they went on drinking and smoking and cutting the cards, until, by an easy transition, sovereigns came to be staked instead of francs, and at length I saw mysterious pieces of paper being handed across the table, with a scrawled signature thereon.

It did not occur to him to ask what was the value of the I.O.U.'s against which he was staking his own signature.

"Hadn't we better stop?" said the eldest of them.

"No, no," said the young man, who was now half-tipsy. "Let us have one or two more—good big ones. I have lost t' much. Luck must turn."

But there was no luck in the matter. There was a dead certainty of his losing; and he lost.

"How these things mount up with your confounded 'double or quits!'" said Burnham to his colleague. "Do you know how much money I have won from you?"

"Haven't the faintest idea!" said the other; and, indeed, there was little reason why he should care.

"One hundred and thirty-two pounds, as near as I can make out."

"The devil!"

"And how much do I owe you, my lord?" said Burnham.

The young man pushed all the bits of paper over to him.

"Look for yourself!" he said, with an indolent, intoxicated gesture. "I can't make head or tail of them."

Alfred Burnham looked over the papers.

"By Jove!" he said, "I find that I owe you £60. Shall I give an I. O. U. for the amount to Mr. Temple, and that will be so much towards what you owe him? Then he can arrange with me, when he pays me what he owes me."

"All right, all right; it will save trouble. Then I owe you something still, Mr.—Mr. Temple?"

"Yes, my lord," said Temple, calmly holding out certain pieces of paper. "I find here I. O. U.'s for £380. With the £60 deducted, the amount will be £320."

The boy was sobered in an instant.

"Three hundred and twenty!" he said, as he rose to his feet, with his face blanched—perhaps more with anger than with dismay.

I think he would have broken into some angry denunciations but that both of the two men kept their eyes fixed on him, and Temple said, coldly—

"Yes, my lord, that is the sum. Will you give me a note of hand for the whole amount, or shall I call upon you at your hotel with these papers?"

"Come to my hotel to-morrow morning," said the lad; and the way in which he said so showed that he now perceived the character of the men with whom he was dealing.

At this moment I walked over to the small table at which they sat, and lit a bit of paper at the gas overhead. While doing so I looked at Alfred Burnham, and he grew suddenly pale.

"Ah, how do you do, Mr. Burnham?" I said; "who would have expected to see you in Brussels?"

The boy looked on in amazement. To hear Sir Charles addressed as Mr. Burnham told him whatever he had not already divined.

"Who the —— are you? I don't know you!" said Burnham, furiously.

"I am sorry for that," I said, lighting my cigar, "for I have just seen several of your friends in England, who would be glad of your address. They seem to have lost sight of you since you left—Westmoreland."

I had nearly said Burnham, but I remembered on the instant that the young lord had boasted of his acquaintance with every family in Bucks, and I thought that he might connect this man with the lady who was known to be the mistress of Burnham House. Had I had less interest in the matter, I should have been even then loth to have Hester Burnham recognized as a friend or relative of a common swindler. Meanwhile, the hint about his address seemed to have maddened him. He swore a furious oath, and jumped to his feet. Franz came over just then, and also produced a cigar.

"Was wünscht der Dummkopf?" he said, coolly.

"For God's sake, let us have no fighting," said Temple.

"As you please," I said; "but perhaps you will give this young gentleman your real names and addresses when next you play with him. And perhaps, before he pays you to-morrow, he will get somebody to inquire about them. Good-evening, Mr. Burnham."

So Franz and I turned and left.

"Lucky for you," said Franz, "that Burnham hadn't a revolver in his pocket. I never saw a man so clearly look murder as he did just now."

The lad who had been playing with them came running down after us, and overtook us just as we were leaving.

"What am I to do?" he said—"what am I to do? I have been swindled. I have been robbed."

"You might have found that out a little earlier," said I.

"But I won't pay these I. O. U.'s—"

"You will be a considerable ass if you do. Go straight up to the Commissary of Police; state your case, and ask his advice. If either calls for payment in the morning—which is far from likely—refer him to your friend the Commissary, and recommend him to leave Brussels."

"How can I ever thank you sufficiently? It is not the amount, but the disgrace of being swindled, that I should have dreaded. How can I repay you?"

"Well, in this way. When you tell your English friends how two of your countrymen tried to swindle you, don't say that one of them was called Burnham. He will achieve fame soon enough. That is all I ask of you."

"I promise faithfully. But—but won't you come and dine with me?"

I believe the boy was actually afraid of being left alone, lest his friends the card-players should follow and threaten him.

"Thank you," I said; "I fancied you had dined sufficiently before you sat down to play cards with two strangers. And we were going to the theatre, when the amusement of watching you and them enticed us to wait. We shall be in time for the operetta, however; and so, good-night!"

"Good-night; and thank you very much."

"Your English families should keep their children in the nursery until they are able to take care of themselves out-of-doors," said Franz.

CHAPTER XXXVII.

IN MUNICH AGAIN.

LINELE was in a particularly kindly mood when we arrived. Franz had merely called at his lodgings in passing, to leave his luggage and top-coat, and bring his zither with him; then we drove on in the droschke to the Königin Strasse, and made our appearance in the Professor's house.

Lena received us with the dignity of a small empress. She allowed Franz to kiss her hand; and answered in a stately manner his inquiries after the health of Annele. But her decorum quite broke down when Franz took out of a box a remarkably pretty fan, and presented it to her. She looked at it all round, and opened it, and shut it, and then kissed it affectionately, and put it in the box again. I think she would have kissed Franz, too, if nobody had been by; for had he not brought a handsome volume of engravings for the Herr Papa, and a wonderful case of housewifely implements, all real English cutlery, for the Frau Mamma? No prospective son-in-law could have done more.

The evening was devoted to the questioning of Franz about his foreign experiences. The Professor would know everything about the galleries, and the architecture of the principal towns, and so forth; Linele's mamma was curious to know how people lived in a land that was so full of money—what and when they ate, and whether everything was comfortable in proportion to its expense; while Lena herself would know how the young ladies of London looked, and where they walked in the constant rains and fogs, and what sort of dresses they wore in such a climate. Then she took out the fan again, and asked Franz if he had seen the opera-house filled with the richest ladies in the world, and whether they were all loaded with diamonds, and gleaming in white satins and silks.

"Papa," cried Linele, petulantly, "I don't believe he has been in England at all. He has seen nothing different, nothing strange; and I believe they have been away hiding somewhere, to escape their painting, and play billiards and go to the theatre. It is wicked of them to deceive us, isn't it, papa? And you won't take the engravings, will you?—and I will give him back the fan, for it never came from England, I know!"

The Professor looked up in mute bewilderment. He had been looking at an engraving of one of Turner's Italian landscapes, and had got lost there. But the mamma said—

"Now, now, Linele, don't bother Mr. Frank, when he has been so kind to you. And you have never even thanked Mr. Edward for the pretty necklace he has given you—"

"But I have put it round my neck: isn't that enough for him?" said Linele, proudly.

"And, instead of bothering the gentlemen, you might go and get up two bottles of the red Rhinewine, since this is a grand occasion—"

"But we have just been drinking beer as we came along," said Franz.

"That doesn't matter," said the Frau Professor, with a sage nod of the head. "You know what they say—

'Wein auf Bier, das rath' ich dir;
Bier auf Wein, das lass du sein!'

There is sense in that. Go along with you, Lena, and make yourself useful."

Presently Lena appeared, making a great fuss about carrying the two bottles of Assmanshäuser, and pretending to be greatly fatigued by their weight. Then she placed them jauntily on the table, and went for glasses, and put them down with a saucy air.

"In England, young ladies don't wait upon gentlemen," said Lena, with a toss of her head.

"More's the pity, then," said her mother, sharply. "What do they do then, I wonder?"

"They drive in carriages, and dress in silk, and sit at table like queens, and have all the gentlemen serve them," said Linele.

"And have the gentlemen nothing to do, either?" said the mamma, with a touch of scorn.

"They can't do anything better than wait upon ladies," retorted Linele.

"Your head is full of wool, Lena," said the mamma; and that stopped the discussion for the moment.

So we settled down to our ordinary work again; and in process of time I got my "Wölundur" finished. The Professor had taken great interest in the progress of the work, and had materially helped me by plenty of sound suggestion and able criticism. I was beginning to feel my way more surely now, and to be able to test in a measure the value of what I was doing. "Kilmeny" had been more of a surprise to myself than it could have been to anybody else; but the technical knowledge I had acquired under the Professor's care, added to the effect of his lectures upon the various qualities of the Pinathothek masters, gave me a better notion of what I could do, and what I could not do, myself. I knew that this picture was freer in manner and altogether more mature than its predecessor; and I was so far convinced of this that I formed the project of offering "Wölundur" to Mr. Webb in exchange for "Kilmeny," which I was desirous, for many reasons, of getting into my own hands.

When it was finished, I consigned the picture to Heatherleigh's care. He had undertaken to send it into the Academy. In the interim, however, I received a long letter from him, expressing his own opinions about the thing, and saying that he had shown it, among others, to the Jew-dealer whom I knew.

"He offers you," he wrote, "four hundred guineas for the work. I hope your brain won't be turned by the announcement, which means more than you fancy. Old Solomons pays a man according to the reputation he has made; merely because it is that alone which has any weight with the majority of his customers; and therefore you may have some idea of what 'Kilmeny' has earned for you. But I would not close with him, if I were you. Send the picture into the Academy, and let it take its chance. If it does what I expect it will do, you will be inundated with commissions, which for yet a year or two you should undertake most sparingly. The results of your stay in Munich are apparent in every part of this picture," etc., etc.

He was strongly opposed to my bartering the picture for "Kilmeny;" but seeing that I persisted in the notion, he went to Mr. Webb and laid the matter before him. Then, as before and since, that gentleman acted in a manner which any one, regarding his dry, timid manner and cold look, would scarcely have expected from him. That is to say, instead of treating me, a stranger to him, in an ordinary businesslike manner, he showed a frank generosity and fairness which, I regret to say, surprised me. For I had not met many English gentlemen; and there still hung about me a half-conscious apprehension, begotten of my experience of Weavle, that every stranger to you must necessarily be on the outlook to take advantage of you for his own benefit.

As before, Mr. Webb placed himself, as a purchaser, in open competition with everybody else. Having seen the picture, he expressed his willingness to give as much for it as any purchaser might offer after it had been exhibited in the Academy—then to deduct from this sum the price he had paid for "Kilmeny," and send me the latter picture, with the difference in money.

The difference, when it came, was nearly two hundred guineas. The draft was made payable on a Munich banker; and when I got the slip of paper, I endeavored to fancy myself ten years younger, and to picture what I should have thought in Weavle's shop of becoming the owner of such a sum.

"Kilmeny" for the present was to remain with Mr. Webb; it was useless to send it over to Munich, when in a few months I might be returning to England.

On receipt of this money, I kept up a good old English custom in a foreign land. I invited the Professor, his wife, and Lena, Franz, Silber, and one or two others, to a dinner at a restaurant. The little black-eyed actress could not be persuaded to come, notwithstanding it was represented to her that we should be in a private room, and unseen by the vulgar gossips of the city. She pleaded a late rehearsal, though I fancy her mamma's notions of propriety had something to do with it.

We were a very merry party; and even Silber forgot to look miserable, and was for carrying his complaisance to the extent of singing a song after dinner—a gratification which we managed to escape. Instead we all went over to a box which I had secured at the Hoftheater; and there Linele, who had dressed her hair in the English fashion, sat like a little princess at the front of the box, and displayed the gleaming fan that Franz had given her.

It was "Linda" they sang; and the good mamma sat and cried a little, covertly, over the pretty story of Linda's trials and faithfulness, and ultimate reward.

CHAPTER XXXVIII.

KILMENY COMES HOME.

Was I free at last, only to be tired of my freedom? I could go where I liked; I could spend my time as it pleased me; I had money at command, and was my own master; I was afraid of no man, and knew that I had the power to compel the future to be serviceable to me, so that I could take up my abode in any part of Europe, and feel sure of being able to live there in comfort and peace.

Or I could travel about from city to city, from village to village, stopping here and there as I chose, and seeing men and manners and things. The world was before me; and, in so much as I cared for it, I was its master. I could make it yield me the things that I wanted, for my needs were not great. The chiefest of them had been all along this freedom from control, and now I had achieved it.

I had achieved it only to find that independence meant isolation. There were no kindly bonds of duty governing my daily actions, and yielding the pleasures of self-sacrifice. There was no obligation connected with my art-efforts; on the contrary, they were the keenest delight I experienced, and following them was in no sense a duty. Outside of this pursuit, I had nothing particular to live for; and I was beginning to weary of too much content, that poor sort of sunshine that lights up the narrow world of selfishness.

"Will Hester Burnham ever come to redeem her pledge?" I used to think. "Will it ever happen that the dream I dreamed in the Tyrol will come true, and we together shall go down through the wonderful valley, all by ourselves? Will it ever happen that each day shall be filled with the numberless duties of love; and that I shall have to watch over my darling, and tend her, and keep her safe from the cold winds and the rain?"

There was no sign or word from her away in England. The many letters I got from various people mentioned her only by chance, and then said nothing definite. She was supposed to be waiting to see how matters should be arranged about the letting of Burnham, and the clearance of the obligations which her cousin's kindness had imposed upon her. Indeed, my correspondents were too busy to waste much time in speculation. Bonnie Lesley was preparing for her marriage; Heatherleigh had married, and was engaged in decorating with his own handiwork a small house he had bought up at Hampstead. He and Polly had persuaded my mother to go and live with them; for Polly, said Heatherleigh, would bother him all day in his studio unless she had somebody else to talk to and make jokes with.

"But you ought not to take a mother-in-law into your house," said my mother, with a smile.

"But I shall want all your help," said Polly, wickedly. "For you don't know what a miser he has grown of late; and unless we are two to one, it will be impossible to keep the house in any comfort. Do you know, my dear, that five minutes after we were married, he took off his gloves, rolled them up, and put them in his pocket, saying they would do for the first time we went to the theatre? Did miserliness ever go further; and on his marriage-day, too?"

I learned, indeed, from my mother that Polly regarded her housekeeping as an elaborate joke, and that she spent the better part of the day in laughing over the eccentricities of an Irish maid-servant who was in the house, and in laying traps to exhibit the artless blunders of that young woman. Yet Polly, in spite of her imitations of the butcher-boy, and her fits of laughter over the courtesies of the milk-man to the Irish maid-servant aforesaid, looked sharply and actively after her domestic affairs, and made a capital wife. Heatherleigh, too, I heard, had grown ten years younger since his marriage; and he and Polly, when all the day's work of each was over, and when they sat down to supper, were in the habit of conducting themselves pretty much like a couple of children, instead of two grown-up and married persons.

Such was the news that came from England; and I was glad

that, amid the din and clamor of eager money-getting, there were some who could find a quiet household for themselves, and peace therein. As for the houseless one—where was she?

I forgot now to look with any interest across the trees of the "English Garden." I had lost all hope of seeing her walk across that patch of level green; not that her coming was any less likely than it had ever been, but that I had grown to see that it had never been likely. The time for such miracles was over, and it did no good to dream of them.

But one morning, as I was passing through the Promenadenplatz, on my way to the Nibelungen frescos, I saw two ladies pass into the courtyard of the Bavarian Hotel. I only caught a glimpse of them as they turned the corner; and yet that glimpse made my heart beat. If it were really she, at last, and the small Madame Laboureau?

I walked up to the front of the courtyard, and looked in. There was no one there but the ordinary troupe of commissionaires, porters, and droschke-drivers. I begged permission, however, to look over the large board on which the names of the various visitors at the hotels are inscribed. I hurriedly went over the bits of pasteboard—meeting with French countesses, German barons, Russian princes, and what not; but there was no mention of the name I looked for, so I turned away. It was not the first time I had been mistaken in fancying I saw the slight, graceful figure I knew so well in the streets of Munich.

I went along to the Festsaalbau, met the Professor and one or two of his students, and remained there for about an hour. Then we left; and, as the others were going down to the old Pinathothek, I set out for a saunter up to the Isar.

I suppose you know the Max-Josephsplatz—the splendid square which is surrounded by the palace and the theatre and the post-office, which looks like another palace. As I turned into this square—all bright and clear as it was in the sunlight—I saw, crossing the corner and coming towards me, the figure I had seen in the morning. Was it true, then, that the wandering possibility that had haunted me through all these long months was at last real and true? Was Hester Burnham really in Munich; and should I actually hear her speak, away over here, in this strange land?

I hastened after her, as she went across the square towards the

Maximilian Strasse. She glanced up at the statue of the king, and I saw the outline of her features. Then I overtook her, and she stopped, and I found her hand in mine. There was a pale, strange joy in her face.

"You have come to me at last," I said.

"Yes."

"For altogether?"

It was her eyes that spoke the answer; and there, in the open streets of Munich, I could have knelt down and kissed her hand.

She and Madame Labourcau had arrived that morning; the hotel people had not yet had time to put their names up. Madame was fatigued; and Hester had come out alone to buy some gloves—hence the meeting. But when I inquired of her what had brought her to Munich, she looked up, somewhat reproachfully, and asked, in that low and tender voice of hers, if I had not expected her. We forgot about the gloves. We wandered away from the city, and past the gates and the suburban houses. There was a clear blue sky overhead, and occasionally a flock of pigeons whirring past and gleaming in the white sunlight. She and I had a whole lifetime to settle, and how fair was that future that lay before us! The light of it shone in her wistful eyes, even while the English modulations of her voice, grown almost unfamiliar to my ear, recalled England and all the by-gone years.

Weavle had at last been cast behind, like Satan. The old days in that Holborn workshop were like a nightmare that had fled before the morning sunlight. But do not think that this deliverance was due to the fact that I had now more money than I had then. God forbid that I should have written this history of my life if I had so poor a triumph to tell in the end. It needed none of Heatherleigh's teaching to show me that money was not the thing that made life most beautiful and valuable; and, as Hester and I spoke of the years that were to come, and as I told her how I had escaped from the stifling atmosphere that hung over the bitter struggle for existence in England, into the sweeter and serener air that now surrounded us, it was no hope of riches that lit up the prospect for us, and no desire of wealth that promised to be the stimulant of our future. Yet we were bold enough to think that some measure of good purpose might be done by us, whether we lived in England or elsewhere, if we could only shed around us the influences of two lives wisely and honestly lived, and made honorable and noble by the kindly servitude of love.

It was not very long after this time that I told my darling a story. She and I were at Rolandseck, over the Rhine, and we were all by ourselves there. It was late in the autumn, and all the herd of tourists had gone home; I think we were the only visitors at the Hôtel Billau, which overlooks the river. The nights were drawing in now; and when dinner was over, and we went out upon the balcony, it was quite dark, and we could scarcely see the great stream, though we heard its rippling down in front of us. But the moon was slowly rising behind the heights of Rolandseck; and so I wrapped my little friend in comfortable shawls and furs, and together we waited for the cold night.

How still it was, and how beautiful too, when the calm, wonderful radiance came over the hills behind, and showed us the magical picture that lay around us. Far in the distance, touched here and there with the moonlight, the great Drachenfels rose from over the river up into the dark, starlit sky. Down at our feet the broad, still stream ran softly past, until it smote and quivered in silver along the shores of the island of Nonnenwerth, that lay out there, half hid in a pale, mystical haze. And high over the island rose behind us, sharp and black, the wooded peak on which the Knight Roland built his tower, that so he might look down on his love, and watch her as she came out with her sister-nuns to walk around the cloisters of Nonnenwerth—until, at last, he saw her funeral procession, and never spoke more. Keener and clearer grew the light, until it shone on the gray buildings of the island, and gleamed along the river that encircled it. Here and there, too, were specks of orange light visible on the other bank, where some cluster of cottages lay under the shadow of the mighty Drachenfels; and we could hear, far down the stream, the sound of some boatmen singing, as they moored their barges close in by the shore.

There was no need of much talking on such a night: it was enough to sit, one great shawl over both of us, and look on the wonderful river and the hills and the stars. But my darling, nestling close and warm under her manifold plaids, bade me tell her yet one more tale; and, as I had exhausted all I knew of Rhenish legendary lore, I told her a story of England. And it was this:

"*There was once a boy who used to wander all over the country by night; and he fell in love with a star. And he said—*

"'*Oh, you beautiful small creature! come down and be my companion, and we will go through the world together, all these coming years.*'

"*But, as he walked on, he saw a Will-o'-the-wisp shining in the dark, and he said—*

"'*Oh, you wonderful creature! with your bright eyes and your streaming hair, I have never seen anything so beautiful as you. Come, and we will go through the world together, all these coming years.*'

"*So they travelled on together. But in a little while the Will-o'-the-wisp began to flicker up and down, and finally flew over a hedge and disappeared; and he was left in the dark.*

"*Then he looked up, and lo! above him there still shone the star, and it was as gracious and as beautiful as ever. And he said—*

"'*Oh, you dear small creature! will you forgive me for what I have done; and will you always look down on me as you do now, and I shall look up to you and love you?*'"

That was the question I asked of my darling as we sat together there, under the shadows of Rolandseck. It is some time since then; and I who write these words am still looking up to this beautiful creature, who has never ceased to shed her soft radiance around me. Perhaps she is a little nearer earth now—but that has only enlarged her brightness; and, thinking over all these things, and of her great affection, forbearance, and sweetness, how can I help regarding her, my most tender and faithful friend, with admiration and wonder and love?

THE END

www.ingramcontent.com/pod-product-compliance
Lightning Source LLC
Chambersburg PA
CBHW020945030726
47496CB00005B/1358
* 9 7 8 3 3 3 7 0 3 9 7 1 4 *